T0367859

Angela's Club

a love story

CARL TURNER

iUniverse LLC
Bloomington

ANGELA'S CLUB
A LOVE STORY

iUniverse books may be ordered through booksellers or by contacting:

iUniverse
1663 Liberty Drive
Bloomington, IN 47403
www.iuniverse.com
1-800-Authors (1-800-288-4677)

Because of the dynamic nature of the Internet, any web addresses or links contained in this book may have changed since publication and may no longer be valid. The views expressed in this work are solely those of the author and do not necessarily reflect the views of the publisher, and the publisher hereby disclaims any responsibility for them.

Any people depicted in stock imagery provided by Thinkstock are models, and such images are being used for illustrative purposes only. Certain stock imagery © Thinkstock.

ISBN: 978-1-4917-2880-2 (sc)
ISBN: 978-1-4917-2881-9 (hc)
ISBN: 978-1-4917-2914-4 (e)

Library of Congress Control Number: 2014904968

Printed in the United States of America.

iUniverse rev. date: 04/01/2014

Dedication

This book is dedicated to all lovers who without knowing it make the world a better place.

Acknowledgments

I would like to sincerely thank my wife who accompanied me on this journey. Thank you so much for all your insights and suggestions throughout the writing of this book and for going over the manuscript so thoroughly. I love you.

Chapter One

HIS BEEPER WENT OFF IRRITATINGLY AT TWO AM. IT was irritating because it was two AM and it was irritating because he had been in bed for only thirty minutes after being up for over twenty hours. Nate sat up on the side of his bed. He couldn't believe his bad luck. He looked at the message on the beeper that consisted of only one word, STEMI. STEMI was an acronym for <u>ST</u> <u>E</u>levation <u>M</u>yocardial <u>I</u>nfarction. The ST referred to a segment of the EKG that, if elevated, indicated that a heart attack was in progress. When a STEMI is called by the emergency room physician, a cardiologist is required to assess the patient, catheterize him or her, and place a stent in the occluded artery—all within ninety minutes of the call. This meant he had to jump out of bed and proceed to the hospital at breakneck speed to start working on his patient in the catheter lab. He had to forget that he was exhausted or that he had a horrendous headache. He could only concentrate on his patient whose life was completely in his hands.

Since he had fallen asleep in the greens he had been wearing since the previous day, all he had to do was to put on his slip-on tennis shoes and grab his keys along with his billfold, cell phone and beeper before heading out. He had done this so many times he could do it in his sleep—which he was essentially doing now half asleep. He went out of his apartment door, caught the elevator to the parking garage, got into his car and then sped out into the street. The traffic was light at two AM so after a brief look making sure he could do so safely, he ran the two red lights that were on the way to the hospital. With one hand on the steering wheel and one hand holding his phone he called the ER physician to get the lowdown on his patient. He knew he shouldn't talk on the cell phone while driving, especially when he was half asleep, but he didn't care.

He raced into the doctors' parking lot, opened the doctors' back entrance using his code, and charged up the stairs to the cath lab. He grabbed a quick cup of coffee in the doctors' area gulping it down hoping it would wake him up. He had lost count of how many cups he had gulped down since starting call. In the cath lab his patient, Mr. Green, was on the table, draped and sedated. He knew there would be no use trying to talk to him or reassure him because of the sedation. Also it was something that he considered non-essential that took up too much time. He glanced at his patient's chart before glancing at Mr. Green through the open door to the cath lab. Mr. Green was forty-five years old and weighed over three hundred pounds. He had awakened in the night with chest pain. His wife wisely called 911 after which he was rushed to the hospital. According to the ER physician, prior to this he had been healthy. Nate laughed at that comment. *This guy was healthy before now?*

Nate scrubbed before putting on his gloves. When he walked into the cath lab the nurses said, "Hey Dr. Williams." He said as usual, "Hey," back. What he was about to do he could literally do in his sleep. He made a cut over the femoral artery, made his way through layers of fat, found the pulsing artery and then plunged a needle into it that enabled him to insert a catheter. He advanced the catheter up the aorta to where it exited from the heart where the coronary arteries branched off. He injected dye that lit up the coronary arteries on the fluoroscope revealing an almost blocked right main stem artery. He was then able to insert a stent where the blockage was, opening the narrowing to such a degree that a reasonable amount of blood was now flowing through it. Nate could tell that the heart had only minor damage. Now that the stent was in place his patient was out of danger, at least for the present.

After pulling out the catheter and sewing up the incision, Nate stood up, shot his gloves across the room as was his usual custom, turned to the nurses and said, "Thanks guys. Let's all hope he won't cause us any more trouble, at least not until morning." They all agreed. After making notes in his chart he began to realize that the headache he had momentarily forgot about was killing him. He knew it was from too much caffeine along with no sleep. Now all he had to do was walk down the hall to the waiting room and briefly reassure the family. Then he might get a couple of hours sleep before he had to get up to start rounds. As he started to the waiting room he felt his headache getting worse by the minute. It was one of the worst ones he could remember.

The waiting room was medium-sized with couches along two walls opposite one another. Two rows of wooden-back chairs with vinyl seats sat back to back in the center. The walls were nicely decorated with paintings that hung over a carpeted floor. It was empty as it usually was at four AM except for a somewhat obese woman in her forties sitting next to an older gray-haired obese man who appeared to be her father. She was dressed in a simple pullover housedress that she evidently had put on in a hurry after she had called the ambulance telling them that her husband had awoken with chest pain. Her hair was that of a sleeping woman in the middle of the night. In a wrinkled work shirt that hung over work trousers, her father also appeared hurriedly dressed. That they were related was evident. They both had the round faces of obesity along with similarly shaped chins and noses. She had a tissue in her hands wet from tears while the man sat uncomfortably next to her leaning forward with his arm around her shoulders. They were sitting at the far end of the waiting room and looked up with surprise when he entered. They both stood up with an expression that at once conveyed both great fear at what was about to be said along with a glimmer of hope. Sue, a new young cardiology nurse, walked into the waiting room at the same time.

"Mrs. Green," he began, "your husband has had a heart attack. However, I was able to find the blockage and put in a stent. He is now stable. The heart damage appears to be minimal. I think he has a good prognosis."

"Thank God," the woman said as she started to cry, wiping her eyes with a much-used tissue turning to bury her head in her father's chest. Her father put his arm around her and said, "I'm her father. Thank you so much, Doctor."

Just then through the doors of the waiting room came a tall, thin, well-dressed woman of similar age followed by a tall rough-looking middle-aged man with a mustache who appeared well built wearing a cowboy hat. "How is my brother, Doctor?" the woman anxiously blurted out.

"I was just telling Mrs. Green that he has suffered a heart attack but he is very stable. It appears that at this point he has suffered only mild damage. With the stent that I was able to put in he should do well. However, there is a chance he could worsen and there can always be unexpected complications, but I have a good feeling at this point." From the expression on her face he could tell that she was relieved. It looked like everyone was assured enough that he could leave to get that couple of hours' sleep that just might help his pounding headache.

The sister became quiet, closed her eyes and then said, "Thank you Doctor." She then turned and looked at her sister-in-law with razor-sharp eyes. Turning again to him she said, "Doctor, please tell her that all that smoking and drinking is what did this to him."

An alarm went off in his head as he thought, *Oh no*. He had been through this before. "Well, it certainly is a major factor," he muttered.

"And tell her that being a hundred pounds overweight and eating nothing but junk food is going to kill him!" The pounding in his head seemed to be getting worse. Before he could respond, Mrs. Green after wiping her eyes with her tissue said, "Leave us alone. Did you hear me? Just leave us alone. We don't need this right now."

The sister in a loud voice started to scream, "Well, I don't need a dead brother right now either!" The pounding was reaching new heights. "Before he met you," the sister continued, "he was in fairly good health but look at him now. It's a wonder at what you feed him that he hasn't had a heart attack before now. But no, you wouldn't listen to me. It's a damn shame, that's what it is. It's a damn shame." Each of the sister's words was now like a sharp knife causing excruciating pain in his brain. She was now on the verge of hysteria.

Mrs. Green shouted, "Get her away from me."

"If my brother dies," screamed the sister, "I will never forgive you!"

Nate could take it no longer. He heard himself shouting, "Shut up both of you. Just shut up! No one needs this, especially me. I don't want to hear another word, damn it!" He looked at both of them with fire in his eyes adding, "Understand? Do you understand?"

They both stopped immediately and looked at him in shock. The new young nurse was also aghast. Then the husband of the sister slowly stepped forward in front of his wife, adjusted his hat, and with a narrowing of his eyes said, "Doc, I thank you for taking care of little Jimmy."

Little? He weighed over three hundred pounds and they call him little. He looked up at this cowboy who was some four inches taller than he was who looked like he had just stepped out of a redneck saloon. He waited to see what he had to say.

"But nobody tells my wife to shut up," the cowboy continued. "I think the lady deserves an apology right this damn minute. Understand?"

Somehow it seemed as if this was a well-rehearsed performance that the sister's husband had been called to put on before. As Nate looked at him he could feel his anger reaching the boiling point. He knew that there were many similarities between sleep deprivation and intoxication, one of which was the loss of inhibitions. Before he knew it he was saying, "How about we go outside and settle this right here and now!" The nurse and the two sisters all gasped together.

Just then an armed security guard came quickly toward them. "I heard a commotion going on here. What's the trouble, Doctor?"

The cowboy spoke at once. "This here smartass doctor just insulted my wife and then asked me to step outside and settle this man to man, which I am more than happy to oblige him." The guard turned to Dr. Williams with a surprised look on his face.

Nate felt his jaws tighten. He could not believe that he was wasting his valuable time with such people. He'd had enough. He abruptly turned and left the room, slamming the door behind him. There was no love lost between him and Mr. Green's family.

He did not love his patients or their families. In fact he didn't love anybody. He was a bachelor, age thirty-two and a damn good cardiologist and that was all that mattered along with getting a couple of hours sleep. The last twenty-four hours had not been good. It could not get any worse. At least that was what he thought.

Chapter Two

Nate decided to sleep in the doctors' call room in the hospital. That way he would get a few more minutes of sleep that would have otherwise been lost driving to his apartment. The call room consisted of a small sitting area with a TV with two doors on each side that each opened to a small room with a single bed. He put his beeper on the bedside table as he fell into the twin bed hoping to go right to sleep but like many times before, all the caffeine that he had consumed kept him awake. He was tired but awake. He was not tired of saving lives. He was just tired.

The last twenty-four hours had been brutal. Actually, when he thought about it, the last twenty years had been brutal. He remembered when he had told his parents and teachers in sixth grade that he wanted to be a doctor. Their immediate response was that there are a lot of people who also want to be a doctor making it very hard to get accepted to medical school. If he really wanted to be a doctor they counseled him, he had to start studying harder than before to make better grades. What they were really telling him was not so much that he had to have good grades, but that his grades had to be better than most everyone else, and he realized it. Secretly, his school buddies became his competitors that he had to outperform. This affected his relationship with his peers throughout high school, college and even medical school where he had to compete for residencies. The result was that he had few close friends.

Nate Williams was pretty smart, but he was not brilliant. Quite a few subjects came slowly to him, which meant he had to study harder than most of his peers. In high school, driven by the knowledge that if he did so he would make better grades than everyone else—which he usually did—he was often up until midnight studying completing his assignments. In college he did not join a fraternity because it simply took time away from studying. A number of his friends enjoyed the party life at school but most of them did not get into medical school even though they had fairly decent grades. It was something he could have predicted, making him wonder how they could have been so careless. Once in medical school, he thought he might relax a little even though there was a lot to learn but then there was competition for the best residencies. Again he had to outperform his peers.

He was now a successful cardiologist. However, lately he had begun to feel sorry for himself when he thought about all of the other things in life that he had missed on his long arduous quest to become a physician. It didn't help that he hadn't slept since the prior morning on top of the fact that his head was still pounding from all the caffeine he had been drinking to help him stay awake. Working twenty-four to thirty-six hours didn't used to bother him but now he dreaded the long hours followed by the increasingly longer time that it took him to recover from such an ordeal.

Since he arrived at the hospital some twenty-two hours earlier he had overseen two long resuscitations, only one of which the patient survived, counseled both the happy family and the grieving family, performed two heart catheterizations, saw one patient in the emergency room along with his regularly scheduled patients finally making it home at one AM. He had gotten into bed with his scrubs on at one-thirty AM and had just began to doze when his beeper went off at two AM notifying him of the STEMI.

The alarm on his phone startled him. He sat up realizing that he had actually been asleep for almost two hours. He wondered if what had happened was a dream. He looked into the mirror which convinced him that he looked a lot older than thirty-two. He brushed his hair but decided he was too tired to shave. He left the doctors' sleeping quarters wearing his very wrinkled greens and headed to the doctors' lounge on the first floor where he grabbed a donut along with a cup of coffee. He wondered, as he did every morning, why the administration provided such unhealthy food for the doctors every day. Maybe it was their way of getting back at the doctors for giving them grief over every little thing in the hospital that was to their disliking.

He first checked on Mr. Green whom he had just catheterized that morning. He entered the cardiac ICU cautiously, hoping there were no family members present, especially ones wearing cowboy hats. He slipped into the doctors' charting area where he peeped around the edge of the door trying to see where Mr. Green was to establish if anyone was with him. Sue, the nurse who was with him when the disaster took place in the waiting room that morning, noticed someone was peering out of the doctors' area who looked a lot like Dr. Williams but it was hard to tell since she could only see one eye. "Dr. Williams?" she said as she walked toward him. Nate immediately straightened up and walked from behind the wall in a very dignified manner.

"Good morning," he said professionally. "Does Mr. Green have any visitors this early?" he asked. Sue looked again to make sure.

"No, he is alone," she said.

"Good," Nate said more enthusiastically than he had intended. "How is Mr. Green doing?" he asked.

"He has been very stable; all his vital signs are good. Now he is mainly sleepy," she said.

"Aren't we all," was Nate's reply. He grabbed Mr. Green's chart and read over it quickly before going to examine his patient who slept the whole time. Nate was aware that occasionally he had begun to envy his patients who were able to sleep most of the day even if it was done in uncomfortable hospital beds. *Envying sick people is not a good sign*, he told himself. He tried to dismiss these thoughts as quickly as they came after which he pretended he never had them.

It was the change of shift. While the nurses had their usual meeting to pass on information about the patients, he grabbed the charts of the patients he would see that morning. He took them back to the doctors' chart room, placing them in front of him trying to stay awake. He was almost through the first chart when he heard the nurses coming out of their meeting. Soon there was Sandy, one of the best cardiology nurses he had ever worked with, standing beside him with his usual cup of coffee in her hand fixed just the way he liked it. He looked up at her with his bloodshot eyes and said, "Thanks Sandy."

"Sounds like you had quite a night," Sandy said as she handed him the cup. He always felt better when Sandy was there. She was good at what she did. The other nurses got on his nerves. They didn't pay attention to details like Sandy did. They couldn't foresee what would be needed in the same way Sandy could. Sandy often had things ready before even he realized he needed them. He could always depend on her.

"I think I'm getting too old for this," he said, staring at the wall.

"No, you're not. You're still young; you just need some sleep,"

Sandy said as she patted his shoulder before leaving to take care of her patients. *Young*, he thought. *I feel like I am sixty.*

The morning seemed to proceed as usual. He saw several patients, two of whom he had catheterized the day before. Around 10:30 he was walking down the hall after leaving a patient's room when he saw the head of cardiology, Dr. Archer, and a fellow cardiologist, Dr. Allen, approaching him.

"Dr. Williams, may we have a word with you privately?" Dr. Archer said with a very straight face. Nate was surprised that Dr. Archer had called him Dr. Williams instead of Nate the way he usually did.

"Sure," was Nate's reply.

"I think the best place would be in the small conference room next to the executive boardroom on the first floor," Dr. Archer said. Dr. Allen stood there silently beside him with a somber expression. *This is very strange*, Nate thought. He began to feel a little apprehensive. They took the elevator from the second floor where the cardiology patients were down to the first floor. In the elevator all three just looked straight ahead without saying a word.

The conference room was small with a polished wooden rectangular table with ten chairs around it. Nate sat on one side while Dr. Archer and Dr. Allen sat on the other side across from him. Once seated, Dr. Archer appeared to relax. He leaned forward to Nate with a half-smile, half-surprised look on his face. "Nate, what in the world happened this morning?"

"Oh, you mean when I had to calm down those two ladies who were screaming at each other?" Nate answered.

Dr. Archer's smile seemed to be getting a little bigger. "I heard that you invited some redneck outside to duke it out. Is that true?"

"Well," Nate said slowly, trying to figure out how to explain what happened in a way so it didn't sound so bizarre. "I did ask him to step outside."

"Well I'm sure you had your reasons. By God, I wish I had been there to see that." Dr. Archer leaned back while Dr. Allen smiled. "Unfortunately this has spread like wildfire around the hospital and the 'redneck' and his wife have filed a formal complaint against you." Nate just looked up and slowly shook his head from side to side in disbelief. "This has reached the administration of the hospital, who in turned contacted Dr. Rogers, chief of staff." Nate slumped down in his chair. He couldn't believe this was happening.

"Dr. Rogers sent us here to inform you that as of now your hospital privileges are suspended until further notice. Dr. Allen here will be covering your patients."

"Now wait a minute," Nate said as he sat up. "This is uncalled for. It was just a simple incident."

"All the nurse stations have been notified. We will tell your patients that you had to leave due to an emergency," Dr. Archer said without responding to Nate's statement.

"I'm glad to cover your patients, Nate," said Dr. Allen.

Nate looked at Dr. Allen briefly before turning back at Dr. Archer. "Surely you can do something."

"I'm sorry but these are orders from the chief of staff," Dr. Archer continued.

"Does he have the authority to do this?" Nate asked.

"He does. It's in the hospital bylaws that we all are supposed to have read when we joined the hospital." Nate remembered throwing them into the trashcan. "He wants to see you in his office tomorrow at 9 AM. Also, you are required to give a urine sample for drug tests along with a blood sample for an alcohol level. Here is a cup for the urine. Dr. Allen will draw your blood."

"You know I don't do drugs or alcohol," Nate said.

"We know you don't, but it's the rules," Dr. Archer returned.

Dr. Williams sat back bewildered. *This can't be happening to me. This only happens to other doctors*. After a long silence of about two minutes he took the urine cup, went into the bathroom shutting the door when Dr. Allen apologized but said he had to witness the collection. After that Dr. Allen drew his blood in the appropriate tube. Afterwards Dr. Archer put his hand on his shoulder and said, "Go home. Get some rest. You need it," Then both of them left.

Dr. Williams sat back on the chair, rubbed his face, and asked himself if this was all real. He then went out into the parking lot, got in his car and drove to his apartment half asleep before collapsing in his bed. He woke up around six that evening hungry. He grabbed a can of beer from the refrigerator then opened a can of beans that he ate sleepily. He turned on the television but nothing interested him. He turned it off then sat in his recliner in the dark staring at the dark screen not really thinking of anything. He was still recovering from the night before. After about an hour he went back to his bed to escape again into sleep.

Chapter Three

HE WOKE UP AT FIVE AM. EVEN THOUGH HE HAD plenty of sleep he was still a little groggy as he stumbled to the kitchen to start the coffee brewing. Usually he would fix the coffee maker the night before setting the timer so the coffee would be ready when he woke up, but last night he was too tired. As the coffee perked he started to remember what all had happened. When the coffee stopped perking he put his usual small amount of half and half with a package of artificial sweetener into the cup before walking out onto the balcony of his apartment.

His apartment was on the tenth floor, the top floor of an old hotel that had been renovated into rather swanky expensive apartments. He signed up for his apartment before the renovation had finished so he could be at the top. The building was ideally situated near downtown restaurants and only three or four stoplights from the hospital.

He stepped out onto his balcony and looked down upon the town of Everston. Everston was an old southern city located some seventy miles from the Atlantic coast. Northwest of Everston were some scenic lakes among foothills along with some small but interesting towns. Southwest was the town of Frankston where he grew up and where his parents lived. It was also where he went to undergraduate school at Central University.

Everston had experienced quite a growth in the last fifty years, almost doubling in size to a population of near two hundred thousand. This meant that it had a number of excellent hospitals each with medical specialists in all fields. It also meant that Everston now had freeways and traffic jams. However Nate lived in the old central part of town, which preserved the small town feeling with small shops alongside of larger modern office buildings. Large old trees lined the streets providing shade for the downtown traffic.

Nate sat down in a chair beside the small round table on the balcony where he could see the city lights that were slowly becoming more in number as everyone began to wake up. This was the favorite thing he liked about his apartment. As he looked out at the early traffic he heard sounds of police cars and ambulances. He thought to himself what a complicated mess humanity was. *But it was an interesting complicated mess.* That was the one thing he liked about medicine, the diversity of the human condition that he was exposed to. He could treat it, observe it but not be a part of it. After working to heal some of it he could retreat to his balcony where life was not complicated and he could look down and count his good fortune.

As the sun started to brighten the city he thought about his meeting with Dr. Rogers. What could come of this meeting, he wondered. He knew of physicians who took drugs or drank to excess or even worse were incompetent and injured or sometimes killed patients, so he thought, surely his little altercation couldn't amount to much. *I had better look and act professional though*, he thought, *because you never know about the politics in hospitals.* This meant he should get out of the scrubs he had lived in for the last forty-eight hours and shave and bathe, which he also hadn't done for two days. This he did dressing appropriately before driving to the hospital to see Dr. Rogers.

St. Joseph's Hospital was an average-size hospital with a little over two hundred beds. It started out in the nineteen twenties as a small Catholic hospital run by nuns and even though it was theoretically still a Catholic hospital, nuns were rarely seen. The hospital was spread out, which meant that it could have all the departments that most hospitals had and yet be only four stories high. The first floor consisted of administration offices, patient admissions, the emergency room, which was adjacent to the department of radiology, the laboratory, the gift shop, the general cafeteria and, somewhat hidden next to it, the secluded doctors' eating area. Obstetrics, postpartum, nursery, and the Neonatal Intensive Care Unit were close together on one-half of the second floor while the other half consisted of ICU, intermediate care, surgery, recovery, and the catheter lab, which Nate and the other cardiologists used daily. The third flood was split between medical beds and surgical beds. That was also where the Gastrointestinal (GI) lab was located. The fourth floor consisted of physical and occupational therapy, the inhalation therapy department, rooms for educational purposes, and a number of rehab beds.

Nate got to the waiting area outside of Dr. Roger's office at 8:40 where Mrs. Vye, his secretary, greeted him. She was fiftyish, well made up with a little too much makeup with a heavily sprayed hair style of the sort that most women in their fifties seem to prefer. Mrs. Vye greeted him with a smile and told him to have a seat because Dr. Rogers had someone in his office at the moment. She then returned her attention to her keyboard. As he looked at her he knew that she probably knew more of what was going on in the hospital than anyone else including the administrator and chief of staff. She sat there typing on her keyboard occasionally glancing at him with a very slight smile as if she knew what this was all about. *I am sure she enjoys her job*, Nate thought to himself. He could imagine the stories that she most likely told her husband each night. He just hoped he wasn't going to be one of those stories.

Just then the hospital administrator came out of Dr. Roger's office and said in a solemn voice, "Good morning Dr. Williams," after which he shook his hand and left. *I wonder what they were talking about*, Nate said to himself, trying to make a small joke. Mrs. Vye then told him Dr. Rogers would see him now. As he walked in Dr. Rogers was standing reading an open file that he had in his hands as he walked back and forth behind his desk. He looked up briefly and said, "Good morning Dr. Williams. Have a seat." Nate sat in a high-backed leather chair that was in front of Dr. Rogers's large wooden desk. As Dr. Rogers continued to read the folder he was carrying, Nate looked around and could not help but be impressed. There was a bookcase on one wall filled with books and journals. On the opposite wall hung a large number of diplomas and honorary degrees. The wall behind Nate was well decorated with artwork, as was the wall behind Dr. Rogers's desk. On the desk were pictures of his wife and grown children with his grandchildren. On one corner of the desk was a round fossilized shell sitting next to what appeared to be a small bowl made from some sort of woven plant fibers that he probably got on one of his trips to the Amazon that he was known to take. Dr. Rogers, in his mid-sixties, appeared healthy and in good shape. He was bald with a rim of gray hair that circled his baldness. He was around five foot ten inches and for some reason wore a white doctor's coat that reached down below his knees even though he did not see patients anymore. He had become rather famous early in his career for research he had done in infectious diseases but now, near retirement, worked as an administrator.

"Dr. Williams, I see here that you graduated from Central

University at age twenty-one. How did you accomplish that in three years?" Dr. Roger's asked.

"Well, I went all year around. It is not difficult if you take advantage of summer classes."

"I see," Dr. Rogers responded. "You were able to achieve an excellent grade point average and you did well on your Medical Admission tests. In medical school your record shows that you graduated number ten out of two hundred. That is really remarkable."

"Thank you sir," Nate said.

"Also in medical school, you stayed during the summer breaks to work on research projects with one of the professors. You then did a three-year internal medicine residency during which time you published two papers. It that true?" asked Dr. Rogers.

"Yes sir," replied Nate. "They were case reports of two interesting patients that required an extensive search of the medical literature," said Nate proudly.

"I remember my residency in internal medicine," Dr. Rogers went on. "It seems that I was almost totally exhausted for three years. I wish I had been able to publish during that time. Then you were accepted for a two-year cardiology fellowship at John Hopkins during which time you did research on stents. Is that correct?"

"Yes sir," Nate answered.

"And I believe that you just finished a paper that was supported by a small grant that you received the first year you were here."

"Yes sir," Nate said again.

"Dr. Williams," Dr. Rogers said as he looked up from his file, "you are now only thirty-two years old and have accomplished all this. May I ask you a personal question?"

"Sure," answered Nate.

"What do you do for fun?"

This took Nate quite by surprise. *Why would he ask that?* Nate asked himself. "Well, I'm pretty busy as you know so I don't have a lot of time for leisure." Dr. Rogers kept looking at him waiting for him to say more. "I guess the main thing I like to do on my off time is have a beer at a local sports bar and watch whatever sport is in season."

"You're not married, are you?" asked Dr. Rogers.

"No, I'm not."

"Do you have a girlfriend?"

"No sir."

Dr. Rogers looked at Nate now over his glasses that had slid down somewhat on his nose. "Are you . . ."

Before Dr. Rogers could finish Nate broke in, "No sir. I'm straight."

"Dr. Williams," Dr. Rogers said as put down the file and sat behind his desk, "as you know, you are one of our most promising new cardiologists. That is why the report of what happened yesterday morning is so surprising. According to the sister of Mr. Green and her husband and according to our interview with the nurse who witnessed the event, you told Mrs. Green and Mr. Green's sister, who were arguing, to 'Shut up! I don't want to hear another word damn it,' or something to that effect. Is that correct?"

"Yes, I think I said something like that," Nate managed to say.

"And then," Dr. Roger's continued, "when you were confronted by the husband of the sister of Mr. Green you asked him to step outside to settle it?"

"I'm afraid that's true," Nate admitted.

Dr. Rogers became quiet. He looked off deep in thought before turning back to Nate. "Your urine and blood tests were clean, which I knew they would be but we had to follow the rules. I know you had been up for almost twenty-four hours and were exhausted in a stressful situation. However, as physicians we are supposed to act professionally regardless of the circumstances or how we feel and you certainly did not act professionally."

Nate looked remorseful. "I am really sorry sir," he said. "This has never happened before. I will apologize to them."

"I think if you will just write a sincere apology I can meet with them to smooth things over," Dr. Rogers said.

"Thanks," Nate responded beginning to feel better. He hoped this little ordeal was over so he could leave soon.

"There is one other thing," Dr. Rogers continued. "Mrs. Green's father who was with her when this all happened is our newest hospital board member and is one of our largest contributors to our hospital foundation." Nate sank back into his chair. The good feeling he had been nurturing began to disappear. "I met with him and he thinks you are one of the greatest physicians he has ever met. He was very impressed with how you saved his son-in-law." Nate perked up. *He should have been impressed.* "When I told him about your credentials he was even more impressed." *Few patients really appreciate what we do for them as much as they should*, Nate thought. *Finally here is one who does.* "That is why," Dr. Rogers went on, "he wants to get you some help."

"Get me some help?" Nate almost yelled as he sat straight up in his chair.

"Yes, get you some help. He thinks you need a therapist or something," Dr. Rogers informed him. Nate sank back into his chair. Maybe this was not going to be a good morning after all.

"He has left it up to me," Dr. Rogers continued. "But he expects, even demands, that I do something." Dr. Rogers paused again. "To be honest, I've been worrying about you for some time. Your work is excellent. However, you don't seem to relate to people well. None of the staff thinks you really like any of them." Nate had never seen the point of trying to get along with or be friends with any of the staff. They all had a job to do and things like that just got in the way. Besides, most of them were not as competent as they should be. That irritated him.

"Dr. Williams, I personally think you are overworked and have been on the verge of burnout for a very long time," Dr. Rogers continued. "This is not uncommon among us physicians. We tend to think we are indispensable for some crazy reason or another and we are not, you know. They used to tell us in medical school that if you think the world cannot do without you, look at your appointment schedule the day after your funeral." They both smiled. "I think basically you need some time off. So I am suspending your hospital privileges for one month."

"A month?" Nate asked as if he couldn't believe what he had just heard.

"Yes, a month," repeated Dr. Rogers. Nate felt himself getting very angry. All this for a simple slip of the tongue wasn't fair or logical. No one appreciated how hard he had worked. No one understood.

"What about my patients?" Nate immediately asked.

"Again, you are not indispensable, Dr. Williams. We have other very capable cardiologists, as you know, who can take good care of your patients." Dr. Rogers stood up and so did Nate. "I don't want to see your face around here for a month and if I do you will be suspended for another two months. Do I make myself clear?"

Nate could tell that trying to argue would do no good. Dr. Rogers's mind was made up. *I've done more for this hospital than most of the other cardiologists and this is what I get for it*, he thought to himself. *So be it.* Nate nodded that he understood.

"Go do something useless. Go on a date. Read a book. Take a trip." Nate started to leave. As he opened the door Dr. Rogers added, "One more thing, Dr. Williams: Don't be so hard on yourself." Nate turned to look at him as he left his office. Outside, Mrs. Vye gave him a slight goodbye smile. He wondered if she had been able to hear all that they had said.

Nate left Dr. Roger's office and walked through the hospital lobby to the corridor leading to the doctors' office building that was attached to the hospital. His office was on the second floor. The elevator was open waiting for him. He liked the fact that the catheter lab and the patients' rooms were only a few steps from his office. He had many times left his office to handle an emergency or two and then was able to return to his office quickly to finish seeing patients. There would be no patients scheduled this morning since he usually only saw patients in the afternoon, keeping the mornings free for his hospital duties.

His secretary was surprised to see him. She was even more surprised when he told her to reschedule his patients with one of the other cardiologists because he would be out of the office for a month due to personal reasons. He went into his office, closed the door and pulled out some stationery with his name on it. He sat behind his desk and wrote what he thought was a good apology sealing it in an envelope before asking his secretary to take it to Dr. Roger's office.

When he had finished he suddenly became aware of how bleak and bare his office was. There was no artwork or anything else on the walls. His desk, cluttered with papers, had no pictures of family or friends in stand-alone frames. Nor were there any interesting souvenirs on his desk from trips he had taken that could serve as conversation starters. A bookcase was on one wall but it was only one-fourth full with books and journals arranged haphazardly. He sat there looking at his office thinking of how maybe his office reflected his life when his secretary informed him that a nurse with a cup of coffee was here to see him. *Ah, it's Sandy,* he thought as he told his secretary to send her in.

Sandy poked her head in and with a somewhat mischievous smile said, "How about a cup of coffee, Doc."

"Thanks," Nate said. "I could use some coffee just now." Sandy came in, gave him his cup and sat in a chair in front of his desk.

"You know you drink too much of this stuff, don't you?" she asked.

Nate smiled, took a sip and said, "Then why did you give it to me?"

"Because I like you," she said. "I'm the only one, you know."

"Thanks, I needed that just now," he said sarcastically. *I don't really like any of them either*, he said to himself silently.

"You're a good doc though. If any of our staff had a heart problem they would want you," she replied.

"That makes me feel wonderful," Nate again said sarcastically. Nate looked at Sandy's face. She had little makeup on probably because nurses typically did not wear much makeup while working but also because she did not really need makeup like most women did. Her face had a natural beauty. She was very attractive with or without makeup. Her light brown shoulder-length hair was gathered in the back with a ribbon, which enhanced her femininity. He looked at her fingers. As usual there was no ring. She looked to be in her mid-twenties. She had a shapely body, which made him wonder why she wasn't married. There was one thing he liked about Sandy. He always knew where he stood with her. No hidden agendas. She didn't irritate him like the other nurses. In fact he liked being around her. Why had he not asked her out? He did not know why.

"So what's the verdict?" she asked.

"I have been given a month's vacation. You can't beat that," Nate answered.

"What is he trying to do, kill you? No lives to save, no

one to boss around; you will go stark raving mad," Sandy said, half-jokingly.

Nate turned slowly and looked out the window, wondering what he was going to do. After a few moments he said in a thoughtful tone, "Yes, I'm a little worried about that."

He kept looking out of the window, trying somehow to accept his fate and convince himself that everything was ok. Sandy interrupted his thoughts. "Look, Doc. I'm going to suggest you do something that is really different for you. I'm having a party at my place tonight for some of the staff. It's a luau. Lots of fun. It might do you good. Here is where I live." She laid a piece of paper on his desk with her address on it. "I'd like you to come."

Like hell, he thought. The last thing he wanted to do was socialize with all those people he didn't really like and who didn't really like him. Sandy was really the only one he felt comfortable with. There was no way he was going to accept her invitation. "Sure, I'll consider it. Thanks," he said with a smile.

She got up and with a hint of a smile on her face as she left.

He immediately wadded up the piece of paper before throwing it in the trash. He gathered up a few journals and his coat turning out the light as he stepped out of the room closing the door. He stood outside the door for what seemed a long time and then went back in and picked up the wadded piece of paper from the trashcan and put it in his pocket.

Chapter Four

ON THE WAY HOME FROM THE HOSPITAL, NATE ATE A sandwich at a fast food restaurant. Once at home he sat on his balcony to decide what to do with himself for a month. He sat there trying to think but decided he needed a nap and headed for his bed. Two hours later he awoke but still felt a little drugged. He opened a can of diet cola before returning again to the balcony.

He thought about just getting in his car and taking a long road trip but this did not really interest him. He got a little excited thinking about catching a plane to Europe to do some sightseeing. But the more he thought about it the more he could see himself wandering alone through museums or sitting drinking coffee in cafés looking out of windows and the excitement faded.

He began to feel depressed and tense at the same time. He knew what he had to do when he felt this way and that was to go to Mike's Sports Bar and Grille, which was located only two blocks from his apartment building. Also, he reasoned, the walk would do him good. Mike's was located on the first floor of an office building with wooden doors with etched colored glass on the upper half that opened to the street that made it easily recognizable as a sports bar. On the inside were televisions placed high on several walls with sports channels playing. There was a long bar across from tables and booths.

When Nate walked in he immediately felt himself relax. He often wondered why that place would have such an effect on him. Basically, Nate thought, if you had enough money to buy drinks and food, everyone liked you. It didn't matter if you were not good at telling jokes or making sharp conversation. It didn't matter what you did or didn't do or whether you were cool looking or just an average Joe. You were more or less guaranteed unconditional acceptance as long as you kept eating and drinking. Nothing else was demanded of you. You didn't have to compete with anyone.

Nate sat at the bar and Mike asked him if he wanted his usual light beer to which Nate answered yes. It was the first of April and the TVs were showing big-league baseball games that had gotten underway. Nate was not really interested in sports. He didn't have time to keep up with all the teams. Also he didn't need it to participate in small talk at work because he never participated in small talk. His work gave him enough excitement so the drama of who did what in sports was really boring. However, when he was at Mike's having a beer his mind would suddenly become blank as he became absorbed in every pitch wondering whether the batter could get a hit or not.

His attention was so focused on the game that he was a little startled when Ernie, an older, always jolly, overweight insurance salesman who often frequented Mike's, sat by him and asked him who was winning. Nate looked around at him smiling because he didn't know who was winning or even who was playing and said, "Hey" with an air of confidence.

Ernie looked around, leaned toward Nate and said in a low voice as if to guard a secret, "I've got a hot deal on some unbelievable life insurance right now. And the way you work, you just might need it. Interested?"

Nate kept smiling. "Now Ernie, why am I going to need life insurance? I'm not married, I have no family, and my parents are secure in their retirement."

Ernie's eyes focused as they usually did when he encountered a tough customer. Then he smiled almost laughing and said, "Well, you could leave it to your favorite charity." At that they both laughed and Ernie slapped him on the back before ordering a beer.

Nate always had a laugh when he had a beer with Ernie. That was probably why Ernie was so successful selling insurance. "Nate," he said, "I've got another proposition for you."

"Oh yeah?" Nate replied suspiciously.

"Yeah," Ernie came back. "I know you have lots of money but I know you're like everyone else and could use a little more and that's why I'm inviting you to my house for poker tonight with me and some of my friends who are actually lousy at poker."

Nate could think of nothing more boring. Before he thought about it he said, "Thanks, I'd really like to but one of the nurses has invited me to a party at her house tonight."

"Ok, I'll let you off this time but there is poker every Friday night at my house and you're invited."

"Just out of curiosity," Nate asked, "what does your wife do on Friday nights?"

"Oh, the missis? She is always busy with her clubs and friends and church. I hardly see her on weekends. Now that all the kids are out of the house and in college, each weekend I get to drink beer, watch sports, and play poker. I tell you, buddy boy, I have got it made," Ernie said with a contented look on his face as he gazed slightly upward as if he could see heaven through the ceiling of a sports bar.

Nate looked at him and thought if that is what is called being happily married, then he wanted no part of it. He said goodbye to Ernie and started walking back to his apartment, wondering what he was actually going to do on this Friday night. He had no patients to worry about, no journals to catch up on, no papers to write, and no problems to solve except the problem of what he was going to do with himself. He really didn't want to go to Sandy's. Sandy was right; no one really liked him but her. For some reason, he just didn't get along with most of the hospital staff. It would be awkward to be at a party with them.

He sat in his living room in front of a turned-off TV trying to think. No lights were turned on but the light from the balcony lit up the room dimly. As the room grew darker with the setting sun he grew more depressed. Finally he stood up. *This is ridiculous*, he said to himself. Maybe he would go to Sandy's.

He found the wadded-up paper with her address on it in his pocket. She lived in one of the older neighborhoods, which was easily found. He got into his car, which was in the parking garage attached to his apartment building, and headed out. The houses in Sandy's neighborhood were all around seventy-five years old, made of wood adorned with large front porches that were built in a day when people sat on them and actually wanted to see and talk with their neighbors.

Several cars were lined up and down the street in front of Sandy's house. He had to park four cars down after which he sat trying to decide if he really wanted to do this or not. He finally got out, walked up the steps to her porch and knocked on the door. He could see party lights inside and he could hear people's voices mixed with music that was being played.

The door was opened and there stood Bobby, one of the inhalation therapists, with a surprised look on his face. He wore a Hawaiian shirt with a lei around his neck. He turned and looked back into the house. Then he turned back to Nate and said, "Dr. Williams, is somebody sick here?"

"Sandy invited me," Nate returned.

A big smile came over Bobby's face. "Just kidding you. Sandy told us you might show up. Come on in," he said as he grabbed Nate's arm and ushered him in taking him over to the snack table. "Here, help yourself. I know all this is bad for the heart, but then it's good for business, right?" Nate laughed as he grabbed a chip. Besides the usual chips and dips and cookies there were also pineapple chunks on toothpicks along with pieces of coconut. Nate had decided that the safest place to be was near the food where he could eat and look very confident without saying anything. Soon, however, everyone came up to greet him, saying they were glad that he came before retreating to the different parts of the large living room and dining room where they had come from. There were four couples along with one young man who introduced himself as Sandy's cousin. They all had on leis with tropical-looking clothes and the ladies were wearing grass skirts. Nate recognized most of them from seeing them at the hospital, but he had never really talked to any of them before now.

Sandy soon appeared out of a hallway, which evidently led to the bedrooms of the house. Nate had to look twice when he saw her. She had a red flower in her hair, a lei around her neck, a flowered blouse that complimented her form along with a long grass skirt that hid tight-fitting shorts. Nate could not help but smile when he saw her.

Sandy smiled back and said, "Hey, you made it, Doc." Before she could finish, a little boy, approximately seven years of age carrying a Star Wars sword, came from behind her and tugged at her hand. Sandy knelt down and he could hear the child say he was thirsty. Sandy said, "Sure David," and got him a drink, after which he slowly went back down the hall looking at everyone suspiciously.

"Hey did everyone say 'hi' to Dr. Williams?" Sandy shouted and everyone raised their glasses in answer. Her cousin began bringing in more trays of food as Sandy again addressed everyone. "We have more food coming and soon this is going to turn into a real luau. I hope you are ready to have some fun." Everyone cheered and Nate smiled again.

"Thanks for inviting me," Nate said.

"I was afraid you wouldn't come. I'm glad you did," Sandy returned.

Nate did not know what to say. He felt uncomfortable. He knew he couldn't just hang around the snack table all evening. He looked around and then managed to say, "I really like these older well-built houses. There is much more of a homey feel here than in apartments."

"I was raised in this house and it is home to me," Sandy replied. "It's old but I have a lot of memories here and I love it."

Nate felt out of place while everyone else seemed to be enjoying themselves. He had been there long enough. He wanted to leave. "This is really a neat place and a neat party. I wish I could stay longer but I just wanted to come by to say hi. I want to thank you for all the help you have given me at the hospital," he said, hoping he could make his exit.

Sandy looked at him closely sensing how uncomfortable he was. "Come, follow me," she said as she led him out the back door to the rather large backyard that was common in a bygone era. "See that tree there?" she said. How could he miss it? It was one of the biggest oak trees he had ever seen, with huge limbs that seemed to defy gravity as they spread all over covering the yard. There were several strings of lights along the limbs that made it resemble a very unusual Christmas tree.

"I climbed that tree when I was nine years old and fell and broke my arm. It was an open fracture that required surgery." She held up her left arm so he could see a long well healed scar below her left wrist.

He looked up at the massive tree and as he gazed at the upper limbs he said, "Are you going to let David climb this tree?"

"For sure," she replied. "There are no other trees he can climb. He can't climb the trees at school or the park anymore because of liability reasons. Everyone is sue happy these days."

"Tell me about it" he responded. "So you grew up here?" he said.

"Yep, My whole life. Dullsville, huh."

"Oh no."

"Surprised that I have a kid?" she asked.

"Well, I guess I am. I have been more surprised that you are not married. You must be rejecting suitors right and left."

"Well thank you, Doc. Did you just pay me a compliment?"

He blushed a little. "I guess I did."

"I got pregnant when I was a senior in high school. My dad and mom said that since I had chosen to get pregnant I had also chosen to get married. Our rabbi was against it but my parents made us get married by the justice of the peace. We were just stupid young kids. He was a cowboy full of fun and drinking and I think that's what he still does for a living. He doesn't visit David. But he's basically a nice guy who just wasn't cut out to be a father. I had my sights on college and wanted to be a nurse. It only lasted a year."

"I guess your parents were upset," Nate said politely.

"I didn't speak to them for six months after that until my mother was accidentally killed in a car wreck," Sandy said solemnly. "I was an only child and my dad had lost both of us. Of course at the funeral I hugged him and asked for his forgiveness but he never got over it." She became quiet. She looked away and a tear came to her eye. Her voice quivered a little.

"Is your dad still living?" he asked.

She looked back. "He was a pharmacist and once alone he started doing drugs. Dad was older than mom and he quickly looked twice his age. The narc agents were closing in on him when he developed fulminant hepatitis and died."

"I am so sorry," Nate managed to say.

She smiled briefly. "My parents were nice people and I loved them. It's just that life threw too much at Dad for him to handle. I got this paid-off house out of the deal and that is my wonderful story. I don't know why I told you all this. Please forgive me. It was not planned."

He stood there not knowing what to say. What a tragic story she had. Yet she seemed to be one of the happiest, most competent, well-rounded people he had ever known. "I really appreciate you sharing all that with me," Nate said sincerely.

"Thanks," she whispered.

"David is sure one cute little guy," Nate said to change to a happier subject.

"Thanks." A smile came to Sandy's face. "When I was younger I never imagined how much I would enjoy being a mother or how much I could love one little boy."

Nate could see the joy in her face. "I think David is one lucky kid to have you as a mom."

"Are paying me another compliment?" she asked.

"Yes I am," Nate responded. They were both silent for a minute. Then he said, "You're Jewish?"

"Yep. What are you?"

"Nothing. I'm nothing."

She looked at him and smiled. "So you're nothing. Does that mean you are an atheist?"

"No, not really. I just don't think about it. I've been too busy for all that," Nate answered. "I've never really known anyone who was Jewish before."

"Well, we don't bite," Sandy said. Nate smiled. "Actually we never went to the synagogue much. I don't think my parents really believed in God and if they did they never talked about it. They did try to keep up some of the Jewish customs of their childhood in our home."

"What about you?" Nate asked. "Believe in God?"

"Not really, I don't know. I've been trying to take David to the synagogue when I can. I want to give him a chance to believe in God, a chance I didn't have."

Just then Bobby yelled out the door, "Sandy, it's time." Sandy looked at Nate and motioned with her head and eyes that they needed to go back inside. Nate had worked with Sandy daily in crisis situations but in the last few minutes he felt closer to her than ever before. He felt a growing admiration for the best cardiology nurse he had ever known.

When they went in Bobby was standing on a chair. When he saw them he began to announce, "Ok, it is time for our hula contest. The ladies will do their best and then the men will vote. Of course each guy will vote for his wife or girlfriend if he knows what's good for him. Sandy's cousin will vote for her so it is easy to predict that we will have a tie. However, we are so fortunate that Dr. Williams is here unaccompanied and unattached to anyone so he can give an unbiased vote so we should have a winner. Let the music begin."

Nate immediately said, "Now wait a minute," but his protest went unheard. The ladies all took off their shoes, stood next to one another and began their dance. Nate found himself watching five lovely young women in their twenties or thirties doing the hula in front of him. Suddenly he felt more relaxed than he had been in a long time. Even more relaxed than he was at Mike's. His eyes scanned all of them but they kept coming back to Sandy. The rhythmic swaying movement of all of her curves mesmerized him, as did her face. She was pretty. She had barely noticeable dimples in her cheeks when she smiled, and she smiled a lot. She was not just pretty; she was beautiful.

Nate was sitting in a chair as they all swayed in front of him. He relaxed even to the point that he forgot where he was or what he was doing until suddenly he realized that the music was over and everyone was looking at him. He sat up quickly, no longer relaxed as everyone waited for him to say who had won. He got up, rubbed his chin and walked back and forth slowly as if he was deep in thought all the while wondering what he was going to do. He told himself that he was used to high-pressure situations so surely he could pull this off.

After a full minute he began. "In my many years of doing intensive research into the fine art of hula dancing I have never really encountered such a talented group of ladies. Each has definitely added new moves and interpretations to the tradition of hula dancing that will go down in history. Thus I am very reluctant to raise one of these fine ladies above the others. However, such a burden has been thrust upon me and I must fulfill my duty. I choose Sandy."

In unison all the men yelled, "Yes!" raising their drinks. Bobby got up and said, "Let's give three cheers for Dr. Williams and all the beautiful ladies." After which commenced much laughter and Dr. Williams entered into playful banter with them all as the men said things like, "way to go Dr. Williams" while the ladies said, "You are something else, Dr. Williams."

When all had died down he found himself alone at the snack table with Sandy. ""You did good, Doc," she said smiling.

He began to feel relaxed again. He looked at her. "Thanks for inviting me. I really must go."

"Sure," Sandy replied. She grabbed his hand as she walked him to the front door. After opening the door she led him out onto the porch. The porch light was off leaving only the glimmer from the window combined with the glow from the nearby lamppost to provide enough light for them to see each other. There was a chill in the air. Sandy squeezed his hand as she moved close to him. Her bare arm rubbed against his as she said, "It's colder than I thought."

Sandy's touch made him tremble. He looked down at her. She was smiling looking back up at him. Her face was aglow. The feel of her soft warm skin against his thrilled and excited him. She was beautiful. Tonight after talking with her he understood just what a beautiful person she really was. He had never held her hand before or felt her against him. It was a new and wonderful feeling that he was experiencing. He definitely liked Sandy a lot. He had often thought that Sandy liked him. Now that she was holding his hand and pressing her arm against his, he was sure of it. He had known and admired her for two years but he had not made any advances toward her. He wondered why and wished he had of. He imagined them being together, being close and having an intimate relationship. He wanted to ask her out for a date. He wanted to kiss her and the way she looked at him, he was sure she wanted him to. Then he started to get scared. The more he looked at her the more he realized how different they were. She was so wholesome, so pure. She was everything he was not. She was loving and he was not. She loved her son David and he wasn't sure if he even liked kids. She had friends and liked people and he didn't. Unlike him, she was a thoughtful person. In summary, she had a big heart, and he had small shriveled up one, and he knew it.

"Thanks for coming," she said, trying to have a conversation still smiling.

"Thanks for inviting me," Nate returned. He stood there paralyzed. All of a sudden he felt ashamed of who he really was. He wanted to hide. As a doctor he was confident. But as a person or maybe a lover he felt inferior and afraid. Sandy was close and it was exhilarating but scary, very scary. It was too scary. He had to leave.

"Come back, ok," Sandy said as he let go of her hand.

"I will," Nate lied. As he walked to his car Sandy stood on the porch in her grass skirt watching him. She waved goodbye before going back into her house. Nate sat there. He couldn't get Sandy out of his mind. She was beautiful. Only now he realized how much he really liked her. Only now he realized how fearful he was of exposing his true self to her. He felt small and lonely. He did not know that sometimes you have to fight for love. Sometimes you have to fight an external foe, but more often than not you have to fight the lesser angels within. Nate knew how to fight. He had fought all his life to achieve to get ahead of others but he had never fought for love. Such a thing was not in his repertoire. When it came to love he was a coward. He sat there filled with regret. He would never have her love. He would never be her equal. He wanted go back to his apartment and sit on his balcony and look down upon the city. It was something he enjoyed doing but now he wondered why the thought of it depressed him.

Chapter Five

THE NEXT MORNING, SANDY WAS STILL ON HIS MIND. He could see her eyes, her smiling face, her beautiful body, and all that was her. The fact that he could not have her was like a weight pressing on his heart. She was simply out of his league. She was a family person. The fact that they lived in two different worlds depressed him.

After finally getting out of bed he went to the kitchen to make himself a cup of coffee. He then sat on the balcony enjoying the cool Saturday morning air. As he sipped his coffee he could see the hustle and bustle of the city below making him wonder what they were all doing.

Suddenly he thought of his parents, which surprised him because he didn't do it very often. He didn't call them but maybe once every couple of months and visited them less, even though they only lived two hours away in his hometown of Frankston. His dad, Pat, taught mechanical engineering at Central University and was near retirement, while his mom, Monica, had been a professor of economics there until she retired a year ago. For some reason he felt a twinge of guilt about not calling them more than he had ever felt before. He had always used the excuse that most doctors have when it comes to personal relationships, that what they do is more important than everything else in life.

He pulled out his phone to call them but then, for some reason, put it down. He always hesitated when the idea of calling them came to his mind. He decided to go ahead. They should be home on Saturday morning because they rarely went anywhere anymore.

His mom answered the phone, "Hello."

"Mom, it's Nate."

"My goodness, Nate, are you ok?"

"Sure Mom. How are you and Dad doing?"

"Oh, we are fine. Are you sure everything is ok?" she asked again.

"Yes Mom. Everything is ok. I just wanted to call and say 'Hi' and see how you guys were doing," Nate replied.

"My goodness then. It is so good to hear from you. Dad, you know, is teaching his last class before retiring at the end of next month. We are both tired a lot, but doing well considering our age. How are you? Is anything wrong?" She couldn't quite believe that he was calling simply to check on them.

"I'm fine, Mom. I know it is unusual but I have the day off and I was wondering if I could drive over and have dinner with you and Dad this evening?" This came out of his mouth before he thought about it.

"You bet. I will cook stroganoff. Is it still your favorite?"

"Yes it is."

"Can you stay the night?"

"No Mom. You know how busy I am; I have to get back but I am really looking forward to this evening. Tell Dad 'Hi.' I will come this afternoon. Ok?" Nate said.

"Ok," his mom replied.

The two-hour drive was pleasant. He felt relaxed seeing stands of trees and pastures with cows grazing. The new environment took his mind off Sandy temporarily. He found their new house in a retirement community with no problem. They had downsized to a small retirement home there because the community offered an exercise center and once-a-month entertainment of one sort or another. Unfortunately all the retirement homes were all in a line and looked the same.

He paused for a minute before knocking at the door. He took a deep breath to calm the unexplained anxiety that he felt each time he visited. His dad opened the door with an open newspaper in one hand. "Nate," he said, "It is good to see you." He gave him a very brief handshake and said, "Come in." Hugging or showing much affection of any kind physically or verbally was simply not in their family tradition, at least not for the menfolk.

His mom appeared from the kitchen, gave him a brief hug and told him to have a seat and talk with his father while she finished preparing dinner.

"Well Nate, how is the medical world. Are you still doing research?" his dad asked.

"Well Dad." He replied, "I have just finished my grant work on stents and I was able to get a publication in a very respectable journal. I am now in between grants and hopefully soon will start applying for my next grant."

"That is wonderful. I am sure you are busy seeing patients every day."

"Yes Dad. I understand you are teaching your last class before retiring."

"Not only is this my last class, which is mechanical drawing, but it is the last time the class will be offered. From now on all mechanical drawing will be done on computers. It is hard for me to believe that future engineers will never use a T-square or pencil again. But that is progress I suppose," his dad said with a slightly sorrowful tone to his voice.

Nate looked at his Dad and wondered. His dad talked with him as he usually did, only occasionally looking at him. He had always been very quiet at home. He was super kind to him growing up, never really correcting him. He never forced his opinion about anything on him mainly because he never really voiced an opinion. He remembered as a child asking him over and over again what movie he wanted to see or what restaurant did he want to eat at. He would always say that whatever everyone else wanted was ok with him.

Carrying a tray arrayed with crackers and cheese and three glasses of red wine, his mom entered and sat down across from them. "This is excellent wine, Mom. Where did you get it?"

"Actually, from the local grocery. It is surprising what they carry these days, and we don't have far to go to shop. In fact we rarely go anywhere that is very far now."

"Now don't grow too old too fast," Nate replied. "You guys have a lot of good years ahead of you, you know. Have you thought of travel, to Europe maybe or a good cruise?"

"Well, maybe some day. Nate, how is Amanda doing? Are you two still in contact with one another?" his mom asked.

Amanda had been Nate's girlfriend during residency. It was amazing how much they had in common. Once they figured each other out they developed a respect for the drive and competitiveness that they both had to reach their academic goals. They soon realized that they both were different from the other residents and thus began to hang out with each other. They eventually shared an apartment and even though they occasionally made love, their lovemaking served only to give them a much-needed break from their busy schedule.

"As you know, Mom, she got accepted to a different cardiology fellowship, which was over five hundred miles from the one I was accepted to." He paused adding, "We were both so busy we didn't have time to keep in touch."

"But didn't you get accepted to the same one she got accepted to?" Monica asked.

"Yes Mom, but I got accepted to John's Hopkins. You and Dad have always taught me to go for the best and that is what I did." Nate began to feel a little nervous. He remembered when he and Amanda went their separate ways after residency that they both felt an unexpected sadness; a sadness that seemed to affect her more than it did him. He had never seen her cry before but that last day she kissed him crying, wondering if they were making a big mistake. He assured her that they were doing the right thing saying that they could keep in close contact with one another. However, they both became absorbed in their fellowship. A year later Nate found out that she had a new boyfriend. He felt he had gotten burned from the whole ordeal even though he had not called or written her the whole time.

His mom announced that dinner was ready in their small dining area. He was overjoyed to have the stroganoff he so loved. The three of them sitting there brought back memories of his childhood. His dad seemed happy. He talked, as he always had done at meals, about the weather and how much he enjoyed Monica's cooking. Their conversations were always polite, pleasant, and superficial. However, he remembered one meal when he was in ninth grade and had brought home several C's on his report card. He remembered their disappointed faces. He remembered his mom saying that with grades like that he would never amount to anything. He remembered breaking into tears and sobbing throughout dinner while his parents continued eating in silence showing no emotion. Their low-key thoughtful praise for him when he did make good grades was the highlight of his childhood, which was about the only time they came close to showing some type of emotion. He dreamt that they would actually hug him when he showed them his report card, but they never did. To disappoint them like he did at the dinner table hurt him more than anything.

He then remembered the two most important days in his life: when he graduated from college and medical school. He was the top of his class each time. It was right after he walked off the stage at college that his dad grabbed his hand and with a lot emotion, which seemed hard for him to control, shook it for over thirty seconds repeatedly saying, "I'm proud of you, I'm proud of you." After that Nate hoped all through medical school it would happen again and it did.

"How about a second helping? We have plenty and then there is cheesecake and coffee for desert." His mom knew how to make him happy. He took seconds and looked forward to the cheesecake.

People often commented how calm his parents always were. He had gotten hints that they were a little freer with their emotions before his older sister was born. She only lived a few weeks before she died of sudden infant death syndrome. After that they just didn't trust emotions. They were both fairly intellectual and had found ways of living and acting that protected them from all the uncertainties of life.

After dinner and desert they talked for a short while. His mom gave him a quick goodbye hug and his dad a brief handshake as usual. He got into his car and thought again about himself as a little boy, a boy with very nice parents, a boy who never felt loved. He felt a deep sorrow within his heart that he always felt after visiting them, a sorrow that maybe he was just now beginning to understand.

Chapter Six

Nate got home late Saturday night tired, sad, and depressed. When he reached his bed, he crashed. The next morning he awoke hoping that he would feel better but he didn't. He made his usual coffee, retrieved the Sunday paper outside his door then sat on the balcony paper in hand. The coffee woke him up. The newspaper caught him up on the world, which seemed to be going along ok without him. He grabbed a bowl of cereal before going back out on the balcony where he sat absent-minded.

At noon he made a sandwich, grabbed a beer and sat in his recliner to watch another baseball game on TV. He went to sleep as he usually did awakening a couple of hours later still in his pajamas unshaven. He turned off the TV and just sat there. *I've got to do something*, he told himself. He got out of his pajamas, put on some jeans with a previously worn sweatshirt and tried to clean the apartment a little. After eating a TV dinner he began playing solitary with an old deck of cards he found in one of his drawers. The game of solitary helped pass the time. It was a mindless game that required minimal thinking and no partner, which you could do over and over again before you tired of it.

He was glad when ten o'clock finally arrived so he could

hopefully again escape into sleep. He slept fitfully awakening Monday morning more tired and depressed than the night before. After coffee he tried to read the newspaper but it did not interest him. He decided he would take a walk. Donning the clothes from the night before along with worn-out tennis shoes he felt ready. His two-day-old beard and the lack of a bath for the same length of time did not bother him because he did not care. He gave his hair one quick swipe with a brush and headed out of the building, where the wind quickly displaced any hair that was in place.

He did not know where he was going, only that he had to go somewhere. It was Monday morning. The streets were busy with traffic bordered by sidewalks that were full of people who were hurriedly going somewhere. Dr. Nate Williams, the young dynamic cardiologist who roamed the halls of his hospital looking for lives to save, now looked like a homeless street person that evoked pity from a number of people who passed him by on the street. The coolness of the early April breeze made him put his hands in his pockets as he walked looking at the pavement a few steps in front of him. He was a bum. No one knew him. Oddly enough he liked the feel of it. There was a sense of freedom that he had not experienced before.

After an unknown length of time and untold number of blocks, he found himself in front of an office building with a bookstore on the corner that occupied one-fourth of the ground floor. He looked up at the name above the entrance, which read, *The Journey Bookstore, For Those Who Are On One. How odd*, he thought. He looked through the glass windows, which had evidently been placed to entice potential customers, and saw quite a few people mulling over books throughout the store. Also there were people sitting in the coffee shop within the bookstore with books in their hands. He thought to himself, *surely these people have something more important to do than hang out at a bookstore on a Monday morning.* He then laughed at the thought that maybe they too had been kicked out of their jobs.

He was about to continue on down the street when he remembered Dr. Rogers suggesting that he read a book, which he hadn't done since his first year in college. With that thought in mind he entered the front door where he discovered a two-level affair with a few steps leading to a lower open room and a short staircase leading to an upper floor. He stood there looking at the two sets of steps as if trying to make the difficult decision of going up or down when a sales lady approached him and said, "May I help you?" He continued to stand there with his hands in his pockets looking at her out of the corner of his eyes. She looked to be around thirty. She was neatly dressed with a long, tight-fitting ankle-length gray skirt and a blue blouse that had *The Journey Bookstore* embroidered above the pocket. Her hair was mid length and perfectly shaped. Her face was both soft and business-like at the same time.

Without turning his head he said, "I'm looking for a book."

"I sort of assumed that. What kind of book. Sports? Travel? History?" she asked.

"A novel," he replied, still looking ahead.

She took a minute to examine this odd-looking street person who wanted a novel. There was something attractive about him despite his disheveled appearance. "Do you read novels?" she asked.

"No," was the short reply. Nate, still looking at her out of the corner of his eyes, noticed how she looked at him. In his career he had learned to tell a lot about a person from their eyes. He could tell when a patient was about to die or recover or when their mind was somewhere else just by looking at their eyes. He could also tell how sharp a person was by the way they focused their eyes. He could see her eyes. She was sharp.

She looked around to make sure no one was close then leaned a little toward him and asked in a lower tone "Are you ok?"

"Sure I'm ok," he managed to get out.

She hesitated and then asked, "Did you break up with your girlfriend or something?"

"No, I don't have a girlfriend."

"Are you…?"

"No, I'm not," was his quick reply. He wondered why people kept asking him that.

"Come, follow me," she commanded and he obediently followed her up the open steps to a small corner labeled classic books that had a small couch to sit on.

"Look," she said. He turned to see her better. She was not wearing a wedding ring. "There are lots of novels. We have thousands of them. There are some good novels today, but there are also a lot of sorry ones. The trouble is we really don't know which ones are the really good ones, the ones that will still be read twenty-five or fifty or one hundred years from now. However, the books in this corner are the classics. They have stood the test of time. I would highly recommend one of these." At that she turned and disappeared.

He stood there still somewhat in a daze. He started to look at the books as he began running his finger over the titles as if some unknown force would make his finger stop on the right one. There was *War and Peace, Return of the Native, Moby Dick* and all the other titles he had heard somewhere in his past but had not read. Then he saw books by Hemingway. He knew something about Hemingway's life. He had been in war zones, was an avid big game hunter, a sports fisherman and had several wives. He was a man's man. He picked up a *Farewell to Arms* by Hemingway and sat on the couch. It obviously had adventure and might, just might, hold his interest.

Just then the saleslady came back. "Did you find anything?"

He held up the *Farewell to Arms* without saying anything. Her eyes focused and her lips tightened. "Well that certainly is a guy's book. Adventure and love and then he is free for another adventure." She went over to the bookshelves, looked over them for a minute, then picked out a book handing it to him. "Hemingway is a good writer, there is no doubt about it. However, I would recommend that you read this one along with it; it will balance you out."

He reached up and took the book. It was *A Tale of Two Cities* by Charles Dickens. She then again walked away. He sat there with the two books in his hands unopened. After a while he got up, went to the checkout to pay, then walked somewhat slowly back to his apartment.

Once back in his apartment he laid the two books on the coffee table in front of him and thought about the very attractive saleslady he had just met at the bookstore. She fascinated him. She was upfront and open like Sandy. He wanted to get to know her better but after today he thought there would be little chance. He tried to stop thinking about her but he could not.

Two days later he showed up at the bookstore again. However, this time he had showered and shaved and put on fresh casual clothes. He ordered coffee at the coffee bar and sat down with the two books in his hand. He wondered what he was doing there. He felt like he was in junior high hoping to run into that "special" girl. *She probably has a serious boyfriend*, he thought. Besides, his first impression had been a disaster. *She may be only part time and what are the chances of her recognizing me?* He sipped his coffee feeling pretty stupid.

The two books lay on the table unopened. He stirred his coffee staring at it like someone looking at tea leaves to determine their future when he raised his head up. To his surprise there she was standing looking at him. For a second he thought it was a dream or maybe she was a mirage. For some reason he had trouble speaking so he just smiled and held up the two books. She stood there holding a couple of books that rested partly on the curve of her waist. After some thought she said, "I have always believed that books could work miracles and now I have proof of it. How much have you read?"

"Well, I've almost read one chapter of each," he stammered.

She smiled again. "You must be a wimp of a reader."

"No, I read a lot," he protested, and he began to feel like his old self again.

"Like what?"

"Well, you know journals and things like that."

"You mean like technical journals?" she asked.

"Well, you might call them that," he replied.

"So you probably read each paragraph three times to make sure you haven't missed any details and get bored out of your mind," she said.

"Well, it is something like that," Nate agreed.

"You know, I think you have an FRD," she said with confidence.

"An FRD? What is that?" Nate asked.

"That is a fiction reading disability. I'm sure you have it."

He smiled. "Does the owner of this store know you treat customers this way?"

"I am the owner," she replied.

"Oh. Well then, do you treat all your customers this way?"

"No," she replied. "Only the ones I like."

That reminded him of something but he couldn't quite remember what. He only knew that he wanted to talk with her more.

"Look," he said before he knew it. "Nothing against your

coffee here, but could I have a cup of coffee with you somewhere else?" All of a sudden the courage he had regained the last few minutes completely left him. He knew he had blown it.

She looked at him thoughtfully for a moment and then said, "Ok. There is a coffee shop two blocks down from here. I can meet you there at three this afternoon, but you're buying."

He smiled. "You bet." As she walked off he said, "I don't know your name."

"It's Angela, Angela Carter. And yours?"

"It's Nate, Nathaniel Williams," he had to almost shout as she walked away.

Chapter Seven

THE COFFEE SHOP WAS IN ONE OF THE OLDER BUILDINGS in town. Inside, the light was sufficient for reading but not bright. There were a few tables, a few comfortable lounge chairs, and a few booths along one wall. A number of people of different ages were sipping coffee, reading books, or typing on computers. A few students were looking intently at open textbooks. Music could be heard in the background that was of such a low and soft nature that it did not interfere with conversation or reading.

Nate grabbed one of the booths and waited. He wished he had prepared something very clever to say but nothing came to his mind. *Oh well, I will just be myself,* he told himself. But the trouble was, when he was not a doctor, he wasn't sure who he was, and unfortunately he did not have quite enough time to figure that out in the next five minutes. Angela arrived before he could finish his thoughts on the subject. He raised his hand slightly as she surveyed the room. Upon seeing him she took the seat across from him in the booth. Nate welcomed her standing up as she sat down.

"What can I get you?" he asked. "Remember I'm buying."

"A latte," she replied. He got up, ordered two lattes and brought them back to the booth.

They both sat there in silence for a few moments sipping their lattes occasionally glancing up at one another. Angela was very attractive. Sitting across from her allowed him to study her more closely. Her makeup was carefully chosen accentuating her beauty. Her lips were not prominent but were of a subtle shade of red that kept his eyes coming back to them. He marveled at how natural she looked while at the same time her cheeks, eyelashes and eyebrows displayed the soft light touch of an artist. She obviously had class. Even the way she sipped her latte spoke of refinement and taste.

As the silence continued it was clear that she was waiting for him to say something. He was on the spot. He had to come up with an opening line. He asked himself why he was not good at things like this. His anxiety was increasing to a point that he finally told himself to just say what was on his mind. "I want you to know that when I came into the bookstore the other day, that, that was very out of character for me. It was very unusual, very unusual," he finally got out. She looked up for a second then began to sip her latte again remaining silent. He looked down at his cup thinking maybe she didn't hear him or maybe she just didn't get it. After a minute that seemed like an eternity, he repeated, "Very unusual, very unusual," shaking his head.

"What do you do, anyway?" Angela inquired. "I know you read journals but that is about all I know about you."

He was afraid that she would ask that question. He had not prepared an answer. He didn't want to be a doctor with her. He just wanted to be a guy. He thought about trying to evade the issue or lying, saying he worked in the lab or something. However, he was not good at lying or pretending so he said, in a somewhat muffled voice, "I'm a doctor."

"A doctor," she exclaimed. "No wonder you have an FRD."

He put his cup down and looked at her. His emotions suddenly went from anxiety and admiration to irritation. "This fiction reading disability, is it actually a disorder or just something you made up?" he demanded.

She didn't seem to hear him. "Fiction reading disabilities are very common in doctors. They are usually incurable. What kind of doctor are you?"

"A cardiologist," he said flatly.

"A heart doctor, my goodness. Now tell me what is a heart doctor doing walking around looking like a homeless person and why does he have so much time off? Are you on vacation?"

"No."

"So did they ask you to leave or something?"

"Sort of, just for a month."

Angela leaned forward with her eyes wide open. "What did you do? Was it drinking or drugs?"

"No," he said firmly becoming more irritated.

"Did you make a mistake and injure someone?"

"No," he said a little louder. Now he was getting angry.

"Did you accidentally kill somebody?"

That was the last straw. He got out of the booth, stood at the end of the table and halfway shouted, "No!" He then looked around. Everyone in the coffee shop had stopped what they were doing and were staring at him. He gave a slight apologetic smile before slowly sitting back down.

"Look," he said in a low tone. "There was a shouting match going on between the wife of one of my patients and her sister-in-law and it was four AM and I couldn't stand it any longer and I told them to shut up and then the sister-in-law's husband demanded that I apologize and I asked him to step outside to settle the issue."

"And did you?"

"No. I just walked away. The next day the chief of staff decided I needed to take a month off." Nate leaned back. "There," he said emphatically.

Angela looked somewhat dreamily. "I wish I had been there. That's real drama. You have a life of true adventure. Unfortunately all my adventures take place between the pages of a book."

Nate calmed down. "I've only known you a few minutes and I have told you more than I ever thought I would. How did you do that?" he asked.

"I don't know. I guess I'm in the habit of asking questions," she replied with a smile.

"Ok, what about you. How does someone as young as you get to own a bookstore?" Nate asked.

"I have a master's degree in English literature. My goal was to get a PhD. However, I ran out of money and got a job at the bookstore. I did such a 'superb' job that, when the owner was ready to retire, he gave me such a good recommendation that the bank loaned me the money to buy it."

"And now you have it made?"

"By no means. I'm able to pay the bills but there is a lot of competition out there and the new eBooks are hurting."

"How did you come up with the name The Journey Bookstore?" he asked.

"We are all on a journey, don't you think?" she replied.

"Well yes, but some of us reach our destination early and then simply have to wait it out."

Angela looked at him more closely. "Boy, have you got it bad."

"I've got what bad?" Nate asked. He was getting irritated again.

"A lack of a sense of wonder. Here you've got a job saving

lives, a job most people dream about having, and you describe it as waiting it out? I think you need help."

I am tired of people telling me that I need help, he thought to himself. His emotions had been going back and forth between admiration and irritation, but for some reason, he was attracted more than ever to this smart, sassy, good-looking woman who was sitting across from him. In a short period of time she had more or less figured him out, and she still seemed to be interested in him for some reason. "Ok, you may be right," he said, hoping to switch the subject from himself. "Let's talk about you some more. I noticed in the bookstore there wasn't a ring on your finger. Mind if I ask if you are engaged or have a boyfriend? I think you asked me something like that the minute I walked into your store, I recall."

"I asked that because I thought you might be suicidal or something." She looked at him, a little perturbed. "I don't ask every young man who enters my store if he has broken up with his girlfriend, you know."

Nate laughed. "I'm glad to know that. Just the suicidal ones then. Now back to my inquiry, if it is not too personal for me to ask." Nate was feeling more relaxed.

"No, it's not too personal to ask. I am not engaged and I do not have a boyfriend."

"Ever been married?" asked Nate.

"Heavens no. I have had a few boyfriends in my life, but they turned out to be jerks. Besides, I don't believe in marriage; do you?" Angela asked.

Nate was surprised by that answer. Marriage? Did he believe in marriage? He felt on the spot again. He didn't really know if he believed in marriage or not. He took a drink from his cup. "I haven't thought about it," he said truthfully. "I think I've been too busy to really consider if I believe in marriage or not."

"Well in my experience a lot of couples are really happy and then once they are married it turns sour and then they either split up or live a life of misery. What about you, ever been married?" Angela asked.

"No. I had a girlfriend in residency but our fellowships were five hundred miles apart and we didn't keep in touch," Nate replied.

"So career took precedence over love?"

"We weren't really in love," Nate replied, not wanting to discuss the matter further. He looked at Angela, wondering what she was going to ask next.

They both sat in silence thinking they had said too much too soon. After a few more sips Angela stood up and said, "What are you doing Saturday morning?"

"Well," he said thoughtfully as if he was mentally checking a complicated schedule, ""actually nothing."

"Meet me at 8:30 on the corner of Main and 5th street and bring running shoes. There is a five mile fun run to promote heart healthy lifestyles."

Nate smiled. "What are you trying to do, put me out of business?"

"Just maybe," she replied. She smiled and as she walked away he couldn't get over how pretty she was.

He picked up some running shoes along with shorts and a sweatshirt on the way back to his apartment. He showed up at Main and 5th street on Saturday morning wondering what he was getting himself into. He had never run one mile before much less five miles. He knew he wasn't in shape. Then there was Angela. He had only just met her but he knew her well enough to know that she was unpredictable. *What will she ask me next*? He wondered. He looked forward to seeing her but she worried him.

There was a crowd of about a hundred people all in running

outfits who were stretching, talking and laughing. There were a few eighty year olds who seemed fit standing next to some younger overweight runners who looked like they would waddle instead of run. There were both middle age and young people who looked in perfect shape who seemed to have their life together. Nate looked at them all and thought to himself, *Oh God, I hope no one has a heart attack today.*

He located Angela near a raised platform that had a megaphone on a stand sitting on it. She greeted him and commented on his cool outfit, which made him feel somewhat at ease. Angela looked great. She wore a fashion running shirt complimented by well-designed shorts along with running shoes that seemed to match everything else. Angela was obviously in good shape. Her legs had the muscles of a runner but they were feminine muscles that made her legs attractive. The temperature was around seventy making the clear morning a perfect day for running. Angela was bouncing slightly from one foot to the other to both warm up and to use up some of the energy she had built up getting excited about the run.

"Are you a runner?" she asked Nate.

"Sometimes I run up and down the hospital stairs when I have to. That's about it," Nate replied.

"You do know that regular exercise is good for the heart, don't you?" Angela asked with a smile. Nate smiled back and didn't say anything. It was almost time for the run to begin. Angela got up on the platform and grabbed a megaphone. The crowd quieted, and Nate realized that Angela was in charge.

"Welcome everyone to our annual heart healthy fun run. Are you ready?" The crowed all said yes in unison.

"I have a surprise for everyone," she continued. "For the first time we have a cardiologist with us and he would like to say a few words. Welcome Dr. Nathaniel Williams."

She motioned for him to come up to the platform looking at

him with a mischievous smile. He couldn't quite believe that she was doing this to him. He had always avoided speaking to any group whatsoever. Now over one hundred heart-healthy runners were waiting for his words of wisdom. He looked back at Angela. With a grim face he climbed upon the platform and mumbled something about how recognizing the importance of having a healthy heart was the first step to heart health.

Angela then grabbed the megaphone. "Let's give Dr. Williams a big hand. You know," she continued, "if everyone had healthy hearts we would put Dr. Williams out of business. What do you say, shall we put Dr. Williams out of business?" The crowd shouted yes and then began to chant, "Put Dr. Williams out of business." The chant grew louder. People who were standing there just to observe began to chant it also. It seemed to energize everyone as they got ready. Nate looked at Angela and shook his head. They all lined up and when the gun went off more than a hundred runners chanting "Put Dr. Williams out of business" started their five-mile run.

Nate was not overweight and looked in good shape, which in fact he wasn't. Nate was in many ways a typical doctor. Despite what he told his patients he rarely exercised and his excuse was that he didn't have the time. Angela took off quickly leaving him. He actually felt good the first ten minutes. Then he began to take deep breaths as he felt the lactic acid building up in his muscles. After twenty minutes he had to stop. He bent over and put his hands on his knees to rest breathing heavily. He wondered what his cardiac output was and wondered if it wouldn't hurt to have a stress test. Then he thought, *Wouldn't it be funny if I were the one to have a heart attack?* The route of the run made a U turn crossing at the corner where he was bent over. He was deep in thought when Angela ran by cheerily and shouted, "Are you having a heart attack, Doc?"

"Very funny," was his reply.

After the race was over there were hot dogs, drinks, and beer, which everyone enjoyed in abundance. There was much laughter and everyone enjoyed kidding Dr. Williams about being out of shape. He felt good being able to kid them back. Throwing lighthearted jabs at one another was something he rarely engaged in but he found himself actually enjoying it. Soon he began to feel a part of the group instead of "the authority" that he seemed to be in every other situation. Angela was right at home. She evidently got along well with most everyone. She laughed a lot and evidently liked to laugh a lot. She even laughed at some of his comments that he hoped were funny and that made him feel good. He hated to see it all end.

As they walked back to their cars Angela thanked him for coming. "Sorry to put you on the spot back there, but you did really well," she said smiling.

"Actually it was quite a unique experience. I've never had crowds of people chant together to put me out of business." They both laughed.

She then looked a little serious. "Next weekend I am having some friends over to my apartment for an old-time fondue party. Would you like to join us?"

"Yes, very much so. Thank you for the invite." He was delighted. She wrote down her address and phone number on a piece of paper. "See you around seven then, ok?"

"Ok," he replied. He smiled as she walked off. Interestingly, he noticed a heaviness that had been pressing down on his heart seemed to be lifting.

Chapter Eight

NATE NOW HAD TWO WOMEN ON HIS MIND, SANDY AND Angela. Just two weeks earlier there were no women on his mind. He had gone so long without a significant relationship that he had convinced himself that he had no need of one. In fact, he feared them and that gave him more reason to avoid them. He tried not to think about Sandy but she kept coming back into his thoughts. He had known and admired her for two years, but now he realized how attracted he was to her. Sandy was so good in every way imaginable and that was the problem. He was not and he was afraid for Sandy to know that. Now Angela had come into his life. She was also good but, for some reason, he didn't feel afraid around her. She seemed closer to his level, but he didn't know why. Also, Angela had figured out who he really was, and it didn't seem to matter. He didn't need to hide anything from her. That was the difference. He decided to put both Angela and Sandy out of his mind for a while, but they wouldn't go away.

The week passed slowly for Nate. He slept a lot and every time he tried to read his two new books his eyes would glaze over until he went to sleep. He decided that since he now had running shoes and running clothes he would give running another try.

He was surprised how good he felt after a short run. After that he started running a little every day at a nearby park. He ate cereal for breakfast but ate out for lunch and snacked at night.

As Saturday came around he began to feel nervous. When he was with Angela he wasn't afraid, but now that he had been apart from her for almost a week, he began worry about his ability to have a relationship with someone like her. His desire to know Angela better and his fear of a relationship with her were two competing emotions within him that fought with each other, but neither could win, until finally they decided to live alongside one another. He was also nervous about meeting her crowd. He had always felt inept at social gatherings. He had a feeling that he wasn't going to like these people even though he had never met them. Trying to talk to people in a social setting was something he did not enjoy. He would much rather have an in-depth discussion on some area of science than play the game of trying to say something insightful and clever to overly polite people.

He showed up a little after seven and Angela welcomed him in. She had a nice apartment of moderate size on the ground floor, which, at the entrance, made it seem more like a house. Inside, the apartment had a modern look with chairs that looked like large buckets in the living room alongside a modern couch filled with pillows. On the walls hung large modern art paintings with lots of seemingly unorganized colors in shapes that did not seem to make any sense to him. In the dining room he could see three couples sitting at an extended dining table talking.

"Hey guys this is Dr. Williams," she said as she ushered him in. They all smiled and said "Hi," and he said "Hi," back. Angela motioned to him to have a seat. He sat down noticing there was one empty place setting at the table.

"Why don't each of you introduce yourself to Dr. Williams and tell him a little about yourselves while I get the fondue ready,"

Angela said as she got up to go to the kitchen. To his left were two middle-aged, moderately overweight, very happy appearing people who wore matching shirts and blouses. The man had a moustache. Standing up he said, "This is Rita my wife and I'm Tony Moretti. Welcome to Angela's club."

Nate was taken by surprise. "Angela's club?"

"Yes, you see, we are all customers at Angela's bookstore. For some reason or another she picked each of us to come to her apartment once a month or so for food and good discussions. Personally I think it is just a scheme to get us to buy more books." He smiled as his wife hit him on the shoulder.

"Tony is a real kidder," Rita broke in. "Tell Dr. Williams what we do for a living."

Tony's eyes brightened as he prepared to make the announcement. "We are the owners of the Silver Lining Restaurant. You may be wondering why we named it the Silver Lining Restaurant?" Nate nodded that he was. "Because we believe that no matter what situation you find yourself in or what life has thrown your way that a good meal and a good glass of wine will help you see the silver lining around any black cloud. That is our philosophy."

"I agree," said Nate emphatically.

"Have you've eaten there?"

"I'm sorry to say I haven't," Nate replied.

"Well you must come there to eat. Your first meal is on the house and the sky is the limit. Of course you will have to pay for your date if you bring one." Tony's wife hit him again. "I'm just kidding. Your date is free too."

"I am definitely coming but only on one condition, that I pay for the meal," Nate replied.

"Ok, you're a hard bargainer," Tony said without hesitation, "but the tip is on us." Everyone laughed as he sat down. Nate's nervousness began to subside. Tony and Rita evidently were nice people full of laughs. He could definitely get along with them. Then the thirtyish, nicely dressed lady across from him reached to shake his hand. "I'm Cindy Miller. This is my husband Rick. I teach third grade and my husband teaches biology at the downtown junior college. We are so glad you are here." Rick shook hands with Nate and Nate reiterated that he was glad to meet them. He thought to himself that since Rick was a biologist he would be a safe one to have a conversation with.

To the right of them sat a tall thin bearded man with hair down to his shoulders who introduced himself as Professor Gregory Johnson, an English professor at the downtown university. Next to him sat his wife Samantha. Professor Johnson wore a tight thin turtleneck over his thin frame and Nate thought he looked like the picture of Jesus Christ that hung in the hospital chapel. His wife Samantha appeared pale and thin and only occasionally smiled. "We are so glad you are here," he exclaimed shaking Nate's hand excessively looking at him with a penetrating gaze that made him nervous. The prolonged handshake left Nate speechless. He looked at the professor's wife who looked back at him readjusting herself on her seat with little expression on her face. Professor Johnson noticed that Dr. Williams was looking with concern at Samantha. "We have two small children, one six months and the other two years and they keep Samantha busy twenty-four hours a day. She is a dutiful mother." Samantha smiled weakly. "Now tell us about yourself, Dr. Williams," Professor Johnson said still looking at him intently.

Angela had just got all the fondue accessories on the table including candles that she had lighted under the pots.

"Well," Nate started, "please call me Nate; that is, unless you are having a heart attack." Everyone smiled. "First, thank you for such a warm welcome. I'm curious; are the professor and his wife the only ones with children?"

"We have an eighteen year old and a fifteen year old, both boys, but I don't think you could call them children," Rita said as she rolled her eyes.

"We have a third grade girl and a sixth grade boy," announced Cindy. Then, mildly blushing with a smile, she added with a touch of pride, "and our third grader is in my class."

"That's great," Nate replied. "I'm cardiologist who has spent most of his life learning how to be a heart specialist with little time for anything else."

Just then the doorbell rang and several people said, "There he is." Angela went to the door and announced that it was Father Jim. Father Jim looked to be near fifty, was of average height and slightly overweight. He had slightly thinning brown hair with a touch of gray around the edges. He wore the usual black shirt and collar of a priest and smiled as everyone greeted him.

As Father Jim took the remaining empty seat Angela said, "I would like you to meet Dr. Williams."

"Oh, we've met in passing at the hospital making rounds but we were always too busy to talk much. Not much time, you know," Father Jim replied.

Nate greeted him and Father noticed he looked perplexed. "Don't worry, Dr. Williams," but before he could finish Rita broke in: "Father, you are supposed to call him Nate unless you are having a heart attack."

"Oh my dear," Father Jim said placing his hand over his heart. "I have been feeling a little under the weather, but I don't think it is my heart. So well, Nate, I wanted to reassure you that this is not a religious group. In fact they are all pagans. I've tried my best to convert them, but I have been singularly unsuccessful. I have been debating if the fault lies with my technique or with the fact that they are incorrigible." Father Jim hesitated as if in thought before adding, "I have finally decided that they are simply incorrigible." They all laughed including Nate who instantly liked Father Jim.

"Let's eat," Angela announced after which they all began to put pieces on the forks and dip them in the hot oil while Professor Johnson held up a meatball and said, "To eat or not to eat; that is the question."

After that the group began eating all the while continuing a relaxed playful conversation. Nate decided to take a chance and start a conversation with Rick. "What biology classes do you teach?" he asked.

"I teach freshman biology and two herpetology classes," he replied. "But my area of research is on the mating behavior of frogs."

Nate almost laughed, but he was able to keep a serious look on his face while he tried to figure out what to say. "If I remember what I learned in freshman biology, frogs have a three-chambered heart," Nate finally said.

"That is exactly right." Rick seemed astonished. "Few people know that."

"The reason I remember it is that occasionally we have an infant born with a three-chambered heart like a frog. In the past they usually didn't live very long but now there are operations that can prolong their lives although their mortality is high. In fact we had one last month that had surgery after birth but died of complications." Nate was starting to feel at home. All of a sudden he realized that everyone had stopped eating and seemed frozen as they looked at him. He had said something wrong. He had crossed some sort of line. Likewise frozen, he looked back at them.

After a few minutes of awkward silence, Rita said, "That is so sad. That poor baby and those poor parents."

Rick spoke up next. "I learned something I didn't know

before. I never knew that infants were sometimes born with a three-chambered heart."

"'Thou know'st 'tis common; all that lives must die, Passing through nature to eternity,'" Professor Johnson said and then added, "*Hamlet.*" Everyone looked at him as if to say, "Gee thanks Professor Johnson."

Nate realized that they were all disturbed by what he had said. He felt embarrassed and out of place. "I must apologize," Nate said as he looked around. "I often start on medical subjects without realizing it."

"Shoptalk," said Father Jim with a smile and everyone looked at him. "People are usually surprised at other people's shoptalk. You should hear us priests. Of course we can't reveal what we hear in confession, but we do talk about what happened to us at weddings and funerals, etc. Sometimes we say things we shouldn't. After the last time I engaged in shoptalk, I had to go to confession. By the way, Rick, I came across a saying the other day that might apply to your research on frogs. I think it went this way, *You do your thing, and I do my thing and if by chance we meet it's beautiful.*"

Professor Johnson said, "I've got that hanging in my office!" Everyone laughed.

Angela stood up. "I think we should all make a toast to Tony and Rita for bringing us such wonderful wine to have with our fondue."

They all made a toast, after which Tony stood up and said, "Actually, Father deserves credit. He introduced us to this wine after one of his trips to Rome. You know the old saying, *Where the Catholic sun doth shine, there is laughter, dancing, and good red wine.*"

"Yes," replied Father Jim. "That is one of the pillars of our faith." Just then he reached into his pocket pulling out a beeper that had been on vibrate. "Oh dear, I must go. Sorry to have to run, always on call you know."

"No one to share call with?" asked Nate.

"No, there is only me and a retired priest who has such bad arthritis he can't get out at night." Nate wondered how Father Jim was able to be on call twenty-four hours a day seven days a week day after day but most of all he wondered why he wanted to do it. As Father Jim got up to leave he asked Angela, "Any new mysteries for me to buy?"

"Yes, come by. I'll show you. Father Jim is hooked on mysteries," announced Angela.

"For after all, life is a mystery, is it not?" joked Father Jim as he stepped out the door.

After that, the evening went fast. After initially feeling somewhat awkward around them, Nate settled down. To his surprise he actually enjoyed the members of Angela's club. As the evening came to an end they all thanked Nate for coming and hoped he would return. Angela turned down their offers to help clean up, saying that they all had children to take care of and that they needed to get home. After everyone had left Nate insisted on helping Angela with the dishes. They carried the dishes to the kitchen and both put on aprons. Nate began washing them while Angela with a dishtowel in her hand dried them.

"I really liked everybody," Nate said as he washed. "I hope they liked me ok."

"They did," Angela reassured him. "I can tell they were all glad to have met you."

"Thanks," Nate responded. "They are all interesting in their own way. However, I was a little worried about Samantha. She seemed so tired."

"That's because she has two small kids, and that is why I do not intend to have any," Angela returned.

Nate looked at her. "So no marriage and no kids?"

"That's exactly right. I really like kids, don't get me wrong, but somebody else needs to raise them. The world doesn't need my help to populate it so I figure I can choose to have freedom, if you know what I mean."

Nate nodded like he understood. Angela had a point there. He had actually never given any thought about having children. In many ways he and Angela were very similar. When they had finished they took off their aprons and walked back into the living room.

"Thanks again for the invite," Nate said politely. Angela stood there looking at him. She remained silent with a pleasant look on her face. She was beautiful. Suddenly he had an overwhelming desire to kiss her. He wanted to say how he felt but the words would not come. He began to get nervous. He had felt so at ease with Angela during dinner, but now he was afraid for some reason. It was no use. He couldn't do it. It would have to wait. He had to leave. After a very awkward moment he said, "I guess I'd better go," and started to walk to the door.

Angela followed him. When he turned around she looked up at him again. "This is the third time we have been together. Don't you think it's time we kissed?" she asked with a smile. Nate's heart began to speed up. How could she be so open and calm when inside he was an emotional wreck? He looked at her smiling face with her eyes all aglow. He indeed wanted to kiss her.

"Why yes," Nate stammered.

"You haven't been too busy being a doctor to know how to kiss, have you?" she asked teasingly.

"I don't think so," he replied.

Angela put her arms around his neck gently pulling him to her. Her soft lips touched his and he felt a thrill race through him.

"I don't think so either," she said after kissing him. She kissed him again and he kissed her back.

Angela looked flushed. She stepped back to regain her composure. "You are a good kisser," she said. Nate also felt flushed and his heart was beating faster.

"Maybe you should go now," Angela said falteringly. "You know before, well, before; you know what I mean."

"Yes," Nate said. "I want to see you soon."

"Me too," Angela said. She squeezed his hand as he left.

Nate stopped outside her door and thought about what had just happened. It was wonderful. Angela was wonderful. He wanted to be with her again as soon as possible. Angela occupied his thoughts and Sandy began to fade from his mind.

Chapter Nine

HE WAS DUE TO GO BACK TO THE HOSPITAL IN LITTLE over a week, but now he was not looking forward to going back to the job he had hated to leave just a few weeks before. It wasn't that he didn't trust himself; it was that he had discovered there was more to life than his career. His mind kept going back to Angela and the kiss they had shared when he was leaving. He picked up the phone, gave the bookstore a call and asked for Angela.

"Hello," she said, not knowing whom it was.

"Hi, this is Nate. I was wondering if you had insulted any of your customers today?"

She laughed. "I'm trying to practice constraint. Have to stay in business you know. What are you doing now that you are not saving lives?"

"Nothing. When I'm not saving lives I do nothing. Would you like to have dinner with me?"

"Sure," she answered.

"How about I pick you up at seven?"

"Great!"

That evening he wore dress slacks and a dress shirt. He had even polished his shoes, which he rarely did. He was eager to see

Angela and looked forward to seeing her and hearing her voice. He knocked at her door and heard her say, "Come on in. It's unlocked."

He stepped in and soon Angela appeared wearing a simple but elegant low-cut dress. Around her neck was a necklace of small, subtle pearls with equally small gold spheres in between each one. Her pierced earrings matched her necklace, each with a similar pearl. Her smartly styled hair was somewhat short not reaching her shoulders. Her lips were red but not brightly so. They were enticing.

Nate was awed by the way she looked. "You are beautiful," he finally said when he was able to talk.

Angela beamed. "You look pretty good yourself, you know."

Nate had made reservations in one of the fancier downtown restaurants. The kind that had valet parking and where the waiters wore tuxes and each table had its own booth. As they sat down Angela looked around somewhat amazed. "Do you eat here often," she said.

"No," Nate smiled. "Actually I have never been here before but I read that if you really want to impress a girl this is the place to go."

"Well, they were right. I am impressed."

The waiter welcomed them and brought them their menu with a wine list. He then told them about the sea bass that was the special of the night before leaving momentarily.

Angela leaned forward and whispered, "There are no prices on this menu."

"I know," said Nate. "Don't worry. I cashed in my 401K so we could come here."

Angela laughed. "Ok, I'll take the sea bass."

Nate also ordered the sea bass and the white wine recommended by the waiter. They sat in silence. Then Nate smiled almost laughing. Angela looked at him questioningly waiting for him to say something. Nate's eyes turned back to her. "I was just remembering our coffee date and you wondering if I had killed somebody."

Angela smiled. "Yes, I found you very interesting." Then she appeared to be excited as she leaned toward Nate with the joyous expression of someone who was about to discover something wonderful and asked, "What is it like to be a cardiologist? What do you really do?"

Nate had never been so relaxed with a woman before. "I basically stick needles into arteries and insert a wire that goes up to the heart where I insert something called a stent that saves the patient's life, most of the time."

Angela sat back looking at him with little expression on her face. "That is the most unromantic description of being a doctor that I have ever heard. You should consider changing professions. Maybe you would like being a car mechanic or something."

"Too much grease," Nate responded. "Blood is easier to wash off."

Angela laughed giving his shoulder a shove with her hand.

"Ok, now tell what it is like to run a bookstore," Nate asked.

Angela thought for a second. "It's like having the whole world right before you. Just by opening a book you instantly travel anywhere and everywhere. You get to know people intimately. You know their innermost thoughts and feelings. You know how they feel when they argue or make love. Plus you can share this with your customers while at the same time make a living at it."

Nate marveled at Angela. She was complex. Disdaining marriage and children, yet at the same time having such a passion for life and love. Unlike him, she knew who she was. Nate felt a void within himself, a void he no longer felt a need to hide. Maybe

Angela could help him discover who he really was and help fill that void.

"That's one reason I like you so much. You have class. I have no class," Nate stated matter-of-factly.

"So you like me?" Angela said, not disagreeing with the fact that he had no class.

"You bet," Nate responded. He loved the playful teasing they engaged in. It challenged him and made him feel her equal.

"Ok, what kind of music do you like," she asked.

Nate thought for a moment. "I mainly listen to public radio," he answered.

"So you are into classical music?"

"No, just public radio," he replied.

"Don't tell me you have no favorite songs or artists," she inquired as if to discover how truly uncultured he was.

Nate again felt he was put on the spot. He did not really listen to music. He had to come up with something so she wouldn't think he was culturally deprived. "I like some of Elvis's songs and some of the Beatles' albums," he said, trying to sound sophisticated. He knew she wouldn't buy it. He waited anxiously to see what she said.

"Me too," she said. Nate could not believe his ears. "There was a lot of great music in the sixties and seventies. I think folks will listen to that music for all time."

Nate sat up straighter and felt proud of himself that he had said something she agreed with. The rest of the evening he talked with an air of confidence that he had never had with a woman before. Their conversation was relaxed and pleasurable. At one point he raised his wine glass and said, "Here is to the prettiest, classiest woman who ever owned a bookstore."

She held her glass up. "Here is to a handsome cardiologist who once was a bum." He had laughs with Angela. She laughed at what he said and came back with jokes of her own. It seems they were evenly matched. They were two of a kind, both injured and searching. They were not exactly sure what they were searching for but with each other they felt they were about to find it.

That evening he walked her to her door. Without saying anything she turned to kiss him. He met her halfway. Her lips excited him, as did her body that she pressed against his. They were both flushed breathing heavily lost in each other's embrace. He pulled her closer not wanting to let go. Angela felt weak. All this had happened too fast. She realized she had to do something. Between kisses she managed to whispered "Do you fish?"

Nate stopped not sure that he had heard her correctly. "I'm sorry, what did you say?" he whispered back.

"Do you fish?" she asked again.

"I have never fished," Nate replied.

"What do you say we go fishing this week? I know just the place upstate and on a weekday we should have the lake to ourselves."

"But," he hesitated.

"Don't worry, I've got everything we need. Pick me up at ten day after tomorrow. Ok?"

Nate tilted his head a little, looked at her with a smile and said, "I actually have been waiting for you to ask me to go fishing."

"Oh shut up," she said kiddingly.

"You've never told me to shut up before," Nate came back still smiling.

"You are too much," she said. "The next time I see you I will have a fishing pole in my hand, ok?"

"Ok," he replied. She smiled, said goodnight and went inside. *Fishing*, he thought to himself smiling. Angela was always full of surprises. He liked that about her. In fact he liked everything about her. He walked back to the car whistling, which was something else he had not done for a while.

He picked her up right at ten. They drove north to a state park that was up in the heavily wooded foothills. The secluded small lake had several small piers. There were a few diehard fishermen on the bank and one or two in boats.

The park was beautiful. The tall pine trees appeared like the giant pillars seen in Gothic cathedrals with long limbs that formed the arches. The spring air held just a touch of coolness. Flowers were blooming and a few bees and butterflies were darting here and there to see what feasts spring had brought them this year. Nate felt delighted as he got out of the car. He breathed the fresh air feeling bigger and lighter inside than he could remember. He helped Angela carry the picnic basket she had brought along with the worms that they had bought on the way.

"My dad used to bring me here to fish when I was a little girl," she said as they set up their folding chairs on one of the piers. Angela had brought two cane poles that she put together after taking them out of the round carrying case that they came in. "You ever baited a hook before?" she asked.

"Never," he replied.

"Well if you're squeamish about it I'll bait it for you."

He laughed as he thought about all the squeamish things he had done as a doctor. He reached into the worm container, pulled out a large wiggling worm and put it on the hook perfectly. "You're a natural," she said.

Nate felt very relaxed as they sat there enjoying the lake surrounded by the towering trees. It was quiet except for the sound of the wind, which would come and go ruffling the new leaves on the trees. The only other sound was the soothing lapping noise the water made as the small wind driven waves broke against the pier. He especially liked seeing Angela's hair move in the gentle breeze. He imagined invisible fingers pushing her hair back like he wanted to do at that moment. They sat there in silence soaking in all that was about them including the light, the easy motion of the lake, the clouds and the trees.

"You mentioned your father. Are your parents still alive?" asked Nate.

"My dad is. My mother died of a blood clot in her fifties for some unknown reason. I was a late in life only child. My dad is in his seventies. He lives in a nice assisted-living complex. He gets around well but he enjoys having his meals cooked for him and the cleaning service they provide. How about your parents?" she asked.

Nate thought about his parents and the fact that someday both or one of them would end up in assisted living. "My mom is a retired economics professor. This is my dad's last year to teach mechanical engineering at his college. I think after my dad retires this year they just plan to settle down and do very little, unfortunately. What did you dad do?" Nate asked.

"Oh, he was a preacher."

"You are a preacher's daughter? I never would have guessed it," Nate said, surprised.

"Why, am I too pretty to be one?" she kidded.

"Yes, you are too pretty," he replied. "Do you," he hesitated, "I mean do you go to…? "

She finished the sentence, "Go to church? Is that what you were going to ask?"

"Yes."

"Heavens no," she replied.

"Do you mind if I ask why?"

"No," she replied, "but do you go?"

"Heavens no," he said, imitating her.

"My dad is the most wonderful, sweet person in the world.

I would do anything for him. He was a wonderful pastor and that's why I guess it hurt so much as a child to see him move from church to church."

"Why did he have to move so much?" Nate asked.

"It was always the same. When we first began at a church everyone was so friendly. But then I would overhear the whispers. Other children would come and tell me that he wasn't bringing in enough new members from the other churches. You see my dad wouldn't get emotional or cry like some of them or shame or scare folks. My dad's sermons were logical and deep, but that didn't fly well with most of the churches he found himself in. I knew as a kid that as soon as the service was over everyone was at home discussing how good or bad Dad's sermons were while they ate their Sunday dinner. I couldn't stand it. After we had been in a church for about a year I usually managed to make a few friends. But then the elders would come to him saying that God was calling them to replace him and that they hoped he could find another church. When I got out of high school I never went back again."

"Wow," Nate replied. "I am so sorry."

"Don't be. I'm grown up now and I've got my dad. I would like you to meet him."

"It would be an honor," Nate replied sincerely.

"Tell me more about your parents," Angela requested.

"They were great, very kind to me growing up," Nate said spontaneously. "We never went to church but once or twice I went with some friends growing up. We never talked about religion, but I am sure they are atheists. They were pretty much consumed by their professions."

Just then Nate's cork went under as his pole bent. "You got something," she hollered as Nate struggled to pull up a nice lake bass. She reached down and helped him bring it on the dock.

"You're not supposed to catch fish like that here, especially with a cane pole, you know. I've only caught sunfish here," she said as she admired it.

"So, what do we do with it now?" Nate exclaimed as he held the wriggling fish on the line.

"We could throw it back but I think one of these fishermen might want it." They walked to the end of the pier where there was a very old, weathered fisherman who sat in an old lawn chair wearing a worn-out baseball cap. He got out of his chair smiling as Nate approached him. His face was deeply tanned and wrinkled and it was obvious that he had no teeth. Yet despite all this he appeared more content and at peace with the world than most people. Nate asked him if he would like the fish. He said yes as he got up. "Wow!" he exclaimed. "You are quite a fisherman! Thank ye son, thank ye," he said as he unhooked the fish. Nate stood and stared at him for few seconds before saying, "You are very welcome."

As they walked away Angela noticed that something seemed to bother him at that moment. "Hey, are you ok? What happened back there?"

Nate kept walking. "Oh nothing really. It's just that he looked very interesting, don't you think?" Nate did not want her to know that it was the first time he could recall anyone calling him son. His own father had never been so personal as far as he could remember.

They found a shady picnic spot under a large pine tree where they could see the lake. From her basket, Angela pulled out chicken salad sandwiches, chips, dip, pickle relish, homemade chocolate chip cookies, and ice tea in a huge thermos. "Wow, you know how to do a picnic," Nate exclaimed as he chowed down.

"I should. I grew up going to church picnics," Angela replied.

"Is your Dad bitter?" Nate asked.

"Oh no. He quickly forgave everyone at each church when he moved on. That's what he preached we should do and he did it. I never could. He is quite a person. He always seemed thankful, even after Mom died. I admire him, but sometimes I think he was a fool, never really looking out for himself."

Nate lay back with his arms folded behind his head looking up at the sky. He thought about all the rivalries he had seen between physicians for academic positions, grants, and patients and all the bitterness that resulted. He thought about all those who had been unfair to him throughout his career. He wondered how anyone could forgive people like that. He never knew of a physician who forgave another physician. None were like Angela's dad.

"Come on, I want to show you something," she said as she grabbed his hand helping him up. She kept holding it as she led him along a small path beside the lake. The path went up a small elevation then turned down into a secluded hideaway surrounded by pine trees except for a small opening where the blue water of the lake could be seen.

She turned around and looked up at him putting her arms around his neck. "This is where I would bring my boyfriends when I was in high school," she said with a soft smile. His arms went around her waist. As he kissed her time seemed to stand still. Her body was close to his and his heart beat fast. It all seemed so natural with Angela.

Angela smiled again and then began to walk slowly up the path, looking at him over her shoulder. He looked at her admiringly for a few seconds before he ran to catch up with her. "Are you following me?" she laughed.

"Yes I am," he replied.

"Do I need to call a park ranger?" she said as she turned around.

"I think you do," he replied as he again took her into his

arms kissing her without thought of where they were. Just then they heard someone coming and began to walk down the path separately both with an innocent look on their face.

They laughed and kidded with each other all the way back to town. It was like both of them had discovered something new about themselves and about life. Nate felt like a regular person. For the first time in his life he felt normal. It felt very, very good. The desires to achieve and overcome that had tortured him all of his life now seemed to have vanished. They were replaced with a desire to be with Angela. It was dark when he pulled up in front of her apartment. He turned off the car then turned to kiss her one more time. Before he knew it twenty minutes had passed. Nate had forgotten what passion was or maybe he never knew what it was in the first place. All he could think about was getting closer to Angela. Yet he wasn't thinking. He was feeling. He liked the part of him that felt. It was a part he had not known, a part that had been asleep for many years. A part that was now waking up and taking over. He was simply loving Angela. Nothing else mattered. For the moment that was all that he knew. He did not know how far he had gone and he did not care.

Angela caught her breath and pulled back for a second. "Here we are acting like teenagers, necking in a car," she said.

"I feel like a teenager," was his reply.

"Nate, what are we going to do?" she asked.

"I don't know," he responded. "I just know I can't go on much longer like this."

Angela looked deeply into Nate's eyes. "Would you like to come in?" she asked softly.

"Yes," he said. However he then became quiet and thoughtful.

Angela was not sure what he was thinking. She sat there silently wondering what he was going to say.

Nate's overwhelming passion began to calm down a little as

his physician self began to come back. Being with Angela would be ecstasy, but he also knew the risks of intimacy. He had no thought for himself but only for Angela. After a few moments he turned to her. "I want you now more than anything." Nate paused for a second. "But I want to do this right. I'm sorry. Maybe it is the doctor coming out in me. I don't want to hurt you. I know I'm ok, but I've been exposed to so many things in my line of work I want to get myself checked out first." Nate for the first time in his life was thinking of another person instead of his immediate needs. He didn't realize it but his small heart was beginning to grow.

Angela understood exactly what he was saying. It warmed her heart. Nate was looking out for her; he cared for her. She knew more than ever that Nate was the person she wanted to be intimate with.

Angela spontaneously kissed him, not passionately but thankfully. "Thank you, Nate, for being so thoughtful," Angela said with a contented look on her face. "I appreciate you so much. I want to do the same for you." She kissed him again. "I want us to be together," she said sincerely.

Nate's heart started to speed up again at the thought of them together and at how open and honest Angela was.

"I want us to be together too," Nate returned. Then, with their lips almost touching, they began to make plans, kissing softly between sentences. When Nate finally said goodbye they were both aglow, filled with joy at having found one another.

Chapter Ten

It was Monday morning, time for Nate to go back to work. He awoke with sweet thoughts of Angela, which he knew would linger throughout the day. He wanted her and he knew she felt the same way. Their desire for each other was almost overwhelming, but they were grown, mature people who knew how to act maturely in the mist of passion. Angela had insisted on having herself checked out also. They had planned for their special day, which was to be on Saturday two weeks away. This would give time for both their tests to come back and Nate would have time to pay back all the calls he had missed. In many ways their special day was like a wedding day that was planned for and looked forward to with anticipation.

The world seemed brighter to Nate. He looked forward to being a cardiologist again. He had never put medicine out of his mind for a month before. For a moment he wondered if he would be as sharp as he had been, but then he quickly dismissed that thought. The coffee was ready. He walked with his cup out onto the balcony wondering what Angela was doing. *What is she thinking this morning? Is she thinking of me like I am of her?* He looked forward to calling her. The next two weeks would be brutal, but that didn't seem to bother him too much. He would have to be on call a lot to pay back the other cardiologists who took call for him while he was gone. There would not be much time to see Angela these two weeks, but he would meet her for dinner the few nights he did have off.

He got to the hospital early. The nurses' station was empty except for a receptionist, which meant that the nurses were still in report. He went back into the doctors' work area, a small room behind the nurses' station situated where patients could not see the doctors. At each doctor's cubicle were computers that he used to check to see who was on his service. As he sat down in his usual seat, in front of him was a square white one-layer cake that said "Welcome Back Dr. Williams." He smiled and then realized that behind him were five or six nurses. He looked back and said, "You guys are something else!" They all smiled and said welcome back as they left to start their day.

The only one left was Sandy who was standing there with a cup of coffee. She sat down beside him and said, "Just the way you like it," as she usually did. She put her hand gently on his forearm. She looked bright and hopeful.

He took a sip and said, "Thanks. It's not good for me, you know."

She smiled. "Welcome back; we missed you."

He smiled back. "Did you put them up to this?"

"No," she protested and then added, "They really did miss you."

Nate looked at her as if to say, "Are you sure?"

Sandy made sure no one else was close by and then said in a low voice, "Be gentle with the nurses today, ok? Remember Louise Stephens?"

He definitely remembered Louise. She was one of the older nurses, in her sixties. She was a good nurse but very slow at times, which irritated him. He nodded that he did remember her.

"Well, her husband was accidentally killed on his job right

after you left. They had planned to retire next year and travel together. This is her first day back." Nate looked at Sandy. He could see the care and concern in her eyes. He felt drawn to her. For the first time he felt a deep sorrow for Louise instead of the shallow sorrow he had always felt before when tragedies like this occurred.

"I am so sorry," Nate said sympathetically. "You shouldn't have made me a cake on a day like this."

"Life must go on," Sandy replied. "We also had a small cake for her in nurses' report this morning. We have been her support for a month. We all have hugged her so much I think she must be sore. She was delighted that we had gotten you a cake also. Things like this take her mind off herself." Nate marveled at Sandy. He thought about all the tragedy she had experienced in her life and the mistakes she had made and yet she was always so caring for others. Sandy was a whole person who one way or another had been healed of all that had injured her in the past. It showed in everything she did. Somehow, she had been able to forgive not only those who caused her injury but also most importantly herself. He thought about that night when she stood close to him on her porch holding his hand. *Maybe things could have worked out between us after all*, he thought. Then he remembered the words from a poem he had read in freshman English that ended with "the saddest words of tongue or pen are these sad words, it might have been." Yes it might have happened. He could not see it happening before but now he could. He felt different now because he was different thanks to Angela. Angela filled his life. He knew that he couldn't keep hold of both of them. He had to let Sandy go. It was time.

"I'll be gentle, don't worry," Nate said. "I will tell Louise how sorry I am."

Sandy looked at him and said, "Thanks." She gave his arm a squeeze before returning to the nurses' station where Louise was.

Nate walked into the nurse's station where Louise was standing looking at a patient's chart. As he walked up to her she looked up expecting one of his orders that he usually barked out. "Louise," he said looking at her seriously, "I am so sorry to hear about your husband." He gave her a quick hug adding, "We are all happy to have you back."

Louise looked up in shock, as did all the other nurses. Nate had never shown any kind of affection to any of the nurses before. Louise thanked him. As he walked back to the doctor's area the nurses looked at each other in amazement.

Just then Kevin, the cardiologist who was coming off call, came in, saw the cake, and commented that it was unfair since the nurses had never made him a cake. Jokingly Nate told him that's because he had never got himself kicked out of the hospital before. They both laughed. Kevin went over Nate's patients that he had taken care of during the weekend and then Nate began his rounds.

The first patient was a fifty-five-year-old male Caucasian smoker and construction worker who was brought to the ER the afternoon before after suffering chest pain while drinking beer and playing football with his boys and their friends. Fortunately he got to the ER in time for Kevin to place a stent that prevented worsening of the small amount of heart damage that was present. He was sitting up in bed and appeared to be in a solemn mood. After examining him Nate explained that his prognosis was very good if he took his medicines, quit smoking, began eating right, and got regular exercise. "But I was exercising when I had the heart attack," he protested.

"Mr. Smith," Nate replied, "it's the weekend warrior-type exercise that is going to do you in. You need an exercise program that is slow and progressive. We will set you up with physical therapy for such a program."

Mr. Smith looked off out the window. "So it's the once-a-week vigorous activity that is dangerous?" he asked.

"Yes," Nate answered. Mr. Smith looked devastated.

"It's not as bad as it seems," Nate reassured him. "There are lots of other activities that you will be able to enjoy."

"You don't understand, Doc," Mr. Smith said as he looked around. "You see, me and the missis, well it's about once a week, if you get what I mean."

Nate smiled. He thought to himself, *Of course. I'm kind of slow this morning.* "I understand," Nate said reassuringly. "If you follow what we have laid out for you I'm sure you can resume your sex life very soon. Most who are in your condition do so without any problem."

"Thanks Doc. I really appreciate everything you guys have done for me and the missis." Mr. Smith smiled and lay back in his bed. Nate felt good about the interaction. He shook Mr. Smith's hand and told him that it was a pleasure meeting him instead of just asking, "Any questions?" as he usually did when he left.

One of the nurses had walked into the room and saw the last interaction between Nate and Mr. Smith; she couldn't believe that this was the same Dr. Williams she had known before. As they both walked out of the room she turned and said, "Dr. Williams, that was great how you handled Mr. Smith. That was the first time I had seen him smile. He seemed pretty depressed earlier."

"Thanks," Nate returned with a smile. "However you guys are a large part of Mr. Smith's physical and mental recovery and I appreciate it." The nurse smiled and again she wondered what had come over Dr. Williams.

His next patient was Mr. Simon, a ninety-four-year-old male who began having chest pain while mowing his yard. "While mowing his yard?" Nate had to read that part twice. Mr. Simon had made it to a phone and wisely called 911. He was then admitted overnight for observation.

"Good morning Mr. Simon. I'm Dr. Williams, the cardiologist who will be taking care of you. How are you feeling today?"

"I'm feeling great, Doctor. I am ready to go home," Mr. Simon replied.

"I've gone over your chart and all the tests that were run on you. It appears that you have had a few heart attacks in the past. Did you know about them?" Nate asked.

"Yes," Mr. Simon replied. "The first one was when I was sixty-five and the last one was when I was seventy."

That was way before stents were invented, thought Nate. "Well, it does not appear that you had another one yesterday, but you may have had some chest pain mowing the yard. I'm sure your heart is not strong enough for you to mow your yard but it is actually in pretty good shape considering your age. If you were younger we would consider doing a heart catheterization to see if a stent placed in your coronary arteries would be beneficial. However, at your age the risks from the blood thinners and the procedure, I think, would outweigh any benefits here."

"So the next time I have chest pain don't bother calling 911?" Mr. Simon asked.

"Oh no, no!" Nate exclaimed as he chuckled a little. "You must call 911 any time you have pain, ok?"

"Ok Doc," was his reply.

"However, I would not recommend mowing your yard anymore. Don't you have a grandson who would do it for you?" Nate asked.

"They are all in their fifties and they don't mow yards anymore," was his reply.

Oh yeah, thought Nate. "How about a great grandson?"

"They are all in their thirties. They are too busy to mow my yard," Mr. Simon replied again.

Nate was smiling now. He cautiously asked, "Any great-great grandsons?"

"Yes I have one. He is fourteen but he doesn't come around much."

"You will have to pay him, you know. But it will give him a chance to get to know his great-great grandpa and you a chance to know him." *Here I am talking like I know a lot about family relationships*, Nate thought to himself.

It was around ten that morning that a code blue was called on one of his patients he was about to see, a seventy-year-old female with moderate chronic heart failure. When he got there, Sandy was giving chest compressions while another nurse was bagging her. As he entered Sandy said, "She's in V-fib. We have already shocked her once. The AED is ready." V-fib stood for ventricular fibrillation, a condition where the heart is essentially quivering instead of having a coordinated beat that would pump blood. They all knew that seconds count in such a situation. An electrical shock to the heart often restores a normal beat; the automated external defibrillator (AED) machine is what is used to give such a shock. Nate put the AED paddles on her bare chest again and told everyone to stand back. He hit the appropriate button and her body jumped and twitched as her arms dangled. Within seconds a normal rhythm appeared but it was slow without a palpable pulse. She was still not breathing. Sandy resumed the chest compressions while the other nurse placed the mask over her face to begin bagging again. Nate grabbed an endotracheal tube from the crash cart quickly inserting it through her mouth into her trachea. The ventilation bag was placed on the endotracheal tube and Nate could tell from the rise of the patient's chest with each squeeze of the bag that her ventilation was much improved.

Shortly thereafter the heart rate picked up and a moderate pulse was felt indicating that finally the heart was pumping an adequate amount of blood with each beat. Nate motioned to Sandy that she could stop the chest compressions. He then ordered a blood gas and after the inhalation therapist had failed twice to get it, he took a fresh syringe, felt the radial pulse in her wrist hitting it exactly. The red blood quickly filled the syringe. He removed the needle and applied pressure as the inhalation therapist rushed the sample to the laboratory. The patient was much improved but still was unconscious and not breathing on her own which she would probably not do for another twenty-four hours.

"It looks like she is stable now," he announced. "Thanks everyone. You all did a great job. And especially thanks to Sandy who got here quickly and started the resuscitation. Now we need to get her to the ICU."

"I've already notified them. They are ready," Sandy spoke up.

Nate thanked Sandy again. He felt back in his old routine. He and Sandy were doctor and nurse again. The more he could interact with her as a nurse the less he would look at her as a possible lover, at least that is what he hoped. He then went to talk to the family who all thanked him profusely before they went to the ICU waiting room.

He went back to his cubicle to finish her chart. He was back in the groove again. He felt as sharp as ever. As soon as his mind settled down, however, he missed Angela. He picked up the phone and called her at the bookstore. This time the store operator recognized his voice. After a moment of silence he heard Angela say, "Dr. Williams, I suppose."

Nate laughed. "Hey, read any good books lately?"

"I'm not into reading books anymore. I've got too many other things on my mind. What's on your mind?"

Nate smiled. "Well, I am not at liberty to say at the moment but maybe we could get together sometime to discuss it."

She laughed and said, "I'm waiting."

The weeks went by fast and each day Nate looked forward to being a doctor because now there was hope in his life, hope as he looked forward to being with Angela and hope that he might actually become a better person. During the two weeks Nate was on call almost every other night. He usually worked late on the nights he was not on call but managed to see Angela several times. They would meet at restaurants that had romantic atmospheres and soft music. They ate and talked and laughed and made plans for their special day. Afterwards he would walk her to her door. They would kiss and hold each other tight for as long as they could, but he would not go in because they were planning to do it right.

Chapter Eleven

THE TWO WEEKS HAD PASSED AND NATE AND ANGELA were ready. She had agreed to come to his apartment Saturday night at seven. He had arranged to have the apartment spotlessly cleaned and all the linens freshly washed. The dining room table was in front of double glass doors that opened onto the balcony revealing the stars that filled the clear night sky. Nate was nervous, but it was a good nervous. He longed for Angela. He had not longed for anything or anyone for so long that his heart had entered a deep uncaring, unfeeling sleep. But now his heart was awake, and it ached for her.

He hoped he had everything perfect for her. He was a little concerned that Angela had been advised not to use birth control pills because of the death of her mother from a blood clot. However, he agreed to provide protection. As planned, they both had tests run on themselves to rule out any possible sexually transmitted diseases. In some ways it seemed cold to have done this, but they both looked at it as a very loving thing to do.

Nate had prepared what he wanted to say to Angela on this special night. He knew Angela felt strongly about freedom and he wanted to assure her of that freedom. Everything would be out in the open between them, no hidden agendas, no secrets. More than anything, he wanted to please her.

Angela arrived right at seven with a small night bag and purse. She wore a simple stylish dress that clung to her revealing the contours of her body. Her hair was down and soft, and she had just the right amount of makeup on. The sight of her took his breath away when he opened the door. He took her bag as she stepped in. He put his arms around her and they kissed. Then without saying anything he led her to the dining table upon which flickered two vanilla-scented candles. Soft music played in the background and the lights were low.

On the table was a bottle of wine already opened with the cork loosely placed back in the opening. Nate poured the rich red wine into slender, crystal-clear wine glasses and gave one to Angela. They stood opposite one another near the table with the glass doors behind while the candles cast dancing shadows on their faces. Intermittently, the reflection of the candles was seen in the enticing darkness of their eyes. Angela was beautiful, and he felt thankful like he had never felt before.

Nate lifted his glass and said, "You are beautiful tonight, as you are always."

Angela's eyes seemed to glisten. "And you are also beautiful," she replied as their glasses touched. They sipped their wine looking into each other's eyes. Then Nate put his glass down and reached for Angela's hand. Angela followed his lead. He stood there in front of her holding her soft hands in his. They were two beautiful people standing there as the candlelight cast a glow about them and as the stars of heaven looked down at them through the glass doors. Nate was eager to say to her what he had ready to say. He was confident because it was from his heart and he knew it would touch hers.

"Angela, you came into my life and opened the doors of my

heart. You gave my heart new life. Thank you." Angela's face brightened. "I care for you so much. That is why there are several things I want you to know," Nate continued. "I promise to you that I will always respect you and your wishes. I promise to always be honest with you. I promise to give you freedom. I know you do not believe in marriage so if you ever want to leave, I will not cling to you or try to get you to stay. I will give you my blessing as you go with no hard feelings." Nate finished feeling proud as he looked at Angela.

Angela's eyes did not seem quite as bright as before. She was a free woman who had cast away all the shackles that had been put upon her as a child. Nate was right. She did not believe in marriage, which often kept a woman trapped in a relationship where she was not respected. She did not really know what she wanted Nate to say. Certainly she did not want him to talk of love and marriage or any kind of binding relationship where freedom was compromised. Thus what he said actually was what she wanted to hear, but then why did she feel let down a little? She looked long and hard at Nate's face. It seemed as if she was looking at him for the first time. She held his hands tightly and tried to say something but the words would simply not come out.

Nate grew a little alarmed. "Are you ok?" he whispered.

"Yes, I'm ok," she whispered back. She then regained her composure and in a low tone said, "I promise everything you promised."

Nate smiled and felt relieved, but he still worried a little. He took her into his arms and kissed her. She was tense at first, but then she began kissing him back passionately. He felt himself tremble as he pulled her close to him and felt the softness of her body against his. Their lips and mouths were intimate, and it seemed unnatural that the rest of their bodies were not intimate also. The shedding of their clothes removed this final barrier and they began to know and discover each other as fully as they knew each other's lips. They lay completely open to each other in Nate's king-size bed. As they explored and caressed every part of each other they became as close as possible to being one as two people could be this side of heaven. They then slept with their bare bodies touching one another in every way possible remembering the closeness they had shared.

The next morning he awoke feeling her softness and her warm bare skin against his. Her gentle rhythmic breathing made him more aware of her softness with each breath. He lay there thinking about how intimate they had been with each other and how he knew her body, her beautiful body. *If there was a heaven then this was the closest thing to it on earth,* he thought. He slowly removed his arm from underneath her so as not to wake her and stood by the bed. He looked at her beauty and wondered how this had all come about.

He slipped on some pajamas and went to the kitchen and started coffee. When he heard her stir he walked back into the bedroom with two cups in hand. She was sitting up smiling. "I hope I made it like you like it," he said as he handed her a cup. She held it with both hands taking a sip. "It's good. Thank you."

It was the first time he had seen her sleepy. Her hair was a mess, she had no makeup on, and her eyelids seemed to droop a little. It was a part of her beauty that he had not seen before, a beauty that was more deep and real and intimate than anything he had experienced before. He could not help but lean over and kiss her gently. She smiled and tried to brush back her hair and said, "I am a mess."

"You're a beautiful mess," Nate replied.

He sat on the bed, sipped his coffee and then turned to her. "You know, getting kicked out of that hospital was the best thing that ever happened to me."

She smiled. "Me too. I never thought I would fall for a bum off the street. That's how you looked that day you walked into the store." They both laughed.

"I've got a surprise for you." He went back to the kitchen where he had warming in the oven her favorite quiche. He walked back carrying two pieces of quiche and two glasses of orange juice on a tray.

"What, breakfast in bed?" she said.

"We try to please," he responded.

"I must stay at this place more often," she exclaimed.

"Please do," he said as he placed the tray on the bed. They ate their quiche slowly and were both quiet and content.

After finishing he took the tray back to the kitchen. She soon followed wearing one of his robes. "This was the first thing I could find. Hope you don't mind," she asked.

"You look great in my robe," he replied.

Angela spotted the two books he had bought at the bookstore on the coffee table and noticed that the bookmarks were on chapter two. "Chapter two?" she said with a smile.

"I have an FRD. At least that's what I've been told," he replied.

"Oh, yeah," she said as if she just remembered that. She went out onto the balcony and leaned on the railing and looked out over the city. He followed her and leaned next to her. "Up here you can start to understand the big picture, can't you," she said as she gazed at the buildings and streets and cars that went as far as one could see.

"How so?" he asked.

"Out there are millions of people who are working, making love, having babies, visiting grandparents."

"And having heart attacks and dying," Nate added.

"Yes," she agreed. "And having heart attacks and dying. It's all part of it. Love, compassion, jealously, revenge, selfishness, and forgiveness are part of each of those millions of lives. It's awe inspiring."

"I agree," he said as he put his arm around her. He thought how he had described what she saw as a complicated human mess.

She smiled as she felt him next to her. "Have you ever wondered," she asked, "if among those millions of people there are two just like us? Two who look like us who met each other and who feel just like us?"

Nate thought for a minute. "I've never thought about it before, but now that you mention it, it is very intriguing to think about." After another moment he added, "Maybe unconsciously we are all searching for our other selves out there hoping that when we find them we can at last understand who we are."

Angela looked up at him. "That is beautiful." She kissed him. "I like being with you," she said. Nate felt euphoric. He felt wanted and loved and accepted. New feelings that amazed him kept springing up from somewhere deep inside. He was in love and someone loved him.

They sat together on the couch with arms around one another saying little but sweet nothings. They explored each other's hands. He ran his fingers through her hair and whispered how lovely each part of her was as he kissed her ear and cheek. For the time being Nate's world had vanished. He was no longer the aggressive competitor trying to get to the top and win everyone's praise and admiration. He was simply a lover, and he wanted to be nothing else.

That evening he started to grill some fish on the small grill that was on his balcony. The glow of the city lights began to appear as the sky slowly let go of its brightness to provide a darkening backdrop for the lights.

They sat at the dining table with the two candles flickering. The fish was cooked just right and lay next to some small potatoes and green beans. Two glasses and a bottle of white wine sat on the table. Nate poured them both some wine and picked up a glass and said, "Here's to us." She raised her glass and touched his.

After a few bites Angela said, "I thought I would go get my dad next week and have him stay with me a few days. I was hoping you could come over and meet him then."

"It would be an honor," Nate replied. "I've never really talked to a preacher before unless I'm resuscitating them," he said with a smile.

"What about the chaplains in the hospital?" she asked.

"I've always tried to avoid them. Not that I don't like them, it's just that we speak a completely different language. But I'm sure your dad and I will get along well," he tried to reassure her.

"You don't have to worry. He is really a nice guy."

"Does he know about us?"

"No."

"And if he did?"

"He would be ok with it. Just like he is ok with me not going to church and not believing in God."

"Not believing in God?" Nate said with surprise. "How could he be ok with that, he being a preacher and all?"

"He loves me, Nate," she exclaimed. "He's all about love. Sure, maybe he would be happier if I was the church lady of the year, but he respects my choices. How about you? Do you believe in God?"

"I don't see any evidence for God," he replied. "I've tried to be an agnostic but basically I just don't believe in all that stuff. "

Angela sat back. That was the answer she expected but for some reason it bothered her. "Do you believe in love?"

"Doesn't everybody?" he asked without looking at her.

Angela's face became serious. "I grew up with everybody saying they loved each other. My dad preached about love every

Sunday and at each church gathering everybody said they loved each other, but few did. Oh there were exceptions like my dad as there always are, but most people just used the word love to get what they wanted and if they didn't, they would turn on you in a minute. No, I don't believe in love. It's just a meaningless word." Angela looked off, lost in her own thoughts.

Nate felt sorry for her but was not sure why. She didn't believe in love or marriage or having children but then neither did he really. His parents never talked about the value of those things, and he never gave them any thought. But he did feel sorry for her for some reason. She seemed to be in turmoil. He had no idea what to say; he had no wise words of wisdom to issue forth, but he wanted to say something that might help. He finally gave up and said what was on his mind.

"You are a strange person, did you know that?" he said with a slight smile. "A preacher's daughter who doesn't believe in love," he added with a bigger smile.

Angela regained her thoughts and again focused on Nate. "Do you like preachers' daughters?" Angela asked.

Nate got up from his chair and stood by Angela. He leaned over and looked at her beautiful eyes and said, "I like this preacher's daughter," and then kissed her.

Angela smiled and her face brightened. "Would you like to take this preacher's daughter to bed?" she asked.

"Very much so," he replied. He held her hand as she stood up. They walked hand in hand to the bedroom, shedding their clothes on the way. They slept in each other's arms that night and did not think of love but only of each other and how they wanted to be as close to one another as they possibly could.

Chapter Twelve

THE FOLLOWING WEEK PASSED QUICKLY. NATE WORKED hard as usual, but he couldn't wait to get back to Angela each night who was now staying at his apartment. She also worked every day but got off in plenty of time to have a wonderful meal waiting for him. Their nights were filled with passion and warmth and sad goodbyes in the morning when they both had to leave. To them the world now seemed new and exciting and their work had new meaning. Near the end of the week Angela moved back to her apartment and then went to pick up her dad so Nate could come over and meet him. They would spend a couple of nights apart, and Nate began to worry about meeting Angela's father.

Nate arrived at Angela's door Saturday afternoon feeling like a high school teenager about to meet the father of his first date. He hoped Angela was right about her father being a nice guy and that Angela was not just another daughter blind to a father's shortcomings.

Angela answered the door, gave him a hug, and ushered him in. Her dad was sitting comfortably in one of her modern living room chairs. He got up as Nate entered. He was of average height and slender build and appeared to get around well. He was gray headed with most of his hair still. He had a very welcoming smile with wrinkles around his eyes and cheeks that appeared to be the result of a lifetime of smiling. Nate could see the resemblance between Angela and her father.

"I have been looking forward to you two meeting each other," Angela said happily. "Dad, this is Nate. Nate, my father."

Nate quickly reached out and shook his hand and said, "It is an honor to meet you, Reverend Carter."

Reverend Carter smiled again. "Angela said I am to call you Nate unless I am having a heart attack. The folks in my churches usually called me either Reverend Randy or Brother Randy. The teenagers referred to me as RR. But now I like plain Randy. So just call me Randy and not Reverend Carter, that is, unless you are in need of a sermon."

Nate gave a nervous laugh as they both sat down. Angela said she would bring them tea and left for the kitchen. Randy continued, "It is an honor to meet you too, Nate. I understand that we are in similar professions."

Nate wasn't sure he had heard him right. "I beg your pardon?" he responded.

"Aren't we both in the business of curing sick hearts?" Randy asked.

Nate smiled. "Yes, when you look at it that way I guess we are."

"Let me ask you a professional question, if I may," Randy ventured. "Do you often see patients that you have restored to a reasonable degree of health only to return sick again because they continued the bad habits that got them into trouble in the first place?"

"All the time," Nate responded.

"When you discharge a patient can you tell if he or she will be one of those?" he asked.

"Usually," Nate answered. He was beginning to relax and enjoy the conversation. "Sometimes I'm wrong, of course."

"The same goes for me," Randy remarked. "I often get my patients, I mean one of my flock, through a crisis of their own making just to see them return to their old ways as soon as they begin to feel well. Most of the time I can tell which ones will be coming back soon."

Just then Angela brought out hot water in a teapot on a silver tray. There were two cups of fine china each with a tea bag in it. "I'm going to let you guys keep talking while I finish dinner if that is all right?" she asked. They both nodded and thanked her.

Randy poured hot water in both their cups and after letting the tea bags soak they laid them aside. Both took a single spoon of sugar. After taking and enjoying a long sip of tea, Randy remarked, "Angela has told me a lot about you and the wonderful work that you do. I haven't seen her this happy in a long time."

"Thank you," Nate returned. "You have a wonderful daughter." Nate was beginning to feel at ease.

"Oh, I think so too, but then I am her father. Tell me about your parents. Are they still living?"

"Yes. Dad is retiring this year from his university teaching job in mechanical engineering and my mom is a retired economics professor."

"Any brothers or sisters?" Randy asked.

"I had an older sister who died in infancy. Other than her, no."

"I know that was heartbreaking for your parents. The death of a child is the saddest and most challenging part of being a preacher. What is even sadder is the effect it sometimes has on the rest of the family. I've seen marriages break apart, and I've seen parents who afterwards remained distant from the other children so they wouldn't be so hurt if they were to lose them also." Randy stopped and took a sip of tea. Nate felt all his defenses disappear. In just a few minutes Randy had penetrated his heart and helped him to understand his parents. He thought about all those times as a child when he wished his parents had hugged him or touched him and now finally thanks to Randy he was starting to understand why they acted the way they did.

Nate was deep in thought when he heard Randy say, "I can tell you were very well raised."

"They were always very kind to me. I can't complain," Nate reported.

"What church were you raised in?" Randy asked nonchalantly as he took another sip of tea.

"My parents never went to church. I guess they were too wrapped up in their professions," Nate replied solemnly.

"That seems to be the modern way," Randy observed. "Angela doesn't go to church. Isn't it funny how many times children grow up and do just the opposite of what their parents have preached to them all their life? However, I have come to believe that if all children did exactly what their parents wanted them to the world would be a very dull place, don't you think?"

Nate smiled and agreed and thought to himself that he had done everything his parents had wanted him to as far as he knew. But then again his parents never really voiced what they wanted him to do other than get an education and that seemed the only way to get their affection.

Randy continued. "Another modern trend that I believe is rampant is for young people to fall in love with love instead of falling in love with each other. I have seen so many couples separate once the thrill of having a love affair is over and they have to decide to love each other."

All of a sudden Nate began to feel nervous again. *Were they just in love with love? Yes, he loved being in love, but his love for Angela was real.* "Yes I suppose you are right," Nate finally muttered.

"I've got this theory about love," Randy said thoughtfully. "I believe that the capacity of the heart to love is in many ways similar to the heart's capacity to pump blood." Nate looked up with interest. Randy continued, "Aren't they both essentially the product of genetics and environment?"

"Yes, isn't everything?" Nate responded.

Randy looked at Nate and smiled as if he had just found out something about him. "I would imagine you have patients who are born with hearts that have a different capacity, don't you?" Randy asked.

"Yes," Nate answered.

"However, with good health habits and exercise, most can improve, true?

"Yes, certainly," Nate answered again.

"That's how I tried to explain it to my congregations. They may be different in their ability to love but with daily prayer and doing small loving acts they can improve their capacity to love." He stopped and sipped his coffee. "You know, I've been talking to you for only a few minutes, and here I am starting to preach." Randy seemed embarrassed. "Please forgive me. Angela tells me she met you in her bookstore."

"Yes, she helped me choose a book." He did not want to go into the details of that first meeting.

"She is an amazing person. Here I go bragging about my daughter again." Nate found that he liked to hear a father bragging about his daughter. "Angela knows almost everything about books. I read a lot of religious books, but I think she has read every kind of book ever written. She wants me to read more fiction. She says I must have some kind of fiction reading disability."

Nate laughed. "That is what she has diagnosed me with. I think my case is hopeless."

"I think mine is also," Randy replied.

Nate could see that Reverend Carter was essentially a happy person just like Angela had described him, and he could see that same trait in Angela. Angela had her demons, but they were like pets on leashes that could only tug at her happiness without threatening it. He was sure Randy had his demons like everyone else, and he wondered how people like Randy and Angela kept them from interfering with their lives.

Angela announced that dinner was ready and they eagerly gathered around and sat at the table. Randy asked if they would indulge him by letting him say grace, to which they readily agreed, after which he said a very simple prayer of thanks.

Angela had prepared spaghetti with a wonderful salad and bread with a hard crust that her dad really liked. The conversation was jovial and lively, which provided several laughs.

"I must tell you about my daughter," Randy said, grinning.

"Oh no, don't, Dad," Angela pleaded.

"Angela always provided her mother and myself with surprises that kept us on our feet. Once when Angela was twelve years old she overheard that our church was in financial trouble. The next Sunday out of nowhere in every hymnal was a note that read 'Give till it hurts, or it will hurt,' signed Reverend Carter."

Nate laughed and Angela blushed. "We all had a laugh about it except for a few uptight church board members. Then there was the time at summer camp when she led a midnight raid on the camp kitchen and the next morning there were no milk or sweet rolls for breakfast."

"Father, please quit," Angela protested.

"Ok, I won't tell Nate about the time when you were seventeen and I was gone the weekend to a convention and you invited your friends, most of whom were daughters of our elders and deacons, over for an all-night drinking party." Randy laughed and went on. "But Angela was a sweet loving girl. When she wasn't pulling pranks on everyone she was helping anyone who was sick or in need, always ready to visit them or take them food. And she always worried that her mom and I were working way too hard." Nate noticed Randy's composure changed when he mentioned Angela's mom. He looked very sad and then he looked at Angela with a look that he had never experienced before with either of his parents, a look that Angela was returning to her father. They both smiled, and Randy seemed his old self again. *He misses Angela's mom terribly*, Nate thought to himself, and he wondered why Angela had never spoken of her mother other than to say that she had died of a blood clot. Nate marveled at the relationship Angela had with her father.

"Now it is my turn," Angela jumped in. "My dad could never say no to anyone. We always had someone in need staying at our house. Once when the circus burned down dad rushed to the scene and offered our house to a family of jugglers. I don't think that I've showed you the juggling tricks I learned that night."

"Yes, that was a crazy night all right," Randy commented.

"And Dad, remember when a nearby church lost their pastor and you volunteered to serve both churches without extra pay until they found someone?"

"Yes," Randy nodded.

"Do you remember once when you squeezed in a funeral between two weddings and when you ended the second wedding you were so tired that as the married couple started to walk out you said, 'May they rest in peace'."

They all laughed at that. Nate felt at home with Angela and her dad, more at home than he had felt growing up in his own home. Angela seemed to have had the perfect childhood. He wondered if there were ever any bad times in her family growing up like most families had. Maybe Angela would tell him someday.

He then realized there were no bad times in his family. He began to feel anxious again and he did not know why.

Angela served Italian crème cake for dessert and when it was all over Nate was sorry to see it end. He stood up and said he had better get back to his apartment. "You're not staying here tonight?" Randy asked. Nate blushed and he and Angela both knew that her father knew.

"No, all my stuff is back at the apartment and besides, I know you and Angela have a lot to talk about. It was an extreme pleasure meeting you," Nate answered. Randy returned the compliment.

Nate and Angela stepped outside the door and closed it behind them. Angela looked at him and said, "Well, what do you think?"

"Your dad is wonderful."

"He didn't preach to you, did he?" Angela asked.

"Oh no. I love your dad," Nate said reassuringly, and he really meant it. He loved his own dad too, but he had never said it and saying it about her dad came easily for some reason.

Angela hugged and kissed him. Nate thought that he saw in Angela the same look that she had shared with her dad, and he felt part of her family. It was a warm solid feeling free of fear or guilt. It was a feeling that he wanted to hold on to for the rest of his life. He left Angela looking forward to when they could be together again.

Chapter Thirteen

AFTER ANGELA'S FATHER LEFT, NATE MOVED BACK IN with her so he could help her get ready for the next so-called club gathering at her apartment. He kept thinking back to his conversation with Angela's father and how much he enjoyed it. It seemed strange to him that he and Angela's father were so different from one another and yet he felt a connection with him that he had not really felt with anyone else he had known. Randy had that ability to connect with essentially anyone regardless of who they were or what they did or what kind of personality they had. *That is a very rare talent*, Nate thought to himself.

Angela had decided to have a pizza party where everyone tossed and made their own pizza. Tony and Rita agreed to bring over pizza dough ready to toss and Professor Johnson would bring wine while Cindy and Rick would supply the salad. Father Jim said he would bring olives from Italy and would give the pizzas a special blessing.

Saturday afternoon Angela began preparing the vegetables, cheese, and other toppings for the pizza that included pepperoni and anchovies. They both had worked hard getting the apartment ready. Angela had her apron on and was busy at the kitchen counter while Nate, with nothing else to do, sat at the table behind her. He rested his chin in his hand with his elbow on the table while with the other hand he played with a spoon, putting his finger in it and making it turn in a circle. Angela hummed gently. He enjoyed glancing at her and just being near to her. It was a rare moment for him. It had never really happened before. What he was doing was totally useless and unproductive and he enjoyed it. He had discovered to his surprise how delightful it was to let his mind just wander aimlessly not knowing where it would lead him, as if he was walking down a path through a meadow filled with flowers that lead to a valley he had not seen before.

After a period of silence, he asked with a smile on his face, "Are all your friends really pagans like Father Jim said?"

"Basically," she replied. "Tony and Rita can't remember when they went to church last. They tried to force their two boys to go by dropping them off but that didn't last long. Cindy is the oldest of six children, and her father was a corporate executive, which meant they moved every two to three years. I think they were simply too exhausted and busy to go to church so she has no experience with church. On the other hand her husband Rick was raised in a very conservative Protestant denomination and never missed church growing up. However, when he began to study science, especially biology and evolution, he quit believing in God. Professor Johnson is almost certainly anti-religion of any kind but oddly enough he and Father Jim get along very well. I'm not sure what Samantha believes."

"You know them very well. Did you choose them because they were pagans?" he asked half-kiddingly.

"No," she laughed. "They are all readers. Tony and Rita read anything, fiction and nonfiction, that involves food. Rita also likes romance novels. Cindy is into classics while Rick likes science and science fiction. I'm not sure what Professor Johnson reads, although he must read a lot, being a college English teacher. He often informs me of books that I need to stock in my store. Samantha will pick up a novel once in a great while."

"And Father Jim?" Nate asked.

"Oh, he is hooked on mysteries. He claims he reads them to understand human nature better, but basically he is a mystery addict."

Nate smiled and then looked puzzled. "Why did you choose me? I'm not a reader."

Angela turned around smiling. "Because you are so . . o . . o pretty."

"I'm just a pretty face?" Nate asked.

Angela dried her hands on her apron and stood in front of Nate holding his cheeks between her hands. "You got it, pretty boy." She then turned back to her work.

Nate looked disconcerted and said in a low tone, "So, I am just another pretty face."

"Yep," Angela said in agreement.

Angela continued washing the dishes and said casually, looking over her shoulder, "I am updating everyone's phone number in our group, and I was going to add your cell phone to the list. You don't mind, do you?" she asked.

Nate turned pale and expressionless. His phone was his protection. Giving out his number would be like opening the gate of a castle to an invading army. He regained his composure and, in a voice used to tell someone a simple fact, said, "You see, my dear, doctors never give out their phone number," with an emphasis on the word never.

Angela's eyes narrowed, and she looked at him the way a schoolteacher looks at a pupil who has just said something stupid. "With us, are you Nate the person or are you Nate the doctor?" she asked.

"It depends on whether someone is having a heart attack or not," Nate replied, trying to make a joke.

"As far as I know, everyone has a pretty healthy heart, so you are Nate the person with us, are you not?" Angela shot back.

"Well, yes. I guess I am," Nate agreed.

"Then, Nate the person, know that persons readily give out their phone numbers to their friends. That's what persons do. So is it ok?"

"But really," Nate protested. "I've only met these people once. I mean I really like them, but they are not close friends." In reality Nate had never had a close friend in his life, never one he would give his phone number to.

"They are my close friends. What are you afraid of? They are good people, and they are not going to abuse it," Angela stated.

Nate sat there contemplating his decision. Angela had brought his poor heart a long way from where it had started. But this for some odd reason seemed too far. It was way out of his comfort zone. He looked at Angela who was looking back at him waiting for a decision. He knew he had to do it.

"Ok," he said, resigned to his fate. "Put my number on the list but I want to ask you one question: How do you do it?"

"Do what my dear?" she asked.

"Make me do things like that," he answered.

Angela smiled and sat in his lap. She gave him a quick kiss and a thrill went through him as it usually did when she did that. "We women have our ways," she answered.

Nate didn't really want to be a doctor around Angela's club but being a physician was something he could hide behind, a barrier he could put up when he needed to, and giving out his cell phone just ruined all that. However, at the moment all that didn't matter anymore. He held Angela and smiled as his heart grew a little.

Their guests soon arrived and as usual Father Jim was a little late. They all met in the kitchen and Tony had the dough for each pizza in separate bowls. Each portion of dough was in the form of a ball, and Tony instructed the group on the fine technique of throwing the dough above their heads to make a perfectly round flat pizza.

"It takes great skill to throw a pizza right," Tony announced. "But if you follow my expert instructions you too can be a pizza thrower." He then flattened the dough somewhat and began to rotate it with both hands above his head when suddenly his two fingers poked through and the dough fell flat around his arm. Everyone cracked up. Tony looked bewildered. "Oh well. Actually I have a cook that does this but I have watched him many times."

Everyone reached for the dough and began trying to throw the pizza without further instruction. They enjoyed making fun of each other's failures and they began making dough jokes. Rick actually had his pizza almost thrown when he started trying to sing in Italian and someone called him a "dough nut." Others when they had dropped their pizza on the floor said in a gangster-like voice, "Gimme the dough." Father Jim commented that he hadn't seen this much dough in a long time and somehow Angela's dough landed on top of Nate's head. Nate looked like a fool and felt like a fool, and he liked it. The kitchen was a mess with flour most everywhere, and no one noticed or cared.

Finally all the pizzas were thrown and the toppings put on. When they were all cooked and ready, everyone gathered and sat down at the table while Professor Johnson poured everyone a glass of wine, a wine he announced that had come from a new vineyard on an island off the South American coast that only he seemed to know about. They were really fortunate, Professor Johnson explained, because this was the first wine to come from that island

and that was why he speculated that he had got it so cheap. Tony asked Father Jim to pray that they would not all be poisoned.

Everyone dug into their pizza bragging that their pizza was the best in the room. Everyone was in good spirits and even Samantha seemed to be enjoying herself. Tony stood up as he usually did when he spoke and announced, "I would like to make a toast to our new member, Dr. Williams, I mean Nate." They all touched glasses. "In honor of Nate I have asked everyone to come with a saying with the word heart in it since he is an esteemed heart specialist. I asked everyone except Angela because she cannot keep a secret and because we all suspect they tend to whisper secrets to each other a lot." He winked at them both. "I will start with an old but very true saying: 'The best way to a man's heart is through his stomach'."

Nate smiled and said, "And I thought it was through his chest or femoral artery." The group laughed and rolled their eyes back.

Rick rose next. "'Small is the number of them that see with their own eyes and feel with their own heart.' Albert Einstein." Everyone became quiet. Rick looked around. "Sorry. I was trying to find something from a famous scientist."

Professor Johnson looked down at Rick condescendingly and then with a slight smile on his face turned to the others and said, "But, 'a kind heart he hath': Shakespeare."

Cindy shot back, "'A woman would run through fire and water for such a kind heart,' to finish your quote from the *The Merry Wives of Windsor*."

Professor Johnson smiled and held his glass up to her and then sat down.

Father Jim broke in. "You might be interested to know that the first heart transplant was described in the Old Testament when God replaced their stony hearts with hearts of flesh."

"Ezekiel 36:26," everyone heard Rick say. They all looked at him with surprise. "I had to memorize about half of the Bible growing up," he explained.

Rita jumped in. "'You've gotta have heart' has always been my motto."

"I thought it was you've gotta have 'a' heart," Nate replied and everyone looked at him as if they expected it.

Angela chimed in, "Now we are getting to the heart of the matter."

Professor Johnson again stood up and took over the stage. "I would like to quote a well-known line from Emily Dickinson." He looked off into the air for a second with a very serious expression and then began. "'The heart asks pleasure first, and then, excuse from pain; and then, those little anodynes That deaden suffering; And then, to go to sleep; And then, if it should be The will of its Inquisitor, The liberty to die'."

Everyone looked blank because no one had heard that quote before. Professor Johnson looked at everyone out of the corner of his eye while still appearing to look off into the distance. Father Jim broke the silence, "'For where your treasure is, there will your heart be also.' From the gospel of Matthew."

Samantha spoke up for the first time and said, "'Home is where the heart is,' or at least it should be."

Professor Johnson, still standing, looked at his wife for a second and then turned to Angela. "I would like to make a toast to Angela." He raised his glass to her. "I would like to thank you for being responsible for such stimulating evenings for us all. The friendship and exchanges that we have here, I'm sure, have planted seeds within us that may affect us the rest of our lives." He then looked around at each person and continued. "Of course we cannot know which seeds will take root; as Shakespeare said in *Othello*, 'If you can look into the seeds of time, and say which grain will grow and which will not, Speak then to me'."

Cindy spoke up. "Actually that was from *Macbeth*."

Professor Johnson looked at her and said, "Are you sure of that?"

"'I speak as my understanding instructs me, and as mine honesty puts it to utterance.' *The Winter's Tale*," Cindy replied.

Professor Johnson said, "I stand corrected," as he bowed and sat down.

After that everyone realized that they were full of pizza and tired of all the quotes, and the conversation shifted to small talk about nothing in particular, which resulted in laughter and the easing of tensions. Nate felt fortunate to be part of the club Angela had formed and he felt a connection with them that he did not quite understand. He felt at ease around them because they were basically nice people but most of all because they treated him like one of their friends and not a doctor. *I don't mind that they have my phone number*, he thought; *in fact, I'm glad they do.*

As they left everyone expressed what a good time they had and thanked Angela for hosting and inviting them. They also all said how glad they were that Nate was now part of Angela's club and they all were grateful to have the updated phone list with Nate's personal phone on it.

When the last one had left, Nate and Angela sat on the couch. He put his arm around her and she snuggled up against him as she was now in the habit of doing. Nate took off his shoes and stretched his legs with the help of a footstool.

"You know," Nate said thoughtfully, "I have to admit something to you."

"What is that?" Angela asked.

"I don't know what's wrong with me but it didn't bother me too much that everyone had my phone number."

Angela looked up at him with her eyes wide and said kiddingly with a smile, "Wow! It's kind of like a miracle has just occurred. We should tell Father Jim about this."

Nate almost laughed. "Oh be quiet. If you are going to make fun of me I'm not going to reveal to you the innermost secrets of my heart."

"But I like making fun of you," Angela said and then kissed him passionately.

Nate pulled back for a second and looked at Angela with a smile and then said, "You're impossible," and then kissed her back. Nate liked Angela making fun of him, but despite all their joking, he knew that something had actually changed within him, something for the better.

That night everyone felt fortunate to be a member of Angela's club, as they always did after one of their get-togethers. They did not realize it but in many ways Angela's club was their church, the only church they knew. There was even clergy present. And unfortunately, like most things, it was not to stay intact for very long.

Chapter Fourteen

THE FOLLOWING TWO WEEKS, ANGELA AND NATE DID not think of the big questions in life or the near or distant future. They just enjoyed each day and each other. Time seemed to them to both stand still and fly by at the same time. They tried to hold onto it the best they could.

Nate took call every fourth night and every fourth weekend. He had finished two busy weeks and he and Angela were now at her apartment again. More and more he began to stay at her place because it seemed more like a home than his. It was Saturday afternoon, and they had just got back from grocery shopping. Their playful banter about what to buy or which melon was the ripest made even shopping enjoyable for both of them.

They had just put the groceries away when the doorbell rang. Angela opened the door, and to her surprise there stood Samantha alone. Samantha appeared somewhat wide-eyed, pale and expressionless. Angela said "Hi Samantha" as she usually did. When there was no response she knew something was terribly wrong. Angela stood there a second looking at her. She then told Samantha to come in showing her where she could sit on the sofa. Samantha obediently did as she was told. Angela sat near her as she signaled Nate to sit across from her on one of the chairs. Angela reached for her hand. "Are you ok, Samantha? Is anything wrong?"

Samantha broke into tears. She wiped her eyes with some tissue that was hidden in her tight hand. "I've left Gregg," she managed to get out.

"Oh my goodness. What happened?" Angela was shocked.

Samantha regained her composure somewhat. "He was caught making out with a nineteen-year-old freshman in his office. She was in his class, and it was the night before finals."

Angela immediately got up and began pacing back and forth wringing her hands. "How could he do such a thing? How could he betray you like that?"

Samantha was able to talk a little better. "His secretary suspected it and told the dean who walked in on them after hours. The dean suspended the student and referred Gregg's case to a faculty disciplinary committee. The parents, understandably, were outraged. They threatened to sue the school if Gregg was not fired. I left with the kids when I found out and I have filed for divorce."

Nate sat there stunned. His face turned red with anger. He had not known Gregg and Samantha very long, but they were friends and he felt close to them. He felt sorry for Samantha but in some ways more sorry for Angela who was obviously very upset. He had always been a calm and collected observer of the good and bad happenings in the families of his patients. However, he was now no longer a distant observer. Like Angela, he was upset also.

"I should have known. I take responsibility for this," Samantha said with her head in her hands.

"How can you take responsibility for what he did?" Angela asked in an irritated voice.

Samantha looked up at Angela. "He began to make advances toward me when I was a student in his class. He told me that he was divorced. Gregg seemed so smart, like he knew everything.

When I became pregnant I found out that the divorce was still pending and that he had lied to me. I wanted to leave, but he apologized and said he loved me and that he would marry me. I was pregnant and alone and I knew that I should not marry him, but he insisted. We were married three days after his divorce was finalized. Then I found out that he had a son whom he has not visited since."

"What a jerk!" Angela exclaimed. She kept walking back and forth repeating "What a jerk."

Nate managed to say that he was so sorry and he meant it from the bottom of his heart.

Angela looked at Samantha. "Well, did he get fired?"

"Yes and no," Samantha answered. "Gregg threatened to sue the school also. It was a big mess. So they let him resign before he was to go before the academic disciplinary committee, which meant there would be no record of the incident."

Angela finally sat down again by Samantha. "What are you going to do?" she asked.

"Cindy and Rick have taken me in. They have an extra room, and I can help them with the kids and any other way I can. I actually have only one more semester to get my education degree and with their help I will be able to do it. I don't know how I can ever pay them back."

"Is there anything we can do? Please let us help you," Angela pleaded.

"Yes there is," Samantha answered. "Gregg has been demanding to speak to me and I can't handle speaking to him alone. Can I let him say what he has to say here at your apartment with you with me? I feel so safe with you."

"Of course, of course," Angela responded immediately.

Samantha looked at Nate. "I would like you here also if you don't mind," she said.

Samantha's request took Nate by surprise. His first impulse was to run from situations like this. He was being asked to be involved in her and Gregg's life in a very close and personal way, in a way that was too close and personal for him. He felt anxious. Any kind of family disagreement upset him. His parents, as far as he knew, had never raised their voices in any kind of disagreement and if they had, their world would probably have fallen apart. He was sure he wasn't needed.

"Are you sure? I don't think I can be of help," he replied to Samantha.

"You're a good man, and you are my friend, and I want you there," Samantha pleaded. "Just having you there will give me great comfort."

Nate could tell from the look on Samantha's face that it was very important to her that he be there and his heart went out to her. "Sure," he replied. "I'll be glad to be there." He felt weak for some reason, but at the same time he felt part of her family, and deep down it felt good to him to be part of a family.

"Thank you," she said. She reached over and gave his hand a squeeze that made Nate feel better. "I have asked Father Jim to be here also if that is ok."

Both Nate and Angela said yes relieved that Father Jim would be present. Samantha then thanked them again. As she left, they agreed that three in the afternoon the following day would be the best time.

After she left Nate and Angela turned to each other with a look of disbelief. Neither one would have predicted that something like this would happen. Finally, Angela said, "This reinforces my belief about marriage. In so many cases it only results in misery."

Nate thought long and hard trying to analyze the situation. "I agree that they should not have gotten married, not because marriage is bad, but because they married for the wrong reasons."

"Like what?" Angela came back.

"I think Gregg married to save face with his colleagues and employer having got a student of his pregnant. I think Samantha married trying to make a bad situation better."

Angela turned and focused on him intently. "What are you trying to do, bring logic into this discussion? I have to get my mind off of all this for now. I can't talk about this anymore." After a few minutes of silence, Angela added, "Let's pop some popcorn and find a good movie on TV and let me snuggle in your arms for a while."

Nate was not into watching movies, but this sounded to him like the best idea he had heard in a while. Angela picked what most guys would call a girl flick, a romantic comedy about lovers and their crazy relatives. To Nate's surprise he thoroughly enjoyed it as they tried to forget about Gregg and Samantha until the next day.

The following day, Samantha and Father Jim arrived a little before three. Angela hugged them both as she ushered them in. Nate shook Father Jim's hand and Samantha hugged Nate just like he was family. Like everyone else Nate was nervous, including Father Jim even though he had been in similar situations before. They had decided that Gregg and Samantha would sit opposite one another with Angela at her side. Nate and Father Jim would sit at each end of the table. Angela offered them something to drink but they politely declined.

Soon the doorbell rang. Angela opened the door and there stood Gregg. He looked somewhat disheveled. His beard was not as neatly trimmed as usual, and his hair was not all in place. He wore a slightly wrinkled button shirt with work trousers and work shoes. He looked in at everyone there without expression. Angela did not say anything but motioned with her arm where he was to sit.

He sat across from Samantha, who glanced at him briefly but showed no other emotion. After an awkward moment in which they all sat there without saying anything, Gregg leaned forward, folded his hands on the table in front of him, and bowed his head for a moment. He then raised it up, looked at Samantha and started to speak. "Samantha, I messed up. What I did was wrong." He briefly looked at the others and then back at Samantha. "I know this has been terribly hard on you and the kids and it hasn't been that great for me either. I want you to know that I am sorry. I ask for your forgiveness."

There was a deafening silence for a few moments. Then Samantha said softly, "I have already forgiven you."

Gregg looked surprised and sat back. Nate couldn't believe it. A family quarrel could be solved this easily? He looked at Angela, who had a bewildered expression. He then looked at Father, who appeared to have been expecting such an answer.

A very brief smile crossed Gregg's face. Then he became serious. "Thank you Samantha. I do not deserve it. I am so looking forward to getting our family back together. When will you come back home?"

"Never," was her immediate reply. Nate almost fell out of his seat.

Gregg looked shocked. "But I thought you said you forgave me?" he asked incredulously.

"I did," she replied, "but I don't trust you. As I told you, I have filed for divorce."

Gregg looked like he was analyzing Samantha before beginning again. "You can trust me. Here I have come confessing my guilt and asking for forgiveness. What more do you want?" he asked.

Samantha remained silent. Gregg turned to Father Jim. "You religious people are all about forgiveness and families. Talk some sense into her head. Tell her our family needs to be together." Nate wondered what Father Jim would say in a situation like this.

"Oh my, oh my," Father Jim said as his thumb and forefinger began to stroke his chin. He thought for a moment and then said, "Forgiveness is one thing but trust is another." *He hit the nail on the head*, thought Nate.

Gregg appeared disgruntled and turned back to Samantha. "Ok, I need to win your trust. Tell me what I need to do and I will do it. Write it down on a piece of paper and I will sign it in my own blood if I have to."

Samantha again remained silent.

"Think of the children. Are you going to turn them against me?" he asked.

Samantha responded, "They will always know that you love them. I hope you will visit them and be part of their lives."

"This is ridiculous," Gregg said, his voice getting louder. "This makes no sense." He stood up quickly, turning over his chair. "I don't understand this!" he said in a loud angry voice as he looked at her.

Samantha in a low whisper responded, "I know."

Gregg walked to the door and half opened it. He looked around at everyone, and then looked briefly at the floor. He shook his head and then left. Nate's emotions had been on a roller coaster. Samantha had remained calm but determined. Angela looked relieved. It was the first emotionally charged family encounter Nate had ever been involved in, and he had survived. In some ways it had been worse than managing a heart attack. He looked at Father and knew that Samantha had gone to him for advice and counseling. He knew that Father, wise in the ways of the heart, had led her down the right path. Nate's heart had grown a little wiser from this intense interaction as it had ever since he met Angela.

Chapter Fifteen

THE FOLLOWING WEEK ANGELA AND NATE COULD NOT get Samantha and Gregg off their minds. Their work gave them some relief during the day, but at night the unhappy couple were on their minds constantly. They wondered what Gregg would do next and if Samantha would stick to her guns. They pledged to help Cindy and Rick as much as possible. Maybe Samantha and the kids could stay with them at times even though their apartments were not large.

Nate was on call the following weekend, which was unusually busy. On Saturday Angela asked if she could come to the hospital to have lunch with him. Nate said he would like that. He told her how to find the doctors' lounge and gave her the combination to the keypad.

Angela was looking forward to seeing where Nate worked. She had actually been in hospitals quite a few times when she went with her dad when he visited the sick as the Bible said he should. They always went during visiting hours. She remembered everyone being happy to see her dad. She also remembered that everyone appeared to be calm like nothing was wrong. Her dad would engage in happy small talk before reading scripture and finishing with prayer. In her mind, hospitals were quiet places where people relaxed and prayed, and nothing else much happened.

She arrived at the hospital and found her way to the doctors' lounge. It consisted of one room with two couches, two recliner chairs and a television on a stand attached high on the wall where doctors could view it laying down. There was a coffee table in the middle on which lay Nate's copy of *A Tale of Two Cities* that he had taken to work with him the week before. She laughed when she saw that the bookmark was still on chapter two. The furniture was old but nice. A small bookcase held some medical textbooks that were at least fifty years old. There was a picture of a hunting dog on one wall but otherwise the room had a sterile look. Overall, it appeared very depressing to her.

So this is where the doctors relax and hide from patients, Angela thought. She wondered how many hours of his life Nate had spent in this room waiting to do the next procedure or because he had nothing to do and nowhere to go.

The phone rang. She was hesitant about answering it but then, after a few rings, picked it up. "Hello," she said in a weak voice.

"This is Nate," a comforting voice said. "Can you hold on for about thirty minutes? Something unexpected has come up."

"Sure," she answered. She had begun to realize that there were always unexpected things in medicine. About forty-five minutes later she heard the keypad and in stepped Nate. He had surgical greens on that fit him well with a surgeon's cap that tied in the back. She couldn't get over how handsome he was. In fact he looked like a doctor one might see on a TV soap opera. *He is so much more than a pretty face*, she thought, but *he indeed has a pretty face.*

"Hey good looking," he said with a smile.

"I was just thinking the same about you," she returned.

"Actually I came here to see if you really were a doctor or that was just a line you used to get girls."

He laughed. "I got you, didn't I?" They kissed a long lingering kiss. She glanced at the book on the table. "I see you have been doing some heavy reading."

Nate said, "Hush." He kissed her again until they heard the keypad being punched. In came a locum tenens physician Nate did not know. They said a brief hello to him as they left.

"Let's get something to eat," he said as they started walking toward the cafeteria. The cafeteria was basically a very large room with a hot meal counter on one side with the other sides filled with open coolers containing various salads, sandwiches, drinks, and desserts. Angela started to go in but Nate said, "Oh, no. Follow me."

They went past the cafeteria to an unmarked door that led into the doctors' eating area. It was a much smaller room with bare walls that resembled the doctors' lounge. There was a table with four chairs, a couch, and a refrigerator containing sandwiches and soft drinks. The room was again depressing to Angela. "Why don't we go to the main cafeteria where the selection is much better?" she asked.

"I avoid that place like the plague," he answered. She looked at him inquisitorially. "You know, it's good to have some privacy," he said, answering a question that had not been asked. Angela was surprised. He was obviously uncomfortable around people in the hospital who were not patients. Angela made a note to herself that she had learned something new about Nate.

"This has been an interesting two days," he said as he munched on his sandwich. "What delayed me was one of my patients, who at least was going to be one of my patients, was brought in dead to the Emergency Room." Angela stopped eating. She looked at Nate who became very quiet as if he was trying to take hold of his emotions. She wasn't expecting him to say anything like this. He took a bite of his sandwich before continuing. "It was a seventeen-year-old football player that his pediatrician had called me about yesterday. He had run an EKG on him because he was about to start medication for Attention Deficit Disorder and found that he had something called W-P-W. It's a defect in the conduction system of the heart that can cause sudden death in athletes participating in competitive sports. It's rare but it happens. Also it is something that is fixable. I advised him to tell the student and his parents that he should do no sports until I could see him on Monday. But that darn little kid slipped out this morning without telling his parents and went to football practice and collapsed on the field." He took another bite and drank some cola. "The EMTs tried to resuscitate him on the way to the emergency room, but he was dead on arrival. I told the ER doc and nurses that I was supposed to see this kid in my office Monday." For a moment Nate looked really sad as he stared off in space. He then shook his head as if trying to clear his mind. "Can you believe that?"

Angela was horrified. She felt sick for the child and his family. "That is so horrible," she said. Nate continued to eat without saying anything. She was beginning to understand what kind of life Nate was living at work.

"Here is something else you won't believe," he said with a smile as he began a new thought. "Yesterday afternoon the ambulance brought in a fifty year old on whom they had been doing CPR the whole way from his home. When he got to the ER he was still in V-fib, which is where the heart just kind of vibrates without pumping blood," he explained. "Well, we shocked him and shocked him and gave him meds and each time his heart would start to beat for a short time then would go back into V-fib." Nate stopped to eat a chip. "I knew it was hopeless so I went out to the waiting room to prepare the family like I usually do before stopping the resuscitation. As usual they were all hysterical. When I told his wife I thought there was little hope, she fainted and the nurses had to admit her. The rest of the family were all yelling and screaming. I was wishing like anything Father Jim had been there. I've seen a lot of hysterical families, but this family took the cake."

Angela was aghast. What a horrible, horrible day. She wasn't sure she could take any more of this.

"Finally after an hour his heart just stopped with no beat at all. We couldn't get it back," Nate continued. He drank the rest of his cola. "We had continued longer than usual. Finally I told everyone to stop, we had done enough. Well as we walked away the monitor showed an occasional electrical beat. The nurses got excited but I told them it was just some residual electrical activity of a dead heart and that we weren't going to restart this whole thing over. There were a few more beats, and the nurses begged to restart the resuscitation. I said it was no use but they could give it one more try. As usual, the doctor was proved wrong. Soon he had a regular beat and a decent palpable pulse but was not breathing on his own." He put away his lunch. "So I said to them 'Great! We have just resuscitated a vegetable. Let's get him up to the ICU'."

Angela did not know what to think or feel. Here was a middle-aged family man who had a heart attack and died and his family went berserk, and then he came back to life. Then without any sign of emotion, Nate had referred to him as a vegetable. She was totally bewildered.

"Well," Nate continued. "As you might expect, when I walk in this morning to see him, he is sitting up in bed and greets me with, 'Doctor Williams, thank you so much for saving my life and not giving up on me. The nurses told me the whole story.' I said, 'You're welcome,' and as he shook my hand I thought to myself, 'You are not supposed to be here talking to me. You're supposed to be dead or at least brain dead'." Nate then laughed. "Things like that are what make medicine so unpredictable and interesting. I learn something new every day."

Angela's emotions had been on a roller coaster. She felt exhausted. *This is real life*, she thought. *This is Nate's life*. It was not the drama and adventure that she was accustomed to in her books. Nate dealt with death every day. She remembered Father Jim explaining about shoptalk. She thought about what she had read about how soldiers protected themselves from the horror of war with humor and distancing themselves from what was happening. This helped her better understand Nate, who lived in a daily war zone.

His beeper went off. Nate looked at it and said that it was something urgent. He kissed her and said he was sorry to have to rush off. He asked her if she could find her way out of the hospital, which she said she could. He then flew out of the doctors' lounge leaving her alone in that quiet, bleak room. She sat there realizing that she had gotten more than she had bargained for when she asked if they could have lunch at the hospital together. How different was her impression now of hospitals compared to her childhood. The drama of hospital life was exciting but at the same time she felt sad and depressed thinking about the patients and the tragedies they endured. She felt scared for Nate. She worried what being a doctor might do to him in the long run. Yes, he received praise and self-satisfaction when he saved a life, but he also exposed himself to a lifetime of guilt when he didn't, for he was human, and all humans make mistakes. He was willing to take that risk. He was willing to put himself on the line each and every day. Her respect for him was more than she ever thought possible. She found her way to the hall leading to the doctors' parking lot. She felt weak and wasn't sure she could actually walk down that long, lonely hall. She managed to get to the parking lot.

She got in her car and headed home to spend the evening alone hoping things would slow down so she could see Nate again that evening.

Angela did not see Nate much at all the whole weekend. He usually arrived very late and left early the next morning. When he left Monday morning Angela knew he was exhausted, but at least he would not be on call that night. That evening Angela had made a very special dinner with candlelight and their favorite wine. She wanted to make everything perfect. When he sat down she gently brushed his hair with her hand and then kissed him. How much closer she felt to Nate. How much more she understood him. Nate was truly her hero. He seemed happy and relieved to be home with her. He chatted off and on as they ate. Angela mainly listened. She smiled as she looked at the man she cared for so much. Nate did not think he had a big heart but she knew that he did. However, she had just discovered how enormous it really was. That night she held him extra close. She wanted to be close to him and close to his heart that she now knew was in many ways bigger than hers.

Chapter Sixteen

It was Friday morning during morning rounds when he received a call from Angela on his cell phone. He apologized to the patient he was seeing and stepped out of the room to take the call. He was surprised to hear Angela crying. "Oh Nate," she sobbed, "Oh Nate."

"Angela, what's wrong," he pleaded.

"It's Dad. He collapsed and they are rushing him to the hospital by ambulance. I'm so worried." She continued to cry.

"I'll be right there. Don't worry." Nate hoped he could find a fellow cardiologist to help him. Fortunately, he saw Dr. Allen at the nurse's station. He explained to him that he had an emergency and would he mind covering his patients the rest of the day. Dr. Allen said sure and then asked innocently, "It is a family emergency?"

Nate didn't know how to answer that question. He hesitated a moment before saying, "Yes."

When he got to Angela's apartment she was ready to go with an overnight bag she had packed for both of them. Nate had never seen Angela so upset before. Deep down he knew that when they got to he hospital the news would not be good. The two-hour drive to the hospital seemed like two days. Angela cried a lot, expecting the worse but not wanting to think about it. She fell asleep for the last half of the trip. Nate's heart ached at what Angela was going through. Such a deep feeling was new to him for his heart had never ached for anyone before. When they arrived at the emergency room they were ushered into a small waiting room off of the main waiting room that Nate knew instinctively was a bad sign.

The ER doctor came in with a nurse and sat in front of Angela. With a somber tone he informed her that her dad had suffered a major brain hemorrhage. They had done everything they could he explained, but he died about an hour before they arrived. When Angela heard the news she turned her face into Nate's shoulder and cried loudly and inconsolably. He put his arm around her. Seeing Angela's grief for her dad broke his heart. He felt like crying himself. Even though he had only met Angela's father once he felt close to him. He would miss him too. After a few moments the ER doctor said he was very sorry and asked if she would like the hospital chaplain to be called. Angela emphatically said no through her tears. She then asked if she could see her father. The doctor motioned to the nurse to show her where he was.

Nate could not count the numerous patients he had pronounced dead or the numerous grieving families that he had counseled afterwards with little inward emotion in his professional role as a physician. Now he was one of those grieving families, and he didn't want to be. He tried to be a tough-skinned doctor to protect himself but holding Angela, he could not. He was grieving as Angela was. When they entered to see her father Angela held Nate's arm tightly as if she was holding on for dear life. There lay Reverend Carter covered with a hospital sheet up to his neck. His face looked relaxed and in an odd way content. It was the face of one who had lived a life of love and forgiveness. It was the face of one who had experienced a deep lifelong inner joy despite the disappointments and hurts that all humans undergo.

Angela looked at him silently with love in her eyes. She bent over and gave him a gentle kiss on the cheek and said, "I love you Dad. Thank you for loving me so. I will miss you so much." She stood there in silence clinging to Nate looking at the father that she loved so much. After a few moments she said, "Goodbye Dad." Nate also said a silent goodbye to a man he greatly admired whom he had known for such a short time.

Afterwards they met with hospital personnel who assured her they had everything they needed. They then met briefly with the funeral home personnel who had arrived. They were very sympathetic as they arranged a meeting with them early the next morning to work out all the details of the funeral. Nate and Angela then got in their car and drove to the assisted living residence where his room was.

The room was one large room that contained his bed along one wall with a couch along the other wall. On the third wall was a desk above which hung a TV set. On his desk were an open Bible, several Bible commentaries, and a number of devotional and prayer books. Angela smiled when she saw his books. "I could never get him to read much fiction," she said picking up one of his books.

On his bedside table were a picture of her mom, a picture of the three of them taken at a church function, and a picture of Angela when she was nine years old. Angela sat on the bed wiping her eyes with a tissue holding the pictures in her hand. She first looked at the picture of her mom that was taken when she was in her thirties. She was smiling wearing a colorful flowered dress that was popular in her day.

"My mom was happy when this picture was taken," Angela said, remembering her childhood. "She was a good woman."

Nate sat on the bed beside her. He could see a strong resemblance between her and Angela. *Beauty definitely runs in their family*, he thought to himself.

"Angela, she was beautiful, just like you," Nate commented.

"The problem was," Angela continued, "that she was not cut out to be a preacher's wife. She wanted the prestige of having a pastor as a husband but did not realize the sacrifice that was involved. I think she pictured Dad as head of a mega church with a very good living, but unfortunately the churches Dad managed to get could barely pay his salary. Also she wasn't prepared to put the church people's needs before their needs like Dad was. But most of all she wasn't prepared to be the last one to get Dad's attention. So basically they didn't fulfill each other's needs. I think men for some reason can live with that sort of situation longer than women. What do you think?" she asked Nate.

Nate was not prepared for that question. "I don't know," he said. "It is not good for either one."

"For the first few years things went well. Mom was the ideal young preacher's wife. Then she began to get irritable. Soon after that she started showing symptoms of depression. It was not noticeable at church, where they seemed the model couple, but at home it was just the opposite. She made his life miserable criticizing him for every little thing. This made my life miserable too. As she got more depressed Dad took her to doctors for treatment but nothing helped. However, my dad kept loving her. He only returned her hateful remarks with kindness."

"I think your dad was a saint," Nate said.

"Yes, but I wasn't," Angela said as she continued to look at the pictures. "I was on Dad's side. I started to hate the way she treated him. I couldn't understand how she felt or why she acted like she did. She wanted Dad to be something he was not capable of being.

133

Now I realize that they were not intimate often. They were both caught in a trap and didn't know how to get out."

Angela was deep in thought, as if she was really analyzing the relationship between her father and mother for the first time.

"I started to not only hate what she did to Dad, but I began to hate her. Then she died of that blood clot, and I couldn't get over my guilt for the way I felt about her for a very long time afterwards. I told myself that I was just a kid, but that didn't help. However, time has a way of healing. Now I just feel sorry for both of them and what they missed in life." Angela brought the picture of her mom to her lips and kissed it. "I love you, Mom," she said. "I am so sorry I treated you like I did. Please forgive me. I didn't understand but now I do."

Nate sat there surprised. He was a little shocked. Angela seemed to have had the model family. Yet it was a family filled with anguish and personal suffering that few people knew about. Nate thought Reverend Carter was the perfect father and family man. But now he realized that he was human and was blinded to his shortcomings like everyone else, shortcomings that had a devastating effect on both Angela and her mother. Nate felt close to Angela. She had opened up to him, revealing to him feelings from the innermost regions of her heart that most people keep hidden. He now felt sorry for Angela. He felt sorry for that cute little nine year old in the picture.

"I know that was tough on you as a kid," Nate said.

'Yep," returned Angela. "Everyone thought my mom and dad had the ideal marriage." Angela paused to wipe the tears again from her eyes. "I decided early on that if marriage was supposed to be like that, then marriage was not for me."

Nate put his arm around her. They sat silently looking at the pictures. Finally Nate picked up Angela's picture. "You were one cute little kid. I wish I could have known you then." Angela was in pigtails, had a Sunday dress on that almost hid her tennis shoes, and on her face was a great big mischievous smile.

"I don't think you would have liked me back then," Angela returned.

"I don't know. I don't think you've changed much," Nate said. "I bet you were an independent little girl back then just as you are now. I bet you didn't let anyone boss you around."

"You're probably right," she said smiling. Angela looked more at the picture of her dad. She cried a little more before regaining her composure. She put the Bible and the pictures in her purse. She took one last look around the room. "It's time to go," she said softly.

They walked down the hall to the assisted living administrator's office and informed him that she would come next week to gather all his belongings and finish any paperwork that needed to be finished. The administrator said that would be fine. He and all the personnel expressed their sorrow and how much everyone loved her father. As they were walking down the hall they passed a very elderly man slumped in a wheelchair who motioned them to come over to him. He had a hard time sitting completely upright but with effort was able look at them. "I want you to know that your dad was a blessing to this whole facility. He made a habit of visiting and talking with everyone here at least three or four times a week, including those who couldn't talk or understand anything. That was real love. He preached on Sundays when there was no one to preach, which happened often. He preached some damn good sermons." He reached up and held her hand. "We will miss him."

Angela smiled and thanked him. She then said goodbye and gave him a hug. It was late when they finally left. They were not really hungry but decided to have a light meal at a nearby restaurant. Nate let Angela talk about her dad and the many memories she cherished. She talked about the good times and how her dad always showed her love and how she felt she was the center of her dad's life. Nate said he felt very fortunate to have met him and was thankful to him for giving him Angela, which seemed to warm her heart.

They found a small motel and checked in. They unpacked their clothes and got ready for bed. As they slipped into bed Angela kissed him and pressed her body next to his. She then looked deeply into his eyes and said, "Love me, Nate."

Nate kissed her back and then remembered he had not brought the protection that he used and said, "Angela, I didn't bring the . . . ," but she cut him off and softly whispered, "Just love me," and held him tight. As they made love that night they did not realize that death and life are often partners in the dance of life.

Chapter Seventeen

THE NEXT MORNING ANGELA AND NATE MET WITH THE funeral home representatives. Randy had enough life insurance to cover the funeral costs so all Angela had to do was work out the details. Her first response was to have a simple small memorial service without a pastor, but she quickly discarded this idea because she knew what her father would have preferred, plus his old friends and former members of his churches would be shocked. The funeral home director said that a fellow retired pastor and friend, Bill Garner, had offered to conduct the funeral if they had no one else in mind. Angela knew him well although it had been years since she had seen him. Reverend Garner and her dad grew up together, and both had become pastors.

Nate accompanied Angela, but he was of no help. He actually had never been to a funeral much less planned one. When Angela asked his opinion on caskets, flowers, etc., he was at a loss. Since her dad was not a current member of a local church the funeral service would be held in the funeral home's chapel. Angela explained to the funeral director that Randy essentially had his own mini church in the assisted living residence where he preached, and that is why he did not otherwise have a church home.

The service was set to be early in the following week. Nate

was able to get off and told everyone without hesitation that it was a family emergency without going into the details. There would be a visitation the night before at the funeral home with the service the next morning at eleven AM. Randy then would be buried next to Angela's mom in the cemetery in the same town. Angela then arranged for a private room in a local restaurant with lunch for anyone who would want to join them after the graveside gathering. Nate was amazed at how knowledgeable Angela was about everything and how she knew just what to do, not remembering that a large part of Angela's life growing up involved helping her dad with funeral arrangements.

Angela and Nate were the first ones to arrive at the chapel for the visitation the night before the funeral. Reverend Carter lay in his casket at the front of the chapel surrounded by stands of flowers. They entered the back of the chapel and hand in hand they slowly walked up to the casket. Nate took a deep breath. He felt more anxious than sorrowful as they approached where he lay. He had seen many a patient dead in hospital or ER beds. That was part of his job. It didn't bother him. However, this was very different. Reverend Carter had the appearance of one who was simply asleep. Nate thought to himself that funeral homes do a marvelous job of creating that illusion. He wore a fine suit and tie and his hands were folded on his chest revealing his wedding ring. They both stood there in silence. After a few moments Angela whispered, "Goodbye Dad."

The visitation was lightly attended. Most were elderly people who had been members of one of the churches where he had been the pastor. Nate marveled at Angela, who took charge comforting everyone. She introduced Nate to everyone as a friend of hers. Many remembered Angela as such a cute little girl. Quite a few said that part of the enjoyment they got from her father's services was seeing her there with her father. Nate smiled picturing cute little Angela at her father's services. They all praised Randy as a loving pastor and wondered why he moved from church to church so much. Angela wondered why they did not visit him more in the assisted living residence.

Reverend Garner arrived midway through the visitation. He hugged Angela and shook Nate's hand. Nate noticed that he too had the demeanor of a happy and contented retired pastor who had life all figured out. He expressed his sorrow but had a twinkle in his eye that gave Nate a feeling that despite their loss everything was as it should be. He began to talk with Angela about the service the next day and the decisions that they had to make about all the details. Angela thanked him and told him that she would leave all that up to him, the music, the scripture, etc. There would be no other family members present because there were no other living relatives. He asked her if she would like to say a few words, and she said that she preferred not to.

The next morning Angela and Nate did not say much to each other. He brought her coffee in bed and sat next to her as they drank it. He would occasionally reach to give her hand a gentle squeeze. She looked at him appreciating the comfort that he gave her. Nate could tell she counted on him during this time of grief. He had a role and a purpose that he had not had before, a role and a purpose that now was more important to him than any other he had ever had before.

When they arrived at the funeral home they were taken to a private sitting room near the front of the chapel until everyone was seated. Then as they were ushered into the front seat reserved for the family they saw right behind them Tony, Rita, Cindy, Rick, Samantha, and Father Jim all in their best clothes with gentle compassionate smiles on their faces. Upon seeing them Angela sighed. Nate could tell how good it made her feel seeing her club, her family, there. She immediately hugged each one of them thanking them for coming and then sat down as the singer, a middle-aged nicely dressed lady, sang two verses of, "I Come to the Garden Alone."

After the song was finished, Reverend Garner got up, opened his Bible and read several Bible verses that he said were the favorites of Reverend Carter before siting back down. The music started again with the song, "What a Friend We Have in Jesus".

Reverend Garner then got up to begin his sermon. He first comforted everyone by saying that although this was a time of mourning and sadness it was also a time of celebration of the life of Reverend Carter. He then recounted what a loving husband and father he had been and what a wonderful devoted pastor he had been to all of the members of his various churches. He told of how they grew up together in the same church and how at the end of a powerful revival at their church they both the same night decided to answer the altar call and give their life to Christ. Even though they were only eleven years old, they understood that the sins that they had committed so far and the sins they were going to commit in the future condemned them to an eternity of suffering in the hereafter but that Jesus would take their place and bear all the sufferings they deserved if only they would have faith in him and walk down the aisle and openly confess their faith. That Jesus would love them so much was so overwhelming that it was hard to fathom. They had both walked down that aisle together, Reverend Garner told them, and with tears in their eyes confessed their faith and were saved. They were both baptized the following week. That was when they decided to devote their lives to Christ and become preachers. Now, he said, Reverend Carter was home with Jesus who had a place prepared for him.

Reverend Garner continued. "We know why there is death in this world. Death was not part of God's plan. Death came into this world because of sin. The sin of Adam and Eve and the sin of all of us is why our beloved Reverend Randy has tasted death. However, Jesus has conquered death and has taken our place on the cross and has offered eternal life to all those who believe in him."

As the sermon continued Angela silently sobbed, not because of what the pastor said for she had heard her father give that same sermon a hundred times, but because she was saying goodbye to a father she loved very much. Nate kept his arm around Angela thinking of her and not paying much attention to what Reverend Garner was saying. When he finished, Nate and Angela walked by the casket to give a last goodbye. They were then followed by the rest who were there. The casket was then closed and taken to the cemetery where most of the attendees gathered behind Nate and Angela as they sat on a row of chairs in front of it. Reverend Garner said similar words of comfort, after which everyone hugged Angela as they left. Angela got up from her seat and touched the casket goodbye. She then picked out a flower from a stand of flowers nearby and, holding Nate's hand, she stepped to her mother's grave, knelt down and laid the flower on it. In a low voice only Nate could hear she said, "Mom, I hope you and Dad will have the love in heaven that you so wanted and couldn't have while you were here." Angela got up, stood straight and walked with Nate to their car without looking back.

Everyone had been invited to a local restaurant afterwards. Nate, Angela's club members, the pastor, and a number of former members of his churches joined them. Angela was no longer crying as she began talking with everyone who shared stories about her father. She laughed and shared her stories along with everyone else. Nate could tell that for a while it was like she was back at one of the many church functions she grew up with. She seemed more relaxed and happy than he had seen her since the death of her father.

On the way home they were mostly silent. She sat next to him using the middle seat belt because she needed his touch more than his words.

Chapter Eighteen

OVER THE FOLLOWING WEEKS ANGELA'S BOUTS OF sadness decreased in frequency. She slowly began to experience a peaceful acceptance of her father's death. She also began to feel again that the light from the good in the world was, in the end, greater than the darkness. It was about this time that one evening she announced to Nate that it was time for them to have dinner at the Silver Lining Restaurant.

The Silver Lining Restaurant was located in a strip mall on the outskirts of town. From the outside it looked very unimpressive. However, there were a number of cars parked outside, which indicated that the restaurant was probably popular by word of mouth. Once inside one was greeted by a very refreshing Italian décor and delicious smells that made you instantly happy that you were there. In the background was music that seemed to be from an Italian opera. There were racks of wine bottles in the corners. Painted on one wall was a copy of Michelangelo's painting from the Sistine Chapel where God, appearing as an old man, had his hand outstretched almost touching Adam, who was very much naked. On the other wall was painted a picture of a vineyard with rows of grape vines along a hillside. There were both booths and tables, each with a flickering candle. They decided on a cozy booth near the corner.

Tony saw them come in and came over to their table. With a big smile he hugged them both. "Welcome to the Silver Lining Restaurant," he said robustly with outstretched arms. "You are my guests tonight, everything is on me."

Nate protested. "Now Tony, remember the first night we met we agreed that I would come and eat here only if I could pay for myself and my date." Angela smiled.

"Ok Nate," Tony responded, "but the wine is on me. I will give you the best in the house. I will not take no for an answer." Nate agreed reluctantly and thanked him. "I will have my son Frankie wait on you. He has only been working here for a short while so be patient with him."

Tony left, and soon Frankie came sauntering up to the table. Angela had met him only once before when his parents had brought him to the bookstore. He was a little taller than his dad with black hair combed straight back. His lips were a little more prominent than normal as was his nose. This, coupled with his very white complexion and dark eyebrows, made him stand out in a striking, handsome sort of way.

"Good evening Miss Angela," he said.

"Good evening Frankie. I would like you to meet Dr. Williams, a close friend of mine."

"Nice to meet you," Frankie responded. "My dad says I am to call you Dr. Williams even though I am not having a heart attack." Nate laughed and said he was glad to meet him also. Nate could see the family resemblance in Frankie in both his looks and the way he talked.

He took their drink orders, which consisted of water and the wine picked out by Tony. Before he left, Angela commented on how nice it was of his dad to hire him to work in the restaurant.

"He had to. It was court ordered," Frankie said as he left to get their wine. When he had come back Angela looked at him and asked, "It was court ordered?"

"Yeah. The cops found some stolen hubcaps in the trunk of my car and didn't believe me when I said I didn't steal them. All the cops in this town have it out for me. It is downright criminal. They gave me probation on the condition that I get a job. So my dad offered me this job, and the judge went along with it."

"Well at least you are making some money," Nate chipped in, hoping to lighten up the conversation.

"Not much with the way my Dad pays around here. What everyone makes around here is the pits; it is simply the pits. The only way one can survive working here is to depend heavily on tips, if you know what I mean," he said, looking at them out of the corner of eyes as he tilted his head.

He then took their orders. They both ordered the specialty of the house, which was chicken prepared in a creamy wine sauce served over pasta. Nate remarked that it was the best Italian dish he had ever tasted. Angela agreed. As they were finishing, Tony came up to their booth and smiled when they told him how much they enjoyed what they ordered.

Tony then looked a little serious. "My boy, Frankie, he has been in some trouble with the law, but he is a good boy. I think finally he has got his head on straight," Tony said as he put his hands together as if he was praying and looked at the ceiling. Then he turned back to them. "I will tell you what I tell all my guests. I hope the meal we have provided not only is pleasing to your taste and your stomach but will also warm your heart so you can better see the silver linings in your life."

Nate held up his glass and offered him a toast thanking him for his generosity. Angela did the same. They then checked out leaving a very generous tip.

As they walked out to their car Angela was worried about Frankie. "Do you think Frankie will be ok?" she asked Nate.

"I don't know," answered Nate. "He worries me. I don't think Tony and Rita know what to do." Frankie actually scared Nate a little, but he didn't want to act too concerned in front of Angela.

"Yes, I can tell they are really worried," Angela returned. They both thought silently to themselves as they sat in Nate's car.

After a couple of minutes Angela became animated. "Let's do something crazy," she said.

"Like what?" Nate asked.

"Let's drive down to the beach."

Nate looked at his watch. It was 7:30 PM and the beach was a ninety-minute drive away. He looked at Angela whose eyes were beaming as she looked back at him expectantly. "Sure, let's go," he said.

When they arrived at the beach the restaurants were starting to close. There was a huge boardwalk on the beach that contained a few carnival rides and a gift shop in which a few customers were still shopping. It was the last of summer and school had not started yet. After Labor Day everything would be closed except on weekends. Nate asked Angela if she wanted to ride the Ferris wheel. She said no because she was afraid of heights, which Nate had not known before.

They walked holding hands along the railing of the boardwalk where they could see and hear the ocean waves. The moon was shining brightly. The night sky was clear except for a few scattered patches of clouds that would occasionally give the moon a break. Nate felt very relaxed. He was glad they had come. Next to the gift shop Angela noticed a picture booth where one could sit inside and for just a dollar four small pictures of them would be taken.

"Come on," Angela said as she pulled his arm. "Let's get our picture taken like we did when we were kids."

"Sure," said Nate.

They both squeezed into the booth and put their heads together as the booth made four flashes. They kissed passionately for the first picture, and then put their heads cheek to cheek for the second one. They made funny faces for the last two by putting their fingers in their mouths and stretching them really big in different ways. The little strip of pictures soon came out, and they both looked at them and laughed.

"I've got another idea," Angela said.

"You are always coming up with ideas," Nate said, smiling.

"Let's drive down to the far end of the beach where no one is," Angela returned. Nate said ok but was not sure what she had in mind. They drove down the beach a far ways where there were no lights as well as no people. They got out and walked down to where the waves gave up trying to breach the beach. The light from the boardwalk that they had been on now seemed like a small lantern in the dark far away. The moon was full and still shining but was surrounded by a few patches of dark clouds. In between the clouds was the deep dark sky filled with small sparkling lights.

Angela was excited. She turned to Nate and said, "Let's go swimming."

"We didn't bring our suits," he protested.

"Who needs suits?" Angela said smiling. He watched her take off her clothes. Her beautiful feminine form appeared illuminated by the moonlight, and it thrilled him as it always did when he saw her undress. She stood there in her full beauty and motioned with her head for him to follow her. He stood there awestruck watching her as she walked into the ocean. He then realized that he was still clothed. He undressed hurriedly and joined her. When he got in he looked around at the well-lit waves from the full moon and said, "It's pretty bright around here."

"If you are worried," she reassured him with a laugh, "just keep what you don't want to show under the water."

Her hair was wet against her head. There were tiny drops of water on her eyelashes and cheeks. She was beautiful. One of the dark clouds drifted over the moon, and it became dark with only a rim of moonlight around the cloud. Nate took advantage of the darkness and drew her to him. They passionately kissed as their bodies came together. The touch of her body against his, her soft lips, and the salty wetness that came around them and in between them in waves as their bodies became one formed a memory that found a place deep within his heart, a place where it would reside forever. The ocean, the world, and the heavens as far as they reached must have been made just for them just for that night. From a distance, if anyone had been watching, two small heads in a moonlit sea appeared to become one among the waves.

They did not get home until two AM. They were still excited and laughing at the fact they had been acting like teenagers and they loved it. They fell into bed and into each other's arms and decided to let the world go on without them.

Chapter Nineteen

For Nate, time off from work was now as precious as gold. His heart had two goals each day. One was to be the best cardiologist he could be. The other was to finish each day as soon as possible in order to get home to Angela. Before, even when he was not on call, he would hang around the wards until eight or nine at night simply because he had little to do at home. In fact, the hospital had become his home. But now he had a real home. Once he was away from the hospital he put work out of his mind. His time away from work was now his time and it was very precious.

This particular day was one of those days doctors dream about. All the problems he faced that day were problems he could fairly easily diagnose. More importantly they were problems he could do something about. There were no gray areas where he was unsure if he was doing the right thing or not, and all the patients thought he was a genius, which was not all that bad either. By five that evening he had all his chart notes done, had looked at all the lab results that he had ordered and had checked out to the cardiologist on call. Nate couldn't believe his good fortune that day. He now only thought of Angela, who was waiting for him.

He left the building and was walking to his car with his car keys in hand when his cell phone went off. The number on it was one that he did not recognize. *Who could be calling me?* he wondered. He cautiously said, "Hello. Dr. Williams here."

"Nate," a man's somewhat frantic voice said in reply. "This is Tony. I am in a bad way, a very bad way."

Nate looked at his phone, not really believing what he had just heard. "Tony, is this you?" he asked.

"Yeah Doc. I need your help bad."

"Tony, what's the trouble?" Nate asked.

"Doc, I'm in the emergency room. I was sure I was having a heart attack but this here ER doctor says it's just my ulcer. He wouldn't page you, but can you come and check me out? I need you bad," Tony pleaded.

Nate was beginning to get mad, and his face turned red. He knew he shouldn't have given out his phone number. He knew something like this would happen. It wasn't like he was needed medically. Tony had gone to the emergency room and was evaluated by a competent physician. Now, unreasonably, he was asking him to give up his valuable private time to check him out.

"Tony, I'm sure you have been checked out thoroughly. I was just on my way home and I'm not sure if I could be of any help to you," Nate tried to reassure him, all the while hoping Tony would say something like, "Oh yeah, sorry I called." However, Tony was to say no such thing.

"Nate, I really trust you. You're my friend, and I need you. Would you please come take a look at me?" Tony pleaded again.

Nate knew he had lost. His choice now was to be downright rude to Tony or go and see him as he requested. He couldn't be rude to a friend of Angela's. *What would she think of him?* He looked at his watch; it was now 5:20. Maybe he could zip in the ER, check his lab and let him go. *This may not take long after all.* "Ok Tony, I'll be right there," Nate told him.

"Thanks Doc, thanks a lot," was his reply.

Nate went through the back door of the ER. He found Tony's chart and looked over all the tests that had been ordered. The young new ER physician that was working the ER saw him with the chart.

"Dr. Williams, what are you doing here? I told Mr. Moretti there was no need for you to be called," the young physician said approaching him.

"He's a friend of mine. He called and asked me to come so I told him I would," Nate replied.

"Dr. Williams," the ER physician replied, "I wish there were more doctors like you around. I'm fairly new at this, but I have known enough physicians to know that few care enough for people to go out of their way for them. Thanks," he finished and shook Nate's hand.

Nate stood there with a blank face not knowing how to respond to the tribute he had just received. He nodded to show his appreciation and then went in the cubicle where Tony was. Tony was still in the white ER gown he had been given. He was lying on his back looking up at the ceiling twiddling his thumbs. When Nate walked in he stopped twiddling and became animated. "Man, am I glad to see you!" Nate couldn't return the compliment.

"Tony," Nate began. "I've checked out all your labs and I'm sure your pain is simply that old ulcer acting up again. I see from your history that you have had trouble with it in the past, so I think it is ok for you to go home now. The ER physician has given you some medicine that should help soon. I'll tell the nurses you can get dressed."

"Doc," Tony said in a quivering voice. "I know what the trouble is."

"You do?" asked Nate.

"Yeah. It's Frankie, my boy. He's been arrested today. That's why this damn ulcer is giving me fits."

"Frankie's been arrested? What happened?" Nate said curiously before he thought about it.

"Possession of drugs. Marijuana. Now he is in city jail."

Nate felt truly sorry to hear that, and he knew Angela would be upset. Frankie was such a good-looking kid. "We better get you out of here fast so you can go visit him," Nate said as he started looking for a nurse.

"Doc," Tony said again. "I hate to ask you, but could you drive me down to the jail. I'm not feeling too good, and I don't think I can drive. Rita is already there. She thinks I have been getting the restaurant ready for tonight. We don't have anybody else."

Nate was just beginning to feel good about the fact that he had taken some of his personal time to reassure Tony and that they were both about to leave, but now he could feel himself getting angry again. He hadn't realized how inconsiderate Tony was. "How about I call you a taxi? It shouldn't take too long," Nate said, hoping this would suffice.

"Doc, Rita would really feel good seeing you there and so would Frankie. You know Doc, what just occurred to me?" Tony said as his face became enlightened.

"What?" Nate said trying not to sound irritated.

"Frankie can have only one visitor. His mom and I have told him everything we know to tell him. It would be really great if you could try to talk some sense into his head. I know he really respects you."

Nate could definitely tell things were going from bad to worse. He could see his evening with Angela disappearing. And besides, he had no idea what to say to a young rebellious kid who used drugs. Then it occurred to him that Angela would want him to go, and he felt a little guilty. "Ok Tony, let's go," he said to Tony's surprised and relieved look.

While Tony got dressed Nate texted Angela. "Something has come up. Will be home late. Sorry." After they got into Nate's car Tony told him how to get to the city jail because he didn't have a clue where it was.

After passing through metal detectors they entered the waiting room at the jail and saw Rita sitting in a row of chairs along one wall with her head in her hands. Next to her was sitting Father Jim in his usual priestly outfit looking rather calm. The waiting room was filled with people, most of who were poorly dressed and appeared not to have bathed recently. As they walked up to Rita, Tony said in a rather loud voice, "I'm ok."

Rita raised her head with a surprised look on her face and said, "You're ok? What's wrong with you?"

"I thought I was having a heart attack so I went to the ER. Dr. Williams checked me out. Thank God it just turned out to be my ulcer," Tony said, smiling. Rita put her head back into her hands without saying anything. "Father Jim, it's great to see you here," Tony continued.

"Rita called me and I came as soon as I could," Father Jim replied.

Rita looked up. "Tony, he can have only one visitor. I think Father Jim should see him."

"I thought maybe Dr. Williams could see him too," Tony replied.

"But he can have only one visitor," Rita protested.

"I've got an idea," Tony said. He went over to the small window behind which sat a secretary and asked to see a policeman. Soon a thirtyish officer appeared. "Officer," Tony began. "My poor son Frankie, as you know, is just a kid and we have our priest here to see him. But we also have his doctor, Dr. Nathaniel Williams, a distinguished physician from St. Joseph's hospital, who has come all the way down here to help, and Frankie needs a lot of help. I was wondering if there was any way possible . . ."

The officer broke in stopping Tony before he could finish, probably because he was not sure how much longer Tony was going to ramble on. "Ok, ok," the officer said, looking over at Nate. "Dr. Williams took care of my grandpa. I tell you what I will do. I will make an exception just this one time and allow one visitor and one medical consultant. Ok?"

"Thank you officer, thank you," Tony said enthusiastically and shook his hand vigorously.

"Father Jim and Dr. Williams, come this way," the officer motioned to them. Nate stood there not quite believing what was happening. He felt like an innocent bystander being pulled into something against his will. He was about to enter a jail for the first time in his life. Father Jim got up and patted Nate on the shoulder as if he knew that Nate was a little reluctant to go with him. They entered a hallway and then through two locked doors into another hallway with cells on each side filled with prisoners. Nate followed Father Jim who seemed to know where he was going. He looked around at the poor specimens of humanity in the cells and thought again what a complicated mess humanity was.

"Hey Father Jim, say a prayer for me," one of the inmates shouted.

"Joe, you know I pray for you daily," returned Father Jim. Joe thanked him, and several other inmates said the same thing. To Nate's surprise, Father Jim knew several of their names. They finally reached Frankie's cell. The officer unlocked the door and let them in. Frankie, who was standing staring at the opposite wall, looked surprised when he saw them both entering his cell.

"So now they are sending in a priest and a doctor. What are they going to do, hang me or something?" Frankie asked sarcastically. Nate looked at him and had no idea what to say. Father Jim sat on his bed without saying anything. Nate followed his example.

"What are you doing here?" Frankie asked.

"We're not exactly sure," Father replied. "Your parents asked us to come."

"I bet they are really pissed," Frankie said, looking again at the wall of the cell for some reason.

"No," Father answered. "They are upset and worried."

"Father, tell them that I was framed; these cops have it in for me."

Father Jim sat there without replying and looked carefully into Frankie's face. After a few minutes Frankie said in a less authoritative tone, "Maybe don't tell them that. I don't know what I am going to do."

Both Nate and Father Jim could tell Frankie was scared. As Frankie paced back and forth, Father Jim continued to sit there silently. Then Frankie turned and said, "What am I going to do?"

"I don't know Frankie," Father Jim said thoughtfully. "All I know is that we are here for you."

Frankie looked at Father, disappointed that he had no easy answer. Then he looked at Nate before looking away as if he felt ashamed of himself. Father Jim then turned to Nate and asked, "Is there anything you want to say, Dr. Williams?"

All of a sudden Nate felt very anxious. What was he going to say? And, more importantly, what should he say? *What I say could influence this young man for the rest of his life*, he thought. This was definitely way out of his ballpark. Then as he looked at Frankie he could see the fear in his face. *He's just a kid*, Nate told himself. He began to feel sorry for him and before he knew it he heard himself say, "I haven't known you very long Frankie, but I'm here on your side. I want to help anyway I can."

Frankie looked at them both. "Thanks and thanks for not lecturing me; I appreciate it," he said sincerely.

"There is one thing I know," Father added.

"What's that?" Frankie asked.

"They are not going to hang you," Father said with a smile.

At that Frankie smiled and almost laughed. He then unexpectedly gave both Nate and Father Jim a quick hug.

Just then the guard informed them that the time of the visit was up. As Father Jim left he said, "Frankie, if you need me for anything, these guys can get hold of me anytime night or day, ok? They've got my number for some reason."

"Ok," Frankie replied with a very slight smile as he watched them both walk away.

When they got back to the jail waiting room Father Jim sat and talked with Tony and Rita. "Frankie is an ok kid," he told them, "who has got himself into quite a bit of trouble, and he knows it. He's the one who has to get himself out of it or it will happen again," Father Jim explained.

"What can we do?" asked Tony.

"I think it is best to let the legal system work like it is supposed to. It would be wise to have a lawyer to make sure he is not taken advantage of, but Frankie needs to know this is not about getting him off the hook. He needs to know that you guys support the laws and the punishment for breaking those laws."

Tony and Rita looked at each other and then Tony said, "Ok."

"He's scared and that's good. Sometimes it takes a crisis to turn things around," Father Jim said reassuringly. Tony and Rita thanked him from the bottom of their hearts, and both hugged him. They then hugged Nate and expressed their thanks.

"This is quite an occasion," announced Tony. "Just to think that my boy Frankie has had both a priest and doctor visit him together. This is something unusual. I want all of us to remember it so Frankie can tell his kids about it." At that Tony pulled out his cell phone and asked one of the less fortunate sitting nearby if they would take their picture, which he was willing to do. Tony motioned for the four of them to stand together and smile.

"That's ok," Nate said. "I'll just stand over here."

"Oh no, no, no," responded Tony. "We have to have you in the picture, Doc," exclaimed Tony. Reluctantly, Nate stood by Tony while Father Jim stood by Rita. The cameraman was in his fifties, had not shaved for at least a week or brushed his teeth. He said with a great big smile that revealed a number of cavities, "Say cheese," and then took several pictures of the four of them. Above their heads on the wall the words *Everston City Jail* could be clearly seen. Tony thanked the cameraman and Nate noticed how odd it was that everyone seemed in such a good mood.

After many thanks from Tony and Rita, Nate and Father Jim walked into the parking lot. "Nate, it was really kind of you to come. It meant a lot to all of them," Father Jim said.

Nate felt guilty for not wanting to come, but now he actually felt good that it had happened. "Father, let me ask you a question if I could," Nate responded.

"Sure," said Father.

"How do you do it? I mean really care for all those folks in jail and everyone else?"

Father Jim smiled and pointed his finger up towards heaven. "Just following orders, that's all. Just following orders."

Nate laughed a little. He liked that answer. He gently slapped Father Jim on the back and said, "Thanks Father. I'll see you soon at the hospital." It was a rare thing for Nate to slap someone on the back the way friends do. It was also rare for him to have friends.

He got home around 9:30. He found Angela sound asleep on the couch. She looked lovely all curled up clutching a pillow the way she clutched him sometimes. Angela had been going to bed earlier recently. She seemed to tire more easily than usual. However now she not only ran a bookstore but also was a lover and worked hard at cooking him meals and making him happy and that could certainly account for it. Nate gently picked her up and laid her under the covers of their bed. She was still half asleep. Without opening her eyes she asked softly, "Where have you been?"

"In jail dear, in jail," Nate replied.

"Very good dear, very good," she replied as she went back into a sound sleep.

Chapter Twenty

THE NEXT MORNING, ANGELA SUDDENLY AWOKE AND realized that she couldn't breathe. She struggled to get air down into her lungs. It felt like she was drowning. She lay on her back trying to figure what was going on. She was frantic. With effort she managed to find Nate's arm. "Nate, I can't breathe. There is something terribly wrong," she said desperately.

Nate woke up immediately. He looked at Angela fighting to breathe and alarms began going off in his head. He quickly assessed her noting that her neck veins were markedly distended. Probing her abdomen, he discovered her liver and spleen were enlarged. Putting his ear to her side he could hear fine rales, an indication of fluid buildup in the lungs. He thought to himself, *My God, she is in acute heart failure.*

"I am going to call the ambulance," he told her as he helped prop her up a little so she could breathe better. He called 911, quickly gave them the information, and then came back to her bedside.

"I'm scared Nate. Am I going to be ok?" she managed to ask.

"I'm getting you help. We are going to take care of you," he said, trying to reassure her. Nate remembered that Angela had seemed to tire out easily the last few weeks, but they had thought it was due to her busy schedule at the bookstore. Now he knew her tiredness was due to the early onset of heart failure. *How could I have missed it?* he asked himself. He quickly slipped on his clothes as he comforted her. The ambulance and the EMTs arrived fairly quickly. They had been trained what do in such cases but were very glad Dr. Williams was there to direct them. A nasal cannula was put in place to provide oxygen. Vital signs were taken, an IV started, and an EKG was taken on their portable EKG machine. Then, all together, they lifted her with her sheet and moved her to the ER stretcher. They then rolled her out to the ambulance where they lifted the stretcher and secured it inside.

Nate sat on a small bench-like seat attached to the wall of the ambulance at her bedside. When everyone was ready he said, "Full sirens, let's go." It was six AM as the ambulance raced through the city streets, which were still mostly empty waiting for the day to start. When they reached the ER the ER doctor and nurses were waiting for them. As they rolled Angela into one of the main treatment rooms, Nate told the ER doctor to start the acute heart failure protocol; everyone knew what to do. The protocol called for stat EKG, blood gas, chest x-ray, blood work, echocardiogram, and chest CAT scan.

Everyone was rushing around with Nate directing them. This was his specialty and he had learned long ago how to turn off his emotions in crisis situations. When the inhalation therapist was hesitant about drawing the blood gas, Nate took the syringe and hit Angela's artery immediately and handed it back to her filled with blood. Angela was having so much trouble breathing she did not notice the blood gas being taken. In between giving orders Nate would hold Angela's hand and bend down and softly tell her that she was going to be ok. He went with her as they rolled her into radiology for her cat scan telling her along the way exactly what was going to happen. When she got back from radiology, Nate asked the nurse to see if Dr. Archer had arrived at the hospital and if so, would he please come down. Dr. Archer, the chief of cardiology, had just begun to make his rounds when he got the message.

Father Jim had just finished consoling a family who had lost a loved one and was exiting through the ER as he usually did in case someone might need him when he saw all the activity. As the nurses went in and out of Angela's cubicle, Father Jim saw Angela in her hospital bed at a 45-degree angle with a very anxious look as she labored to breathe. His heart sank. He said a quick silent prayer for her and then slipped behind everyone to the head of her bed without getting in the way of anyone. He touched her shoulder and said, "I'm here." Angela turned to him with a look of relief, "Oh, thank you Father for being here." He smiled and squeezed her hand and whispered, "I will be here anytime you need me." Despite Angela's distress a slight look of relief seemed to cross her face.

Dr. Archer arrived and Nate stepped outside the cubicle. "Thanks for coming. This is a friend of mine who appears to be in acute heart failure for some unknown reason. I would appreciate it if you would take her on."

Dr. Archer replied, "I'd be glad to." They went together to the nurses' station and reviewed the entire lab with the other results obtained so far. Dr. Archer agreed that she was in acute heart failure. They both knew that she needed to go to the ICU as fast as possible. Besides oxygen, Angela was given a diuretic to help remove some of the fluid that accumulates with heart failure along with nitroglycerin, which dilates the coronary arteries. By the time an ICU bed was ready her breathing was a little easier, and she felt a little less anxious. Her bed was rolled down the hall to the elevator that would take her up to the ICU. The nurses in the ICU were waiting for her and helped transfer her from the

ER stretcher to the ICU bed. They attached her to the monitors and took her vital signs. Afterwards, being exhausted, Angela fell asleep.

Nate knew that everything that could be done had been done. He went to where the doctors normally did their charting and laid his head on his arm on the desk. He kept going over in his mind how she looked and acted the last week. He kept asking himself why, oh why, he, the heart specialist, had missed all the subtle signs. He felt like a total failure as a doctor. Now the thought of losing Angela produced a sick cramping feeling in the pit of his stomach. He could not stop sobbing. There were no other doctors present. It was quiet except for his sobbing when Dr. Archer walked in. He put his hand on Nate's shoulder and said, "Are you ok?"

Nate sat up and wiped his eyes on his sleeve and responded that he was. With a very serious face, Dr. Archer began talking. "As you know, she is in critical condition. Her ejection fraction is down to twenty percent." The ejection fraction is the percentage of the body's blood that is pumped out of the left ventricle during a contraction, which is normally fifty-five to seventy percent. Both knew that a twenty-percent ejection fraction meant the heart was seriously weakened and that she might not survive to leave the hospital.

Nate looked grim and remained silent. Dr. Archer continued. "So this is a friend of yours?" he asked.

"Yes," Nate replied.

"Just a friend?"

"Well, my girlfriend," he replied again.

"There was another test we ordered," Dr. Archer said, looking straight at Nate. "We ordered a pregnancy test and it was positive. She is about two and a half months along."

Nate sat back, shocked. He put his left hand on his forehead and slowly brought it down over his face. He thought to himself, *It was the night of her father's death. That was the only time I did not use protection.* He then leaned forward and rested his forearms on his legs and looked at the floor. He thought about all of the comments he and other doctors had made about stupid teenagers who could not figure out how to prevent pregnancy.

He looked up at Dr. Archer and said, "I will tell her in a day or so when she is awake and can fully understand."

"Since this pregnancy is pretty likely to end her life if it goes on, would you like me to inform her that the pregnancy must be terminated?" Dr. Archer asked.

"No," Nate responded. "Thanks, but I'll take care of it."

Dr. Archer got up, touched Nate on the shoulder, and said he was sorry before walking out of the room. Nate sat there alone staring at the wall wondering how all this had come about.

Chapter Twenty-one

As Sandy entered the nurses' station of the intermediate care, one of the night nurses pulled her aside. "You won't believe this. This morning we admitted Dr. Williams' girlfriend to ICU with acute heart failure, plus she's pregnant. Dr. Williams has requested that you be her nurse in intensive care."

Sandy felt like cold water had been thrown in her face. "Dr. Williams' girlfriend? And she's pregnant?" Sandy heard herself saying.

"Who would have thought that grumpy old Dr. Williams would have a pregnant girlfriend? It is the talk of all the nurses," the night nurse said.

Sandy was dumbfounded. She felt numb. This was not something she could have even dreamed of happening. The nurse asked her if she was ok. Sandy mumbled that she was but that it was just so unexpected. A rumor had been going around that a woman had visited Dr. Williams in the hospital one Saturday when he was on call. Also there was much speculation as to why Dr. Williams had become so nice to everyone recently. Sandy somehow had managed to dismiss all this and refused to believe that he really had a girl friend.

In a daze, Sandy began to walk to the ICU nursing station. There was a sudden emptiness deep inside of her and for some reason she had lost all hope, hope for what exactly she did not know, hope for something she didn't want to admit to herself but hope none the less. She reached the nursing station, where the nurses welcomed her and began filling her in on Angela's condition. Sandy did everything she could to keep her mind from drifting in order to listen to what was being said.

She walked in cautiously to Angela's room and saw her lying asleep with only a slight labor to her breathing. There was an IV in her right hand and an oxygen cannula in her nose. She looked very tired and weak. A nurse had tried to straighten out her unbrushed hair. She had no makeup on and this, combined with the way her hair looked, would have made most women seem less beautiful than they were but not her, thought Sandy. Sandy could tell why Nate was attracted to her, and she felt jealous and then ashamed for feeling so.

As Sandy gently put her fingers on her wrist to check her pulse, Angela opened her eyes and looked anxiously at her. Sandy immediately said, "Hi, I'm Sandy, your nurse."

It took some effort for Angela to respond. With a hoarse whisper she said, "Thank you. Nate has told me all about you."

"He has?" Sandy said before she could stop herself.

"Yes." Angela had to catch her breath. "He said you were the best nurse he has ever worked with," and with that she dozed off again.

Sandy stood there surprised. Suddenly she was filled with a sadness that Nate only thought of her as a good nurse. Sandy told herself that it was time to get professional, and she began to expertly assess Angela and go over her medical management plan. On her examination she noted the bulging neck veins and the enlargement of the liver and spleen and some edema in her legs. On Angela's finger was an oxygen saturation monitor, which read ninety-five percent. That was good, but being on oxygen, this should have been near one hundred percent. She checked her IV fluids to verify that the correct solution was hanging and was at the rate ordered. She went over all her medications and orders for tests throughout the day.

She was just finishing her initial assessment and had knelt down beside the bed to check the urine output in the bag that was connected to a catheter that had been inserted into Angela's bladder when Nate walked in. Nate did not see Sandy as he went to Angela's bedside. Sandy watched as he held Angela's hand and kissed her on the cheek. Angela opened her eyes. "Nate, oh Nate," she said.

"I'm here," he said.

"I'm so scared," she said looking at him.

Nate put his cheek next to hers, and Sandy heard him whisper, "I am going to take care of you." He kept his cheek next to hers for several minutes. Angela took a deep breath and closed her eyes and seemed to tremble at the touch of Nate's warm, unshaved cheek against hers. Sandy saw Angela open her eyes again and look at Nate's hair close to her face. She could tell that Nate's presence comforted her greatly. As Angela became visibly calm, Nate slowly backed away and looked at her lovingly. Sandy stood up and asked herself if this was the same Nate Williams she had known for the last two years, the Nate Williams she so adored and the Nate Williams that nobody else liked. Angela looked at Nate and said, "Sandy's here." Nate turned and saw Sandy, who gave him only a brief look and smile and went back to work, not noticing the smile Nate tried to give her.

"It's my heart?" whispered Angela.

"Yes," Nate said, "Now try to get some rest." Angela slowly

closed her eyes and rested. Nate turned to Sandy. "Thank you so much Sandy for taking care of Angela."

Sandy could not look at Nate directly. It simply hurt too much to look at someone that you really liked or maybe loved who didn't love you. "I'm more than happy to," she said in a professional voice and continued to check Angela's vital signs.

Nate left for a short period of time and came back shaved with a new set of greens on. Nate stayed with Angela most of the day. Sandy kept as busy as she could and said very little. She was a professional taking care of a patient and nothing more.

Chapter Twenty-two

NATE HAD ASKED THE OTHER CARDIOLOGISTS TO COVER his patients so he could be by Angela's side, which they were glad to do. Dr. Archer came in several times during the day to check on Angela discussing with Nate her condition in detail. One moment Nate would be the heart specialist who thought in terms of anatomy, physiology, and chemistry and as a heart specialist he would not think of Angela but only the functioning of her heart. The next moment he would be a lover sitting next to his beloved. Angela was critically ill, but he felt relief knowing that Sandy was taking care of her. He watched Sandy check and recheck all of Angela's medications, and he saw her examine Angela closely for any subtle changes in her condition. He was filled with respect and admiration for Sandy as a nurse, but he also realized that just having Sandy close by gave him great comfort for some reason. Nate stayed by Angela late into the night, and then when he was sure she was stable, he tried to get some sleep in the doctors' call room. However, he could not really sleep. Several times during the night he made short visits to check on her.

The next morning Angela was a little more awake and had a little more strength. She was sitting up still with her nasal cannula under her nose attached to leads and her IV. Nate marveled that a person who was so ill could at the same time look so beautiful. Nate sat by her bed and held her hand. Knowing how critical her situation was, he was sick with fear and wished he could instantly cure her; unfortunately, as a physician, he knew that was impossible.

Angela managed to smile when she saw her Nate close by her side. She looked at him lovingly and said, "Are you ok?"

"Yes, I'm ok," Nate answered. *Angela is on her deathbed and she is concerned about me?* he thought. A lump came in his throat. He couldn't bear the thought of losing her.

She caressed his hand gently and felt the strength of his fingers and the smoothness of his palm, concentrating on his every movement, and it seemed to give her great comfort. After a short while she said, "It's my heart, isn't it?"

"Yes," Nate said softly.

"What's wrong with it?"

"For some reason your heart has become very weak and not able to pump blood as well as before, and that is making you tired," Nate said.

Angela looked thoughtful. "Is there no reason for this?" she asked.

"Most likely it is from some sort of viral infection," Nate responded.

"Does my condition have a name?" she asked again, still holding Nate's hand.

"Yes," he answered.

"What is it?"

"Well there two names really. Acute congestive heart failure is what we doctors call it, but your heart is not in total failure, just not as good as before."

"And the other name?"

Nate was amazed that she had been so close to dying yesterday and today her condition was only slightly improved, and yet she could ask questions in a logical and thoughtful way. "The other name is viral cardiomyopathy."

"Would you please write them down for me?" she asked. Nate pulled a note card from his pocket and wrote the two names down and put it on her bedside table.

"Thank you, Nate," she said. Then she turned to him and with a smile said, "Kiss me." He leaned over and kissed her and then she said, "Again." Angela looked contented and peaceful. "I think I will rest now." Nate said yes, she needed to rest.

The next day Angela was even better. Her ejection fraction had increased from twenty to twenty-five percent and she was able to sit up and start drinking clear liquids. She was sipping a little hot tea when Nate came that morning. Nate had slept again in the doctors' call room. Nate kissed her and commented on how much better she looked. Her hair was well combed, and she had just enough makeup on to reveal her beauty.

"I'm feeling better every day thanks to you," she said.

"Well, Dr. Archer is officially your doctor because if I was your doctor I might get too distracted examining you and forget what I was supposed to do," Nate replied with a smile.

Angela pulled his hand to her breast and said, "You know what you're supposed to do."

Nate blushed and looked around to make sure they were alone and then said, "And that is the problem." They both laughed a little.

Angela slept most of the day. The next morning Angela felt even better. On her bedside table were a few get-well cards. "Look at all the cards my club members have sent me. I'm sure they are waiting for me to get better to visit."

"They are," Nate assured her. "Somehow they got hold of my

cell phone number and have been calling me constantly asking about you." They both smiled.

Nate then looked serious. "I have something important to talk to you about," he said as he looked into her eyes.

"And everything else hasn't been important so far?" she said smiling.

"Oh, yes, everything else has been definitely important," he answered, "but this is also very important. I don't know exactly how to tell you this."

"Nate, get to the point," she said in a parental-like tone.

Nate took a deep breath. "A pregnancy test was ordered, and it was positive."

Angela just stared at him with a blank expression for a minute. She then regained her composure, took a sip of tea, and said, "You mean, I'm pregnant?"

"Yes," he responded.

She took another sip of tea. "What does this mean for my condition?" she asked.

"The pregnancy is not good for your condition. Each week it will put more strain on your already weakened heart, a strain I'm afraid your heart cannot bear. I've asked Dr. King, chief of obstetrics, to visit you when you are a little better, if that is ok with you."

She looked at him, and he could see her mind thinking. He was sure she knew what this meant. After a long thoughtful silence, she said, "I certainly know how to pick 'em."

"What do you mean?"

"Here I am with a critical heart condition and a heart specialist for a boyfriend." She smiled.

Nate waited for her to say something else, hoping she would want to discuss her pregnancy more, but she just sat there thinking and sipping her tea. "You know, I had better rest now," she said as she lay back on her pillow. Nate was at a loss for what to say. He wondered what was going through her mind and hoped she was thinking rationally. He kissed her without saying anything more and as he walked out, she said, "So, I'm pregnant, huh?"

"Yes," he returned and as he walked out he could see her lying there with a slight smile on her face.

Chapter Twenty-three

THE NEXT DAY, ANGELA HAD IMPROVED TO THE POINT where she could sit in a chair. She also was able to walk slowly to the bathroom with the help of a nurse. Afterwards she was exhausted and breathless, but she was proud that she was able to do anything out of the bed. The following morning, she was sitting in a chair beside her bed when Dr. King, chief of obstetrics and gynecology, knocked at her door and asked if he could come in. He introduced himself and told Angela that Dr. Archer had asked him to consult on her case. Angela thanked him for coming.

Dr. King looked around fifty years of age, was of average height and weight and had the look of someone who kept himself fit. He sat in a chair across from Angela's bed with her chart in his hand.

"How are you feeling?" he began in a soft-spoken cordial manner.

"Today is my best day so far. I'm starting to get my strength back," Angela answered.

"Well, you look very good. Considering what you have just been through the last few days you are a remarkable woman."

Angela smiled. "Thank you," she said.

"I have reviewed your chart like Dr. Archer asked me to," Dr. King said becoming very serious. "Dr. Archer was worried about your pregnancy and what effect it was going to have on your heart and to be honest I am very worried also." Dr. King opened her chart and looked at it briefly before closing it. "During a normal pregnancy the demands on the heart increase by thirty to fifty percent, which is stressful on a normal heart but dangerous for a heart weakened by disease. Unfortunately, your heart has been significantly weakened. It is now functioning at a level of less than one-half of a normal heart." He stopped to see if what he said had frightened her, but he saw no evidence that it had.

"Go on," she instructed him.

"The bottom line is that if the pregnancy is allowed to progress your life would be in danger," he said and waited for her response.

"How much danger?" she asked calmly.

"It is difficult of course to know exactly because each case is different," he responded.

"Can you give me an educated guess?" she asked.

Dr. King's face tightened. "I think the chance of you not surviving the pregnancy could be as high as fifty percent."

Angela remained quiet. Dr. King could tell she was in deep thought. She then asked, "Have you ever had a patient in my condition who went through with their pregnancy?"

"I had two during my residency and one in private practice, " he answered.

"What was their outcome?" Angela asked.

"Of course conclusions cannot be made from such a small sample. I hope you understand that."

"Yes, I understand," Angela replied.

"One died during pregnancy, one died at birth, and one survived."

"Thank you," Angela said in a professional voice like she used when she was considering the facts before making a business decision in her bookstore.

They both sat there not saying anything. After a few minutes Dr. King broke the silence. "It is a general consensus of the medical community that in such cases termination of the pregnancy should be considered to save the life of the mother. It is a procedure that can be performed before you leave the hospital, if you so choose."

Angela looked out of the window again deep in thought. She then turned back to him. "Dr. King, thank you. You have been so informative." She reached to shake his hand. "I will give everything you said serious thought."

"Thank you and if I can be of help in any way, please let me know," Dr. King replied and with that he left.

At lunchtime Nate arrived, kissed her, and asked how she felt, trying not to reveal to her that the main thing on his mind was her decision about terminating the pregnancy. After some small talk, he casually said, "Did Dr. King come by?"

"Yes he did. I really liked him."

"Good. What did he say?"

"Basically what you guys have been telling me."

"Well," Nate said softly.

"Well what?" she answered.

"Well what did you decide?"

"Nate, I need to go home to my apartment and think this over. Dr. Archer said I might be going home in a few days. How has your day been?"

Nate sat there frustrated. His day was the last thing on his mind. The decision seemed so clear. *What did she have to think about?*

The next three days Angela continued to improve. During this time she avoided talking about her pregnancy despite Nate's attempt to bring it up in conversation. Dr. Archer felt that she had improved so much that she might be able to go home as long as her activity was restricted to bed rest and she continued on her medications. The hospital arranged for an aide to be with her during the day. Nate would be with her at night. When he was on call she could call him if she needed anything. The aide was a nineteen-year old part-time college student who went to school at night to study nursing.

Angela awoke with a feeling of hope and excitement the day she was to be discharged. The nurses went over all of her medications and instructions. Nate insisted on pushing her in the wheelchair down to the entrance where his car was waiting. Angela thanked all of the nurses and staff. She especially thanked Sandy, whom she gave a tight hug. Nate also thanked the nurses and Sandy. He brought them several boxes of expensive candy that the nurses loved but did not need to eat.

The nurse's aide was at Angela's apartment when they arrived and was eager to help. Nate carried Angela in and laid her in bed, after which she fell immediately to sleep. Nate went over the recommended daily schedule with the nurse's aide, including when her medicines were to be taken. He stayed there that first day to make sure everything went well. Angela slept through the night, and, to Nate's relief, she looked even better the next morning.

He brought her morning tea to her bed. "You are the most beautiful sick lady I have ever seen," he exclaimed before kissing her.

Angela smiled. "I will definitely take that as a compliment since I have a lover that has seen more sick ladies than anyone else I have known." They both laughed a little. Angela continued, "Now I don't want you to be late for work. You missed so much work on account of me they might fire you, and then I would have to go back to work so my bookstore could support us."

"Ok," Nate said. "If you insist, but the reason I am going back to work is because you are better, my dear. I think with the nurse's aide you will be all right. But I am going to check on you often so don't get mad at me if I make myself a pest."

"It's a deal," Angela returned.

Nate went back to work and true to what he said he checked on her often. At night he cooked her the best meals he could come up with. Her improvement definitely made him feel better, but he knew that her heart was permanently damaged and that she would have a shortened life span. He felt depressed but tried his best to hide this from her. He had learned what most physicians had learned and that was to take life one day at a time. Even though through his training and experience he knew what lay ahead, he tried not to think about it. He had learned to concentrate on each day's problems as they came up. The one main problem that now was looming over them and threatening them was her pregnancy. He knew they had to confront it soon because each week the danger to her was growing. Yet he could not get her to talk about it when he brought it up.

Angela kept the card that Nate had written her diagnosis on in her purse. She always seemed to have more energy in the morning. For several mornings she broke doctor's orders and would call a taxi after which she and her aide would be gone for an hour or two.

Angela saw both Dr. Archer and Dr. King on a weekly basis, who answered all her questions and repeatedly informed her of her risks. However, she still would not talk to Nate about the pregnancy. One evening after dinner she turned to Nate and asked, "So you think I should terminate this pregnancy, don't you?" Nate thought to himself, *How can she ask such a question after all that has been said to her?*

"Yes, I do," he said.

"Tell me again why," she responded.

Nate felt angry. His first impulse was to go over all the medical facts and statistics again, but he stopped himself. He looked closely at her. His anger was replaced by fear and sadness at the thought of her death.

"I'll tell you why," he began but then emotions overwhelmed him. His throat became tight. He swallowed and regained his composure. "It is because I don't want to lose you. I want you with me as long as possible." Then his voice cracked a little. "I don't think I can live without you."

At this tears came to Angela's eyes. She got out of her chair and sat in his lap. She put her arm around him and kissed him. Then she said, "I will call Dr. King tomorrow and arrange it."

"Oh, thank you, thank you," Nate said as he hugged her never wanting to let go.

The next day Angela, as she promised, made an appointment with Dr. King's office to terminate the pregnancy. Nate scheduled to be off that day off so he could be with her and drive her home. The night before she was to have the procedure Nate was called out, as he often was when he was on call. After he left for the hospital early that evening Angela sat alone thinking. She then picked up the phone and called a taxi.

It was around seven PM and Father Jim entered the Sacred Heart Catholic Church where an hour before he had held Mass. He was returning to the sanctuary to straighten up and extinguish the candles. The sanctuary was large with central columns holding up the decorated ceiling. Several candles flickered making a glow around the altar. The low lights made the rest of the church seem dark but not too dark for one to see. Father Jim could hear someone softly crying in a pew midway back from the front of the church. He did not want to disturb anyone who was praying, so he pretended not to hear as he straightened the hymnals in the pews while leaving the candles burning. As he bent over to pick up a hymnal from the floor he glanced over and saw that it was Angela.

He slowly went to where she was and sat in the pew in front of her. "Angela, are you ok?" he inquired.

"No, I'm not, Father," she said between tears.

"Can I help?" he asked.

"No, in fact I'm sure you don't want me here."

"Goodness," Father Jim said, surprised. "Why would you say that?"

"Because I'm prochoice, Father," she replied.

"I know," he responded softly. "You know, if we kept everyone out of here who didn't agree with everything we said, then, goodness gracious, I'm afraid the church would almost be empty."

"But this is one issue that you feel very strongly on, don't you?" she asked.

"Oh yes, we do feel very strongly about abortion. However, we also feel very strongly that everyone should love their neighbor as themselves, and unfortunately I think there are very few who do, but we let them in each Sunday."

"Father," she said wiping her tears again, "I am going to have an abortion. Do you want me to leave now?"

Father's face seemed to relax. "Can I ask you just one question Angela?" he said.

"Yes," she whispered.

"Why did you come here?"

Angela looked up at the huge crucifix where Jesus hung, with nails in his hands and feet and blood coming from a wound in his side. "That guy up there. When I see him, he affects me in a way I don't understand. I have come here a number of times just to sit and look. I didn't want you to know."

Father Jim turned and looked at the crucifix for a moment and then turned back to Angela. "Yeah, he has always affected me in ways I think only my heart understands. Do you know why it is called the passion of Christ?"

"Not really," she answered.

"Most people when they see Christ on the cross can only think of the horrible unbearable pain and suffering that it represents and they don't want to see it or be reminded of it. But when we see Christ there, we think of a love so passionate and so intense that it wants to undergo such suffering for the ones who are loved, which includes all of us. Thus we see the passion He has for each one of us."

Angela was quiet a second. "Are there no exceptions?" she asked.

"Exceptions?" Father Jim asked.

"Does the church allow for any exceptions concerning abortion?" Angela asked.

Father Jim sat back and thought for a second. "In rare cases where the pregnancy will result in the death of the mother, certainly a case could be made." He then turned and looked seriously at Angela. "The church realizes that we are all on a battlefield here and that in the midst of battle we all make mistakes. We're only human, you know." He stopped for a second. "So do the best you can, Angela."

Angela and Father Jim stood up and she gave him a hug. "It is always so helpful to talk to you. Thank you, Father. The taxi outside is running so I had better go."

Father Jim said as she left, "Do you remember what I whispered in your ear in the emergency room; if ever you need me, I'll be there." Angela nodded that she remembered and left with a peaceful look on her face.

Chapter Twenty-four

NATE GOT BACK TO THE APARTMENT AROUND MIDNIGHT. Angela was curled up sleeping soundly. They had to be at Dr. King's outpatient surgery clinic at 7:30 the next morning, so he set the alarm for six AM and gently crawled into bed so as not to awaken her. When the alarm went off, Angela was not in bed. He sat up wondering where she was. After taking a minute to wake up he went into the kitchen where he found her sitting at the kitchen table drinking a cup of tea.

"Angela, what are you doing?" he exclaimed. "You are not supposed to eat or drink anything before the procedure."

"I've decided not to do it," she said calmly.

Nate was dazed. He thought he might be dreaming. "You're not going to do it?" he repeated, looking at her confused.

"That's right," she answered.

Nate tried to clear his mind. He sat in one of the kitchen chairs and silently went over again all that had happened. He thought about their last conversation when she said she had decided to terminate the pregnancy. He looked at her across from the table and wondered who this woman was. Was she the same one he had slept with last night? With a distressed look on his face, he said, "I don't understand."

"I've thought it over and have changed my mind," Angela said, thoughtfully sipping her tea.

Nate's face hardened. He felt a growing anger overtake him. Angela was being irrational and illogical, which meant that everything he had said or would say would have no effect. He stood up and began to slowly walk back and forth in front of her shaking his head. Finally he said, "This is crazy. Yesterday it was all decided. You agreed it was the logical thing to do."

"I know," was her reply.

"You know how dangerous this pregnancy is to your life; why in the world would you change your mind?" Nate was obviously irritated. She was silent. He looked at her, "You told me you were prochoice."

"I am prochoice," Angela returned. "This is my choice."

"Ok, ok," Nate said as he tried to analyze this. "I don't know much about religions and all that, but I do know that almost all religions would allow this to happen to save the life of the mother."

"That's very true," Angela responded. "This is not about religion."

Nate's anger subsided. Now he was afraid. He felt panicky. He was about to lose the most precious thing in his life and he didn't know what to do. His heart ached at the thought of it. He turned pale. In a voice full of anguish he asked, "What is this all about?"

"Sit down Nate," she ordered. She placed a cup before him with a tea bag in it and then poured hot water into it. He sat there kind of numb watching her. She took the tea bag out after a minute or two. "Would you like some sugar?" she asked.

He said no emphatically and wondered how she could be so calm while he was an emotional wreck.

Angela sat down across from him and fixed her tea. She looked at Nate with loving and sympathetic eyes that indicated she felt what he was going through. "Once you said that you've got to have 'a' heart," Angela said as she stirred her tea. "Well, I don't have one or much of one and the chance of me getting a new one by transplant is slim." Nate very slightly shook his head in agreement. "This past week I have been taking a taxi to the medical library while you were at work trying to learn all I could. I know that medicine is an inexact science and cannot accurately predict how long I will live. But from what I have been able to discover it seems that patients with my particular type of cardiomyopathy may have only a fifty percent chance of living five years. Is this not true?" Nate looked surprised at what she had learned.

"In some studies that is the case, but other studies have had better outcomes. Each year we hope we will improve the survival rate," Nate answered.

"Here's the way I see it," she said looking at him. "If I terminate this pregnancy the baby dies and I might live five years but possibly much less than five years, who knows? If I continue with this pregnancy and we both die then I have lost only a few years of living."

"But important years," Nate returned.

"However, there is a chance," she continued, "I know a slim chance, but there is a chance that I might carry this child long enough to where he or she can live. I am willing to give my life to give my baby, I mean our baby, that chance."

Nate put his elbows on the table and rested his face in his hands. He had a sinking realization that he could no longer get her to change her decision.

Angela put her hands over her womb. "Nate, don't you see? I want to give this little girl or boy a chance to be a little girl or boy. A chance to become a young man or woman. I want he or she to grow up and be like you or me and experience life and love and maybe be a parent someday. Can't you see?"

Nate looked at her. He could see her face full of joy. He could see love radiating from her. He thought he knew what love was but now he realized he had only scratched the surface.

Angela went on. "I know this means a lot of pain and suffering on both our parts, but the love I have for this little one makes me want to do this with all my heart." She stopped and thought a second. "This is probably selfish of me. I have made this decision hoping you would agree with it." She got up and walked over to Nate, had him scoot back in his chair and then sat in his lap facing him with her legs on each side of his. Even in his anguish he felt a thrill as her body touched his. He realized to his sorrow that he would not be able to change her mind. She put her arms around him and pulled his head to her chest.

"Oh Nate," she said, gently rocking him back and forth. "What have we got ourselves into? I've got to leave you sooner or later. I know it will be very hard on you. I am so sorry."

Nate felt the comfort of her breasts and the beat of her heart soothed him. He put his arms around her waist and pulled her tight against him. Angela continued to hold his head against her. Nate began to sob silently. "What am I going to do without you?" he said softly. "What am I going to do?"

"I know," Angela said lovingly. "I know." Tears came to her eyes. They sat there in each other's arms soothing each other with the warmth of their bodies. Their eyes decided that enough tears had been sent on their way and now it was time to be simply lost in each other's love.

Nate sat back. Angela could see that he had calmed down. He looked at Angela's stomach feeling it gently. "We should get married," he said.

"There is no need of marriage," Angela replied. "We know what we have. Putting a name on it doesn't change anything." Nate decided not to argue the point.

Later that day they met with Dr. King who said he completely understood when they apologized for cancelling the procedure. When they asked him to be Angela's physician he said he would be honored. He said there would be a team consisting of him, a perinatologist who specialized in high-risk pregnancies, and of course Dr. Archer. He explained that some of the medicines that were used in her condition were contraindicated in pregnancy and that she would require a lot of rest along with a special low-salt diet. She was now about twelve weeks along. When she was twenty weeks she would be admitted to the hospital for the remainder of the pregnancy. At that time a sonogram would be performed to check for any problems. Infants have been known to survive at twenty-five weeks gestation he informed them, but if they survive, they often have significant complications. He would like her to make it to thirty weeks or more if possible. He then added with a smile, "Not too many of my patients have their own personal live-in cardiologist." Angela smiled and agreed that she was indeed very fortunate.

They both thanked Dr. King profusely. That afternoon they met with Dr. Archer who also pledged to do everything he could to help her. That evening when they got back to the apartment Angela lay on the couch exhausted. They both were in a daze emotionally drained. Nate fixed a light meal that satisfied the small amount of hunger that had built up. They went to bed early that night. As the three of them lay together Nate slept with his arms around the two people he loved because he wanted to hold them as long as he could until he could hold them no more.

Chapter Twenty-five

LIFE WENT ON FOR ANGELA AND NATE AS IT DOES FOR everyone, but for them, each hour was precious. They hated to see each day end. Tony, Rita, Cindy, Rick, and Samantha worked out a schedule where each family would bring over a meal each week cooked according to the dietary guidelines recommended by the dietitian. Each night Nate would serve the meal and clean the dishes. He would then sit by Angela's side to talk or read journals. One evening Angela said, "You know what I would like?"

"What?" asked Nate.

"I would like you to read to me," was her answer.

"Anything you want, my dear," he said while still looking at his journals.

"Read to me *A Tale of Two Cities*," she said.

Nate looked troubled because he could not remember where he had laid it last. "If you are wondering where it is, I saw it in the doctors' lounge when I was there," Angela said to relieve his worry.

"Oh, yes. I left it there so I could be sure and read at work every chance I got," he lied.

"Sure, "she said mockingly.

The next morning, the first thing he did was go to the doctors' lounge to see if it was really there. Sure enough, there it lay where he had left it with a bookmark at chapter two. He put it on his desk to make sure he would remember to take it home.

He was glad to start his rounds because for brief moments it took his mind off everything else in his life. He was glad for the intense busy moments that his profession provided for him. In between these he looked forward to calling Angela. He wanted to check on her, but he also wanted to simply hear her voice. He liked talking to her about anything, even the weather. Their short pleasant conversations were little bright spots in his day. After finishing one of their conversations he was on his way to the cafeteria where the selection was better when his cell phone went off. It was the emergency room calling. *Oh no, not an emergency,* he said to himself. He only had thirty minutes until his next catheterization, and he was looking forward to a quick lunch.

"Dr. Williams?" the young ER doctor asked.

"Yes," said Nate in a low controlled voice.

"We have a Professor Johnson down here who came in with simple hyperventilation. We had him breathe in a paper bag, and he is totally ok. However, he insists on seeing you. I told him you were not needed, but he says if we didn't call you he would call you himself since he has your private number."

Nate's pleasant disposition disappeared like a popped balloon. He turned red with anger. Professor Johnson was a jerk who cheated on his wife and kids. Now he had come into the ER simply because he was breathing too fast making unreasonable demands. And lastly he was about to take away the only lunch break he would get all day. *I should tell the ER doctor to tell him to kiss off,* he thought. *Yes, that is what he needs to do, just kiss off.* Then he heard himself saying, "Sure, I'll be right down."

As Nate walked to the emergency room he shook his head back and forth. *What's wrong with me?* he thought. *I must becoming weak or something. I'm not the guy I used to be.* He continued an in-depth self-analysis until he reached the ER. He went over his chart carefully. It was as the ER doctor said; Professor Johnson was simply hyperventilating.

"Professor Johnson," Nate said cordially as he entered his cubicle. Professor Johnson looked up with no significant expression on his face. "I have carefully looked at everything, and I am sure there is nothing serious going on here."

Professor Johnson did not smile. "Nate, I could barely catch my breath when I walked in here. I thought I was going to suffocate. Surely there is something wrong with me," he said in a demanding tone.

"How you felt is the way one normally feels when they hyperventilate," Nate explained. "You see, when you breathe too fast you blow off too much carbon dioxide, and this makes your body think you are not getting enough air, which made you breathe even faster. It becomes a vicious cycle. That's why the ER doc had you breathe into a bag, which captures the carbon dioxide and helps restore the normal levels."

Professor Johnson looked like he was analyzing the situation. "So why did I hyperventilate in the first place?" he asked.

"Some people just have a tendency to do it for no obvious reason. Others do it when they experience anxiety."

"Well, I certainly have anxiety. Samantha will not call off the divorce," Professor Johnson said angrily. "Can you give me some medicine for this, Doc?" he asked.

Nate had so far remained calm, but now he was starting to get angry again. "No I can't. Try your family physician. You may want to see a counselor."

"Counselor? They're useless, and I don't have a family physician."

"Why don't you talk with Father Jim? He's pretty wise on all these things. I really have to go. They are waiting on me in the cath lab," Nate said as he turned to leave.

"I'll give it some thought," Professor Johnson said.

Nate walked to the elevator. *He didn't even say thank you. He is something else*, Nate said to himself as he got into the elevator.

When Nate got home that night he kissed Angela as he usually did and then went into the kitchen to fix one of the prepared dinners her club members had brought. Angela followed him and sat in one of the kitchen chairs.

"Soon I will be able to fix our dinner like I did before. I am feeling better every day," Angela said.

"Oh no," Nate came back. "You're the queen, and I am your servant, and I intend to keep it that way." Nate bowed like a servant might.

"Well I like being a queen, but I feel bad that you end up with all the work," Angela said sadly.

"It is my pleasure," Nate said, and then he kissed her. "You won't believe who I saw today."

"Who?" Angela asked.

"Professor Johnson, of all people. He came into the emergency room hyperventilating and demanded to see me."

"Did you go see him?"

"Yes, and I didn't get lunch because of him."

"Nate, you are a nice guy. Most people would have told him to kiss off," Angela said firmly.

"Well I thought about it, but I think hanging around you and your club is ruining me."

"You mean we are turning you into a nice guy?"

"Yeah, something like that. He asked me for medicine for anxiety. I told him to go and talk with Father Jim."

"Very wise advice, very wise," Angela said. Angela sat there thinking. Nate could tell she was disturbed, thinking about Samantha and the kids.

"I brought the copy of *A Tale of Two Cities* home," Nate said in hope of cheering her up.

Angela smiled. "Are you going to start reading it to me?" she asked expectantly.

"Yes, right after dinner," he replied. The dinners were always well prepared, balanced, and tasty. Angela was always tired after eating and went to lie on the couch. After a quick cleanup, Nate grabbed the book and sat in a soft chair by her.

"Where shall I start?" he asked.

"It has been so long since I read it last, and I know that you can't remember what you have read so I think you should start from the beginning," Angela answered.

"You don't know that I can't remember what I have read," he said defiantly, "but just because I like you I will start at the beginning."

Nate opened to the first page and read the beginning of the first sentence, "It was the best of times, it was the worst of times'," and suddenly a lump came to his throat and then a tear to his eyes. He stopped and pulled out his handkerchief.

Angela turned to look at him. "Hey Doc," she said. "Is this fiction too much for you to handle?" He lifted the book and acted like he was going to hit her with it and then put it in his lap to put away his handkerchief. "You know, if each line of this book affects you like that we will never get through it," she said kiddingly.

"It's not nice to make fun of disabled people, you know," he returned.

"Disabled?" she asked.

"Don't you remember? I have an FRD, a fiction reading disability."

Angela thought for a minute and then said. "Yes, I do recall that you have that disability. I wonder," she said looking off thoughtfully, "if it is genetic?"

"So now you are wondering if maybe I have passed FRD genes to our child. That is something you should have thought of before because it is too late now, sister. So there," Nate said authoritatively.

"Well, I am sure you have some other good genes in your gene pool," Angela replied.

"I hope so" he replied. "But now how about getting back to this book before it gets too late." And Nate began to read without getting choked up and stopping at every line.

Chapter Twenty-six

ANGELA WAS NOW SIXTEEN WEEKS INTO HER PREGNANCY and she was tiring more easily. Dr. Archer could see no improvement in the functioning of her heart. Nate tried to put on an upbeat air around her, but she could tell that he was becoming more and more worried as the weeks went on. Angela did her best to cheer him up but did not know exactly what to do.

It was Wednesday morning when Samantha arrived at Angela's apartment with a prepared meal consisting of meat loaf, vegetables, and salad. The aide let her in. She said "Hi" to Angela and then placed what she had brought into the refrigerator before fixing them both a cup of tea as she had started doing each time she visited. Samantha never brought the kids with her because they seemed to get sick often. She did not want to expose Angela to any type of infection.

"It's good to see you, Samantha. Thanks for the meal," Angela said as Samantha sat down by her in the living room. Angela was sitting up in a chair, which she could do for about forty-five minutes before she got too tired.

"It's good to see you too," Samantha returned. Both of them wondered what to talk about next. "Are you getting some reading done?" Samantha asked.

"Actually, Nate reads to me every night. He has never been much into reading anything other than medical journals, but I think he is starting to enjoy it," Angela answered.

"Greg used to like to read to me. He would even act out Shakespeare as if he were in front of a huge audience instead of just me. I would clap enthusiastically, and he would take a full bow. Kind of crazy, huh?"

"Not so crazy," Angela said. "It seems you and Greg had some good times."

"We did. He really treated the kids and me very well. He always liked to be the center of attention, which I didn't mind. I think that came from his childhood."

"What do you mean?" Angela asked.

"He was neglected by his single alcoholic mother. When he was six, child welfare placed him in foster care. Unfortunately, he was never in one foster home for a long time."

"I never knew that about Gregg," Angela said as she sat there beginning to understand a little more about him. "Oh Samantha, I am so sorry for you both of you." Angela reached over and squeezed her hand.

Samantha began to cry softly. "I love him so. I know he loves me. I don't know what to do."

Angela had no words of advice to give. She could only be a friend to someone who desperately needed a friend. They both sat in silence holding hands. Angela then caught Samantha's eye and said, "Anytime you want to talk, I am available. There are no easy answers but given the chance, the heart will find a way. I'm sure it will."

"Thank you," Samantha responded. "And thanks for being my friend." She hugged Angela warmly and then left.

Father Jim came by after lunch to visit Angela as he had been doing the last several weeks. After an hour's visit Angela thanked him as he left to go back to his office. The nurse's aid noticed that Angela always seemed so much better each time Father Jim visited.

Father Jim got back to his office and sat in his chair behind his desk leaving the door to his office open as he usually did. He cleared his desk hoping to start writing his homily for the coming Sunday when he heard a slight sound. He looked up and there was Gregg leaning in the doorway with his hands in his pockets. He had on a simple button shirt and a nice pair of pants. He was well groomed but appeared very thin.

When Father Jim saw him he immediately stood up and said, "Professor Johnson, please come in and have a seat."

Professor Johnson entered and sat down. "No need to call me professor anymore because I ain't one," he said with an emphasis on the word *ain't*. "If you haven't heard, I resigned from the university at their request."

Father Jim looked at him, trying to figure out why he was here. "Yes, I heard that you did. What are you doing now?" he asked.

"I've been substitute teaching at the high school. I have a degree in secondary education that I got before I received my PhD. One of the high school teachers is out for six weeks having a baby so I now have some steady income."

"How is that working out?" asked Father as he shifted his position in his chair.

"It has been good. I think I'm making a good impression so they might at some point offer me a full-time job."

"Good, good. I'm glad to hear it. What brings you here today?" Father inquired.

"I know I asked you this before but I want to ask you again; can you convince Samantha that it is time for us to be back together again?" Gregg asked earnestly.

"Oh I wish I could help you, but I'm not the one who needs to convince her," Father replied.

"Samantha needs to give me a break," he said angrily. "I know I messed up, but everyone messes up now and then." Father noticed that one of his fists was clenched and turning white and that he looked very depressed. Father Jim didn't say anything. He just waited while Gregg stared out the window. Gregg finally stopped looking out the window and turned to Father Jim and said, "Yesterday I went to the ER hyperventilating because of the stress I've been under. Nate saw me and suggested I come see you." He then looked at the floor and added, "I guess this was a wasted trip."

Father Jim sat back and began to gently rub the crucifix around his neck with his thumb and forefinger. He finally asked, "You ever heard of Longinus?"

"No," Greg returned without looking up.

"I know you are not religious, but bear with me for a second while I tell you about Longinus."

Greg looked at him briefly and seemed to offer no resistance as he sat down.

"Longinus," Father continued, "was one of the soldiers at the foot of the cross who nailed Jesus to the cross and mocked him. Then at the end Longinus stabbed Jesus in the side with his spear."

Gregg looked again at Father Jim as if to say "so?"

"Have you ever been to St. Peter's Basilica in Rome?" Father asked.

"No," was his reply again.

"Well, it is the largest Christian church in the world, over two football fields long inside. About two-thirds of the way down is this unbelievably huge altar designed by the great artist Bernini. Set back from the altar surrounding it are four colossal statues of saints. These four saints are really impressive. They are over fifteen feet tall."

Father paused and began rubbing his cross again. Greg looked up and asked, "'Why are you telling me this?"

"Because one of those saints around the altar is Longinus." Greg looked surprised. "You see, he later converted, took instructions from the apostles, and died a martyr's death. Some of course consider his story just to be a legend that was passed down over the centuries, but even if it is a legend I think the fact that the church cherished his story so much that he was given such a place of honor says something to each one of us as we live our lives. Judas would have made it there also if he had not given up on himself."

Greg stood up. "I don't know about all those stories," and then added, "but I'll give it some thought."

"Please do," Father said as he left. Father quickly said a prayer for him, as he did for everyone who had made a mess of their life and could not see a way out.

Chapter Twenty-seven

DESPITE ALL OF NATE AND ANGELA'S ATTEMPTS TO slow down time, before they knew it Angela was twenty weeks into her pregnancy. It was time for her to be admitted to the intermediate care ward in the hospital where she would stay until the baby was born. Nate, Dr. King, and Dr. Archer were all growing increasingly worried and anxious because, if anything, Angela's heart appeared to be getting weaker. Each week the baby put increasingly greater demands upon her heart, demands that could only be met by taking away from the needs of the mother. Angela fully realized this but wanted to give of herself to the infant as long as they both could be kept alive.

After she was admitted she hoped to see Sandy but was cared for by a nurse she hadn't met before. However the next morning to her surprise Sandy walked in. "Hi, remember me?" Sandy said smiling.

"How could I forget you, Sandy? Thanks for being my nurse today," Angela said with enthusiasm.

"I was off yesterday, but most of the time you are here I will be taking care of you."

"Wonderful," Angela replied.

Sandy began her usual routine. She did a physical assessment of Angela to make sure there were no changes from the previous shift. She then went over all her medications and orders thoroughly. After she finished, she looked at Angela. "I want you to know that all of the nurses here admire you for your decision. It must have been terribly hard."

"Not really," Angela said. "Once I considered all my options, it was one of the easiest decisions I have ever made."

"We all hope that if we were in a similar situation we would do the same."

"I'm sure you would. Are you a mother, Sandy?" she asked.

"Yes, I have an eight-year-old son named David."

"Tell me about David," Angela requested.

Sandy smiled and Angela could tell that she had made her happy asking about her son. "David is one of the cutest little boys in the world. Of course I would think so, being his mother. He is smart, sometimes too smart. He can almost talk me into anything within reason. He gets so excited over little things, like me taking him for doughnuts before we go to the synagogue or staying up past bedtime or playing baseball."

Angela thoroughly enjoyed listening to Sandy talk about her son. When she had stopped, Angela asked, "And his dad?"

"He doesn't come around very often," Sandy said sadly. "He's a good person, but he was just a young mixed-up kid when he got me pregnant. My parents made us get married, but it didn't last long. David wishes his dad was around like those of the other kids."

Angela looked at her sympathetically. "I'm so sorry."

"Enough about me. I'd like to hear more about you and Dr. Williams, how you met, etc. I have to see my other patients now, but we will talk later."

Angela and Sandy both knew that they would become best of friends, which they did. As the days went on, Sandy learned all about her and Nate. After a while she felt part of their relationship. Sandy better understood what they had together. She began to feel less jealous, only a little sad that it was not she.

That afternoon Cindy dropped by her room. "Cindy," cried Angela, "it's so nice to see you."

Cindy apologized for not visiting more, but being a third grade teacher and mom took up a lot of her time. Today was a day off for teachers, and she had been looking forward to visiting her in the hospital.

"Thank you for all those wonderful meals," Angela exclaimed. "You did twice your part. You shouldn't have." Cindy blushed. "The hospital food is really ok,"

Angela continued, "but I will miss all that home cooking."

"Maybe I can slip a meal or two past the guards," Cindy said jokingly.

"How's Rick?" Angela asked.

"We have some good news. Rick has been working on his PhD in the summers. He will graduate in a few months. He got two papers published on the mating behavior of frogs, and he has been offered a position at the university. It's rare for that to happen to junior college teachers," she said proudly.

"Tell Rick I am so proud of him. I'm sure he will meet some very interesting people at the university."

"He already has," Cindy answered. "Each Friday afternoon he has been invited to the home of the chairman of the biology department where they drink beer and discuss biology and anything else that comes to their minds. Rick simply loves it."

Angela looked off and dreamily said, "That sounds so good to me. I miss our club meetings."

"Me too," Cindy said sadly.

Cindy had to leave but promised to come back soon. Angela thanked her and told her not to forget to tell Rick congratulations.

Sandy came back in before the end of the shift to tell Angela that the ultrasound was scheduled for the next morning.

"You mean I will get to see the baby?" Angela asked.

"Yes," said Sandy with a smile.

"Will we get to know whether it is a girl or a boy?" she asked again.

"Most probably," Sandy answered.

Angela lay back smiling. "I don't think I can wait that long."

Sandy laughed and said, "Tomorrow would be here before you know it." Angela looked at the ceiling and in her heart, thought, *How true, how unmercifully true.*

Angela lay awake most of the night thinking about the ultrasound the next morning. She wondered what her baby would look like and how she would feel when she actually saw him or her. Then despite her best efforts her thoughts would return to the reality of the precarious situation they were both in. If they both died together then they would both meet in heaven that very same day. This comforted Angela a great deal. If the baby lived and she died, then life would go on, without her for sure, but she didn't care as long as the baby lived. She could not even hope or think about them both surviving because it was so unlikely. Then she thought of Nate. She thought of what it would be like for him if he lost one or both of them. Her grief for him over powered her. She did not want him to be alone.

Nate came to her room at 6:30 that morning to see her. He had some catheterizations to do, but he had planned it so he would be there at 10 AM, the time of the ultrasound. The transport technician came at 9:30 and began getting ready to roll her bed out of the room. However, Nate was not there. Angela asked where he was. Sandy called down to the catheter lab and came back and said that Nate told the nurses that he would meet her in the ultrasound room.

The bed was slowly rolled down the hall to the elevator that led to the ultrasound floor. Once in the room where the ultrasound machine was located the young female technician told her to relax that there would be no discomfort.

Angela looked around. "Where is Dr. Williams? He said he would be here," she asked anxiously.

The technician seemed in a hurry. "Those doctors are always getting tied up. We can go ahead and do this quickly. I will record it all so he can see the pictures when he is less busy."

Angela rarely got mad. In fact she prided herself on her self-control, but now she felt a growing anger within. "I would rather wait until he is here," she said firmly, trying to be calm.

"I'm sorry," the technician replied, "but we have a very busy schedule. If we can't do this now you will have to come back in a few days when we will have an opening. "

"I am not having this ultrasound without Dr. Williams being present," Angela again said firmly, trying to control herself. Unbeknownst to Angela Sandy had decided to slip down to see the ultrasound and was standing in the doorway when she saw that Angela was getting upset. She went into the waiting room where she discovered that the mother next in line for an ultrasound had come early. Sandy talked to the ultrasound tech who agreed to do the other mother first. Maybe this would give Nate time to break away to be there, she thought. Sandy helped roll Angela's bed back out into the hall.

"Sandy, I don't know what I would do without you. I was about to lose it back there," Angela said gratefully.

"Don't worry. I called the cath lab and there was a minor unexpected complication. I'm sure Nate will be here soon," Sandy responded.

The ultrasound of the other mother was just finished as Nate walked up somewhat out of breath. "I'm am so sorry, but I just couldn't get away. I was so scared that I would miss it."

"Sandy saved the day," Angela said happily. "I want her right there with us when we meet him or her." Nate agreed.

They were ushered into the ultrasound room again. The technician sat on her stool beside the bed and placed a clear lubricant jelly on Angela's abdomen. As she placed the probe on her below the umbilicus, the technician began looking at a TV screen searching for an image.

"I will point out what you will see," she said, "but you can pretty much tell yourself. I will be taking measurements of the size of the infant, the size of the head, and other measurements so if I am quiet for a while you will know why."

Nate, Angela, and Sandy were all close together with their three heads almost touching as they looked at the screen when all of a sudden they saw a small hand come into focus and then a small arm attached to it. Angela gasped with excitement, "Oh, look, would you! There are five fingers, how cute."

While Angela counted fingers and toes and talked happily, Nate remained quiet. He was nervous. His trained eye was looking for abnormalities of the head, spine, abdomen, kidneys, and especially the heart. The baby's face was blurry at first but then came into focus. It looked strange, almost like from outer space. Then it turned a certain way where it indeed looked like a baby, the cutest baby Angela had ever seen. Nate could see the tiny heart beating. He pointed it out to Angela and Sandy, who sat in wonder. The heart looked normal, as did everything else. Nate began to relax.

Nate and Angela had agreed beforehand that they wanted to know the sex of the baby, which they let the technician know. It seemed like a routine decision, but both knew that Angela might never know the sex otherwise. Then the technician said, "Look right here, between the legs. It looks like three lines. It's a girl."

Angela forgot she was critically ill. She did not think about all the possible outcomes. She did not think of death. All she could think about was the beautiful little girl who was inside moving about and who depended on her mother for life.

Nate suddenly stopped being a hardened, highly trained physician and became the father of a baby daughter, a father who felt giddy, a father who laughed at her every move, and a father who was in love with his daughter. *I am sure she will look like Angela*, he thought to himself, *and I am sure she will be just as independent.*

When the ultrasound was over everyone was quiet as Angela was taken back to her room. Everyone, including Sandy, was immersed in their own thoughts about the miracle of life and about the little girl they had just met. Without them realizing it, the experience of witnessing that ultrasound together had formed a bond between the three of them that would help bind the four of them together for the rest of their lives.

Chapter Twenty-eight

NATE'S CELL PHONE RANG AT THREE AM. HE HAD BEEN sleeping in the doctors' call room ever since Angela had been admitted to the hospital. He was not on call so he wondered who it could be. The number was not one he recognized. He awoke enough to say hello in a very sleepy voice.

"Nate, this is Cindy. I am so, so very sorry to call you at three AM in the morning," he heard an apologetic voice say.

"That's ok," he responded still wondering why she was calling.

"Our little boy Joshua awoke with a stomachache two hours ago, and it is getting worse," Cindy informed him in a very concerned voice. "Do you think we need to take him to the emergency room?" she asked.

Nate thought for a second. "Does he have any vomiting or diarrhea?" Nate asked.

"No," Cindy replied.

"Does it hurt when he moves or when you touch his stomach," Nate inquired.

"Yes. He is holding his stomach and won't let us near it."

"I think he may have appendicitis. You should take him to the emergency room now to make sure," Nate instructed. "I will call the ER doc and tell him you are coming."

"Thank you so much, Nate," Cindy said gratefully. "You are a real friend, and I am so sorry to wake you."

"I'm glad to be of help. Call me any time," Nate said as he ended his call. *Cindy and Rick are really nice people*, he thought to himself. *I'm glad they called me.* He felt fortunate to have them as friends. He worried a little about their son Joshua, but then he knew he would be well taken care of. Nate went back to sleep not realizing that it was the first time he did not mind being called in the middle of the night.

At six that morning Nate got up and showered and shaved before going to Angela's room to say good morning. He told her about Joshua adding that he would check on him first thing. Angela was proud that Cindy felt close enough to Nate to call him in the middle of the night. She was even prouder of Nate. Nate seemed in a hurry and started to leave.

"Are you forgetting something, my dear?" Angela said before he could get out of the room.

"What?" Nate replied. He looked at Angela who lay there with her lips puckered. Nate almost laughed as he walked back to her bed to kiss her. "How could I forget such a thing," he exclaimed. It was not just a simple goodbye kiss that Nate gave her.

Angela looked very happy. "Give them my love dear," she instructed him.

"I will," Nate replied happily. *Angela always knows what's most important*, he thought to himself. He found Cindy and Rick in recovery standing next to Joshua who was asleep having just gotten out of surgery.

"You were right, Nate," Rick said. "It was appendicitis but we got here before it ruptured thanks to you."

"I'm just glad he did ok," Nate responded.

Cindy hugged his neck. "Thank you so much," she said thankfully. Nate liked being thanked; it felt good to him.

"I'll check back after rounds. It looks like Joshua is going to do fine," Nate said as he left.

Later that day Joshua was taken to his room. When Nate finally finished his rounds he peeked in Joshua's room so as not to disturb anyone. Cindy saw him and said to come on in, that Joshua was so conked out nothing could wake him. Cindy sat on the bed while Rick sat in a chair reading some journals. Sitting in the other chair in the room was Father Jim who always seemed to show up when he felt he might be needed. Father Jim got up when Nate entered, but Nate told him to keep his seat.

"We really appreciate you two guys," Cindy said, looking at them both.

"Thanks," responded Father Jim. "You know you are like family. Isn't that right, Nate?"

"You bet," Nate said with a smile. He indeed felt like he now had a family.

In the meantime Rick continued to be absorbed in his journals.

"Rick, stop reading all that and talk with us," Cindy demanded.

"Oh that is ok," Father quickly put in. "I know that you have a lot to prepare for with your new position at the university."

"Thanks Father but I wasn't really doing work. I found an interesting article on the appendix."

"Always learning," Cindy piped in.

"It's not just that," Rick answered. "I have always had a lot of respect for science but when an experience like this has touched me and my family personally, my faith in science has just increased one hundred percent."

"Oh, science is indeed a marvelous thing," Father said, agreeing with him.

"Just to think that, due to the understanding that science

has given us," Rick returned, "a doctor can come in, feel a child's abdomen, and be almost completely sure that he has appendicitis. Then he knows the body so well that he or she can cut into it and remove the diseased appendix. Just a little over a hundred years ago, appendicitis was fatal." Turning to Nate he continued, "And this is nothing compared to what you can do to help the heart." Nate smiled appreciating the compliment.

"I can see why you chose science as a career. I wish more people had such an appreciation for science that you have," Father said thoughtfully.

Rick smiled. "Father, this article I am reading, gives evidence that the appendix may have evolved over thirty different times in evolutionary history." Rick then became quiet. He looked at Father seriously, "I'm sorry if I have offended you talking about all this science stuff."

"Oh no, my goodness. There is no quarrel between science and religion as far as I am concerned," Father said as a matter of fact. Nate looked at Father Jim with interest as if he had just heard something new.

"Sure, Father," Rick said in a mildly mocking tone.

"No, really. I'm serious," Father returned.

"You should tell that to the group I hang out with every Friday afternoon," Rick said.

Cindy broke in. "Rick has been invited to a biology discussion group at the chairman's house where they drink beer and try to solve all the unanswered questions in the world," Cindy said with a smile.

"You're familiar with the big bang theory, I'm sure," Father asked.

"Of course, the evidence for it is overwhelming," returned Rick.

"How old does it say the universe is?" asked Father again.

"Around thirteen billion years," answered Rick.

"Did you know that a Catholic priest was the one who proposed that theory?" Father politely asked again.

"You're kidding," said Rick.

"Oh no. It was Father Georges Lemaitre. He was the first to propose it in a paper in 1931. He received his PhD from MIT. Then there is Gregor Mendel, the father of genetics, who was an Austrian monk, and I can't leave out Pasteur, one of the greatest scientists of all times, who said the rosary daily." Nate was shocked.

Rick looked thoughtfully at Father Jim, "How do you know all this stuff, Father?"

"I read a lot about everything, and that's one of my faults. Sometimes I think I am better at theology than service, and I pray every day for God to help me with that problem."

Nate smiled and almost laughed. *Father is something else. You never know what was on his mind*, he thought to himself. "Well I hope he doesn't help you too much because I enjoy listening to you talk about all this," Nate said enthusiastically.

"Me too," said Rick.

"Thank you. Now I'd better be going," Father Jim said, standing up.

"I've got to go too," Nate added. "We are so glad Joshua is ok." Cindy gave them both a hug as they left. As they were walking down the hall together they ran into Samantha bringing Cindy's little girl Ann to visit her brother. Samantha greeted both of them and asked how Joshua was doing and was happy to learn he was doing well.

"I have what I think is good news to tell you, Father," she announced.

"Good, what is it," he returned.

"Gregg on his own initiative has seen a counselor and has enrolled in a therapy program."

"That's excellent," Father exclaimed.

"I still don't trust him, but he seems less angry. Only time will tell. I asked him what came over him, and he said something about Longinus. When I asked him who Longinus was, he said to ask you, for some reason."

Father stroked his chin and then said, "That name does ring a bell, but I really have to get going. I have other parishioners who are ill that I need to see."

As she left neither of them realized his slip of the tongue about "other parishioners." Nate looked at Father Jim. He admired this gentle soul who cared for so many and who was so smart. He thought back to what Angela's father had said about how loving acts help the heart to grow and how much he, the heart specialist, had learned about the heart recently. He concluded that Father Jim had one of the biggest hearts of anyone he had ever known.

Chapter Twenty-nine

A FEW DAYS AFTER THE SONOGRAM, ANGELA BEGAN TO feel the baby kick. At first, she didn't realize what it was but then as the baby repeatedly kicked she was sure of it. The first time happened at night. She put her hand over her womb and smiled. For that moment the world stood still and faded away as Angela made contact with her baby. She gently whispered, "I love you."

The next morning, however, Angela's joy had turned to brooding and sorrow as she thought about the future. Sandy came in with her usual smile to begin her morning routine. She noticed that Angela was very quiet. She appeared reserved and despondent. "'Are you ok this morning?" Sandy asked.

Angela lay there looking at tear soaked tissue that she held in her hand. After a few moments without looking at Sandy she said, "Tell me what's it's like to be a mother."

Sandy was a little surprised. "I couldn't begin to describe that in words," she said.

"Try," was Angela's reply.

"Ok. Well, let's see. It's like something awakens in you that you never knew was there. All of a sudden you feel a connection with all the mothers who have ever lived since the beginning. When you see your little one, the whole world seems new. Everything in it, from butterflies to flowers, takes on a whole new meaning." Sandy stopped and looked at Angela who still was not looking at her but who appeared to be taking in everything she said.

"Go on," Angela whispered.

Sandy thought again for a minute and continued. "Being a mother means you must over and over again say 'Hello' and 'Goodbye.' You say hello to your infant and then quickly you say goodbye, as that infant becomes a toddler. Then you must say goodbye to your precious toddler as he or she turns into a six year old. Six year olds are especially hard to say goodbye to because he will never again want to tell you every detail of his likes and dislikes and all the drama that goes on in his life with his friends. David is now eight. I will soon say goodbye to him, but then I will say hello again when he is twelve and fifteen and eighteen. I think the hardest goodbye will be when he leaves home, but then hopefully I will get to say hello to a daughter-in-law and grandchildren." At this Angela began to cry, with tears streaming down her cheeks. "Did I say it wrong?" Sandy asked desperately.

"Oh no," Angela said between sobs. "I'm just afraid I will never get to say hello."

"Oh Angela," Sandy said. Sandy put her arm around her shoulders and put her head next to hers. Sandy continued to hold her until she seemed to settle down. Sandy stood up still holding her hand. "There is something better than all this, at least that's what I've been told."

"What could it be?" asked Angela in a weak voice.

"It's having a lover, one who is close to your heart, one who is your soul mate." Sandy now had a hint of a tear in her eyes.

Angela looked up at her and saw her sadness. "That's true. It is a wonderful thing." She squeezed Sandy's hand and softly said,

"It will come to you." Sandy smiled sweetly and hugged her and then left the room.

Nate had cut his patient load in half and with the help of his colleagues he was able to take each afternoon off to stay with Angela. During this time they talked while Angela rested. He also continued to read *A Tale of Two Cities* to her, which she looked forward to each day. They had actually made a lot of progress. Now that they were over halfway through, Nate was very interested in finding out what was going to happen. Lucie, the perfect daughter, had restored her physician father back to physical and mental health in England after he had been in a French prison for eighteen years. The French revolution was in full swing and Lucie's very good and honorable husband who was a French nobleman decided to return to France to save his former steward. Nate and Angela of course knew that this was not a good move on Lucie's husband's part. Both were anxious to continue the story.

That afternoon he read a lot but still the fate of Lucie's husband, Charles Darnay, was up in the air. "This guy, Charles Dickens, sure uses a lot of words, doesn't he? I wish he would just quickly get to the point here," Nate said somewhat kiddingly as looked at Angela for her reply.

"You know, Nate, this may go against your basic nature, but sometimes the journey is more important than the destination," she replied.

That was something that had never entered Nate's mind before. He had always thought the most important thing was the final goal in almost everything he did. The journey was something simply to be endured. To think that the journey might be more important than the goal seemed absurd. He then looked at Angela. Angela seemed to know things that he didn't. Her mind worked in different ways than his, and that was one of things that made her so attractive and interesting. He had slowly begun to realize that there were certain aspects of life that he was totally blind to, to which Angela was helping him find his way. This meant that he had to trust her just like a blind person has to trust the one guiding them through a maze. "Is that why you named your bookstore 'The Journey'?" Nate asked.

"I think so," Angela responded. She then held Nate's hand as she looked into his eyes. "We are on a journey Nate, you and me. I don't know where it will eventually lead, but that doesn't matter, you see. A lot of journeys do not end well for many people, but everyone can experience the adventure of a journey. This is our journey, and I consider myself the luckiest woman in the world."

Nate could not describe how he felt. Maybe it was awe that filled him or maybe it was a sense of wonder that she once said he lacked. Whatever it was, he felt less afraid and more hopeful even though he knew there was little hope.

Nate sat there in deep thought. A small tear came to his eyes. "Do you know why I like you so much?" he finally said.

"Because I'm beautiful and sexy?" Angela asked.

"Well yes, that's very true," Nate answered. "But believe it or not there is another reason."

"What in world could that be, my dear?" Angela asked with a smile.

"It's because you have something that I lack," he said.

"What's that," she asked.

"Wisdom," was his reply.

Angela smiled again. "Does that mean I can count on you sticking around?"

"Wild horses couldn't drag me away, my dear," Nate replied.

"You're becoming very poetic. I think this reading is having a good effect on you," Angela came back.

"Then I guess I had better read some more," and that is what he did until almost nine o'clock. They were both tired at this point and Nate closed the book. "I think it is time for me to go to the call room and let you get some sleep."

"I want you to stay," she said.

"Stay here?" he asked

"Yes, I want you here next to me," she said pointing to her bed.

"But that's against the hospital rules," he protested.

"Someone told me that you are a doctor here," she replied.

'Yes, that's true," he answered.

"And I believe that the nurses do what the doctor says, is that not true?" she asked.

"Most of the time," he answered again. Angela's bed looked very inviting, but it seemed a little strange being in bed with her with the nurses coming in to check vital signs during the night. *But then why not?* he said to himself.

Nate turned out the light and started to get into the one-person bed with her when she said, "Not with your greens on."

"But," he stammered.

"You can get under the covers. Nate, I want to feel your touch. I want your heart next to me. I want to listen to you breathe all night."

Now this seemed even stranger to him, lying there with just his underwear on. He looked around to make sure no one was about to come in and then quickly got undressed and lay beside her. "Touch me like you always do and place your hand here," she said as she placed it over her womb. Nate followed all her instructions. He gently felt the softness of her body and explored all of her curves. As he pressed his body against hers it seemed like it did before she had gotten sick. He then put his hand over her womb. They lay there together as their hearts beat close to one another. They felt the warmth of each other's bodies, and they both felt the kick of their daughter.

Nate lay awake as long as he could, concentrating on everything he was experiencing because he wanted it all somehow to be etched into his soul so that it would never fade away. However, before he knew it, he and Angela fell into one of the most restful sleeps either had had in a long time.

Chapter Thirty

Angela was now twenty-eight weeks into her pregnancy. Infants born at this time often survived, but there were still great risks for complications. Angela was definitely worsening. The retention of fluid by her body was showing in her face, and the edema in her legs left lasting indentations after pressure was applied to them. Except for quiet talking, almost everything Angela did left her breathless. Her heart would occasionally develop an irregular rhythm, which was of great concern to Dr. Archer and Dr. King and especially to Nate because of the chance of these irregular beats turning into a fatal arrhythmia. Because of this, Angela had heart monitor leads on her chest and side twenty-four hours a day so that her heart rhythm could be seen by the nurses at the nurses' station. However, she was still in a private room, and the wires and leads were not a hindrance to Nate sleeping with her and caressing her all night long.

Father Jim had been visiting Angela on a daily basis, usually in the morning when Nate was seeing patients. He carried his Bible as he usually did but he also had another book or two with him each time he came. When Nate wasn't there he would spend up to an hour with her. However when Nate was present when he arrived, he would make a brief inquiry about how she was doing and then quickly leave.

Angela was asleep when Sandy came in in the morning to start her daily sponge bath. She gently woke her up after which Angela nodded her head that she knew about her bath. Sandy had two basins, one for soapy water and the other for the rinse water. She uncovered one of Angela's swollen legs and began to gently wash it with a soft soapy cloth.

"I'm not going to make it," Angela said.

"Oh, we can't predict the future. Just relax and enjoy your bath," Sandy replied.

"I know I am not going to make it," Angela said again. This time Sandy remained silent and continued the bath.

"How long have you known Nate?" Angela asked.

"For about two years," was Sandy's reply.

"Nate is a good man."

"I know, "said Sandy.

"He has a big heart."

"Yes, I know," Sandy returned.

"Before I met him, Nate didn't think he needed love in his life. Now I don't think he can live without it," Angela said, taking a breath. "We are soul mates, Sandy. When I am gone he will need another soul mate or I'm afraid he will die, spiritually if not physically."

Sandy looked at her briefly with a questioning look and then continued washing her.

Angela with some effort grabbed Sandy's hand, making Sandy look at her. "Will you please take care of my Nate when I'm gone?" Angela asked.

"Let's not talk about such things now," Sandy said. "Besides, Nate is a mature person who is very capable. And yes, if it will make you feel better, I will do my best to help him."

At that Angela smiled and fell back to sleep as Sandy finished her bath.

Nate had finished a busy morning and now was relieved of his duties. He was able to get to Angela's room around two o'clock. Angela had eaten a little lunch and was asleep. Nate marveled at how she looked. Her face was swollen with edema and she looked tired, oh so tired. There was no smile. Her face was very still with no movement of her facial muscles that were usually so lively when she was awake. And yet she was beautiful. A stranger may not have thought so but to Nate, her face filled him with joy. He could not stop looking at her. Yet mixed with this joy was sadness. How one could experience such joy and sadness and sorrow all at the same time he did not know. He wanted to lie next to her. He wanted to hold her forever, but he knew that would not happen. He wanted what all lovers want but cannot have and that is for their minds and hearts and bodies to be together, to be one flesh, forever and ever. If only there was more time. Their time had been cut short but in some ways the time that they had been given seemed like an eternity. For that he was thankful. Nate knew they did not have long. He could only sit next to her as the moments slipped by.

Angela woke up off and on during the afternoon. Each time when she saw Nate she smiled and then went back to sleep. Around seven that evening she became much more awake. Nate had been there all along holding her hand. When her eyes finally opened and rested on him they seemed to sparkle. She pulled his hand to her lips and kissed it as she looked at him lovingly.

"I am so happy," she said and then kissed his hand again. *Oh Angela*, Nate thought to himself. *How can you be so joyous? What do you know that I do not?*

Her eyes focused on him again. "Nate, my dear Nate. How are you?" she said softly.

"I'm ok," Nate said with a tear in his eye.

"Do not cry, my love," she said. "I want to remember you as the happy guy I first met."

"You mean that bum off the street who came into your bookstore?" he asked.

"Yes, that bum. That wonderful bum who swept me off my feet the first time that I saw him. Did I ever tell you that?" she said.

"No. I was afraid I had made such a bad impression on you that I would never have a chance with you," Nate returned.

"And I was afraid you would never come back. But you did, how wonderful you did." Angela became quiet and then said, "I have a confession to make to you."

"Oh Angela, you don't need to confess anything," Nate said earnestly.

"Yes I do. I told you that I did not believe in love. But that was not true. I do believe in love. I believed in love from the moment I saw you. I love you so much!"

Nate's eyes could not hold back his tears. He held Angela's hands with both of his next to his heart. "I love you too," Nate said his voice almost cracking. "I have been wanting to say that to you for so long."

"Will you forgive me, my love?" Angela asked.

"Forgive you for loving me? Never," he said strongly.

They both sat there holding on to each other wondering how they got to be the luckiest people in the world. Angela then said, "Will you do something for me?"

"Anything my love," Nate replied.

"Would you please call Father Jim and have him come now if he can make it. He will know why."

"Father Jim?" Nate asked surprised.

"Yes, Father Jim," she replied.

Nate picked up the phone and called Sacred Heart Catholic

Church expecting to get an answering machine, but to his surprise Father Jim answered. "Hello, this is Father Jim."

"Father, this is Nate," Nate said.

"Oh Nate. It is so good to hear from you. How is Angela?" he asked.

"She has been very tired and has been sleeping a lot. She asked me to call you and ask if you could come over tonight. She said you would know what for," Nate said.

"Of course," Father Jim replied. "I will be right there."

Nate sat down by Angela, who had fallen back to sleep, and waited. Soon there was a very faint knock at the door as Father Jim slowly opened it and came inside.

Nate got up to greet him. "Thank you so much, Father," he said.

Angela had awakened and said, "Father, thank you."

Nate stepped back while Father Jim bent over to whisper something to Angela. Angela responded also in a whisper. Nate noticed that he had a priestly cloth around his neck. In his hand he held a small book and a small container. Standing by her bed he said a prayer after which he read quietly some passages from his book. He then dipped his finger into the small container he had opened which contained oil. With loving care he rubbed the oil on Angela's forehead. Angela then extended her arms on the bed and slowly opened her hands exposing her soft palms. Father Jim with the same care gently rubbed the oil into her palms, palms that had so many times caressed Nate, palms that he now ached for as he watched this mysterious and ancient ceremony unfold. Nate heard Father Jim say, "Through this Holy Anointing, may the Lord in his love and mercy help you with the grace of the Holy Spirit. May the Lord who frees you from your sin, save you and raise you up."

Angela looked at Father Jim and said, "Thank you Father."

Father Jim said, "You are welcome." He gave her a gentle hug and put his hand on her forehead and began to pray. "Lord, bless Angela. It seems funny to ask for something that we know is already freely given, but that is how lovers talk. We know you are close to Angela every minute because that's how lovers are." He then laid his hand on Angela's womb. "Lord, if we ever forget what an incredible force love is in this world may Angela and this beautiful little girl within her remind us. We know that this child is loved and blessed by you and that she is in your hands. Lord, we also pray for Nate, her father, who has loved and stood by her and her mother."

An eerie feeling came over Nate. He felt like the three of them were no longer in a hospital room but were somewhere else that was otherworldly and supernatural. He didn't know what to think. It was against his very nature to be a part of anything like this, but somehow all the tension and worry over Angela and their child that had built up in him began to subside, and he felt at ease for the first time in a long time. And contrary to all reason, for a moment Nate felt that all was right with the universe.

Father Jim continued, "We ask you to protect Angela and Nate and their daughter. We ask that they will know the reassurance of your everlasting love." With this Father Jim made the sign of the cross, after which Angela also made the sign of the cross. When he had finished he turned around and with a compassionate expression looked at Nate. He then gave him a hug and quietly left. Nate would never forget that hug and the care and concern on Father Jim's face that night.

Nate was left speechless. He had never seen anything like it before. He was greatly moved in way he had never been before. He slowly sat down by Angela with a surprised look on his face.

Angela appeared very tired. She held his hand and looked into his eyes and with effort began to speak. "Yes, I am now Catholic," she said. "Father Jim has been giving me instruction. I didn't want you to know about it. I'm sorry."

"Don't be sorry," Nate said quickly. "Why did you not want me to know about it?" he asked.

"Because I thought you would think that I am that atheist in the foxhole who cries out to God for help," Angela answered.

"Oh Angela, I would never think that, "Nate responded.

"Well, I thought that about myself at first, but I am not afraid to die. You know that, don't you?"

"Yes," he responded.

"I think I rejected everything my dad taught not because what he taught was wrong, but because I saw him hurt so much. But then I realized it did not bother him, it only bothered me." She thought for a minute. "Maybe I just couldn't shed all that religious stuff from my childhood as much as I wanted to."

"Your dad was truly a wonderful person," Nate said.

"I know that he sees me now and is extremely happy over the decision I've made. I know in my heart that he is praying for me and will continue to pray for me until we meet in heaven." She thought for a minute. "Nate, it's just not what my father taught me that has made me rethink the whole question of God. We can't just be molecules, can we? Can what we have, the three of us, just be a chemical reaction?"

Nate had tears in his eyes. "Now it seems absurd to think so," he replied.

They were silent for a few moments. Angela appeared to be resting and then seemed to gain her strength back and said, "I want you to name her Catherine. And when she is older, take her to Siena." Nate agreed, not having any idea why Angela had chosen Catherine or why she wanted him to take her to Siena. He could only say yes and not question why. There was so little time.

"Also, I want you to raise her in the church," Angela added.

Nate looked a little blank and then said, "Which church?"

"Your choice," she answered.

"But I don't know anything about churches. I would guess now the Catholic Church," Nate answered honestly.

"The Catholic Church is not the only church, you know," Angela informed him. Nate looked totally lost. "Also, Christianity is not the only religion," she added.

Now Nate was really lost. "What do you mean?" he asked.

"Well, there's the Hebrew faith, for example," Angela explained. "Jewish people are wonderful people, some of the most wonderful and loving people I know."

"Ok," said Nate falteringly, with no idea what Angela was really talking about.

"But," Angela continued, "whatever church or religion you choose for her, will you take her to church? Will you promise me that?"

"I will, I will," he promised earnestly.

Angela was now more tired than she had been all day. "Can we talk more in the morning? There is something important that we need to do. We will talk tomorrow, but now I am simply too exhausted. There is so much more I want to say to you, so much more." Her voice faded as she spoke these last words. She started to drift to sleep. She then opened her eyes and looked at Nate, who was still holding her hand and looking at her. She had a look of love on her face, and this sent a feeling of joy through him. She smiled and said, "I love you," and then fell to sleep. Nate returned, "I love you too, my love." Nate's heart ached. It amazed him how much it meant to him to hear her say those words and how wonderful it felt to say them back to her.

Nate lay in bed with Angela that night and held her as he had been doing. He felt her all over and then put his hand over his daughter, hoping to feel her as she awoke to stretch and move about. That night he had a multitude of thoughts about things he never dreamed of thinking about before. He realized that his love and respect for Angela was deeper and fuller than he ever thought possible. But he also knew that the end was near. Fear and love so overcame him that his whole body trembled. He took a deep breath. Beads of sweat appeared on his forehead. For several hours he lay in agony realizing there was no escape, no solution even though he kept desperately searching for one. Finally all he could do was to put his arms around Angela and place his body next to hers. That let him for a brief time forget the future, to forget the inevitable. His mind and heart were filled with her touch. Her warmth and the beating of her heart soothed him so that his fear knew that for now it had lost the battle, and it retreated from the scene. Nate relaxed and actually had a slight smile on his face as he went to sleep.

Chapter Thirty-one

He could hear "Code Blue" coming from somewhere. It seemed just to be in the air everywhere, but he couldn't figure out where the code blue was. He found himself racing down the hospital hallways asking anyone he saw where the code blue was, but they did not know and did not seem to care. They just kept walking like zombies doing their job. He became frantic and started running faster wondering what was wrong with everyone when he felt a hand on his shoulder and heard a nurse's voice say, "Dr. Williams, Dr. Williams. I'm sorry to wake you, but one of your patients on the third floor just arrested, and they need you."

"Yes, yes. Thank you," Nate said sleepily. He got up quickly and put on his greens and his slip-on tennis shoes. Angela opened her eyes. Nate bent down and kissed her. "I have to go," he said after their kiss.

"Bye," she said softly and added, "I love you."

"I love you too," Nate said as he kissed her once again. Saying I love you seemed to come naturally now, as natural as breath and just as important. He began to back away holding her hand as long as he could until their fingers parted. He stopped at the door to look one more time at her beauty. Their eyes focused on one another for a moment of silent communication that said things only their hearts could understand.

Once out of the room he raced to a stairwell that went up to the third floor. He ran to the nurses' station where a nurse told him that the resuscitation was in Mr. Taylor's room 3011. Mr. Taylor was a 68 year old who had had multiple stents in the past and was admitted to have a colonoscopy. Nate was the consultant for the gastroenterologist. He could see Mr. Taylor's tearful wife outside of the room in the hallway being comforted by relatives. Inside, a nurse was administering chest percussions, and an inhalation therapist was bagging. Nate entered and quickly assessed the situation. The nurses had already shocked the patient who now had a very slow heart rate of thirty beats per minute. Nate immediately ordered epinephrine and a blood gas.

The pulse began to pick up a little but then decreased again. Nate ordered more epinephrine and asked the inhalation therapist to intubate the patient. The chest percussion was stopped momentarily while the inhalation therapist attempted intubation. He had difficulty inserting the endotracheal tube into the trachea and stopped after one try. The bagging and chest compressions began again.

Nate moved to the head of the bed to attempt the intubation himself. When he was ready he ordered the chest compressions to stop. With his left hand he inserted the laryngoscope into the mouth lifting the tongue up in order to see the vocal cords. At the same time he could faintly hear the operator say, "Code Blue" over the public speakers. *What a coincidence, having two code blues at the same time*, he thought to himself. With a little adjustment of the laryngoscope he could now see the vocal cords. With a slow sure motion of his right hand he advanced the endotracheal tube gently into the opening between the vocal cords. He heard "Code Blue" once again. Once the tube seemed to be in its proper place he attached the ambu bag to it and started bagging. He requested someone to listen to the chest to make sure he was ventilating both lungs when a nurse said, "Dr. Williams, there is another code blue."

Nate said abruptly, "I can't cover two code blues at one time. They will have to find someone else."

The nurse appeared shaken as she said, "but it is your wife, I mean, your girlfriend."

He was sure he didn't hear her right, but then when he saw the distress in her face he knew he had. He felt weak. He thought he was going to faint. It seemed like all of a sudden there was an empty gaping hole where his heart used to be and that there was nothing left of him inside. "What can I do?" he stammered to himself. He felt like his very soul was being torn apart. The wife and family of Mr. Taylor depended on him to do everything he could to save him while at the same time the woman he loved and his daughter were both at death's door desperately needing him. He was about to do the unthinkable and abandon his patient when Dr. Allen stepped in the door and said, "I'll take over. Dr. Archer is with Angela."

Nate quickly handed the ambu bag to the inhalation therapist and ran down the flight of stairs to Angela's room. He entered with only one thought in mind and that was to start helping save Angela, but he found only a cold empty room. Her bed was gone. The floor was littered with pieces of tape and empty plastic syringe covers. His heart sank. He stood for a second frozen not knowing what to do. Then a nurse entered and said they had taken Angela to the operating room for an emergency C-section.

Nate frantically ran down the hallways to the obstetrics area. He was shaking when he got to the surgical suite. He was about to enter when Dr. Archer came out with a grave look on his face. "Nate, I am so sorry. We did everything we could. We resuscitated

Angela all the way here. Dr. King did an emergency C-section and saved the baby, but we could not save Angela."

Nate at first was in denial. Surely this could not have happened so fast. He had just said goodbye to her thirty minutes before. But then his medical knowledge came crashing down on him, and he knew that she was gone. Father Jim was in the hospital and joined Dr. Archer and Nate. They both helped Nate to the small conference room where relatives could start the grieving process.

Father Jim and Nate sat on the couch together. Father Jim put his arm around Nate's shoulder and began to rock him back and forth gently as Nate sobbed with his face in his hands. Nate had never known grief before, the grief that is so totally encompassing that there is no thinking, only the overwhelming anguish and cry of a heart that has lost its soul mate. Father Jim motioned to Dr. Archer that they should be alone and Dr. Archer left. Tears blinded Nate's eyes as he felt Father Jim's comforting embrace. After a while Nate's sobbing slowed down and he managed to say, "Doctors aren't supposed to cry."

Father Jim wiped his own tears with a handkerchief and said, "Neither are priests." Father Jim then said, "Nate, do you mind if I say a prayer?" Nate managed to say no, he didn't mind. Father Jim kept rocking Nate and prayed, "Father, this is too much, this is simply too much. I don't think we can bear it, Lord. I just don't think we can bear it." Nate had never heard a prayer like that before and somehow it comforted him a little.

After a short while one of the surgical nurses entered their room and asked if he would like to see Angela now. They got up and walked slowly into the surgical suite. Angela was lying on her back and looked asleep. A fresh sheet covered her body, and all traces of blood had been removed. Her arms were outside the sheet on the bed. The fluid that had caused swelling in her face now kept her cheeks from appearing sunken, as was often the case.

Father Jim and the nurse were on each side of him as he stood by her side. The nurse then pulled one of the stools in the room over for him to sit on. Nate sat on it and gently picked up one of her hands and asked if he could be alone with her. Father Jim said of course. Then he and the nurse left.

Angela's lifeless hand still had a little warmth in it as he held it with both of his. There were tears in his eyes but he was not crying now, he was looking at Angela. Angela was beautiful even in death. He wiped the remaining tears from his eyes with his sleeve and began to talk slowly.

"You are so beautiful, Angela. The most beautiful woman in the world. I love you so much." There was no life in her face, but her face still thrilled him as he looked at it.

"Why did you have to go? Why did you have to leave me?" He gently rubbed her hand. His tears came back, his voice cracked. "What I am going to do without you?" Nate felt a hurt within him that almost doubled him over. It was as if his heart had twisted onto itself in a severe cramp of agony that was wringing the life out of it. Nate let go of Angela's hand and grabbed his stomach and bent over. After a moment the hurt subsided a little. He sat back up and held her hand again.

"Angela, you said you loved me. It felt so good to hear you say that."

Nate wished that Angela had said it a hundred times before. "But we didn't really need to say it, did we?"

He looked closely at her. In his mind he could see her smile and laugh. He thought about how she kissed him at the lake and how she looked that night at the beach as she walked into the water. All their intimate times seemed to flash before his eyes.

"I had a cold heart when I met you but you took care of that, didn't you? I know because cold hearts don't break and mine is breaking right now." Nate again broke into sobs.

He took a deep breath and sniffled. "I wish I could have told the world that I would love you until death do us part. But then we showed the world that, didn't we?"

He leaned a little closer to her. "I would have liked to have pledged my love to you forever, but you didn't believe in marriage for some reason." Then he thought for a moment. "Could that have been the important thing that we were supposed to do?" He looked off for a second and then softly said, "I wish I could say that you were my wife." Then he turned to her, "Angela you were my wife, I know you were. We just didn't let anyone else in on it."

He thought about little Catherine. "Angela, we have a little girl. I haven't met her yet. She is very premature. She may not make it. But you gave her a chance. You gave her a chance to grow up and love and maybe be a mother. And you gave me a chance to be a father. You gave your life for us, Angela. Thank you, thank you, oh, thank you."

He wiped new tears from his eyes. "I'm going to finish that book, you know. I just wanted to let you know that."

Nate sat there thinking of the first time he saw her in her bookstore.

"I had no idea what awaited me that day I came to your bookstore," Nate said thoughtfully. "It was you, yes it was you, that awaited me. You took my heart on a journey and what a journey it was."

He stood up and kissed her hand that he had been holding and gently placed it back onto the bed. "I need to go and meet our daughter now. I know how you longed to say hello to her and to hold her. I wish you could have held her just once and kissed her." Nate had to stop for a moment to clear the lump that was there. "Angela, I will tell her hello for you, and I will hug and kiss her for you every day. I will tell her that she is the luckiest kid in the world to have had a mother like you, a mother who loved her so much. Oh, I love you, Angela. I am going to miss you so much. I don't know how I am going to live without you, but I must go on because there is this little girl who needs me. Goodbye, my darling." He bent over and kissed her on the cheek and then walked to the door without looking back.

Chapter Thirty-two

WHEN NATE WALKED OUT OF THE SURGICAL SUITE there stood Father Jim and Sandy with tears in her eyes waiting for him. They both noticed that Nate had an unexpected look of peace about him as he approached them. There seemed to be a silent communication between them as they hugged him. The three of them stood there like the sole survivors of a shipwreck in a vast and lonely sea. Nate felt a calmness that he did not quite understand. He had stopped crying and was getting back the focus in his eyes. All he could think about now was the little girl that he had felt kicking each night as he held Angela. He looked at them. "I want to see my daughter now," he said calmly. Father Jim and Sandy both said yes at once and the three of them started walking towards the NICU.

The neonatal intensive care unit was on the same floor. After going down several hallways they came to the NICU where Dr. Janet Warren was waiting for them. "Dr. Williams, I am so, so sorry about your loss. Would you like to meet your daughter now?" she asked.

"Yes," was his reply.

The NICU was a large room with about ten open radiant warmers and ten incubators. The incubators looked like large enclosed glass boxes with two round doors on each side that could be opened to gain access to the infants inside. The radiant warmers were open beds under large rectangular hoods that provided warmth and heat for the infants. The hoods were attached to large arms that came from the back of the open bed. At first glance the infants seemed unprotected in a bed with no walls except for a four-inch plastic side railing on all four sides. The NICU was filled with sounds, the rhythmic swishing of the respirators pumping life into the underdeveloped lungs, the beeping sounds reassuring everyone that the little hearts were still beating, and the occasional alarms that said, "Hey, this baby needs attention."

Dr. Warren asked them all to wash their hands before entering and then escorted them to a radiant warmer on one side of the room in which lay a very tiny thin infant with doll-like hands and feet and a head that was disproportionately large for the rest of her body.

"Here she is, your daughter," said Dr. Warren as they approached the radiant warmer. "She weighs two and a half pounds or a little over eleven hundred grams. She has what most infants at twenty-eight weeks' gestation have, respiratory distress syndrome, but it is not severe at this point. Otherwise she looks very healthy for her age."

Nate stood there in a dazed trance. He could still see Angela lifeless on her deathbed while at the same time he was looking at their daughter, who was very tiny struggling for life. He reached down and touched her foot, which moved a little. Out of her mouth came a small endotracheal tube that was attached to a respirator that gave her oxygen and a breath sixty times each minute, which made her tiny chest expand then contract slightly with each breath. The tube was held in place by a small plastic ring-like structure that was secured by tape.

Nate thought how beautiful and vibrant Angela had been.

To think that this tiny infant could someday be a mature women who could love a man and give life to children of her own seemed impossible. Even though at this stage his daughter seemed like she came from outer space, he thought he could see some resemblance to Angela.

"How is her heart?" asked Nate.

"It seems perfectly normal as far as we can tell," replied Dr. Warren. "She is about sixteen inches long and her physical exam is normal for a twenty-eight-week gestation infant. Her respiratory distress syndrome will probably get worse before it gets better. We expect that. However, we gave her surfactant and hopefully that will help."

Three wires secured by small round adhesive pads that had been placed on each side of her upper chest and on her leg monitored her heart rate. A fourth wire was taped to her abdomen, which recorded her temperature and automatically adjusted the overhead radiant warmer to keep her temperature at the optimum level. Around her foot was taped a pulse oximeter sensor, which measured the oxygen saturation in her blood. Coming out of her umbilicus were two small catheters, which were attached to a three-way stopcock valve that was attached by tubing to IV fluids.

"What are her chances for survival?" Nate asked.

"She has a little better than a 95% chance of surviving. However, she is still at high risk, but we will try our best to prevent any complications."

Nate stood there just staring at his daughter letting the sight of her soak deep into his soul. Somehow this seemed to heal the emptiness that was there. He thought of how much Angela loved this tiny infant. "Her name will be Catherine Angela Carter Williams," he announced as he held her hand. He then he started to feel weak. After a few minutes he thanked Dr. Warren and said he would return soon. Dr. Warren said that she would notify him of any changes. As he walked out of the NICU he felt faint. He walked to a couch in the waiting room where Father Jim and Sandy helped him sit down.

All of a sudden the tears began to flow again. This time Sandy held him in her arms and tried to soothe him. Father Jim said he would stay with him at his apartment today because he didn't think there was anyone else to be with him. Sandy said she knew that he had parents within a two-hour drive. She asked Nate if she could call them. Nate said ok and showed Sandy their number on his cell phone.

Sandy went into the nurses' lounge, which was empty, and dialed the number Nate had given her. An elderly female voice answered, "Hello."

"Mrs. Williams?" Sandy asked.

"Yes, this is she," the voiced returned.

"My name is Sandy Abraham, I am a nurse who works with your son, Nate. I am calling you about him."

"Is Nate ok?" Mrs. Williams asked with alarm.

"He is ok, but his girlfriend died this morning, and he is very sad and distraught."

"Nate has a girlfriend?" his mom said questioningly. "He never mentioned her to us. But then again we really don't talk much. I am so very sorry to hear this."

"There is one other thing that I must tell you," Sandy said slowly.

"What is that?" Mrs. Williams asked.

"His girlfriend died in childbirth giving birth to their premature daughter, who is now in the neonatal intensive care unit."

"Oh my, oh my," Nate's mom said repeatedly. "Nate has a daughter, and I have a granddaughter. I never would have expected such a thing. My goodness, my goodness. His father and I will leave immediately and come down there as soon as we can. Will Nate be at his apartment?"

"Yes," Sandy replied. "Father Jim or I will stay with him until you arrive."

"Father Jim? There is a priest there?" his mom asked.

"Yes," Sandy answered.

"This is a morning full of surprises, my goodness," she said spontaneously. "Sandy, thank you so much for helping Nate. We will be there soon. I hope to meet you."

Sandy hung up the phone and then walked back to where Nate and Father Jim were. Nate had stopped sobbing. He said he felt better and wanted to go home.

Father Jim drove Nate to his apartment while Sandy went to the store to buy some simple meals because she rightly figured that his apartment was probably empty. She bought eggs, milk, cereal, bread and the makings for a few simple meals. Soon after she arrived at Nate's apartment Rita and Tony brought several meals that could be frozen from their restaurant. Father Jim had notified them along with Cindy and Rick and Samantha who brought more food later that evening.

Nate's parents arrived late in the afternoon, both looking very worried. Nate had taken a small nap and was up and about. He would get occupied with minor tasks like making coffee that would take his mind off Angela and then her memory would bring overwhelming sadness back into his soul. When his parents arrived, he seemed all together. He welcomed them and thanked them for coming and said he was sorry that they had to be involved in all of this. His mother hugged him with a hug he had never experienced from her before, while his father shook his hand and patted him on the shoulder.

His mother even hugged Sandy and Father Jim and thanked

them profusely. As they left, they gave Nate's parents their phone numbers and said they would check in with them the next day.

Nate felt numb and dazed. He sat in his usual chair in a trance. His dad asked him if he wanted to turn on the television, and Nate said ok. His dad was at a loss for what to say so he sat pretending to read the newspaper. His mom worked busily in the kitchen making a nice spaghetti dinner with French bread and wine. When it was time to eat his mom called them to the table. Nate was not hungry, but he knew he needed to eat since he had not eaten anything all day.

"I am so sorry about Angela. She sounds like a wonderful girl. How did you meet her?" his mother asked.

"I met her in the bookstore that she owned," Nate replied.

"I wish I could have met her," she said sorrowfully. His father joined in with, "Me too."

"I'm sorry I didn't tell you about her," Nate said his voice cracking. Nate was glad that his parents were there. Their presence comforted him. However, he did not feel like talking but oddly enough, when he did talk, he felt a little better.

After a few moments more of eating, his mom broke the silence with, "Tell me about our little granddaughter, will you?"

"She is very premature," Nate answered. "She weighs only two and one-half pounds. She is on a ventilator, but I think she is going to make it."

"I can't wait to see her. Are we allowed to?" his mom asked.

"Yes, tomorrow we will go together," Nate reassured her.

"Good," his dad managed to say.

After dinner Nate and his dad sat in the living room while his mom washed the dishes. Little else was said until it was time for bed. They all said goodnight before going to their rooms. His mom with her nightgown on went to the kitchen for a glass of water when she heard Nate sobbing in his room. She quietly opened his door. There she saw him lying in a fetal position in his bed crying. She sat on the bed next to him and gently sat him up. She put her arms around him and started to sing a soft lullaby that she had sung to him as an infant.

"Oh why didn't I hug you more growing up?" she said softly. "Why didn't we touch each other and tell stories and do all sorts of silly stupid things that we would never forget? Why were we so practical?" A shudder of relief and warmth went through Nate's body as he heard her soothing words and felt the warmth of her as she hugged him. He missed his mom. He had missed her his whole life. Now she was back.

Nate looked up at her and said, 'I love you, Mom."

"I love you too, Son," she said back to him. That was the first time he could ever remember them saying that to one another. After a while she tucked him in as he lay back down. "Thanks Mom," Nate whispered.

"You're welcome," she said as she left.

She went back to her room where her husband was waiting. His face showed little emotion or expression, as it normally didn't when he was feeling afraid or anxious. She sat with him on the side of the bed with her arm around him. "I love you," she whispered. He mechanically returned, "I love you too."

She then whispered, "Nate's going to be ok. He is strong, and so are we."

He smiled a little at this. "But what can I do?" he asked. His voice quivered.

"Just be here for us," she answered. "You have always been here for us, and I love you so for that." She kissed him. He smiled a little for the first time since they had received the phone call from Sandy. That night she, in a small way, helped save the two men in her life that she loved.

Nate woke up around midnight. He could not sleep. Little

Catherine was on his mind. He had to see her. He got dressed and went down to his car and drove to the hospital. He went up to the NICU where the nurses let him in. The neonatal unit seemed a little less busy. There were still all the beeping noises, but there were fewer tests being performed, and the lights were a little lower. The neonatologist was in her call room nearby, leaving only the nurses to look after all the infants.

He pulled up a stool beside little Catherine's bed. He reached over the plastic railing to gently stroke her hand. He was very gentle as he touched her paper-thin skin. This tiny fragile infant struggling to breathe was his daughter. He loved her already. He wondered how he could love such a little creature that most would not even want to look at. But he did love her. He loved her with all of his heart. To him she was simply beautiful. He thought to himself that he was indeed different than he had been only a year ago. Now he was beginning to get to know the new person that he had become. It felt strange wondering what he would discover about himself.

Catherine's tiny hands somehow reminded him of Angela's hands. Then it occurred to him that he had a daughter to take care of. Initially, he felt a need to solve some problem, like which college she would go to or what clothes she would wear when she got home. Then the problem-solving part of his mind either just gave up or went to sleep after which he was able to just be a father admiring his daughter. Before he knew it, over an hour had passed. He said goodbye to Catherine before heading back home to his apartment and his sleeping parents.

Chapter Thirty-three

THE NEXT MORNING, NATE'S MOM GOT UP EARLY thinking about the granddaughter she was going to meet that day. She had given up on grandchildren. With the retirement of her husband she looked forward to a very quiet and comfortable life of boredom. Now she knew life would not be boring or dull, but she also knew that there could be unbearable heartache. She already had been worrying about little Catherine, worrying that she might not live or that she would suffer complications that would make her life challenging.

Nate looked refreshed. Even his dad looked a little brighter than he had been. They ate quickly before heading to the hospital. Nate took them up to the NICU where they were welcomed by Catherine's nurse. She informed them that the rules only allowed two visitors at a time due to space limitations, but if they didn't mention it to anyone, she would make an exception. After washing their hands the nurse led them to Catherine's warmer.

Nate's parents had never seen a premature infant before. Catherine looked like the scrawniest, most fragile tiny thing they had ever seen. They at first could not believe that this was their granddaughter. She looked like she was from another world.

Wires were attached to her and a machine was breathing for her; all in all, she seemed unreal.

Nate's father began to analyze all the mechanical equipment there to take his mind off this little creature. His mother, after recovering from her initial shock, touched her hand and said, "Oh you poor little thing."

Nate took a deep breath when he saw her. A lump formed in his throat as his mind again went back to Angela. Dr. Warren walked over to them and Nate introduced her to his parents. Dr. Warren informed them that she had to turn up the settings on the ventilator a little because her respiratory distress syndrome had gotten a little worse, which was to be expected. She went on to explain that otherwise she was stable. Also antibiotics had been started to cover any possible infections. They all thanked her after which the three of them stood there for almost an hour amazed at the small little infant in front of them.

As they left the NICU they saw Father Jim who was waiting for them in the waiting room. He asked if there was anything he could do. They all thanked him but said everything was under control. Father Jim then asked if he could talk with Nate alone. Then he and Nate went into a small adjacent conference room while Nate's parents waited in the main waiting room.

"Nate, I know how rough this has been on you," Father Jim began. "I want you to know that you have been in my prayers. Rita, Tony, Cindy, Rick and Samantha all are sick with sadness about Angela. They are also very concerned for you right now. They all want to help any way they can. Even Gregg called to say how sorry he was."

Nate said he appreciated all that.

Father Jim continued. "I want you to know that Angela had arranged for almost everything before she died. She made all the arrangements for her funeral. She also in her will left her bookstore to her assistant. It seems that the monthly income from her store was about equal to the monthly debt payments, so there was not a lot there to give away. She cancelled the lease on her apartment and had her clothes given to charity." Father Jim then pulled a small jewelry box from a briefcase he had with him. "Angela gave me this box, which holds her jewelry. She did not have a lot but she wanted Catherine to have it." Nate realized that he had never given her a present of any kind, not even a ring. "Also, she wanted you to have this," Father Jim said as he handed an envelope to Nate. "I believe these are family pictures to show to Catherine when she is older," Father added.

Nate was amazed at the efficiency and thoughtfulness of Angela. "Thank you, Father," Nate said. "Did Angela have any other family?" he asked.

"No, Nate." Father answered. "She was very alone in this world. She only had her father who, as you know, passed away. She had her employees as casual friends but her little club was evidently the only kind of family she had. Then of course she found you." Nate had always thought that Angela loved him but did not need him. Now for the first time he realized how lonely she was. Part of her happiness that he so loved about her came from his love for her. Nate looked off for a second. He could see Angela smiling at him.

Nate turned back to Father Jim. "Can you tell me about the funeral?"

"Yes. Tomorrow night will be the visitation at the funeral home where we will say a rosary. That's a Catholic custom that we do the night before the funeral. Then, the next morning, Thursday morning, we will have the funeral at my church, the Sacred Heart Catholic Church. Afterwards we will have a graveside service where she will be buried next to her parents."

Nate thanked Father Jim again.

"There is one other thing," Father Jim added. He reached into his pocket and pulled out a small envelope and handed it to Nate. "The day before she died, Angela told me that she had come to terms with many things in her life that she had not been able to before. These included her issues with God, marriage, and love. She was afraid that she might die suddenly before she could tell you so she wrote this note. She was very weak but she managed to write this. She asked me to give it to you if she died before she could talk to you."

Nate opened the envelope. On a sheet of her stationery Angela had written in very labored handwriting:

Nate my love,
If you are reading this I know your heart is broken.
Know that my heart is broken also being separated from you.
Also know that I love you and that I do believe in love
I love so very much!

Angela

Nate trembled upon reading what Angela had written. He felt both an agony and a joy that was unexplainable. Father Jim put his hand on his shoulder and said, "Angela taught us all about love." Nate nodded his head in agreement and softly said, "I know." Deep inside Nate did know. He knew it with all of his heart. He would never forget it. Angela indeed had taught him about love. "Thank you Angela," he whispered. After a few minutes Nate regained his composure and hugged Father Jim, something he had never done before. He then joined his parents.

The next day, Nate and his parents visited Catherine again. Her respiratory distress was about the same as the night before. In the afternoon they all went back to the apartment to rest. That evening they went together to the funeral home. The funeral home looked a lot like a church with pews and a center aisle. At the front lay Angela in her coffin with several stands of flowers on each side. Nate trembled as he entered and felt faint. His dad walked beside him and his mom held his arm supporting him as they approached Angela's casket. She appeared asleep with her hands folded over her chest holding a small rosary. Around her neck was a small cross. She looked beautiful lying there dressed in a fine gown. His first impulse was to say something to her to wake her up, but the longer he stood there the more he realized that this was not Angela. Angela was no longer there.

The visitors that night included Cindy, Rick, Tony, Rita, and Samantha. Gregg arrived late and sat separate from Samantha. There were also Angela's three employees, several nurses from the hospital, and Sandy, who sat in a back pew. Each one paid their respects to Angela and expressed their sorrow to Nate before taking their seats.

When everyone was seated Father Jim went to the podium. He thanked everyone for coming. "We are here to say goodbye to Angela whom we all loved," he began. "We grieve and we feel deep sorrow and that is how we should feel at such a parting. Jesus, our model in all things, wept at Lazarus's death. So we weep for Angela. However, we are not without hope for we know that Angela is with our Lord and that we will see her again someday."

Father Jim paused for a moment. Realizing that neither Nate, his parents, or anyone else as far as he knew were Catholic, he said, "It is our Catholic custom to say a rosary together the night before the day of the funeral. The rosary dates back to the Middle Ages. It is a form of meditation that helps us meditate on God's love for each one of us."

Father Jim continued. "Angela gave birth to a very small beautiful daughter who is very sick and in need of our prayers, so we say this rosary to meditate not only on God's love for Angela but also for His love for Catherine her daughter and for Nate, whom she loved so much."

Father Jim paused before continuing. "Angela was a very recent convert to the Catholic faith and only had time to say the rosary a few times. When she learned of our tradition of saying the rosary at this time she was pleased. After the rosary I would like to invite anyone who would like to say a few words to come up here and share with us. With that we will now begin."

Nate had heard of the rosary, but he and his parents knew nothing about it. There were two nurses there who were Catholic who had rosary beads to hold during the service who knelt on their knees during the recitation. Father Jim began by crossing himself and reciting the Apostle's Creed, which was followed by the Lord's Prayer and three Hail Marys. He then announced the first decade would focus on the annunciation of the angel Gabriel and Mary's response of "Let it be." As the rosary began, Nate at first felt he was part of an ancient ritual that was in some ways not much different from that of primitive cultures throughout the world. However, as it went on, the words, "Pray for us sinners now and at the hour of our death," seemed to stick in his mind. He realized that Angela was comforted knowing that Mary was praying for her at the hour of her death. The repetitive rhythm of the voices joined in prayer soothed him in a way he had not expected.

Father Jim completed the rosary after which he invited those that were there to come forward and say a few words. At first everyone sat there silently without moving. Then Rita got up and walked slowly to the front. "Tony and I have known Angela for a few years. We own a restaurant where we interact with our employees and our customers but in reality we are lonely people. We met Angela when we were looking for something to read about food, and she really took an interest in us. She not only was our advisor, but she became our friend. We will miss her greatly."

As Rita took her seat, Rick and Cindy got up together to go to the podium. Cindy began. "Rick and I also met Angela in her store. I was into classics and we had a lot of great discussions. We are very busy parents of young children and have little time for anything else besides our children and our work. Angela knew this. When she saw that a local theater group was performing Shakespeare's *All's Well That Ends Well*, she bought us tickets and offered to babysit."

Rick joined in. "I had never seen a Shakespeare play before and I loved it. Angela also helped expand my reading in science and science fiction. She was our dear friend."

Samantha then got up. "I've never really read much, but that didn't matter to Angela. She was willing to talk to me about anything under the sun and was there when I needed her." Gregg sat quietly observing.

"I must add some of my own reflections," Father Jim said. "I have known Angela for quite some time. I frequently went to her bookstore because, and I must confess this, I was hooked on mystery novels." He smiled, as did everyone else. "Angela helped me find the latest and best such novels. She then asked me to join her and some of her friends once a month to talk about what we have read. She treated me just like everyone else despite the fact that I always wore my collar. I must confess again that it was a pleasant change just to be one of the gang, so to speak." He again smiled. "She was a wonderful loving person. All who knew her were touched by her love." After he had finished no one else came forth to say anything. As everyone started to leave Father Jim asked the club members along with Nate's parents and Sandy to stay. He made a special effort to catch Gregg who was starting to walk out.

"I'd like you to stay too. I know Angela would also," Father Jim said to Gregg earnestly.

Gregg looked a little sour and a little suspicious. "Are you sure Father?" he asked.

"Yes, I'm sure," Father Jim responded.

While they were waiting for everyone else to leave Nate's mother approached Father Jim. "Father, I never met Angela but from what I have learned about her I am so grateful that she was part of Nate's life." She then paused. "I am not religious, we have never been, but if you would pray for our little Catherine, I would appreciate it." Nate's father added, "I would appreciate it too, Father." Father told them that he had already been praying for Catherine. He said that the fact they have requested his prayers made his prayers more special than ever.

When everyone else had gone, Father Jim asked them all to sit in the front pews. Nate sat with his parents in the first pew while everyone else sat in the two pews behind them. Father Jim moved a chair from behind the podium so he could set in front of them. He sat facing them with a small folder in his hand. Once seated everyone became very quiet.

"Thank you for staying," Father began to the group. "I wanted this chance to talk to you for just a minute." Nate hoped Father Jim would not take too long. He just wanted to go home. He wanted to be alone.

Father Jim continued. "Angela knew that she would not live long. That is why she asked me to convey to each one of you just how much she loved you. She wanted you to know how much she will miss you." Several wiped the tears from their eyes. Father Jim opened his folder and retrieved some cloth-like objects. "Angela wanted you to have a special gift from her," he said as he passed out one to everyone including Gregg. He did not hand one to

Sandy. In their hands was a ten-by-two-inch silver bookmark made of the finest silk with their name on it embroidered in gold.

"Angela wanted it to be silver to remind everyone of the silver linings that are around every dark cloud." At that Rita burst into tears. Tony, with a few tears in his eyes, put his arm around her to console her. Father smiled then added, "She also said maybe it will encourage you to continue reading books as you continue on your journeys." This brought a smile to everyone's face including Nate's.

Then Father took out one more bookmark and handed it to Sandy. "Angela asked me to give this to you separately and say a special 'Thank you'. She asked me to say thank you for listening and being her friend." Sandy, who had been dry eyed up to that point, had tears streaming down her cheeks as she accepted it. He then took out another one and handed it to Nate. "This is for someone special who couldn't make it tonight." The gold embroidered letters read, "To Catherine from Mommy." Nate's heart went out to Angela. He put his hand over his eyes as more tears came. "This one is specially for you," Father Jim said as handed Nate one more bookmark that had 'Nate' on one side and 'Love' embroidered on the other. He heard himself saying, "Angela, oh Angela." He then felt the much-needed comfort of his mother who put her arm around him.

Father Jim then said, "I want you to know that I love everyone of you. All of you are in my prayers every day. That includes Angela and Catherine by the way. Please let me know if you need anything or if I can be of help in any way." Everyone thanked Father Jim profusely then hugged Nate as they left.

Afterwards, Nate and his parents made a brief visit to the NICU where Catherine was stable, not getting any worse but not improving either. That night after everyone went to bed, Nate got up again around midnight to visit Catherine. Catherine seemed asleep as she lay on her back with the endotracheal tube protruding from her mouth. A swishing sound continued incessantly and rapidly as the oxygen went in and out of her lungs at the command of the respirator. She lay exposed, frail, naked, and unprotected. She looked cold. However, Nate knew that the radiant warmer overhead was keeping her warmer than covers would.

He held her little hand and said, "I've got a special present to you from Mommy." He then carefully laid the silk bookmark that was almost as long as she was by her side. The smoothness of the silk in some way symbolized precious little Catherine to him. Nate then bent down, and as he promised he would, whispered in her ear, "You are the luckiest kid in the world to have had a mother who loves you so much." He would whisper that in her ear each time he visited. As he held her hand and thought of Angela he began to feel that he was lucky too. Somehow he started to have hope, hope that he had thought he had lost.

Chapter Thirty-Four

FATHER JIM AWOKE WITH ANGELA, NATE, AND LITTLE Catherine on his mind. He had said a prayer for them before bed, and another one before he got out of bed. He had awakened on his own fifteen minutes before the alarm was to go off. He turned it off and sat on the edge of the bed. Growing up, funerals had always been sad occasions for him. When his dad had died when he was a teenager he remembered not only how he felt but also how much his mother had cried. He had never seen her cry before. She seemed different, almost like a stranger. He cried too, but he felt so sorry for her that his desire to help her took his mind off his own grief. It was then he discovered that helping other people was the key to dealing with his own suffering and the demons within him, demons that he discovered everyone had. After the funeral, he and his mom began going to daily Mass. He eventually decided to be an altar boy again, like he was when he was younger. The Mass became a special time when the world seemed to stand still. He was with his Lord where he could see the big picture and the really important things of life. Soon he wanted to share the joy that he had with others. However, preaching or trying to convince others to believe what he believed was not up his alley. What made him happy was simply serving others. He hoped by doing this those he encountered in this life would experience the love of Christ through him. When it came to converting souls he would be ready to help God in whose hands it was in rather than his own.

His mother was overjoyed when he told her he wanted to become a priest. However, Father Weber, their kindly elderly priest, was more reserved. He saw the beginnings of a priest within Jim but knew they were only the beginnings. Father Weber began having wonderful weekly talks with him over tea or coffee, where they explored a world of ideas that included all religions as well as science and atheism, which seemed to be so prevalent in modern society. They talked about the love of Christ. Father Weber suggested that Jim start volunteering at the soup kitchen and homeless shelter. He knew that when many good-intentioned young people faced the poor and unfortunate directly, they would become discouraged not only at the depressing situation of the poor but also at the sometimes ungrateful attitude they would encounter. However, this did not discourage Jim whose desire to become a priest became even stronger.

The seminary was definitely a challenge. He enjoyed the structured life, the daily Mass and the prayers, but Greek and Latin were hard. Philosophy and history interested him the most. He contemplated becoming a professor teaching others what he had learned. However, he got his greatest joy simply helping people. He discovered that people were very complicated interesting beings intriguing each in their own special way. While he thanked God for all the religious people in his parish, he enjoyed being around all those folks who were simply concerned with making it through life who didn't give much thought to theology, God, or eternity. He didn't try to convert them but only to help them. He only hoped that his presence would help them along spiritually in some way.

He enjoyed performing weddings and hearing confessions where he could express God's mercy and forgiveness. He especially enjoyed Mass where he was *in persona* of Christ. The only priestly duty that he had at first found stressful was conducting funerals. Funerals brought back memories of his father's funeral and of his mother overwrought with tears. Over time however, he was comforted, knowing that all would be reunited in God's time. He began to realize that funerals were a family event that often brought families together who had been separated by distance or conflicts or old unresolved hurts. He began to understand that even death was part of God's love.

He thought back to when he first met Angela. He had been going to her bookstore buying detective novels when she approached him one day as he poured over new selections. He could hear her words still. "What's this? A priest reading fiction?" she asked. When he had said yes she said, "Well, you are my kind of priest and I don't even believe in God." They both laughed, and soon after that they became close friends. He felt honored when she invited him to her club. When she warned him that she didn't think anyone in the club believed in God, he said he liked hanging around pagans, and they both laughed again.

Father Jim went through his usual morning routine of going to the Eucharistic adoration chapel and saying the morning prayers that all priests throughout the world say each morning. He knelt before the exposed Eucharist, the body of Christ, and prayed and asked God to give him the right words to say at Angela's funeral. He did not eat breakfast so he could be in a state of fasting for the funeral. He then headed from the small rectory where he lived toward the church to make sure everything was ready. It was January, and the air was cold but clear. A fresh snow had covered the earth with a white shining blanket. He walked through the snow to the church but stopped before going in and looked up. He was almost shivering, but the sun's rays gently warmed his face. He gave a prayer of thanks for life and then said another short prayer for Angela, Nate, and Catherine.

He entered the sanctuary. Flowers from the funeral home were already there. New candles were in the candleholders and everything seemed in place. He had arranged for a vocalist, a pianist, and someone to read scripture along with an altar girl to help him during the Mass. He put on the special robe that he wore for funerals and walked to the church entrance to greet the people as they entered and to await the arrival of Angela's coffin.

He wondered if there would be very many attending the funeral. Then to his surprise a young man followed by fifteen or so people were walking up the steps to enter the church. He thought maybe this was some tourist group. He decided that he should inform them of the impending funeral.

However, before he could say anything the young man shook his hand and said, "Hi Father. I'm Jeff Story, Angela's assistant and the new owner of her bookstore." Father smiled and shook his hand. The young man continued. "All these people here consider themselves Angela's friends although they only knew her from talking with her in her bookstore. Angela had this special talent for establishing relationships with people easily. Now you know why, in this age of electronic books, that Angela's bookstore was successful. I just hope I can follow in her footsteps."

Father Jim smiled. "I'm sure you will. I will pray for the success of what is now your bookstore, and I will pray for you."

"Thank you, Father," the young man said. With that he shook Father's hand again. He motioned to those behind him to follow him into the sanctuary.

Afterwards, Angela's club started to arrive. First to arrive were Tony and Rita, both looking very solemn holding hands. They both hugged Father Jim for a long time and didn't seem to want to let go. Then Cindy and Rick along with Samantha entered. They all gave Father Jim a brief but meaningful hug. Arriving by himself was Gregg, who shook Father's hand and then took a seat in the back while the rest of the club sat right behind the first pew on the right that had been reserved for Nate and his parents. Sandy also hugged him as she entered by herself. Soon a group of nurses from the hospital arrived, most of whom he knew from his rounds in the hospital. Even a few of them hugged him. *Hugs from people who love you are one of the perks of being a priest*, he thought to himself.

He looked out at all the guests and did not recognize any from his parish. It crossed his mind that this might be the first time he would hold a Mass with no Catholics in the congregation and that when he stepped down from the altar to offer the Eucharist possibly no one would come. *Oh, well*, he thought, *there is a first time for everything*. He looked around and Angela's casket had arrived.

Chapter Thirty-five

NATE AWOKE DREADING THE FUNERAL. HE JUST DIDN'T see the point in having it. Angela was gone. Nothing would bring her back. Funerals were for the living but he didn't need it. His sadness returned. The reality of Angela's death kept coming back to him in waves, feeling like a lead weight in the pit of his stomach. Angela was really gone. He would never see her again. He would never hold her or love her passionately or hear her voice again. He didn't want to go to the funeral. He just wanted to be alone where he could mourn for her. He had to figure out how to go on with life without her but that would have to come later.

That morning he and his parents said very little to each other. His mother gave him a hug when she first saw him and his dad awkwardly patted him on his shoulder. They had a small breakfast before the funeral home escorted them to Sacred Heart Catholic Church where an elderly nun welcomed them. The nun introduced herself as Sister Mary Catherine. She expressed her sorrow at their loss as she accompanied them to a small chapel located at the front of the sanctuary off to one side. When everyone was seated, she led them to the first pew on the right, which had been reserved for them.

Neither Nate nor his parents had ever been in a Catholic church before. It was like walking into a different world full of stained glass windows and statues. The sanctuary was huge with three aisles, one down the middle with two smaller aisles on each side. Nate looked up at the top of the sculptured columns that were in a row on each side of the center aisle. They seemed to reach up to heaven. Arches radiated from the top of each one that seemed like arms holding up the church protecting everyone inside. The stained glass windows on each side were brightly lit from the outside sun. Each one revealed in ornate detail a saint or some biblical character. In between the windows above eye level were sculptured scenes that depicted the different events of Christ's crucifixion. Nate just wanted to sit there and not focus on anything, but the details of his surroundings would not let him.

Nate sat in the front pew with his parents on each side of him. For the first time Nate saw the large crucifix on the wall behind the altar with Christ hanging on the cross with his bowed head bearing a crown of thorns. There was graphic detail of the nails through his hands and feet. Blood was seen flowing out of his side where he had been stabbed. As he looked around he saw to the left of the crucifix a statue of Mary with a queen's crown on her head. She was looking heavenly with her hands together in a praying position. To the right of the crucifix was a statue of St. Joseph carrying baby Jesus in his right arm while holding a staff in the other.

Nate felt like he had stepped back five hundred years into the medieval era. He wondered if all Catholic churches were so far behind times. This was a world so much different from the one he lived in. It was a world of symbols and beliefs about things for which there was no real proof. It was the world of mankind before the modern age of science and reason. It was a world outdated and meaningless. Nate was feeling more and more like an alien in a strange world when he heard the doors to the sanctuary open. He looked back and saw Angela's casket being rolled into the back of the church. He then saw Father Jim put a white cloth over the casket. Then Father Jim held a small metal ball with holes in it by a handle that protruded from the bottom. He proceeded to dip the metal ball in a small container of water after which he walked slowly around the casket sprinkling water on it. Next he was handed a silver container on a chain from which the smoke of incense arose. Father Jim swung it back and forth as he again walked around the casket. The smoke of the incense had a slightly sweet smell as it slowly drifted upward forming a slightly hazy cloud above the casket. Nate now was sure he was in the wrong place. He wondered how Angela could have associated herself with such superstition and ritual.

The casket was then rolled to the front of the church. Father Jim followed the casket down the aisle walking behind an altar girl who carried a brass pole with a crucifix at the top. The vocalist began to sing *Be Not Afraid*, a song that was often sung at Sacred Heart.

When Father Jim approached the altar, he first bowed and then turned around and made the sign of the cross. He noticed that about half of the congregation also made the sign of the cross, which let him know that there were Catholics present. He then welcomed everyone and thanked them for coming to this celebration of the life of Angela Carter. He then spoke the usual greeting, which were the words spoken by Paul to the Corinthians, "The grace of our Lord Jesus Christ and the love of God and the fellowship of the Holy Spirit be with you all." The congregation responded with, "And with your spirit." He then prayed a prayer from a large red book held by the altar girl before sitting in his chair. A woman then got up and went to the podium to read scripture.

Nate decided to listen to the woman as she read from Ecclesiastes 3:1–8.

> *There is an appointed time for everything.*
> *And there is a time for every event under heaven –*
> *A time to give birth and a time to die*

Nate did not hear the rest of the reading. The words *A time to give birth and a time to die* echoed in his mind. He asked himself—or was he asking God, he wondered—*Why was its Angela's fate to give birth and die at the same time?* Tears started to flow. He thought he had no more tears but he was wrong. Until it is healed, a grieving heart will never run out of tears. After the first reading, the vocalist sang the Twenty-third psalm with a voice like that of an angel from heaven. Next the woman read from Romans 14:7–8:

> *Not one of us lives for himself, and not one dies for himself, for if we live, we live for the Lord, or if we die, we die for the Lord.*

After she had returned to her pew, Father Jim arose carrying a large red book above his head as he walked to the podium. Everyone stood up as he read from John 15:12–13:

> *This is My commandment, that you love one another, just as I have loved you. Greater love has no one than this, that one lay down his life for his friends.*

Father Jim paused before closing the book of the gospels. He looked first at Nate and then the congregation before beginning the funeral homily. "We are here today to celebrate the life of Angela Carter and to celebrate what she believed. We are also here to grieve at our having to part from her for we dearly miss

Angela. Even though we know about the life to come we weep over her death, just as the Lord wept over the death of Lazarus."

Father Jim continued. "The white cloth we placed over Angela's casket is the same white cloth we give to the newly baptized. At baptism we are born into God's family, and death in this life is our birth into the heavenly kingdom. The Holy Water we sprinkle reminds us of baptism and these two births. The incense is a symbol of our prayers that rise into heaven. It is also a symbol of Angela's spirit rising to meet our Lord."

Father Jim now looked as if he was about to speak from deep down in his heart. "It may seem a little odd, but when I think of Angela I am reminded of the Garden of Eden story in Genesis. The story of God putting Adam into the garden and telling him to keep it is worded very similarly to the accounts of priests in the Old Testament that were commanded to guard the temple with their life. Adam was very much like a priest who was to protect the garden and his wife with his life from any evil that would come into it. However, when evil did come, where was Adam? He was hiding behind Eve as she confronted the devil."

He smiled, as did a few others. "You see, facing evil meant facing danger and suffering. Eve, unlike Adam, chose to face suffering for the sake of love. Of course she lost the battle with the devil, but the ancient rabbis applauded her for stepping forward in the face of danger."

Father Jim continued. "Angela was like Eve; she stepped forward. She chose to face and accept suffering because of her love for her daughter; a suffering that she knew would end her life prematurely. Unlike Eve though, the threat of suffering did not defeat her. Her passion, her love for her daughter was greater than any fear of suffering she might have to endure." Father Jim looked back at Christ on the cross for a solemn moment before turning back to the congregation. "That is what Christ on the cross is all about. We call this his passion because of the love and passion he has for all of us. He didn't have to die on the cross. He could have forsaken us and avoided the terrible painful death he endured. However, the love he had for all of us was more powerful than the greatest suffering that was thrown at him. Christ showed us the awesome power of love. Angela had that love, that awesome power within her. She could have avoided suffering. However, she chose love instead. Like Christ she showed us that love dominates suffering in this world. Thus she chose to give her life so that her daughter might have a chance to live."

Father Jim's words struck at Nate's heart. That was Angela. Angela said she didn't believe in love when they had first met, but now he knew that she really did believe in love all along. She tried to convince herself she didn't, but she was not successful. She showed love more than anyone he had ever known. Tears began to flow again as he thought of how she loved him. He could see her now, smiling with open arms. Nate's mom held one of his hands, and he felt for the first time his father's arm around his shoulder. In some ways he felt like a little boy again, frightened and alone. Having his parents next to him comforted him. They cared for him; they were there. He could depend on them. Their touch was like an island in a stormy sea, and he would never forget that feeling.

"That brings us back to love," Father Jim continued. "Love is the basis of our faith, for God is love. Christ commanded us to love one another as he has loved us. It is this love that breaks all the barriers of time and space. Christ showed us what love is. He showed us that love results in the resurrection. He showed us that love continues after death. Thus we know that Angela loves us now as she did before she died. It is our Catholic faith that she is praying for us and that she is now one of those in the cloud of witnesses that Paul talks about. I know in my heart that Angela is now praying for Nate and her daughter, whom she loves very much." Father Jim finished this last sentence looking at Nate who was looking back at him with open eyes.

"Angela," Father Jim continued, "rediscovered her faith shortly before she died. However, she never really lost the faith of her childhood, which shows us how important it is to raise our children knowing God's love. Angela was raised by loving parents who were full of love for God. You see, her dad was a wonderful pastor. His love and teachings were forever written on her heart despite the fact that she tried to deny it. That is how God's love is for us. We may try to run from it but we cannot. When we come to that point in our lives where we can no longer be in denial of God's love we find a joy and a courage that we did not know we had. It is then that God's love within us will overflow to our families and our fellow human beings. It is this that will make every minute of our lives worth living no matter what life throws at us. Finally it is this love that will thrust us from this life into an eternity of love with God and with those whom we have loved on this earth. Angela knew that love. Maybe her example will help us all rediscover God's love within ourselves. Angela would want that, I know."

Father Jim then went on with the usual Catholic Mass, which included reciting the Nicene Creed, prayers of the faithful, and the Eucharistic prayer said at the consecration of the bread and wine. Everyone stood to say the Lord's Prayer together. At the sign of peace almost everyone came up front and hugged Nate with more hugs than he had ever had in all of his life. It seemed each person's hug brought a little more peace into his soul.

After Father Jim finished the prayers of thanksgiving he stepped down, and about half of the congregation came forward to receive the Eucharist. Before the end of the service he invited everyone to join them at the graveside, which was to be where her parents were buried, about a two-hour drive from the church.

When they arrived at the cemetery, Angela's casket was on a velvet-covered stand under a tent-like structure where folding chairs were lined up in rows beside it. The wind had started to blow; the snow began a heavy downfall. The open grave had snow following into it and looked cold, very cold. At the graveside were only Nate and his parents and the club members except for Gregg. Sandy stood silently behind everyone. Nate sat in the first row looking at Angela's casket. The wind seemed to go right through his clothes. A numbing cold penetrated him reaching the innermost chambers of his heart.

Father Jim again said some comforting last words before making the sign of the cross over the casket. Everyone hugged Nate as they said goodbye to Angela. Nate was the last to leave. As he left he touched his finger to the cold smooth wood of the casket letting it slide along the edge as he walked away. When his finger lost contact with the casket he remembered the last touch he and Angela had that morning as their fingers parted.

Father Jim had arranged for a lunch at an Italian restaurant not far from the cemetery. They all entered the private dining room in a somber mood that they tried to hide with small talk about the weather. The table was already set with wine glasses. When they had sat down, the waiters immediately poured everyone a glass of wine. Father Jim stood up with a glass of wine in his hand. "I've asked that the wine be given to us first because I want to make a toast to Angela whom we love and miss very much." At that everyone stood up touching their glasses and taking a small taste of the wine. Father continued, "I hope everyone will enjoy this restaurant. Tony, I apologize that it is Italian, but it was the only one with a separate dining area."

"As long as the food is not better than the food in my

restaurant, I won't mind," Tony said, smiling. Everyone seemed to relax a little.

"I ordered the specialty of the house, spaghetti," Father added. Everyone smiled a little more.

As the waiter began to put bread on the table and serve the salad, Tony stood up and began to speak. "I want to tell a story about Angela. Angela would come to my restaurant on a fairly regular basis. Once she pulled me aside and said she had an idea that would make me rich and famous. I told her I could use an idea like that." Everyone laughed a little. "She said, 'Tony, why don't you start another restaurant where, when people order food, they could also choose a famous writer like Charles Dickens or Tolstoy. Then when the food is brought out everyone would get an easily read handout with the most famous sayings of each author that they could discuss while they ate. You could call the restaurant *Food for Thought.*' Well, I told Angela that might be a wonderful idea, but unfortunately most of my customers only had thoughts for food."

At that they all laughed including Nate, who chuckled a little. Everyone began to share stories about Angela as the food was served. Rick told how Angela insisted that he read the original *Frankenstein* by Mary Shelly. He was surprised that the book had some really good insights on the frightening power that science was giving to mankind. However he said after reading it he awoke one night from a nightmare where he had dreamed his laboratory had created a monster. However, he then reassured himself that since he only studied the mating behavior of frogs, there was little danger of that happening. Another small laugh followed.

Cindy said that Angela helped her lighten up. "Unfortunately, I'm sort of a control freak. I like schedules and routines. I was mainly reading serious classics and I read them like I was preparing for a college exam. Angela insisted that I break out into something not quite so heavy. She gave me *Three Men in a Boat,* which is totally silly but I laughed. Then she insisted I read Erma Bombeck. I started with *Motherhood: The Second Oldest Profession*, and I have been laughing ever since. I still read my classics, by the way."

Hearing others talk and laugh as they remembered Angela helped Nate. Maybe it wasn't the end of the world after all. Maybe remembering and being thankful for all the fun times and laughs that they had together could help him escape at least momentarily from the depths of depression and sorrow and feel happy once again.

Father Jim joined in. "Once when I was going to purchase another mystery novel Angela looked at me and said, 'Father Jim, from now on all your books are free.' I said, 'How come?' She said because I had taken a vow of poverty and she just felt guilty charging me. I then told her that I had also taken a vow of chastity and that I had no family to support, although there were a couple of hundred kids who called me Father each Sunday."

Nate found himself laughing with everyone else and before he knew it, he began to talk about Angela also. "Well, it's my turn. As you know, we doctors think we are pretty smart. When I first met Angela she quickly diagnosed me with what she thought was an incurable affliction." Everyone was paying close attention. "She said I had a fiction reading disability." Everyone laughed. "So I asked her if I had such a disability, why had she invited me to be part of the club. She responded because I had a pretty face. I said with much indignation, you mean I'm just another pretty face? And do you know what she said?" They all shook their heads no. "She just said, 'Yep'." They all cracked up. Nate's mom put her arm around him and told everyone that she always thought he had a pretty face, at which Nate said, "Gee, thanks Mom." Sandy had remained quiet during the meal but she looked at the club members and at Nate and a smile could be seen on her face.

Finally everyone was in a good mood as they were ready to leave. Father insisted that he was going to pay for the dinner, but they all agreed that someone who had taken a vow of poverty should not pay even though they had also taken a vow of chastity.

Chapter Thirty-six

AFTER THE FUNERAL, NATE AND HIS PARENTS WENT TO visit little Catherine. The nurses made an exception to the rules again and let all three of them in. Catherine still had the endotracheal tube coming out of her mouth. The tube kept her mouth open, giving her face a slightly fish-like look. Her chest rhythmically expanded as the respirator pushed oxygen into her lungs. Besides the two umbilical catheters, the nurses had been able to start a peripheral IV in her left hand. Her left hand was secured by gauze and tape to a very small arm board that extended half way up her elbow. The IV entered on the top of her hand, which also was secured by tape.

She seemed even smaller than before. She lay under a layer of clear Saran wrap that was attached to the four-inch plastic side rails on each side of her radiant warmer. This had been put in place to help retain her body heat. Nate and his parents were surprised to see her wearing a mask in the shape of glasses over her eyes. Dr. Warren walked over and explained that she had developed hyperbilirubinemia, or jaundice. Since Nate was a physician, Dr. Warren went into more detail than usual, explaining that the molecule that caused the yellow jaundice was bilirubin, something that Nate already knew. The bilirubin that is naturally released each day from the breakdown of red blood cells must be metabolized by the liver and passed into the gut for elimination. Nate knew all about this. However, in all infants and especially in premature infants, Dr. Warren explained, the liver takes a few days before it is able to process the bilirubin. Thus it builds up in the blood and deposits in the skin, giving the skin a yellow color. The danger from this is that if it builds up too much, it will cross the blood brain barrier depositing itself into the brain causing brain damage. This caught the attention of Nate's parents. The yellow lights, known as phototherapy, Dr. Warren continued, make the bilirubin in the skin water-soluble so it can be eliminated through the kidneys while waiting for the liver to mature thus reducing the jaundice. This explanation went completely over the head of Nate's parents. Catherine's eye mask is there, she explained, to protect her eyes from the phototherapy.

Catherine was now two and one-half days old. She continued on the same respirator settings, which indicated that her lungs had not improved. Dr. Warren again explained that it often took a number of days to see improvement. She also informed them that she had ordered parenteral nutrition known as hyperalimentation to be given through Catherine's IVs. The IV nutrition consisted of elemental proteins, lipids and glucose that would not be sufficient in themselves to completely supply her nutritional needs but would be of great benefit until she could be given feedings through a tube that would be inserted through her mouth or nose into her stomach.

Nate took it all in with interest, but his parents were overwhelmed with all the medical information given to them. They simply kept looking at Catherine acting like they understood everything. After their visit they all went back to his apartment where they all took a nap. Afterwards, Nate's mom fixed another simple nutritious meal that they ate while engaging in sparse small talk because it was too difficult to talk about Angela at that point.

After going to bed he got up around midnight as he had done before to visit Catherine. He pulled up the same stool he had sat in before and looked at her holding her hand. Suddenly he noticed a slight change. She seemed to now have a dusky color. Her chest began to have retractions, indicating labored breathing. The pulse oximeter, which measures the amount of oxygen in her blood, dropped from the normal ninety-five percent to eighty-five percent setting off an alarm. Nate became alarmed but before he could call the nurse she was quickly there, assessing the situation. She asked the other nurses to notify Dr. Jones the neonatologist who was there that night in his call room while she grabbed a stethoscope to listen to Catherine's chest. Dr. Jones arrived immediately, dressed in green scrubs with his hair all awry. He listened to both sides of Catherine's chest then said to the nurses, "There are decreased breath sounds on both sides. Suction out the endotracheal tube quickly."

The nurse disconnected the ventilator hose from the endotracheal tube, put a small amount of saline down the tube, inserted a small suction catheter and then slowly pulled it out producing a sucking sound the whole time. She then attached an ambu bag and started giving her respirations manually. Catherine's status did not change. Her saturation was now eighty percent and her heart rate was dropping from one hundred eighty to around one hundred beats per minute.

Nate realized his little daughter was dying. He was afraid. He had experienced fear before in medical emergencies but this was a different kind of fear. Before, the fear was one of not figuring out what was wrong with his patient. It was a fear of a patient dying. It was a fear that excited and challenged him. If his patient died then it was one of those sad things that one learned to get used to. However, now this fear went to the pit of his stomach. He felt a panic he had not experienced before. He felt the horror a father feels when he is losing his child.

Dr. Jones then said, "Let's extubate her." He quickly peeled off the tape holding the endotracheal tube in place and pulled it out. The nurse gave him the ambu bag with a small rubber mask attached, which he put over Catherine's nose and mouth. He began squeezing the bag with slow forceful squeezes. Catherine's chest began to rise as Dr. Jones was able to pump fresh oxygen into her lungs. After several breaths her oxygen saturation began to increase, first to eighty-four percent, then eighty-nine percent, and finally to the normal ninety-five percent. The nurse showed Dr. Jones that the endotracheal tube he had removed contained a mucous plug that had blocked it.

"Fortunately it was just a blocked tube," Dr. Jones said to Nate in the very calm voice of a doctor "We will put a new one in and then get an x-ray to check for tube placement. It looks like she will be ok." Nate was relieved. He knew it could have been much worse. It could have been a collapsed lung or fluid in the lungs or a number of other things that could have ended her life.

Nate thanked him. He tried to act and talk like a doctor who was used to things like this. Dr. Jones and the nurses, however, knew how he really felt but went along with his pretense. Dr. Jones was able to easily insert another endotracheal tube. The follow-up x-ray revealed it was in the right place.

Nate sat back down next to Catherine. He leaned over and whispered, "You almost scared me to death you know, little girl. I'm sure you scared your mother also. I'm sure glad it was just a blocked tube." He held her hand gently squeezing it while he talked to her. After he was sure she was stable he went back home weak and exhausted and fell into a deep sleep. It was the first of many crises that he would experience as a father. He had been scared. He was grateful that it was over.

The next morning, his mother had breakfast ready for him. She gave him a hug; his father gave him a pat on the shoulder. It was Friday and his parents had decided after their visit to Catherine that morning that they would go back home to take care of a number of odds and ends before returning on Monday. When the three of them visited the NICU, they received some good news. Catherine's respiratory distress appeared to be getting a little better. She required less oxygen and less pressure with each breath. Also, her jaundice had leveled off and was slowly returning to normal. With that reassurance, Nate's parents left in good spirits.

Chapter Thirty-seven

WHEN NATE AWOKE EARLY SATURDAY MORNING HE knew what he had to do. It seemed clear to him now. He had been restless most of the night. There was something unfinished that had been weighing heavily on his mind, but he did not know exactly what it was. However, at four AM, it came to him. He got up a couple of hours later and put a folding chair into the trunk of his car along with his book, *A Tale of Two Cities*. He grabbed a cup of coffee and began driving; two hours later, he was at Angela's cemetery.

The cemetery that Angela and her parents were buried in was a large old cemetery that originally was on the outskirts of town, but now many years later was so surrounded by development that it seemed in the center of town. The cemetery had many old trees that threw shadows on the tombstones. The lush green of the well-kept lawn gave it the appearance of a park that was like a breath of fresh air in a world of cement and freeways. Parts of the cemetery were elevated due to the slight hilly aspect of that region. Angela's grave was next to her parent's graves on one of these elevations. There were small paved roads that ran through the grounds in a maze-like pattern. Angela's dad had bought their lots soon after the cemetery had opened. Thus they were near the front of the cemetery where they could be easily seen on the left as one entered the cemetery entrance.

Nate parked his car near Angela's grave. As he got out, he looked up to where Angela was buried, and it all came back to him. Angela flashed before him. He was at her funeral again sobbing at her gravesite surrounded by everyone there. Tears began to roll down his cheeks. He felt weak. He sat back down in the car. *I've got to get control of myself,* he heard himself say. After a few moments, he took a deep breath to calm down. He had an urge to drive back to Everston but then he thought, *I have to do this.* He opened the trunk of the car and took out the chair and the book. He took another deep breath to slow the beating of his heart then walked up to her grave. The grave had been covered the day before with sods of grass so that from a distance it did not appear new. With the chair in one hand and the book under his arm he stood there staring at the spot where he had left her just two days before.

Nate discovered that he felt close to Angela there. He knew what he was about to do was irrational, but he could not deny his feelings. He rarely did irrational things, so he thought, but this was simply something his heart told him that he had to do. Listening to his heart was new to him. He realized by doing so he might be led to far off, unfamiliar places. The thought of that made him apprehensive. However now, unlike before, he heard the siren whispers of his heart, whispers that he could not resist, whispers that he was learning to love.

He sat the chair down by her grave. "Angela it's me, Nate. I've come back to say hello and to say how much I miss you already." He opened the chair and sat in it facing her grave. He leaned forward with his hands together as if she could hear him better. "Angela, I miss you next to me at night. I miss feeling you. I miss hugging you before I go to sleep. I miss the sound of you breathing and the beat of your heart. I'm sure you miss me too wherever you are." Nate sobbed a little. He took out his handkerchief and dried his tears.

"I also wanted to let you know our daughter is doing ok. She gave me quite a scare the night of your funeral, but now she is doing better." Nearby, a groundskeeper was doing his usual trimming and raking while a number of visitors began to enter.

He opened his book and looked at it for a second and then turned to Angela's grave. "Remember that I told you that I was going to finish *A Tale of Two Cities*. I've read most of it to you already. I thought I would read it to you like I did before. I thought you would like that."

He wiped more tears from his eyes. "I will start from where we left off." He sat in the chair and began to read out loud. He didn't read in a whisper. He read just like he did when Angela was alive. He first read leaning forward and then after a while he sat back and crossed his legs. When he got tired of sitting he stood up and slowly walked around Angela's grave with the book open, continually reading. The visitors would pause as they entered the cemetery because they could hear him reading and because they had never seen such a sight before. The groundskeeper noticed him and edged closer. Nate stopped reading when he noticed the groundskeeper because he could see that he wanted to talk. The groundskeeper was a thin, elderly man with a leathery face that seemed to always be smiling. His smile revealed shiny white, loosely fitting false teeth that made his speech a little unusual. He wore an old straw hat for shade.

"Was she your wife?" he asked.

Nate hesitated for a moment. "Yes, she was my wife."

"I am so sorry. There are a number of graves here with young people in them and it is so sad, especially the babies. Did you have children?"

"Yes," said Nate rather proudly. "We have a daughter."

"A daughter who has lost her mother. I am sorry to have interrupted you but I like to pray for the folks buried here when I work. The more I know about them the better I can pray for them. It's one of the perks of my job. Do you mind if I pray for your wife?" the groundskeeper asked.

"Not at all," Nate replied. He didn't believe in prayer, *But what can it hurt?* he said to himself. "I would appreciate it. So would Angela," he added.

"So Angela is her name," the groundskeeper said thoughtfully. "I think it is the perfect name because now she is an angel," he said, smiling. He seemed kind of proud of himself. "Do you see?" he continued, "Angela, angel."

"Yes, I get it," Nate answered. "I'm sure she is an angel."

"There's lots of angels around here. That's why I am so fortunate to have the job I have. You know most folks don't believe in angels, but they are real. If people only knew that they were surrounded by all their loved ones they would feel a whole lot better when they came here." He looked around. "I think though that after a while, they start believing in angels. Know why?"

"Why?" Nate asked

"Because after a few visits they start to look calm and peaceful. I can tell. I can tell when the angels start talking to them, I sure can."

Nate just looked at him. He did not know what to say.

"Well I'd better get back to my work and let you get back to your reading. I do my best to keep this cemetery nice and clean for all of the visitors and of course for all of the angels."

"The cemetery looks nice," Nate replied, looking for something to say.

"Thanks," the groundskeeper said with a smile nodding his head. He then slowly drifted off continuing his work.

"Well Angela," Nate said with a smile, "that makes two who are praying for you. Father Jim said he was praying for you too. I'm not so sure about this prayer stuff so if it's ok with you, I'll just keep talking and reading to you for now." With that he continued reading for a little longer.

"You know Angela, I'm actually enjoying this book," Nate said, looking at his book after pausing from his reading. He then smiled and said, "Maybe there is hope for my disability." He looked at Angela's grave. "Fiction reading disability. You are something else, Angela. Who ever heard of such a thing? Only you could come up with something like that." A smile came to his face. He continued reading, and after about an hour he closed his book. "I don't think I can read anymore today. I think I am read out. I know I am a wimp when it comes to reading so please forgive me. I will be back because there still is a lot more to go. I will check on Catherine and let you know how she's doing. I'm going back to work Monday, Angela. Maybe you can pray for me. I will need all the help I can get." With that he folded up his chair and started to walk back to his car. After he had taken only a few steps he turned around. "Did I tell you that I love you? I don't think I did. I love you. I miss you terribly." With a tear in his eye he turned and went back to his car. As he left, visitors whispered to one another about what they had seen.

Chapter Thirty-eight

NATE WOKE UP MONDAY MORNING AND REACHED FOR Angela, but she wasn't there. For a moment he wondered why then he remembered she would never be there. The relief from the heartache that sleep had provided him was over. He sat up rubbing his face. He felt the deep longing one heart has for another heart that it was once one with. He wondered if it was all a dream. Then he thought about when he first met Angela and little Catherine. He couldn't decide if was a bad dream or a good dream. It seemed to be both.

The coffee pot had just finished brewing thanks to the timer. He poured himself a cup before going out onto the balcony. He had gotten up early so he could visit Catherine before he started rounds at the hospital. The city lights could be easily seen because the sun had not yet began to lighten the sky. He thought about that first night when he stood by Angela looking out over the city talking. He wondered again if out there somewhere there was someone who was just like Angela, but of course it wouldn't be Angela.

How life had changed the last nine months. How he had changed. He knew the thrill and joy of being a lover, the thrill of being lost in someone's love. Thanks to Angela his heart was able to love. Now that she was gone life had to go on. *I am the father of a little girl. I will be her father the rest of my life*, he thought to himself. He wondered what kind of father he would be. What would Catherine think of him when she was a grown woman? This was too much for him to think about now. There had been some good news the last few days. Dr. Warren said that Catherine's lungs were improving to the point that she might be able to come off the respirator soon. He started to feel a little happier.

Nate had gone to work many mornings when he was dead tired wishing he could stay in bed. This would be the first time he would go to work feeling empty inside. He wondered if he would be able to make it. However, the thought of seeing Catherine gave him the energy to get dressed. He then remembered that his mom and dad would be coming into town to stay with him for a few days. Unlike before he looked forward to them coming. He thought that his heart was filled only with darkness but the thought of these things brought a little light into it like the rays of the first morning sun.

When he got to the hospital he was surprised that there was no tube coming out of Catherine's mouth. Instead there was a small nosepiece that covered both nostrils that was attached to oxygen tubes. Nate knew that this was CPAP, or continuous positive airway pressure, which through her nose kept a gentle pressure in her lungs to keep them open while administering oxygen at the same time.

"She is a little fighter," the neonatal nurse said as Nate approached. "Yep, she just wiggled out that endotracheal tube all on her own. She did so well we decided all she needed was a little CPAP."

Nate bent down to look at her and whispered, "You are something else, you little girl. You are strong, just like your mother."

He smiled. He visited for about twenty minutes before going the to see patients. In the doctors' chart room the cardiologist who was on call briefed him on his patients he had taken care of during the weekend. He would make rounds in morning then to go his office in the afternoon to see patients.

After the on call doctor left he sat there looking at his charts. He thought he heard something. When he looked around there was Sandy with his usual cup of coffee. "Welcome back," she said.

He could always count on Sandy. She was the one thing he could always be sure of. "Thanks," he said as he took the cup from her. He took a sip. "I want to thank you for taking such good care of Angela and for being there at the visitation and funeral. I really appreciate it." Sandy could tell that this was from the bottom of his heart.

"Angela was a wonderful person," Sandy replied. "I knew the first time I met her why you had fallen in love with her. You two were really fortunate to have each other." She paused for a second. "I'd better get back to my patients." Nate felt comforted by what she had said.

He started down the hall to see his first patient when he saw Father Jim coming out of a patient's room. "Father Jim," he said to get his attention. Father Jim smiled when he saw him. "I want to tell you how much I appreciated you being there for Angela and myself all this time. The funeral was exactly what Angela would have wanted."

"Thanks, Nate," he replied. "I have been praying for Angela."

"I know," Nate said. "I told her so."

Father Jim looked surprised. "I am praying for you also."

"Thanks Father, but I don't think that works in my case."

"You never know," replied Father Jim as he walked on. "You never know."

Nate's parents arrived at the hospital before noon. Nate had finished rounds in time to join them as they visited Catherine. The nurse explained to them about the CPAP. She also said that they were going to put down a nasogastric feeding tube in order to start a special formula for premature infants that would be given in small amounts every three hours. They took it all in with a sense of wonder at the sophistication of modern medicine. Nate's mom then began talking to Catherine. He had never seen her act that way before. She was talking baby talk telling her about all the fun they were going to have when she was bigger. Nate wondered if this was really the same mother who had raised him. His dad as usual did not say much, but he smiled more than usual and seemed happier than he had seen him before. He thought to himself, *He never hugged me or told me he loved me, but he was always there just like he is here for Catherine.* He felt like hugging him but knew it would only embarrass him.

As the week went on Catherine continued to improve. On Tuesday, the CPAP wasn't needed anymore. She was moved to an incubator that was enclosed with see-through walls with four round doors that could be opened. Nate broke away at ten that morning to quickly visit Catherine. As he entered the NICU he saw Sandy standing by Catherine's incubator smiling at her. "She is a cutie pie," Sandy said when she saw Nate.

"She certainly is," Nate responded. Sandy had to leave quickly to go back to her patients. After a few minutes Nate had to leave also. Nate's parents came shortly afterwards. They would visit during the scheduled visiting hours before returning to Nate's apartment. Around three-thirty that afternoon Nate was surprised to see Gregg with a boy that looked to be around twelve years of age standing in the hallway looking through the glass window into the nursery. "How is she doing?" Gregg asked.

"She is doing well, improving every day," Nate replied.

"Glad to hear it," Gregg said. "I would like to introduce you to my son Henry. Henry, this is Dr. Williams, who I have been telling you about."

Nate remembered Samantha saying that Gregg did not visit his son from his first marriage; he was surprised to see them together. "Nice to meet you, Henry," Nate said as he reached out and shook his hand.

"I have been picking up Henry after school to help his mom, who works," Gregg said. "Henry says he wants to be a doctor. I thought you might be able to give him some advice."

Nate thought back to when he announced to his parents that he wanted to be a doctor. He remembered the pressure they put on him by telling him how difficult it was to get in medical school. He remembered them telling him he had to make better grades than everyone else. He wondered what he should say to this young man recently reunited with his father.

"Henry, I think you would make a good doctor," Nate began. "I enjoy being a doctor because I enjoy helping people. To be honest, I sometimes wish I had also considered one of the other many professions in the health care field that help people, like the nursing profession for example. They are all very rewarding. Whatever you choose I know you will be happy."

Henry said, "Thanks," and smiled.

Gregg held out his hand to Nate. "Thanks Dr. Williams. I'd better get Henry back home now."

To Nate there was no doubt that Gregg seemed like a different person. He now had a quiet manner. He thought before he spoke and he seemed to care for his son. As they walked off, Nate wondered if he would see him again. The other members of Angela's club also came by during the week, all expressing their relief that Catherine was doing better.

In the evenings, Nate's mom cooked some really delicious meals during which time they began to talk more than they ever had. They talked about everything from the weather to their family history. Nate's mom said that when Catherine came home, if he wanted them to, they would be more than happy to live there as long as needed to help with Catherine. Nate was greatly relieved because he had not really thought about how he was going to care for a small infant twenty-four hours a day.

By the next Saturday, Catherine had actually began to gain a little weight, first only a half an ounce a day then a whole ounce a day as her feedings increased. She still was not up to birth weight because she, like most premature infants, had lost about ten percent of her birth weight. She would probably not reach her birth weight until after two weeks of age. She continued to be tube fed because she would probably not nipple feed for another month at least.

Nate got into his car Saturday morning to go to the cemetery again because his heart was telling him that his task was not finished. This time he brought a thermos of water and a large umbrella that was on a pole with a sharpened end that could be inserted into the ground in case it rained. It would also provide shade. When he got there the sun was shining and the groundskeeper was nearby clipping the bushes. The groundskeeper saw him take his giant umbrella, chair, thermos, and book up to Angela's grave. Nate stopped at the foot of the grave. "Hi Angela. I'm back. Catherine's better." Now talking to Angela at her graveside seemed more natural than before. He was surprised that the wrenching pain he had experienced the first time he visited her grave was not there the second time. He put his chair under the large umbrella that he had stuck into the ground. The thermos sat by his chair with a large straw out the top. He had just opened the book when the groundskeeper came up.

"Hey," he said. Nate said "Hey" back. The groundskeeper continued. "I was curious if I might ask what you are reading."

"It's called *A Tale of Two Cities* by Charles Dickens. I was reading it to my wife before she died so I come here to finish reading it to her," Nate replied.

"That's mighty nice of you. I'm sure she enjoys it," the groundkeeper said. "Over the years, I've seen grieving relatives do a lot of different things. Of course, the most common thing is to leave flowers on the grave, but can you believe it, some folks leave food like fruit and stuff. It's like they think their loved ones are going to come out at night and eat it. Does that make any sense to you?"

"No it doesn't," Nate replied, wondering what the groundskeeper was going to say next.

"There are lots of folks who leave letters on the grave. I figure that they are only going to blow away and what good is that, so I usually collect the letters at night. It prevents the graveyard from becoming all cluttered, you see."

"Sure," said Nate.

The grounds keeper continued. "I have a whole collection. It's amazing what they write. Some of course simply say I love you, but others are really pitiful, confessing all sorts of things from having affairs the person didn't know about to stealing money and all sorts of things. I've come to the conclusion that confessing things to dead people is a lot easier than going to a priest, if you get what I mean."

Nate smiled. "I think you are right. I plan to pass this bit of wisdom on to a friend of mine who would especially appreciate it."

"Well, my name is Sam." He stuck out his hand.

"Mine's Nate."

"I want you to know you are the first and I think only one who has come out on a regular basis to read to the dead and on behalf of the dead I want to thank you."

"You're welcome," Nate replied and smiled, thinking Sam seemed a lot happier than a lot of people he knew.

The groundskeeper told him he had better get back to work. He slowly moved away as he clipped the nearby bushes. After he had left Nate started to read aloud. He was walking back and forth in front of Angela's grave reading aloud when he heard a young child's voice say, "What are you reading?" Nate looked down. There was a young girl around the age of eight or nine looking up at him.

"It's just a book," Nate said.

"My mommy reads me books sometimes but my dad doesn't."

"I'm sorry to hear that," Nate said.

"Yeah, I wish he did. We are here visiting where my grandpa is buried. He would read books to me." The little girl looked at the chair and umbrella.

"It looks like you are at the beach." Nate smiled. Then he heard her mother say, "There you are."

"Yes Mommy," she replied.

When the mom walked to the grave she stood speechless looking at Nate standing by his chair and umbrella. "He's reading a book, Mommy, can I listen?" the young girl asked.

The mother looked at Nate. "She's welcome to. I am reading *A Tale of Two Cities*," Nate said. "I have a baby daughter I hope to read to someday."

The mom smiled. "Can I listen too?" she asked.

"Sure," Nate replied as the mother sat down. When the grounds keeper saw the three of them he joined them at the grave. The three of them sat listening to Nate read. As people drove into the cemetery that morning, most stopped to observe a sight they had never seen before.

When he had finished reading, the three thanked him before leaving. He said goodbye to Angela. He told her that he would be back the next Saturday because he hadn't finished the book yet. He packed everything in his car and looked forward to visiting his little Catherine.

Chapter Thirty-nine

ANGELA BEGAN TO VISIT NATE AT NIGHT. SHE WOULD sometimes stand by his bed with a contented look on her face. Sometimes she would be in the kitchen at the sink. When he would speak to her she would turn around and smile but would not say anything. When he saw her he heard himself saying this is not a dream over and over again but he would then usually awaken in a sweat. He soon learned that when he found himself trying to convince himself that he was not dreaming he always was. Sometimes he and Angela were in a field together. Sometimes she would come close to kiss him, but their lips would never meet. He was both happy and confused when he had such dreams. He looked forward to them and dreaded them at the same time. For several weeks the dreams came often. Then slowly Angela began to visit him less and less and when she did, she did not stay long.

One evening he decided to open the packet of pictures Angela had asked Father Jim to give to him. He had seen them before. They were pictures of her and her parents as she grew up. They appeared to be taken using an old box camera. Some were in black and white; some were in color. Many of the pictures had creases across them, but you could still see Angela with either her mom or dad in their house or yard or on some vacation with mountains in the back. They were always smiling with their arms around one another. Nate thought to himself, *What a lucky kid she was to be loved like that.*

Then he saw a small strip of four pictures that had somehow gotten covered up. They were the pictures of him and Angela taken in a photo booth on the beach that wonderful night. He picked them up to see them closer. The first picture was of he and Angela kissing passionately without a care in the world. In the next picture they had their heads together smiling. The other two pictures were of them making funny faces. In each picture was the Angela he remembered. He couldn't believe that these were the only pictures of them together. He thought about all the pictures most lovers have of each other, pictures of their wedding, pictures from their showers, and pictures of themselves in different places. However they had no pictures like that. Catherine would only have these four little pictures of them together when she was grown. Nate sat back. Sadness came over him. They had never even given presents to one another. Only once had they dressed up and gone out together. He tried to comfort himself that he and Angela had something special, something that so many never have in their life. The fact that it was not recorded in pictures or by a wedding ceremony did not diminish it. He propped their pictures up against his bedside lamp as he got into bed. The next day Nate went to a card shop and purchased a card that he placed in front of the pictures. The front of the card said "To My Lover." Inside he had written, "Dear Angela, I will always love you. Nate." Each night thereafter he would look at their pictures before going to bed.

Catherine was considered a grower. She was still tube fed and in an incubator, but all her IVs were out. Her temperature was now easier to maintain, which meant she could be held swaddled in an infant blanket for short periods of time, which Dr. Warren encouraged. Dr. Warren said the human touch and cuddling was very important to Catherine's health and development. Catherine seemed more alert each day. She would stretch her arms and legs a lot and would seem to look around. She responded to sounds and startled easily. Nate and his mom would hold her as much as possible. Even Nate's father held her at times. Sandy asked if she could hold her occasionally to which Nate readily agreed.

When Nate held her he would look into her open eyes, which fascinated him. He could imagine how all the sights and sounds were imprinting themselves into her young mind. He hoped his face, his voice and his touch were helping shape a part of her unconscious that would give her strength and comfort in her life. The depth of her eyes captivated him. Her eyes were like a portal into the past with all of human evolution recorded in the workings and structure of her brain. Looking into her eyes was much different than looking into the eyes of a pet or other animal. There was something so different that it was a little frightening. It was as if he was staring into another dimension, something not of this world. It occurred to him that maybe he was glimpsing the spiritual realm, but then he quickly discarded this thought. Whatever it was, he could not help but look into her eyes as much as he could.

Keeping busy helped Nate not think about Angela. Sometimes, when he was conducting a resuscitation or doing a catheterization, he would not think about Angela at all. But then at unexpected times he would almost double over with an ache he could not soothe. It would come like a severe muscle cramp that took its own time to go away. However, as the weeks went on, these aches came less often.

He had just finished morning rounds with the charts under his arm when he headed to the doctors' charting room behind the nursing station. He had just opened the first one when an overwhelming sadness took over his whole being. He could only think how much he missed Angela. He put his head in his hands and began to weep silently. He did not know how long he had sat there when he heard a chair being dragged beside his. He looked up, and there was Sandy with a kind concerned look on her face. "How about a cup of coffee?" she asked as she held a cup in her hand. "I know this is not that good for you, but here it is if you would like it."

"Thanks Sandy," he said as he took it.

"It's not that easy, is it?" Sandy said.

"No it's not," Nate replied.

"Well, hang in there, Doc. We need you." With that she put her hand on his shoulder giving it a gentle squeeze as she walked back to her patients. Nate sipped his coffee as he realized that the ache inside of him was beginning to slowly go away. How thankful he was for Sandy.

That afternoon he went to his office. Seeing patients in his office was usually less stressful than seeing the sicker patients in the hospital. His first patient was a twenty-eight year old who complained that his heart seemed to race off and on. His EKG and laboratory tests were normal. He denied excessive use of caffeine or alcohol, and he did not smoke. Nate ordered him a Holter monitor, which was a recording device that he would wear for twenty-four hours that would record any rapid or irregular heartbeats. Nate felt fairly confident that anxiety was the underlying cause of this young man's symptoms. He felt sorry for him. He was beginning to understand the sorrows and suffering most people underwent now that as a physician he had both his heart and mind engaged. He realized that the joy of being a physician was beginning to come back to him, or maybe it was appearing for the first time.

His second patient was an eighty-four-year-old grandmother

accompanied by her sixty-year-old daughter. She was in for her routine check of her aortic stenosis, which was a narrowing of the opening of the heart valve that opened into the aorta. The stenosis was slowly but progressively worsening, which meant her heart had to pump harder to push the blood out of the narrowed opening as she aged. The stress on her heart had caused her to be in moderate heart failure, but she was in no distress and seemed to be tolerating it well.

"Will it be long before I die?" she asked innocently.

"Oh, I don't think you are anywhere close to death, Mrs. Kelly," Nate replied. Her daughter smiled and looked relieved.

"I'm sorry to hear that," her mother said.

"You are?" Nate replied in an effort to be polite and carry on a conversation.

"You see, my husband died last year. I want to join him soon."

"I'm sure he will wait for you," Nate said with a smile. He had said similar things many times in his career, not because he believed it, but because it went over well with patients. However, to his surprise, this time it seemed to come from his heart instead of the collection of phrases that he had found over time worked. Her daughter grabbed Nate's hand and thanked him for being such a kind caring doctor. This made him feel good. He did not dismiss it as useless sentimentality as he usually did.

Saturday rolled around again, and he needed to go to the cemetery one last time. He only had a couple of chapters left, and he was determined to finish them. He got to Angela's grave early glad that there was no one around. Her grave no longer frightened him or threw him for an emotional roller coaster ride like it did the first time he visited it. Now it only brought a feeling of sweet sadness of what they had together. He was thankful for the time he had with Angela because now he had a grateful heart.

He set up his chair and umbrella as before. Then, looking

at the gravesite, he began talking. "Angela, little Catherine is continuing to do very well. She is in an incubator, and we are getting to hold her. When I hold her I am already telling her about you. Angela, today I will finish our book. I may not be able to come as often after today. I know that you are not really here, but it comforts me to come here."

He sat down and began to read out loud. Sam, the groundskeeper, was nowhere to be seen. He finished one chapter, took a drink out of his thermos and then stood up reading as he walked slowly in a circle. Near the end of the last chapter he noticed the little girl he had met before sitting there listening. "Hi," he said.

"I told my mom you would be here, but she didn't believe me. Can I listen?" she asked.

"Sure," he replied." He started to read and soon came to the famous last line of the book, "It is a far, far better thing that I do now than I have ever done; it is a far, far better rest that I go to than I have ever known." That last line struck deep within his heart. A tear came to his eye, but he did not cry.

The little girl thought for a minute and asked, "What does that mean?"

It took Nate a second to regain himself. "There was this man named Sydney Carton who gave up his life in order to save the life of another man."

"You mean he died?"

"Yes."

"Did that really happen?" she asked.

"No, it is only fiction," Nate responded.

"Have you ever known anyone who did that?"

A lumped formed in Nate's throat. He managed to say in a low voice, "Yes, I have."

"Are you a preacher?" she asked.

"No, I'm not."

"Do you go to church?"

"No, not really."

Do you believe in God?" she asked again.

Nate thought a second. "Everyone believes in God a little."

"My dad doesn't," the little girl responded. "He says it's all made up. He won't go to church with my mom and me. My mom says that what we believe will help him."

"I think that's true," Nate heard himself say.

Just then her mother appeared and approached them both. "I hope she is not bothering you," the mother said.

"Oh no. She is a very nice young lady," Nate replied.

"Well, we have to go now. Tell the nice man goodbye, Catherine."

Nate looked surprised.

"Goodbye," said Catherine.

Nate watched them walk away. He then said softly, "Goodbye Catherine." He wondered about the relationship between Catherine and her father. He hoped it was good.

Nate stood by Angela's grave not saying anything for a few minutes. "Angela," he began, "I may not come back for a while. I know you are not visiting me at night as often either. That doesn't mean we don't love each other as much as before. It's just that I'm sure we both have a lot to do and life must go on." He paused before continuing. "You know my busy schedule and soon little Catherine will be coming home. I don't know what you have to do, but I'm sure it is very important. However, I will let you know if anything major happens. I'd better go now. I love you. Goodbye." He took one last look at Angela's grave and felt the heartache of her loss again, but now it was not an overwhelming heartache as before. Now he knew that life could go on. He knew the heartache he had would become like a well-healed scar, not painful but always there to remind him of the love they once shared.

He folded up his chair and got into his car and drove back home. He would not come back to her grave again until Catherine was old enough to inquire about her mother. But for several years afterwards, the townspeople talked about the man who read to the dead.

Chapter Forty

THE WEEKS BEGAN TO SLIP BY QUICKLY. CATHERINE continued to grow and be the model premature infant. Nate's parents would stay with him during the week and go back home on weekends. Nate would always arrive early each morning at the hospital to have time to see Catherine before starting rounds. He would leave late holding Catherine before he left. Life was busy leaving little time to think beyond his daily interactions with patients, Catherine, and his parents. Each morning, Sandy was there with a cup of coffee and her smile and her encouraging words. Slowly but surely the pain of the loss of Angela lessened and feelings of gratitude for the precious time that he had with her increased.

Catherine was now four weeks old and weighed close to three and one-half pounds. She still was fed with a small feeding tube. It would be another two weeks before she would be able to coordinate her suck and swallowing to be able to be bottle-fed. She was beginning to fill out and look more like a normal infant with her increased body fat. She also had longer periods of vigorous stretching and wiggling. All of her five senses seemed to be coming into high gear. She would startle at noises. She would look around at everything, and was comforted when being held. Nate would always tell her that he was her daddy when he held her.

Cindy and Rick organized a baby shower for Nate and his parents, which was perfect timing because the three of them were starting to get worried about being ready for Catherine when she came home. Nate's mom was starting to feel a nesting instinct. She began to make lists of everything they would need. It was hard for Nate to think of much more than a baby crib, bottles, and diapers. Before they did further planning, Nate and his parents decided to wait until after the shower when they would know what they had.

Cindy and Rick's house was a nice four-bedroom, typical suburban home with a landscaped front yard and a fenced backyard. It was about ten years old and was very clean and well kept. Most of the interior of the house looked like what one would expect as far as furniture and decorating goes except for one bedroom, which Rick had turned into a study. Here there was a couch with rustic wooden arms, a wooden desk with a cane back chair and a couple of floor-to-ceiling wooden bookcases filled with science books. The walls were decorated with various pictures of nature.

When Nate and his parents arrived, Cindy, Rick, Tony, Rita, and Samantha were already there along with Sandy who had also been invited. To everyone's surprise, Gregg also showed up separately. He was very quiet but seemed friendly nonetheless. Father Jim was not there, but Nate figured he would be late as usual, which was the case. Cindy had gone to the trouble of putting up some baby decorations and ribbons above the doors. Nate had never been to a shower before and was sure it was something for mothers only. He smiled and greeted everyone but he felt uncomfortable. *How does one act at a baby shower?* he asked himself. Cindy offered them all punch along with some snacks as they all engaged in lighthearted small talk.

They then gathered in the living room. Nate sat in a large chair in the middle. Nate's mom had a pen and paper ready to record who gave what presents so they could write thank you notes. Sandy sat by Nate's mom and offered to help, which she appreciated. Nate smiled at everyone as he looked at the pile of wrapped presents in front of him. He tried to hide the fact that he didn't like being at the center of attention. Before he could start there was a knock at the door and Father Jim entered, made the sign of the cross in the air and said "Peace be with you." He smiled then took a back seat. Everyone smiled when they saw him. Somehow this impromptu blessing for folks who didn't believe in blessings made them feel good.

Before Nate could start to open any presents, Tony stood up as he usually did when he wanted to speak and be the center of attention. "Nate," he said. "We all know that you know a lot about hearts, but when it comes to babies we are not so sure." Everyone laughed a little. Before he could go on, Cindy spoke up.

"So we asked ourselves what would Angela want us to do and we all agreed that this is what she would want." She looked at Rick who then went into another room and came out with an armload of books. He went back again and the result was a huge pile of books of all sizes and shapes. "We bought every book on taking care of an infant that Angela's bookstore had. We expect you to read every one before Catherine comes home." They all laughed again.

The books covered every conceivable topic relevant to infants. There was Dr. Spock's book. There were books on feeding and schedules. Some advocated very flexible schedules while others insisted on rigid schedules. There were books on what music infants should listen to and what were the best crib side mobiles and how to combat colic and how to get some sleep. Nate had never realized there were so many things to consider when taking care of a newborn.

The presents consisted of a used baby crib that looked like new from Cindy and Rick. Inside was a baby book of insects. Rick said it was never too early to start to learn some science. Tony and Rita's present was a set of bottles with nipples designed for a premature infant along with a baby bottle warmer. They also gave him a book on Italian recipes for children. Tony added that Nate could wait a little while before starting the Italian cooking. Samantha gave a cute baby hat and mittens. Gregg's present was a small but beautiful silver spoon. Father Jim's present was a very nice pink silk blanket with pictures of tiny infants in the corners that could almost pass for angels.

The last present to be opened was from Sandy. It was beautifully wrapped with ribbons and bows. When Nate finally got it opened, there beneath thin white tissue, was a beautiful, elegant infant formal dress, the kind of dress that every parent would be proud to have his or her newborn's picture taken in. Even Nate was impressed. As he thanked Sandy he could not help but notice the glow of her eyes as she looked back at him.

Nate looked again at all the books and presents from everyone around him. Inside of him feelings of warmth, peace, and joy all blended into one feeling, which only be described as what one feels on coming home.

"I want to say something to you guys," Nate began. "My mom and dad are the only family I've ever had, and unfortunately up until recently I've been so busy that we were not together as much as we should have been." He looked at his mom and then gave a special look to his dad that he knew would probably make him uncomfortable. "I am happy to say that has now been rectified. I am also happy to say that my family has grown recently. Now I have a daughter, as you all know." They all smiled as he held up the dress Sandy had given him. "But I am also so fortunate to have you guys. You are my family now, like it or not." Nate smiled as he said it. Everyone else smiled also. "So thank you for being my family. Thank you for caring so much for Catherine and me. Thank you also for all these presents and most of these books." Everyone laughed a little.

Cindy immediately brought out wine glasses and poured everyone a glass of red wine. "Here is a toast to Nate and Catherine," Cindy said, raising her glass.

Then Tony stood up. "I would like to make a toast to Nate and Father Jim. As you know, my son Frankie has been in some trouble recently. However, Father Jim and Nate had a good talk with him and now he is doing good. He's on probation and has to go to boot camp, but he is trying hard and doing well. Here is to these two super fathers." Tony raised his glass and everyone raised his or her glass also.

Father Jim stood up. "Tony, Nate and I know you appreciate us talking with Frankie, but it's your and Rita's love that has saved Frankie. That is what saves all of our children. Parents are not perfect. We make mistakes, sometimes serious mistakes, and there are things not in our control. When I hear grown children talk about their parents, it is those parents who simply stuck by them and loved them through thick and thin that helped them the most despite their parents' failings. You and Rita have done that and I offer a toast to you." Everyone put down their glass and clapped. Nate sat there astonished at what Father Jim said. *So it all boils down to that*, he thought. How simple and how true was what he had told them. Nate would go on to read many books on parenting, but he would never forget those words. Nate realized that what Father Jim had said was the most valuable present he had received that night.

Everyone enjoyed the rest of the evening, which was filled with smiles and laughter and warm conversations. Nate and his parents loaded up all the presents and books and thanked everyone again.

That night, Nate's mother made a list of everything else they needed. She then made a plan of what and when to buy next. For some reason, Nate was exhausted. He said goodnight to his mom and dad and got ready for bed. He was tired, but it was a pleasant tiredness, and he looked forward to a restful sleep. He walked into the bathroom and saw himself in the mirror. He looked older than he had before. As he stood there he realized that he was looking at a father who would soon bring home a baby daughter who would be completely dependent on him. He became terrified. He knew nothing about taking care of a baby. His hope for a restful night's sleep vanished as worry filled his mind. Nate did not know this was something he would have to get used to as a father.

Catherine was now six weeks old, which meant she was at thirty-four weeks gestation and was beginning to take all her feedings by nipple. The feedings were slow, taking about thirty minutes every three hours, but she was gaining weight and maintaining her temperature in an open crib. Dr. Warren thought she might go home in about two weeks if everything went well. Nate suddenly become very busy with patients but slipped down as often as he could to hold and feed Catherine. His parents would stay with him during the week and go home on weekends, but now they were making arrangements to stay all the time once Catherine came home. Sandy often dropped by the NICU to hold Catherine. During this time she and Nate's parents became good friends. Nate's mom mentioned to Nate several times how much she liked Sandy. Nate would agree that she was a wonderful person then go about his work.

The day finally came for Catherine to go home. Nate and his parents had arrived that Friday afternoon with a car seat and Sandy's special outfit. She was now two months old and weighed four and one-half pounds. She gulped down her feedings in twenty minutes but still needed to be fed every three hours. The day before she had gotten her routine two-month immunizations, which, after a short cry, did not seem to bother her. The nurses reported that she was a model baby. She did not cry except right before her feedings. After each feeding she would go right to sleep. When she was awake she was the most pleasant premature infant they had ever seen. They all felt she would give them no trouble at home and that is what Nate and his parents expected to happen.

The NICU nurses had put ribbons on Catherine's crib and had a poster board attached to the back of the crib that said goodbye to Catherine and that they would miss her. After the three o'clock feeding the nurse told Nate he could dress her. Nate had brought the special outfit that Sandy had given him at the shower. Nate slowly took off the small infant gown. With much pride he carefully put Sandy's dress on her. Everyone smiled, especially Sandy who was standing by her crib the whole time. All the nurses including Sandy stood together as a group to say goodbye as they left.

Catherine slept in her car seat all the way home. She even stayed asleep as Nate carried her up to the apartment. She slept soundly until five PM when she awoke, stretched and looked around. Nate held her in his arms and said, "I love you little girl." He then walked around showing her the apartment. She fed again at six and went right to sleep as usual. Nate's mom made a wonderful dinner. They all felt very happy to have Catherine home with them. Nate's mom said that Nate had not been a model baby. She went into detail how he cried and kept them awake for months. She was so thankful Catherine was not like her dad. At eight Catherine again woke up, looked around and seemed content. Starting around eight thirty she became a little fussy. By nine she was starting to cry until Nate's mom fed her, after which she again seemed very content going right to sleep.

Nate could not believe how easy it was to care for an infant. All three of them were thankful for their good fortune.

At nine forty-five she began to cry. It was not whimper, it was an all-out cry that startled them all. Nate immediately checked her over. Everything seemed all right. He then tried walking her around, during which she would stop crying maybe for a minute before starting back again. Nate's mom theorized that she was having trouble having a bowel movement, but Nate reminded her that she had had a good bowel movement right before leaving the hospital. Nate's dad said that maybe she had gas and needed some sort of gas medicine. Nate responded that the nurses at the hospital never mentioned a gas problem. Multiple theories as to the cause of her crying were bantered around amongst the three of them until midnight when she fed again and went right to sleep.

They were all relieved. Every infant has an occasional fussy spell they told themselves. They decided that they should try to get some sleep. Nate's mom volunteered to do the three AM feeding after which they all hit the sack immediately. Their rest was short lived when they were awakened by a piercing cry at one AM. They all rushed to the crib to see what was wrong. As they looked at Catherine, Nate and his parents could not believe such a loud shrill cry could come from such a small infant. Nate picked her up and began walking around the apartment. Catherine settled down and seemed sleepy. After twenty minutes, Nate very gently put her in her crib. He turned around and quietly tiptoed away but was only able to take about three steps when the piercing cry returned.

It was now two AM. Nate and his parents began to get worried. Maybe she was hungry, but she had taken such a good feeding at midnight that that was probably not the case. Nate's mom said maybe she was getting sick and that Nate should call the pediatrician. Nate considered it for a moment then said he was not going to be one of those parents who pediatricians talk about who called them in the middle of the night because the baby is crying. Finally at three AM Catherine again fed like a champ and went to sleep for about an hour but was back at it at four AM. Now it seemed that she was fairly content as long as someone held her and walked around the room, but as soon as she was put in her crib the piercing cry came back. This routine continued until her nine AM feeding after which she slept like a baby for two and one-half hours.

Everyone was exhausted. Their nerves were shattered. Nate's mom said she was getting too old for this and didn't know if she could take it. Nate's dad said he couldn't remember when he had been so tired. Nate said that the night was worse than taking call. All day Saturday Catherine was again the perfect infant, feeding and sleeping and looking around, but as evening came she again started her loud cry unless she was held and walked around. This perfect day and miserable night routine would keep up for a couple of weeks until finally she began to sleep a little more at night. At her one-week appointment the pediatrician said he was proud of all of them including Catherine. Catherine had gained over a half a pound and looked the perfect picture of health. When Nate's mom asked about the nighttime crying and Catherine's need to be held at night, the pediatrician smiled and said this would all improve with time. The three of them thought to themselves, *How much time, Lord, how much time.* Nate's mom thought to herself that maybe Catherine was like her father after all.

The pediatrician was right; after another week or two, Catherine began to settle down and sleep more at night. She was now on an every-four-hour feeding schedule. Each week she seemed more bright eyed and more interested in her environment. Nate and his parents decided that they were going to survive after all.

Chapter Forty-one

NATE WAS NOW A FATHER. HE PURCHASED A DIGITAL camera and began to take pictures. He took pictures of his parents holding Catherine. They took pictures of him holding her. He took pictures of her feeding and sleeping and stretching, and he retook all these pictures on his phone. One morning he went in to feed her and he was amazed to see her looking up at her animal mobile smiling. He looked closer to make sure. He had seen what he thought was a smile before while she slept but figured it was just a reflex, but now she was smiling at her mobile. As he picked her up she quit smiling for a second, but when he said "Good morning sweet girl," she smiled again. She was now a little more than four months old, which meant that she would be a little over a month in age if she had been born at term.

Nate rushed into the kitchen where his mom and dad had staggered in to make coffee. "You won't believe this. She's smiling," he blurted out. The three of them gathered around and for twenty minutes looked at Catherine talking baby talk to her in between their exclamations of wonderment. Nate said he knew she would be smart. He let his parents know that many babies did not smile until almost two months of age. He whipped out both his digital camera and phone and took numerous pictures.

At work that day almost all of his conversations with the nurses and fellow physicians ended with, "You won't believe what my little Catherine did today." He would grab his phone and show them her picture. This set a pattern that he would repeat over and over again every time Catherine did something new like reaching out at four months of age or rolling over at six months and everything in between. The nurses were pretty good at pretending to be impressed, but his colleagues' eyes would glaze over as they looked at the small picture of a bald-headed baby that to them looked like every other baby in the world. Then they would usually say something like, "Thanks, but I'd better be going. Lots to do you know," before quickly disappearing leaving Nate alone looking at his phone. This, however, did not discourage Nate who looked forward each day to showing off Catherine.

Catherine was now over six months old and Nate's mom was starting to get a little worried about her son. He essentially did nothing but go to work and obsess over Catherine. She was surprised that he didn't go out with friends before she realized that he really had few friends. His mom kept thinking about what a cute sweet girl Sandy was but she did not want to interfere by saying anything. Finally one morning at breakfast before work she decided to say something.

"Nate, I think you need a break or something. It would be good for you to get out of the house occasionally."

"Sure, Mom," Nate said as he continued eating, not really paying attention to her.

"I read in the paper that this Saturday local artists are having an art sale at the city park," she said as she buttered her toast.

"Great," Nate replied in a non-interested tone.

"You could use a nice painting in the apartment. Why don't you go down there? Dad and I will babysit Catherine before we go back home Saturday night. We will be back Sunday night but at least you could get out of the apartment Saturday during the day."

"I'll think about it," Nate replied.

"Maybe you could take one of your nurse friends with you who might have a better appreciation for art than you do," his mom added.

Nate put his arm around her. "Mom, are you trying to tell me I have poor taste in art?"

"Oh get out of here," she said playfully pushing him away.

At lunch that day Sandy saw Nate sitting in the main cafeteria eating by himself. She noticed that had his phone lying next to his plate and that he was smiling to people he knew as they passed by. She grabbed a sandwich and asked if she could join him.

"It's unusual to see you here," she said. "You usually eat in the doctors' private lounge, don't you?" she asked.

"Yes," he responded. "But the selection is much better out here." He smiled.

Sandy took a bite of her sandwich. "You know, Nate, you are a changed man."

"How so?" he responded.

"Well for one thing you are eating out here with the common folk. For another, you are being friendly to everyone. This is very strange, you know."

Nate smiled again. "Who can understand the working of the human heart? By the way, did I show what Catherine did yesterday?" he asked.

"Yes you did," Sandy responded flatly.

"Oh," Nate said as he put down the phone he had just picked up.

"I've got to tell you something, Nate." Sandy shifted in her seat. "Everyone here, well, that is almost everyone here, has their own family and their own children and as much as you would like them every day to be overly delighted hearing about your family, they just aren't. If you want people to stop avoiding you like the plague, I would recommend not talking quite as much as you are about little Catherine."

Nate looked thoughtful for a second. "You think so?"

"I think so," Sandy replied.

"I guess I do tend to overdo things a bit," Nate said again thoughtfully.

"A bit," Sandy replied. "But I like you anyway." She smiled and took a bite of her sandwich.

Nate liked being around Sandy. For some reason he felt better when she was around. She always seemed to have him figured out somehow. He sat there thinking of what his mother had said that morning.

"I think my mother is right," Nate said as he ate.

"Right about what?" Sandy asked.

"She says I need to take a break from Catherine and get out and do something. How about you, you ever feel that way?" he asked.

"Sure. All parents feel that way sometimes. The best parents do, at least that's what I've been told," Sandy said. Nate knew she was kidding him a little. He felt a little stupid.

"Did you know that starving artists are having a sale in the city park this Saturday?" Nate asked.

"No I didn't," Sandy responded. "I hate to see artists starve," she added.

"Me too," Nate replied. Nate sat there in silence. He wanted to ask Sandy to go with him. *What if she turns me down?* he thought.

Sandy also sat and waited for Nate to say something. Finally she finished eating. "I guess I'd better get back. You know how these doctors are if everything isn't done just the way they want it." She started to get up.

"Wait Sandy," Nate finally said. "Would you like to go with me to the park? We just might find a painting we like and help some future Van Gogh to eat."

Sandy sat back down and looked at him. Her eyes narrowed. "Are you asking me out to go with you to the park?" she asked like she didn't hear him correctly.

"Yes," Nate said. He began to feel weak. Maybe he had crossed some line or said the wrong thing. *It's all mother's fault*, he told himself.

"I'd love to," Sandy replied with a soft smile.

Nate felt relieved. "How about I pick you up at two?"

"That would be great," Sandy said as she walked off.

As Saturday approached, Nate felt a little nervous about his outing with Sandy. *I shouldn't be nervous*, he told himself. She was now only a friend, and friends hang out together sometimes, that's all. Saturday morning he walked into the kitchen wearing a nice pair of slacks and a sports shirt. His mom was sitting there drinking coffee. She looked surprised.

"I'm taking your advice, Mom," he said as he entered. "I'm going to the artist sale you recommended."

His mom looked up and asked, "Alone?"

"No Mom. Sandy is going with me," Nate answered.

His mom's eyes widened. She put down her cup. "Sandy is such a nice sweet girl. I just love her."

"Now don't get any ideas. We are just friends and nothing more," Nate reassured her. His mom just smiled and seemed to have a slight twinkle in her eye.

Nate picked up Sandy at two in the afternoon as they had planned. Sandy had arranged for David to visit a friend that afternoon so she could be free. As Nate walked up to her door she came out shutting the door behind her. Sandy looked lovely. Her hair had been recently styled with a cut that made it seem to flow around her ears to the back of her head. She was wearing a cute blouse that tied at the bottom in front that did not quite reach her well-fitted denims that had embroidered flowers on each leg at the bottom. She was smiling and looked fresh and vibrant; Nate could not help but take a deep breath when he saw her.

"You look very nice," Nate said as he looked at her.

"Thank you. Do you think I'm appropriately dressed for starving artists?" she asked.

Nate thought she looked wonderful. "Yes, definitely," he said with enthusiasm, not thinking about the little joke she had made. Nate felt free. For a few hours they wouldn't be parents or professionals. They would be free from all the worries that normal people have. They would simply be two friends who for a short time would pretend to be art critics and enjoy life.

The Everston city park looked a lot like Central Park in New York only in miniature. From the air it appeared to be a green postage stamp in the middle of a sprawling city. It was large enough to have running and bike trails, several tennis courts, and multiple concrete picnic tables that sat under large old oak and pine trees. On one side of the park was space designated for vendors to set up booths to display everything from home crafts to home cooking, which happened once or twice a month. This week, starving artists had come from miles around to display their paintings hoping someone would finally appreciate their artistic ability. Alongside were booths selling homemade ice cream, turkey legs, cotton candy, and pastries of various sorts.

Nate found a parking space about a block from the park. The afternoon was pleasant with the temperature in the seventies with just a few clouds in the sky. Around the displays a moderate crowd had gathered that consisted of parents, kids playing, old folks, and a few dogs on leashes. Everyone was in a joyful mood. Between the oohs and ahs that emanated in front of each painting could be heard laughter and joking. Not everyone looked like an artist. There were a number of grandparent artists along with a few normal-appearing people. Apparently a few true artists were there with long hair and beards dressed in simple wrinkled tee shirts. Prices ranged from thirty-five dollars for small five by seven paintings to three hundred dollars for larger ones.

Sandy became animated when she saw all the paintings. "Some of these are really good," she said as she grabbed Nate's arm to show him one she liked. There were a lot of nature scenes of mountains and meadows and lakes, but Sandy pulled him in front of a painting of a very thin Texas long horn steer that stood in an obviously overgrazed pasture who looked right at the viewer as if to say, "There's gotta be something better than this."

Nate smiled. "Now that is an original. I really feel for that cow," Nate said as he studied the painting.

Sandy laughed. "Me too. I think there is a hidden message in there somewhere," she said.

"Yeah, like don't eat me," Nate said with a smile.

"Aw, come on," Sandy said, pulling him to another painting. The next one was a canvas full of paint dabs of different colors with several patterns weaving in and out of one another that didn't seem to make sense. "What do you see here?" Sandy asked.

Nate put his hand to his chin and looked closely at it. "I think it represents an explosion in an Easter egg factory."

Sandy pushed his shoulder and said, "You're hopeless. Let's get an ice cream."

Nate got a plain vanilla cone while Sandy ordered one with nuts and chocolate chips. Nate watched as Sandy tried to eat hers, catching every little drip with her tongue before it left the cone. He couldn't get over how cute she looked.

"What are you, just a plain vanilla guy?" she asked.

"Yep. I'm also a man of few words but many actions," Nate replied.

"Ok man of few words, let's go and look at some more paintings," Sandy returned. As they walked, Sandy put her arm inside his. It just happened naturally when she moved close to him to let someone by. She left it there. Nate acted like it was perfectly natural also, but deep down inside he felt a little thrill stirring. The air was cool, the sun was shining, Sandy had hold of his arm, and Nate realized he hadn't felt this good in a long, long time.

Sandy stopped in front of the next painting and just stared at it in silence. It was a painting of a cottage. It had pale stone walls with a light brown roof that had a chimney made of light red bricks arising from the far side. The two windows in front were simple and square. In between the windows was a door with an arched top that had a curved natural walkway leading up to it. Flowers and colorful bushes adorned the outside walls of the cottage that sat on a lawn that had a stream that curved in front of the house. A stone bridge crossed the stream that was lined with larger stones. Two or three small ducks could be seen near the bank. Overshadowing the house from behind were large trees in autumn foliage. To the left of the house was a vine-covered trellis from which was suspended a wooden swing that could hold three people. Upon closer examination, one could see next to the swing a mother in a blue dress looking out at the stream holding an infant in a white blanket.

Nate stood alongside of Sandy looking silently at the scene with her. "I feel like a happy family lives there," Sandy said solemnly.

"Me too," Nate agreed. The picture was three by four feet with a price tag of two hundred dollars. Nate noticed a small tear in one of her eyes.

"I like that painting," Sandy whispered. After a moment more she walked away without saying anything. Nate watched her leave. He knew deep within his heart what he wanted to do.

Sandy was walking fast, but Nate caught up with her quickly. "I have to go to the little boy's room. How about I meet you back at the ice cream place."

"Sure," Sandy said with a slight smile as she continued walking. Nate headed to the other side of the park where the restrooms were but as soon as he was out of her sight he turned and went back to the painting. The painter who had stepped away had returned. He was delighted that Nate was interested in his painting. He was obviously in his seventies, had a full gray beard, and was slightly overweight with a very contented and peaceful look on his face.

"I have a close friend who really likes your painting. Can you tell me about it?" Nate asked.

The elderly man smiled. "That is the house I always wanted to grow up in," he said. "The woman holding me is my mother who also dreamed of a cottage like that. My dad left us when I was a baby and my mom and I talked a lot about our dream house when I was growing up. I promised to buy her that house when I grew up but I never had the money so I decided to paint her dream house for her but she died just as I was finishing it. Unfortunately she never saw it."

Nate couldn't believe how much this painting meant to him and how fortunate it was that Sandy had found it.

"I just want someone to have this who also dreams of having such a house," the old man added.

"I know someone who fits that description exactly who would love to have your painting. May I buy it?" Nate asked.

"Yes," he responded. "It is two hundred dollars if you can afford it."

Nate pulled out his checkbook. He wrote him a check for

three hundred dollars and thanked him for the painting. The elderly man was obviously moved "God bless you son," he said thankfully. Nate smiled at being called son. The artist hung a brown paper covering over it to protect it. Nate took it back to the ice cream vendor and hid it to one side.

Sandy walked up looking for him. "I've got a surprise for you," Nate said, pulling the painting out to where she could see it. He lifted the brown paper covering slightly so she could see. Sandy gasped.

"Nate," she shouted. "Oh you shouldn't have. I can't accept this," she exclaimed.

"Nothing could stop me from getting this for you," Nate replied. "You have helped me so much; this is just my very small way of saying thank you. It's yours and that's final," he said authoritatively.

Sandy hugged his neck and bounced up and down like an excited kid. "Thank you," she said over and over again.

Nate smiled. He felt very proud. "I hope you have a place to hang it," Nate said.

"Yes, I have the perfect place. Would you help me hang it?" Sandy asked.

"You bet," answered Nate.

They drove home quickly. There was an empty wall space in her living room that was in need of a painting. Sandy found a picture hanging kit with nails and wire. Nate first attached a wire to the back of the frame. After some serious analysis as to how high it should be, he was able to get the nails in the wall at the right place. Sandy was right by his side handing him nails and wire and anything else he needed. He stepped upon a stepladder to reach everything while Sandy stood close to him holding the ladder.

"Oh Nate, it's going to be beautiful, just beautiful," Sandy commented as he worked. He had never felt so happy hanging a picture before. He was glad to see Sandy so ecstatic. He hung it up and after a few adjustments to get it level they both stood back to admire it. They then both sat down on a nearby couch with their shoulders almost touching and looked at it in silence. They leaned back and rested their heads on the soft back of the couch letting the painting fill their mind.

"I want David and I to live in that cottage," Sandy said wishfully.

"Actually, in some ways it reminds me of this house," Nate responded.

"Yes it does," Sandy agreed. "I want David to have a happy childhood more than anything."

Nate turned his head toward hers and looked at her as she gazed at the happy home before them. He couldn't help but be amazed at her beauty. He felt a longing for this beautiful loving person next to him. The feeling that he had the night she stood next to him on her porch started coming back to him. Only this time he wasn't scared. She no longer frightened him. She simply filled him with an overwhelming desire to know her and be close to her.

Sandy somehow sensed that Nate was looking at her. She turned and looked into his eyes. She could tell from how intently he was looking at her that he was attracted to her, as she was to him. It seemed as if there was a force drawing them closer to one another. The glow from her face warmed his. He could feel the sweetness of her breath as it gently joined his and filled the small space that separated their lips. Her lips were slightly open. She gazed at him with an expectant look as their eyes communicated what their hearts were feeling. Nate was completely under her spell. He could no longer think or reason. He knew only one thing and that was he wanted her lips against his. He moved slowly toward her and as he pressed his lips against hers he found the ecstasy that he sought. She pressed back. He stopped momentarily and looked at her and then sought her lips one more time.

Nate laid his head back realizing what he had just done. His eyes widened. He felt the fear of a heart that has overstepped its bounds. "Oh Sandy," he said. "I'm sorry. I shouldn't have done that." *This is all too soon*, he thought. *What will she think of me he?* he wondered? He felt guilty. His stomach started to cramp.

"Don't be sorry," Sandy said softy. "Oh please don't be sorry," she repeated again.

Nate took a deep breath at the reassurance of Sandy's words. The tension he felt began to subside. He looked at Sandy. Her lovely face and beautiful eyes mesmerized him. He had to see her again soon. "Oh, Sandy, I must go now, but I want you and David to come to my place tomorrow. I want to get to know David, and I want David to get to know Catherine, and I want to cook you something nice," Nate said with his face aglow.

Sandy's eyes brightened. "Yes," she answered. "That sounds wonderful."

"Great," Nate said enthusiastically. He got up from the couch. Sandy stood by him. He reached out and held one of her hands. "Thank you for such a wonderful day and thank you for everything," Nate babbled excitedly.

"I had a super time, and thank you for buying me the most beautiful painting in the whole world," Sandy said with enthusiasm.

"Goodbye and I look forward to seeing you and David tomorrow," Nate said as he started to leave.

Goodbye," Sandy returned. She reached and squeezed his hand softly like she had done once before. Nate smiled when she did it.

When he left Sandy, Nate felt like he was walking on air.

For the first time since Angela's death, he felt happy. He was giddy with excitement at the prospect of getting closer to Sandy, wonderful Sandy. Sandy also was giddy with excitement that she and Nate, the person she had been in love with for so long, might begin a relationship. Both of their hearts were now filled with the beginning of a joy they had been longing for. That night these two hearts had trouble sleeping because of their excitement. One heart had been so filled with grief and loss that it thought it could not love again while the other heart had given up all hope of being loved. Now, they both had hope. Nate had hope that his heart was now big enough to love Sandy. Sandy had hope for that love. They ached for one another but did not want to admit it. It was way too early to think of such things. But despite their best efforts, they did think of those things, and it kept them awake.

Chapter Forty-two

NATE AND SANDY FINALLY WERE ABLE TO GO TO SLEEP, but both awoke thinking of what had happened between them. They both relived the kiss they had shared; they both looked forward to seeing each other. When David walked into the kitchen where Sandy was, she grabbed both of his hands and with a big smile went in a circle and said, "We are going to visit Dr. Williams and little Catherine today." When Catherine woke up, Nate held her like she was a dance partner and danced with her around the room and said, "Sandy and David are coming over today sweet girl. We have to get ready for them."

Nate wanted to fix something very special. He decided to grill shish kabobs, thinking David would like taking food off a little spear. For desert he would buy apple pie and ice cream. Nate had a backpack to carry Catherine in when they went shopping, which she seemed to enjoy. They made it to the store where they found everything they needed and were able to get back in plenty of time before noon when Sandy and David would arrive

Sandy and David arrived right on time. They were greeted by smiles from both Nate and Catherine. Sandy looked beautiful. She had on a tailored blouse and tight-fitting jeans and wore a little more makeup than she usually did. Nate held Catherine as he welcomed them. Sandy was carrying a Tupperware container full of salad along with salad dressing and a silver-serving spoon.

"You shouldn't have," Nate said as he looked at the salad.

"You can't expect me to come without bringing something," she replied, smiling.

"Thanks," Nate said. "This is just what we needed."

Nate noticed that David was looking curiously at Catherine. Nate squatted down to lower Catherine to his level. "You can hold her hand," Nate said. David reached and gently grabbed her hand. "Does she cry much?" he asked.

"Well yes and no," Nate responded. "When she gets her way she doesn't, but if she doesn't get her way, watch out." They all laughed.

Sandy asked if she could hold Catherine. Sandy smiled as Nate handed her Catherine who didn't seem to mind. Sandy walked around with her humming a soft lullaby that soothed Nate as much as Catherine. Catherine at first seemed very content but then began to get a little fussy. "It's her feeding time. I bet she is getting hungry," Nate said.

"Can I feed her?" Sandy asked.

"Sure," Nate replied.

Sandy sat on the couch and gave Catherine her bottle continuing to hum her lullaby. Catherine seemed to look deeply into Sandy's eyes as she fed. Nate kept glancing at Sandy and Catherine together. He couldn't quite keep his eyes off of them. Sandy had such a gentle way with babies, just like she was gentle with her very sick patients. *Catherine needs that gentleness*, he thought. He wasn't able to provide it for her, and his mom couldn't do it forever. It warmed his heart seeing them. His respect and admiration for Sandy increased more than he thought possible.

"My mom says you are an expert on hearts," David said to Nate.

"Well, yes that's true," Nate tried to say in a humble way.

"Do you know how big a giraffe's heart is?" David asked.

Nate thought for a moment. "No, I don't think I do."

"It is two feet long and weighs twenty-two pounds," David said.

"That is a big heart. I will have to remember that."

"Do you know how big a blue whale's heart is?" David asked again.

Nate was starting to feel a little embarrassed. "No, I don't."

"It weighs thirteen hundred pounds and is as big as a Volkswagen bug."

Nate looked again at this eight-year-old smart little kid and had to laugh a little. He certainly had his mother's smarts, that was for sure. "Where did you learn all this?" Nate asked.

"I read books," David said and then went to look out the balcony.

"We have lots of zoo and animal books around," Sandy said, smiling.

David looked out over the city from the balcony and exclaimed, "It's just like riding in an airplane up here."

"Yeah, I pretend I'm flying one all the time when I go out there," Nate said to David in a loud voice so he could hear him. Nate and Sandy smiled at one another.

"This is so cool," David exclaimed again.

Catherine finished feeding and then went to sleep. Sandy gently put her down in her crib, which was in Nate's bedroom next to his bed. The shish kabobs were warm in the oven since Nate had finished grilling them right before they arrived. Sandy went back into the kitchen.

"Let me help," Sandy said.

"You've already been a great help putting Catherine to sleep. She feels very comfortable with you," Nate replied.

They both began setting the table and getting everything ready. They smiled at each other but kept busy being overly polite as they got in each other's way. Occasionally their eyes would meet briefly. They would smile and quickly look away because they felt uneasy wondering what the other was thinking. *Maybe yesterday didn't really happen*, Nate thought. *Maybe I just dreamed it.*

Everything was ready. The three of them sat down. David's eyes got big when he saw what looked like a slender spear on which had been cooked pieces of steak separated by grilled vegetables of various kinds.

"I don't think David has ever had shish kabob before," Sandy said.

"I hope you like it," Nate said to David.

"Wow," David said. "Can I keep the spear?"

"You bet," Nate replied. Sandy smiled with approval.

"Wow, I like this, Mom," David said as he started to gobble down his shish kabob.

"Me too," Sandy joined in.

Sandy's salad was put in one of Nate's big bowls. Her salad looked wonderful. It was an amazing mixture of lettuce, tomatoes, artichoke hearts, olives, and a number of other salad vegetables all lightly coated with an Italian dressing. In it was her silver spoon.

"This has got to be one of the best salads I have ever had," Nate said with enthusiasm.

"My mom is the best cook ever," David exclaimed.

"I believe it," Nate returned.

"It's just a salad. That's all," Sandy said.

Nate felt extremely happy with the three of them all eating together. "She makes a good cup of coffee too," Nate said, looking at David. "Every morning she makes me a perfect cup of coffee at work."

"I think my mom likes you," David said.

"Kids," Sandy exclaimed. "They will say anything."

"I like your mom too. I also like you, David," Nate said, smiling. David smiled as he continued to eat.

"I know your parents are helping a lot, but is there anything I can help you with?" Sandy asked.

"No, I'm really lucky to have them. We are doing just fine," Nate answered.

"Well I'm available any time you need something." Their eyes kept meeting briefly. Then they would pretend to concentrate on their food.

After the shish kabobs were finished, Nate brought out the apple pie and ice cream. David was ecstatic. "Mom, can we come here every Sunday," David asked.

"You bet," Nate said quickly. Sandy smiled again.

"David, why don't you watch one of those nature shows you like so much while Dr. Williams and I finish the kitchen," Sandy said when they were finished. Nate turned on the TV and found one of his favorite shows.

"David is one smart little kid," Nate said.

"That's what scares me," Sandy said half-jokingly. "He already knows how to outthink me. He usually gets what he wants."

Sandy got up and started to clear the table. Nate got up also. As they both reach for the pie dish their hands came together. They both froze with their hands touching each other. Their faces became serious as they slowly turned to one another. Their eyes met. Then they looked down and realized that they were bent over the table holding each other's hands while at the same time holding onto a half-full apple pie dish. After a tense moment they started laughing. Sandy said, in the midst of her laughter, "You can hold my hand any time you want, you know. You don't have to pretend it was an accident."

Nate came back, "Thanks, that will make holding your hand

a lot easier." Nate felt at ease with Sandy. He had been waiting for the right moment and now was the time. Still smiling, Nate said, "Sandy, will you go on a date with me?"

"Yes, any time," Sandy said enthusiastically.

Nate felt wonderful. "Next Saturday Catherine and I are leaving with my parents for a week's trip up east. She wants to show off Catherine and maybe me too to some distant relatives. Would Friday night work for you?"

"Yes," Sandy answered.

"I want to take you somewhere special and have a nice dinner," Nate added with a big smile.

Sandy's eyes brightened. "Will you also take me dancing?" she said in an excited schoolgirl's voice.

"Yes, I will take you dancing, but you will have to teach me how so I don't step on your toes," Nate answered playfully.

"We will start off slow, and you'll do fine," Sandy reassured him. Nate was excited at the thought of dancing with Sandy next to him. Just then they heard a small whimper from Catherine. "I'll check on her," Sandy said.

"Thanks. I'll finish in here," Nate replied.

Sandy went into Nate's bedroom. Catherine's crib was by one side of his bed. Sandy wondered how Nate could sleep in the same room with a baby all night. Sitting on the edge of the bed, Sandy reached into the crib and gently patted Catherine and hummed a soft tune. Catherine was a beautiful baby. She looked like Nate, she thought. Sandy had always wanted a little girl. As she soothed her back to sleep she dreamed of how wonderful it would be to have a daughter. After Catherine finally went back to sleep Sandy decided to remain on the bed for a short while in case she woke back up.

Nate's bedroom is definitely a guy's bedroom, she thought. The walls were empty of any pictures. The bed and the chest were made of nicely polished dark heavy wood. The bedside tables were of the same wood. When she glanced at the bedside tables she noticed a strip of small pictures leaning against the lamp on the table near her. Her heart sank as she picked them up. There were Nate and Angela passionately kissing in the top picture. They had their smiling faces together in the next, and they were making funny faces in the last two. Sandy felt empty inside as she looked at them again. Then she noticed a card on the table that said, "To My Lover" on the front. She opened it and read what Nate had written, "Dear Angela, I will always love you. Nate."

Sandy swallowed to clear her throat. Her eyes watered a little. She knew Nate loved Angela so why did she feel this way? How could she be jealous of someone who was dead? She felt ashamed. She didn't want to replace Angela or erase her memory. She just wanted Nate to love her at least as much as he did Angela. But how could she compete with someone who was not living? If she and Nate developed a serious relationship, she didn't want to be second in his love her whole life. She again felt guilty for thinking such selfish thoughts. *But could he love her as much as Angela?* Only time would tell but deep down in her heart she felt he could not. This filled her with an overwhelming sadness. She stood up and wiped the last remaining tears from her eyes. She then put on a false smile because there was no more joy in her heart before walking back into the kitchen.

"David, we had better go now. Thank Dr. Williams for such a wonderful meal," she said as she entered the rest of the apartment.

Nate looked surprised. "So soon?" he asked.

"Yes," Sandy returned. "We had a wonderful time. Your parents are coming soon, and it is for the best."

"Ok," Nate said, not exactly sure why she was leaving. "Can I pick you up at seven on Friday then?" he asked.

Sandy felt a little better because Nate looked disappointed at their leaving and because he seemed excited about their date. *How foolish to think all those thoughts in his bedroom.* She would simply put them out of her mind. She felt like smiling again. "Yes, that would be great," she said with feeling. She reached and gave Nate's hand a quick squeeze.

Nate felt relieved and Sandy knew it. In fact he now felt happy. "Wonderful. I look forward to seeing you at the hospital tomorrow," he said as she was leaving. Sandy carried her empty Tupperware salad bowl in one hand. Her silver spoon was in the dishwasher mixed in with all of the other silverware.

"Oh, I forgot. David is out of school this week. I have taken the week off to be with him."

"So I will see you next Friday at seven then," Nate said, waving goodbye.

"Yes, see you at seven," Sandy returned and then she and David were gone.

Nate wondered about Sandy. *What she was thinking?* He worried that he might have done or said something wrong, but he had no clue as to what it could be. But then he felt better that she had reached for his hand as she left. She really seemed to look forward to going out with him on their date. He would make it the most perfect date ever. Deep down he was sure she liked him. After all, she had kissed him and had come to his apartment today and said yes to go out on a date with him, he reassured himself. Catherine began to wake up. As he walked to get her, he told himself that it would all work out just fine.

Chapter Forty-three

SANDY WOKE UP MONDAY MORNING AND DECIDED THAT she needed to shake it off. What she had thought and felt the day before was ridiculous. Nate had loved Angela, but she was dead. Now Nate seemed to be open to new love. It was that simple. Life must go on. It was going on and that was all there was to it. *But he had known me for two years before he met her,* kept going through her mind. For all that time Sandy had hoped he would make advances toward her and finally that night at her party they seemed close to one another. When she stood by him on the porch he seemed attracted to her. *So why didn't he choose me? Why did he choose Angela so soon after that,* she wondered. Would he always view her as his second choice? *Widowers remarry all the time,* she thought. But they usually marry someone they had not met before so the second wife could always think that she would have been first if he had only met her first. Sandy was denied the luxury of that thought.

Sandy finally decided that she was thinking too much. She needed to give Nate a chance. That's what she would do. She would give him a chance. *Who knows what will happen?* she told herself. She needed to give him a chance.

Sandy made plans for the week. On Monday, she went

shopping for a new dress. She had a good idea what she wanted so she was able to take David with her. She kept him busy with books and games that he took into the store while she tried on different dresses. She was able to decide on the perfect dress, which was stylish and dressy but sexy at the same time. Next, she made an appointment in one of the high-end stores downtown to have a makeup evaluation. David was able to visit a friend so she was free. Her evaluation took about an hour while the makeup specialist determined her basic natural colors and then matched makeup, eyeliner, and lipstick to these colors. When Sandy left she felt she looked more beautiful than she had ever before. The next day she had appointments to get her hair styled and her finger and toenails polished. Her hair was short but not too short and had a wave to it that she thought Nate would like.

Friday seemed to have come too quickly. David was to spend the afternoon and the night with a friend. Friday afternoon, she showered early and then spent the rest of the afternoon getting ready. She applied the makeup and lipstick and eyeliner just perfectly. When she had finished it was six o'clock. She put on her new dress and then had an hour to relax. For the first thirty minutes she thumbed through some magazines. Then at six-thirty she put the magazines down and sat back and thought about Nate. She put aside all thoughts about Angela. In her mind she pictured Nate knocking on her door. A smile came to her face when she thought about how he would look when he saw how beautiful she was.

Even though Nate had a busy workweek, the thought of his and Sandy's special date never left his mind. He made reservations for them at one of the very fancy downtown restaurants that were located on top of a tall building that overlooked the city. Afterwards, they would go to an upscale nightclub where the more mature hung out and where the live music provided for both slow and fast dancing. One day he slipped away early from work and went to a high-end men's store to get advice on the latest in men's fashion. He walked out of there with new slacks and shoes and a sport coat that was suited for the young and debonair while at the same time mainstream enough to be considered formal. Nate's mom was extremely happy about the new clothes and that he and Sandy were going out.

Nate had arranged to get off at noon on Friday to make sure there would be no last-minute emergencies, which often happened and delayed him. That morning as he was getting ready, his mom came in holding Catherine.

"Nate, Catherine seems a little fussy for some reason this morning," she said with a slightly worried look on her face.

Nate quickly looked her over. She had no cold symptoms, no vomiting, or diarrhea, and she did not feel warm. "I think she will be ok. Sometimes she is fussy in the mornings for some reason," he reassured her.

Nate finally got home around two in the afternoon in plenty of time to get dressed. "Catherine is still fussy," his mom said as he walked in the door. "She hasn't eaten much today," she added.

Nate briefly looked her over again and could not find anything obvious. "We should take her temperature to make sure," he told his mom. She retrieved the rectal thermometer that Nate insisted on using because he thought it was more accurate than the kind that was placed on the forehead. Catherine was a little fussy but didn't seem to mind too much. After three minutes Nate removed the rectal thermometer and read it aloud. "It says 100 degrees," he announced.

"She's getting a fever. What shall we do?" Nate's mom said in alarm.

"Mom," Nate said in an authoritative tone. "When you take the temperature rectally you subtract a degree to see what it would be in the mouth so she really only has a 99-degree temperature, and that is not a real fever," Nate reassured her.

His mom seemed somewhat relieved and decided to try to feed Catherine while Nate got dressed. Catherine ate about one-half her usual amount and then at three thirty went down for a nap that was at least an hour later than usual.

At six Nate was ready. Catherine was still asleep for some reason. At six fifteen they all heard her whimper. Nate picked her up and became alarmed. She was burning up and seemed limp. "Mom, let's take her temperature again," he said. She quickly got the thermometer after which Nate inserted it rectally. It worried him that she lay there without resisting. When he read the thermometer he could hardly believe his eyes. "It's 104," he said, more alarmed.

Nate's mom blurted out, "Oh my God!" Her mind flashed back to Nate's older sister who died in infancy. Growing up, Nate knew this story well. His mind raced back to Angela and her death. Now the thought of losing Catherine sent a sickening fear to the very depths of his being. He was almost on the verge of panic, but then he quickly regained himself as the father and the physician that he was took over.

"We've got to get her to the emergency room," Nate said in a shaking voice. He pulled out his cell phone and dialed the emergency room number and asked to talk to the emergency physician. Nate told him about their situation and that they were heading his way. *To be able to talk directly to the emergency physician is one of the perks of being a physician*, he thought. Just then his mom, who had been holding Catherine, came into the kitchen where Nate was.

"Here, hold Catherine while I get her bag," she said. Nate laid his phone on the kitchen table and grabbed Catherine. His dad remained silent as usual but looked very, very worried. With

Catherine's bag in hand the three of them rushed out of the apartment to the emergency room. Nate's phone lay by on the kitchen table where he had left it.

When they got to the emergency room a little before seven, the triage nurse was waiting for them. Catherine was even more limp than she had been, which Nate knew was a bad sign. He felt desperate. Nothing was on his mind except little Catherine. They were ushered immediately to an ER cubicle, where the nurse took Catherine's vital signs and verified that she had a 104-degree temperature. The ER physician came in next. He talked with Nate and his parents as he quickly assessed Catherine. Nate explained that Catherine had been well with no other symptoms but fussiness during the day. The ER physician thoroughly went over Catherine and then said, "I think first we should do blood tests and a urine test after we give her some ibuprofen.

"Do you think this could be serious?" Nate's mom said, trying not to appear too alarmed.

"At the moment I do not think this is serious," the ER physician answered. "Let's see how she does and what the tests show." Nate agreed, but they were all still worried.

First the nurse came in and gave her ibuprofen that was in a syringe without a needle, which she slowly squirted in her mouth. Catherine gulped it down. Next the nurse loosened Catherine's diaper after opening a kit she had brought. With the help of an aide she cleaned her off with an orange betadine cleansing solution to make the opening to her bladder as sterile as possible. Then with gloves on she began to insert a sterile catheter between her labia into the urethral opening. At this Nate's mom and dad decided to go to the waiting room saying they just couldn't take it. Nate remained. He was a father and wanted to be with his Catherine no matter what. He was also a physician; maybe he could help in some way. After about five minutes the nurse finally got the catheter in and out came about an ounce of clear urine that drained into a sterile urine cup.

After this was accomplished the nurse got ready to draw her blood. She had three tubes, one for a blood culture, one for a blood count, and one for chemistries. The nurse put a small tourniquet on Catherine's right upper arm and applied betadine to the bend of her arm and slowly advanced a small needle in search of a vein. However, the veins were not cooperating and after several tries she switched to the other arm. Catherine was starting to resist and cry more, which made it even more difficult. When the nurse was unable to hit a vein in her other arm, she then put the tourniquet above her wrist, looking for a vein on the back part of her hand. Nate was starting to get nervous. Maybe they were not going to be able to get a blood sample from her. He thought about trying himself but hitting an infant's vein was something he had never done before. Finally, with a small butterfly needle, the nurse hit a small vein in her hand, and blood slowly advanced through the tubing into the laboratory tubes. When she was finished she wiped away all the betadine and applied small Band-Aids with cute animals on them to the three sites.

The nurse then retook Catherine's temperature and it showed 102 degrees. When Nate's mom and dad came back in Catherine was more alert and looking around. They all felt somewhat relieved even though they were still worried. It was now around eight o'clock. The nurse came in and said that the ER was extremely busy and that the lab was behind but hopefully it would not take too long. About twenty minutes later the ER physician came in again to reexamine Catherine apologizing for the delay.

The ER physician pulled up a stool and sat in front of Nate, who held Catherine facing him. The ER physician smiled at Catherine. He then began playing peek-a-boo with her while at the same time tickling her toes. Nate's parents began to wonder about his competence. Catherine then smiled and actually laughed when the ER doctor's face appeared from behind his hands.

The ER physician appeared relieved. "I think she is going to be ok," he said confidently.

Nate's mom sighed. She felt better than she had all day. Now she realized that this was one of the most competent doctors she had ever known, except for Nate of course. She felt like hugging him. "Thank you Doctor, thank you so much," she said. Nate was also greatly relieved.

"Oh, you're welcome. I will go and check on her lab now. Thanks for being so patient," the ER physician said as he left. It was now after eight-thirty and everyone was in much better spirits.

Sandy was both excited and nervous as seven o'clock approached. At seven fifteen she looked out the window. It was very unusual for Nate to be late. There was always a good reason. At seven-thirty she began to be worried. At seven-forty five she decided to call Nate's cell phone. His phone rang as it lay by itself on Nate's kitchen table. Sandy heard the recording with Nate's voice say, "This is Dr. Williams. Please leave a message, and I will get back with you as soon as I can." By eight fifteen Sandy's stomach was churning as she walked back and forth wringing her hands. *Maybe something serious has happened. Why doesn't he call me?* she asked herself. *He is never without his cell phone so why isn't he answering it?* she wondered. By nine o'clock she was exhausted with worry and just sat on the couch in misery.

It was nine o'clock when the ER physician finally was able to break away from all the other emergencies and review the lab that had just come back. He entered with a smile as he saw Catherine and Nate and his parents who had been waiting patiently. "I have good news," he said. "All of her tests were completely normal. Her urine was clear of infection and her blood count indicates if anything a viral infection. I think you guys can go back home and just give her fever medicine and watch her and I'm sure she will be ok. Of course if she worsens in any way come right back." Catherine was smiling and reaching for things in a playful way and seemed perfectly normal.

"We had planned a car trip tomorrow. Do you think we can still go?" asked Nate's mom.

"See how she does. I have a feeling this is one of those twenty-four hour viruses that we have been seeing and that tomorrow she will be better. If she still has a fever don't let any relatives hold her or be near her. They can just admire her from the other side of the room." They all smiled and thanked him and headed back home.

As they walked into the kitchen Nate saw his phone on the kitchen table. He picked it up and panicked when he saw several calls from Sandy. How could he have forgotten to call her? His heart seemed to shrink, leaving an agonizing painful wound in its place. He immediately called her. It was now ten o'clock.

"Hello," Sandy said solemnly.

"Sandy, I am so sorry. Catherine developed a high fever. We had to rush her to the emergency room," Nate explained in a very stressed and urgent tone.

Sandy became alarmed. "Is she all right?" she asked immediately.

"Yes, it turns out it is probably one of those twenty-four hour viruses. She is acting normal now. Sandy, I am so sorry but in all our rush I simply forgot to call you. Can you forgive me?"

Sandy remained silent for a moment processing everything that had happened. Catherine was ok. That was most important. But Nate had forgotten all about her. Surely he could have called her from the emergency room. Sadness and disappointment now filled her heart. She couldn't shake it off.

"That's ok," she said halfheartedly.

"The doctor says we can probably still go on our trip tomorrow but when we get back I want us to have the date we missed tonight. Ok?" he pleaded.

"Ok," was all Sandy could say even though she didn't mean it.

"Promise?" Nate asked.

"Promise," she again said, not intending to really keep it.

"Wonderful," Nate returned. "I will call when we get back." With that they both said goodbye.

Sandy put her phone down and walked into her bathroom. She sat in front of the mirror where she had put on her makeup. She looked at the smoothness of her skin and the perfection of her lipstick and the mascara stained from her tears. As she looked at herself she thought about her life. She was getting older. She was alone. Time was running out, and now she had lost hope of finding the love of her life. Briefly she thought about giving up and accepting her life as it was. Then she sat up straight. Life was painful especially when the heart was involved, but she was tough. Her and David's life had to go on. She had a plan in mind.

Chapter Forty-four

NATE WORRIED ABOUT SANDY THE WHOLE TIME HE WAS gone. He berated himself for forgetting to call Sandy and standing her up. He hoped she would forgive him. He thought repeatedly how he was going to make it up to her and show her that he really cared for her.

By the next morning Catherine had only a 100-degree temperature. When they reached the relatives two days later she was acting normally with no fever. Still, about half of the relatives admired her from across the room while the other half held and played with her with abandon. They all also complimented Nate on being a fine physician making Nate feel like a kid again.

The trip went by excruciatingly slowly for Nate. All he could think about was Sandy and getting back to her and apologizing again for his total lapse of consideration for her. They finally got back late Sunday afternoon. After Catherine went to asleep, Nate got into bed looking forward to seeing Sandy and saying he was sorry.

The next morning he went to the nurses station as usual grabbing his charts before going to the doctors' area to wait for Sandy to bring him coffee. When she didn't appear, he approached one of the nurses. "Is Sandy here today?" he asked.

"Why no, Sandy took another week off," she said politely.

"Do you know if she is at home again with her son?" Nate asked, thinking maybe David had another week off for some reason.

"I don't think so. She just said she was leaving town and could not be reached," was her reply.

Nate stood there quietly for a moment as the reality sunk in that he would not see Sandy for another week. "Thanks," Nate said. He went back to the doctors' area wondering what Sandy was doing. *Where was she? Why had she left?* He felt a brooding uneasiness that Sandy felt really hurt, but he did not know what to do about it. He finally opened his charts and with a grim determination began his rounds.

The week went by slowly for Nate. He had trouble sleeping and concentrating on his work. At work he tried to act like nothing was wrong, but he counted the days until the next Monday when Sandy would be back.

Monday morning finally came around. Nate went to work eagerly. He looked around for Sandy but did not see her. He sat back in the doctors' charting area hoping that Sandy would appear. Instead a nurse appeared looking for a chart and Nate asked, "Is Sandy working today?"

"Don't you know?" she replied. "Sandy doesn't work here anymore."

"What?" Nate said, shocked.

"She doesn't work here now. She took a job with a traveling nurse company that sends nurses all over the states to where nurses are needed."

"When did this happen?" Nate demanded. The nurse could tell that he was upset.

"All I know is that she had applied and was accepted a while back. They were just waiting for her to say yes. The nurses usually stay three months in their new location and if they like it, they can stay permanently."

Nate stood there. He couldn't believe it. He felt himself getting angry, angry with Sandy for leaving and angry at himself for blowing it with her. After a minute he regained his composure. "Do you know where they sent her?"

"No." The nurse was starting to leave. "All we know is that she would not tell anyone and said she could not be reached." With that said the nurse found her chart and went back to the nurses' station.

"Thanks," Nate said loudly as she left. *Why would Sandy do this?* he wondered? Why would she be this upset over his forgetting to call her? Maybe he was mistaken about Sandy really liking him. Or maybe she liked him a lot and was really hurt and thought that he didn't care for her. Whatever it was, he wanted to go to Sandy and explain it all. He wanted to tell her how much he cared but now it was too late. He had no way to reach her. He'd had his share of sadness but now he mainly felt remorse and regret, which quickly led to depression.

He had to continue his life for little Catherine. He had to go on and he would go on. It was just now there would be no joy in his life except when he was at home playing with little Catherine. She had an ability to temporarily make him forget his cares.

Both the nurses and his mom noticed a change in him. The nurses talked about it behind his back. At home his mom would repeatedly ask if everything was ok. Nate would repeatedly say it was. He began having trouble sleeping at night, he became more irritable with the nurses; invariably, he would feel guilty when he did and would apologize to them. He stopped eating in the main cafeteria and went back to the isolated doctors' eating area where he could be alone. He did not feel kindly to his patients anymore but he was a professional and did not let it interfere with the quality of his work. In many ways, he seemed to have reverted to his old self. Everyone was worried.

At night, after playing with Catherine, he would just sit with his father and watch something mindless on TV. He put the four pictures of he and Angela away and did not look at them each evening before bed as he once did. He would lie in bed hoping sleep would relieve him from the misery he experienced thinking about Sandy.

After two months Nate had given up on finding Sandy and was on the verge of clinical depression. Nate knew the signs of depression. He knew that he was depressed but then he would go into denial mode pretending he wasn't. One evening while he was staring at the TV his mom walked up to him carrying a silver serving spoon.

"Nate," she said, looking at the spoon. "I've just noticed this spoon that I don't remember seeing before. It looks too nice to be one of yours. Do you know anything about it?" she asked.

Nate looked at the spoon and shook his head that he had no idea. "Sorry Mom," he replied and turned back to the TV as his mom walked back into the kitchen. Spoons were the last things on his mind. Then suddenly it came to him. It was Sandy's spoon, which she must have left that day she and David had visited. He went into the kitchen where he found the spoon laying on the counter. He sat back down with it thinking about Sandy. His mom noticed him with the spoon.

"Did you figure out where that spoon came from?" she asked.

"Yeah," Nate answered flatly. "It's Sandy's. She left it here."

"How is Sandy?" his mom asked.

"I don't know. She's been out of town working for a traveling nurses' group. I'm not sure if she is coming back," Nate answered.

"That's a shame," his mom said. "She was such a nice girl and cute as she could be. I was secretly hoping you two might hit it off someday. But oh well, such is life."

Nate continued to look at Sandy's spoon when it came to him. Why had he not thought of it before? A tiny spark of hope was instantly lit within him. He got up and said goodnight to his parents. He solidified his plans as he got ready for bed.

The next morning, he went down to the accounting office of the hospital where the employee checks were written. There behind a desk sat a young lady he recognized as being the daughter of one of his patients.

"Hey Doctor Williams, what are you doing down here?" she asked.

"First, how is your dad doing?" he inquired.

"He is doing great, thanks to you. He and mom are finally taking that vacation they always wanted. How can I help you?"

"Do you remember a nurse named Sandy Abraham that used to work here?" he asked.

"Do I remember her? How could I forget her? She took excellent care of Dad and we all fell in love with her," she replied. *Me too,* thought Nate.

"Well," Nate cleared his throat, "she left something special, and I wanted to send it to her. Would you happen to know where I could send it?" He felt he wasn't really lying. The serving spoon could be something special, who knows. For some reason he wondered what Father Jim would think about all this.

"I have the address of where we sent her last check," she said as she looked around. "I'm really not supposed to give it to anyone, but I would do anything to help Sandy." She found it on her computer and wrote it down on a piece of paper handing it to him. Nate said thank you. As he walked away he couldn't help but feel a little guilty, but then he quickly shrugged it off.

The address was in a town named Woodsville, California.

It was located in the northernmost part of California nestled amongst the redwoods and a fifteen-minute drive from the coast. He looked it up on the Internet. It had a population of twelve thousand and only one hospital. It was three thousand miles away. Nate thought to himself, *When Sandy does something, she does it all the way.* If Sandy had signed on for only three months then she had only four weeks left there. Who knows where she would go next. Nate had to act quickly. He arranged for some emergency time off, not telling anyone the exact nature of the emergency, but he had been through so much lately that no one dared to ask. He got a flight on the next Thursday morning to Woodsville and a return flight four days later on Monday.

The one hospital in Woodsville was predictably small. There were only four or five family physicians, a general surgeon, an obstetrician, an anesthesiologist, two nurse anesthetists, and an ENT specialist who came two days a week. Nate figured out that the nurses there worked eight-hour shifts instead of the twelve-hour shifts that most hospitals had gone to. The flight of over three thousand miles was ten hours in length. He would fly into San Francisco and then take a small plane to Woodsville getting there Thursday night.

His flight left early in the morning. He was ready for a long day. He tried to read some journals but quickly gave that up. He looked out the window. The plane was above the clouds, and below the plane the clouds made a fluffy white carpet that extended as far as the eye could see disappearing into the blue horizon. He thought about Angela and wondered if she was out there somewhere. He remembered his conversation with Sam the cemetery groundskeeper. Maybe Angela is an angel, who knows? He thought about how much different of a person he was thanks to Angela. In his mind he began talking to Angela, which he still did on occasion. *Angela*, he thought, *you really changed me.*

I was happy, at least I thought I was happy, living alone, not being close to anyone. You took my heart and showed it what love is. You knew my heart would need love after you were gone. That was pretty sneaky of you saying that Christianity was not the only religion and then suggesting the Hebrew faith. I'm a little slow at these things, but finally I now know what you were up to. You know what, it worked. Thanks for looking out for me.

"Excuse me sir, would you like something to drink?" the stewardess asked.

Nate, deep in thought looking out the window, startled for a second and then said yes, he would like some coffee. The stewardess handed him a cup with a little packet of creamer and artificial sweetener. As he sipped it, his thoughts turned to Sandy and how much he missed her. He had been attracted to her from the very beginning. Each morning he looked forward to seeing her. He missed her smile and the dimples in her cheeks. She was always upbeat. He always felt good when he was around her. He wanted to hold her hand. He wanted to kiss her. He wanted to be close to her.

Then a dark shadow entered his heart as if a black cloud suddenly blocked the sun. What if this is all too late and she had found someone else? He began to feel sick as his stomach turned over. *What if she just doesn't love me?* If she is not married or really in love with someone, he told himself, he would do everything to win her love no matter how long it took. This made him feel a little better.

His huge jet landed in San Francisco. Then he boarded a small turbo plane that held only twenty people for the last leg of his ten-hour flight to Woodsville. He had always been anxious about flying in small planes but that quickly passed once the plane was in the air and his thoughts again turned to Sandy. His flight arrived in Woodsville late that evening. The Woodsville airport was unbelievingly small with only a few planes and a two-story control tower. Fortunately he had been able to reserve a rental car, which was waiting for him. It was almost eight that evening before he was able to drive into town. He found a room in a small but nice motel and checked in.

Nate had a plan for the next day. He would go to the nurses' parking lot and be sitting there when the nurses got off at three in the afternoon. If she weren't with them then he would go to the head nurse and introduce himself as Dr. Williams who was passing through and wanted to say hi to Sandy. However, if he could catch her in the parking lot and talk with her alone that would be best. He parked his car at the far end of the parking lot and sat inside waiting.

Nick began to feel stupid. Why was he doing this? He thought about going in to the head nurse when the nurses began to come out to their cars. Nate's heart sank. She was not with them. He was about to give up when he saw her. She was walking with two other nurses, talking and smiling. She looked beautiful. From a distance he could see her hair as it flowed around her ears. Even though she was wearing nurse's greens he could see the curves of her body. He started to get out of his car when he saw a cowboy looking guy walk up to her and start talking. He was a little taller than her and wore blue jeans, boots, a plain shirt, and a cowboy hat. They talked for a second, and then he put his arm around her shoulder. Then they walked to a truck and got in and drove off together.

Nate sat there frozen. His worst fear had come true. She had someone else. He felt sick and depressed. He had lost her, and it was his fault. He wiped a tear from his eye. He would go back to his motel and try somehow to cope. Now he had lost the two women in his life that he loved. He didn't know if he could survive. He started his car. He would have to be alone until his plane left in three days unless he could get a flight out sooner.

Chapter Forty-five

NATE GOT BACK TO HIS MOTEL AND ENTERED THE LOBBY with a grim face. Behind the check-in desk was now an elderly man instead of the young girl who had checked him in the night before.

"Can I help you sir?" the elderly man said.

"I've already checked in," answered Nate.

"Are you the fellow from Everston?" he asked again.

"Yes," Nate answered again.

"You're a long way from home, aren't you? Isn't Everston something like three thousand miles from here?"

"That's correct," Nate said, hoping the conversation would end soon.

"What brings you all the way out here?" the elderly man asked with a friendly smile.

"Just passing through. I was hoping to run into a traveling nurse friend of mine who I thought might be here," Nate answered.

"That must be Sandy, Sandy Abraham," the man said confidently.

Nate was surprised. "You know her?"

"In this small town everybody knows everybody. The hospital was glad to get her. Everyone likes her. To be honest, it is a little surprising she is dating Ned Thurman's boy. They're a rough bunch."

"Oh?" said Nate, now very much interested in the conversation.

"Yeah, but overall they're ok if you don't cross them. If you wanted to bump into her they will be tonight where they always are on Friday nights and that is at the Silver Bullet."

"The Silver Bullet?" Nate asked.

"It's a combination dance hall and bar on the square. There is usually some local cowboy band that starts playing around eight."

"Thanks," Nate said. "Maybe I'll try to make it down there."

"Good luck," the elderly man said as if he knew that Sandy was more than a friend.

The Silver Bullet Saloon was in a very large old wooden building that took up over half a block on one corner of the town square. The town square consisted of a two-story ancient stone courthouse surrounded by red brick streets. Across from the courthouse on all sides were two-story buildings built in a bygone day. Some of the buildings contained stores, one a lawyer's office, another a small café. The Silver Bullet consisted of one super large open space with a ceiling two stories high that made you feel like you were in a barn when you entered. In front to the left was a small platform situated in front of a dance floor. On the platform were two guitars resting on stands and a microphone on a pole. To the right of this area was a long wooden polished bar with a metal foot rail. Behind the bar was a large mirror and along the bottom of it were lined up liquor bottles of every imaginable type. To the right of the bar was a door leading to the restrooms. Round tables and chairs occupied the rest of the room so customers could sit either in front of the dance floor or near the bar depending on their proclivity.

Nate entered the Silver Bullet Saloon around seven-thirty. Since the music and dancing did not start until eight, the tables were only one-fourth full. He was wearing blue jeans, a sport coat, and regular dress shoes. He walked to the bar and sat at the far end near the entrance to the bathrooms and ordered a beer. The bartender was an elderly man in his late sixties. He had a bright face that sported a very gray beard and was overweight to a moderate extent. He greeted Nate with a smile.

"New in town?" the bartender said, wiping the bar.

"Yeah, just passing through," Nate said. "Thought I would catch some music tonight."

"Welcome to Woodsville. My name is Joe, and this is my place," the bartender said as he reached to shake Nate's hand. "The band starts at eight and is pretty good if you like country music," he added. Joe had the kind of eyes that revealed a wisdom within that came from listening to innumerable customers over many years who sought a drink and an ear to tell their troubles to. Around eight o'clock three lanky cowboys stepped onto the platform. Two grabbed the guitars and one, who was the lead singer, took hold of the microphone. They welcomed everyone; the tables were now half occupied. They began a song about someone cheating on someone, which would remain the main theme for the night. Nate looked around. There was no Sandy. The feeling of hopelessness that was within him got even bigger.

Around eight-thirty three cowboys with cowboy hats entered accompanied by three ladies, one of which was Sandy. Nate couldn't believe it. She was actually here. Nate continued to drink his beer and looked at them out of the corner of his eye as the three of them sat down at a table in front of the dance floor. The waitress walked up to their table and then brought them all beers.

Sandy was striking. She had tight-fitting jeans and a western shirt that complimented her form. Her hair seemed a little longer than he remembered and was gathered in back with a ribbon in the shape of a bow. Sandy looked great but she did not look happy.

The three of them just sat there with stone faces drinking their beer and listening to the music as a few couples danced.

Nate's heart went out to Sandy. She stood out like a rose among thorns. *What is it about her and cowboys?* he wondered. He wanted to go over and ask her to dance and pull her body next to his but at the same time he had a sinking feeling that it would not happen. It was all too late; his Sandy was gone, gone from his life.

The cowboy that was with Sandy stood up and grabbed Sandy's hand and pulled her up to dance without saying anything and Sandy followed. They danced some sort of two-step and he with his cowboy hat looked down at her, but she seemed to look away. Neither one smiled or said anything as if this country dancing was very serious business. After the dance they sat back down. Nate felt sorry for Sandy. She deserved so much more than this. He decided he would finish drinking his beer and then silently slip out never to see her again.

After a short while Sandy got up and headed to the restroom located near the end of the bar. When she got a few feet from Nate she stopped with an amazed look on her face.

"Nate, is that you?" she exclaimed.

Nate turned his head and said, "Hi Sandy."

Sandy looked troubled. She turned back to look at her table and her companions and then turned to Nate. "What, what in the world are you doing here?"

"I came to see you," Nate said solemnly.

"How did you ever find me?" Sandy asked, still totally surprised.

"I have my ways," Nate responded.

Sandy became flushed. "Why are you here?" she asked again in a lower tone.

"For two reasons. One I wanted to return something you left at my apartment." Nate reached into an inner pocket of his sport jacket and pulled out Sandy's serving spoon and handed it to her. Sandy looked at it with wide eyes not knowing what to say.

"The other reason was to collect on a promise," Nate answered.

"To collect on a promise?" Sandy said, her voice rising unexpectedly.

"Yep. You promised me a date, remember?" Nate said matter of factly.

Sandy began shaking her head as she became more flushed. "This isn't going to work," she said, looking at the floor still shaking her head. Just then her cowboy friend, noticing that she was talking to some stranger at the bar, walked over to them.

"Is this guy bothering you?" he said, standing with his hands on his belt as if he was ready to draw a gun or something.

"No," Sandy said, glancing briefly at him. "He's an old friend, that's all."

"Well, I think it's time you came back to the table," he said firmly.

"He's come over three thousand miles to say 'Hi' and I want to talk with him a minute," Sandy said, not looking at him.

"I don't care where the hell he came from, come back to the table," the cowboy ordered, grabbing her arm. Sandy tried to jerk away but the cowboy, with a mean face, tightened his grip and pulled her arm even harder.

Anger exploded inside Nate like a bomb. He jumped off of his chair and with both hands gave the cowboy a shove, pushing him back several feet forcing him to let go of Sandy.

"Get your hands off of her," Nate ordered. Sandy stood there speechless with a surprised look on her face.

As fast as lightning, the cowboy punched Nate in the stomach. Nate felt an excruciating pain shoot through him to his spine as he doubled over and fell back against the bar. His eyes went blurry as he tried to catch his breath. Sandy screamed and tried to grab his shoulder. Nate held stomach as his breath returned. Sandy was crying. Tears were streaming down her face. The pain in his stomach began to subside. As the focus of his vision returned Sandy's face appeared in front of him. He would never forget how she looked at that moment. He turned back to the cowboy who stood there proudly looking down at him with clenched fists. Then something snapped in Nate. It is the same thing that happens in great athletes when the mind stops thinking and the inner animal wakes up and takes over. Nate's inner animal had been asleep far too long. Nate had been a fighter all his life, but he had never fought for love before. Now it was time.

Nate recovered and came out swinging fast and furious catching the cowboy off guard. One of Nate's fists found its mark on the cowboy's forehead as he ducked. The other hit him below the chin near his windpipe, which made him choke and grab his neck. As Nate advanced on him throwing punches, the cowboy staggered back several feet, losing his balance until he backed into a table with a couple sitting at it. When he hit the table he fell backwards on the table between the couple, scattering bottles and glasses everywhere. The couple jumped back surprised and confused. Several ladies began screaming.

The cowboy managed to get up with clenched fists. He and Nate faced off, both slowly walking in a circle. In the background someone yelled, "Call the police!" The music stopped, and the three cowboys on the stage looked at the scene with their mouths open and then put down their guitars and quickly left. Joe disappeared from behind the bar.

Nate and the cowboy exchanged several blows hitting mainly each other in the shoulders or sides. They kicked chairs aside when they got in their way. They seemed to be an even match, which surprised Sandy as she watched horrified and sick with worry for Nate. Nate managed to hit him again when it happened. The cowboy's right fist landed squarely on Nate's left eye. Suddenly, Nate saw a million black dots and for a second did not know where he was. When his vision started to return he could hear Sandy screaming, "Nate! Oh Nate!" He found himself on the floor. He had backed into a table that had overturned resting against it. There were broken glasses and beer bottles on the floor beside him. Nate's left eye was swollen almost shut, and there was a gaping laceration below his eye that was bleeding.

He looked at the cowboy and started to get up. Sandy was on the floor beside him and screamed, "Nate, don't!"

Nate gently pushed her aside and said, "Out of the way, Sandy," as he got up.

It was when he got up that everyone said the fight was over. That was when the cowboy turned pale and began to back up as Nate approached him with clenched fists and fire in his eyes. No one was supposed to be able to get up after a punch like that. The cowboy looked scared. One of his friends grabbed his arm and said, "Let's get out of here. We've had enough trouble with the law." At this he turned with his friend and made a swift exit, kicking more chairs out of his way.

Nate stood straight and tall and watched them leave. The screaming had stopped, and Sandy stood there totally stunned. Joe came running into the saloon carrying a shotgun pointed at the ceiling. His face was beet red, and he was sweating profusely. He yelled, "No more fighting! No more fighting!" He then stopped. A puzzled look appeared on his face. He dropped his gun and put his hand to his chest and then dropped to his knees before slumping over. Nate saw him and in an instant knew what was happening. He quickly turned him over and began CPR. Nate looked at Sandy and motioned for her to help him. Sandy came out of her stunned state and began giving mouth-to-mouth resuscitation.

"Does this place have an AED defibrillator?" Nate asked, looking at Sandy.

Sandy looked up at him between breaths and said, "Are you kidding?"

"Call 911," Nate ordered. Nate and Sandy knew how to coordinate the chest compressions with the mouth-to-mouth breaths. This was something they had done together many times before, and they were once again a team. The police arrived and the two young officers, expecting to see a ballroom brawl, were somewhat confused to see a stranger with a black and bleeding eye resuscitating Joe the bartender. Soon an ambulance arrived and two EMTs entered with their equipment.

The EMTs recognized Sandy from the hospital and looked surprised. "It's Sandy," one exclaimed.

Sandy looked up. "Hey guys, this is Dr. Williams, a cardiologist from my home town."

"That's great! Boy, we're glad you're here," they both said and then noticed that Dr. Williams had a black eye and was bleeding. They stopped for a second, wondering what was going on. "Thanks," Nate responded. "Get the defibrillator ready, ok?"

They said, "Ok," and stopped looking at Nate and whipped out their defibrillator. Nate put the paddles on the bartender's chest, which confirmed that his heart was in fibrillation like Nate suspected. "He's in V-fib. Everyone stand back," Nate ordered as he shocked him. The bartender's body jumped and twitched and then Nate resumed chest compressions while one of the EMTs began bagging him with oxygen. "Sandy, get a line in," Nate said. One of the EMTs gave Sandy an IV catheter while he got a bag of IV fluid ready. Sandy swiftly inserted the catheter into a vein in the right antecubital area and taped it in while the EMT placed leads. The EKG revealed that the fibrillation had stopped and that there was a regular but slow rhythm. "Epinephrine, Sandy," Nate said, and Sandy knew exactly what to do. The pulse picked up.

"We've got a good rhythm and pulse," Nate said, feeling the bartender's pulse and stopping chest compressions. "He's not breathing. We had better intubate him," he added.

The EMT pulled out an endotracheal tube. "I've only intubated manikins before," he said.

"Well now it's time to do the real thing. I'll help you," Nate said, no longer needing to do chest compressions. Nate stood by and gave him guidance and encouragement as the young EMT expertly placed the endotracheal tube in the right place. "Good job," Nate complimented him.

Smiling, the EMT said, 'Thanks Doc."

The EMTs placed leads on Joe's chest and attached them to a monitor. A gurney was brought in and he was placed on it. Then while still being bagged he was taken to the ambulance. Inside the ambulance Nate sat on a bench near the head while the EMT continued bagging. Sandy sat next to Nate. Her hand was on Joe's wrist so she could monitor the strength of his pulse. The ambulance turned on the sirens and headed to the hospital. Nate glanced at Sandy who had a worried look as she looked back at his swollen eye and laceration. He wondered what she was thinking and then decided he didn't really want to know. Everything had gone so very wrong. He had to quit thinking of Sandy for the moment and be a physician and nothing more. Afterwards he would try to make amends, but he had a sinking feeling that would be impossible.

When they reached the ER the lone ER physician was tied up with an automobile wreck and was glad that Nate and Sandy were there. Once in the ER Joe was stable but unconscious and not breathing on his own. A respirator was attached to his endotracheal tube giving him breaths. A helicopter was called to transport him to the nearest cardiac unit, which was some thirty miles away. Nate took charge and ordered blood gases and other lab tests along with a chest x-ray while they waited for the medical evacuation team to arrive. The helicopter and the team soon arrived, and Nate filled them in on Joe's condition as they assessed him. After determining that he was stable enough to make the trip, the team put him on one of their stretchers that was equipped with a respirator and monitors that resembled a mini ER on wheels. They then lifted the bed into the helicopter as they all disappeared inside.

Nate and Sandy stood outside watching as the helicopter rose off the ground turning its tail to them before slowly disappearing into the night sky. Sandy had moved close to him and held onto his arm as the helicopter took off. Nate looked down at Sandy and remembered that night long ago standing on Sandy's porch with her next to him. *So much has happened since then*, he thought. He wondered if he had any chance with her after what had happened.

Sandy carefully looked at Nate's swollen eye and bleeding cheek. "Now it's time to take care of you," Sandy said and pulled him back into the ER. The ER physician was now free. After examining Nate closely he ordered x-rays to make sure there were no fractures.

"Dr. Williams," the ER physician announced after Nate returned from the radiology room. "Your x-rays show no fracture and your eye looks good inside so I think there is no permanent damage."

"Thank God," said Sandy.

"Now we need to take care of that laceration," the ER physician added.

Nate lay on the bed. After his laceration was cleaned with betadine a sterile drape with a hole in it was placed over his face revealing only the laceration.

"Dr. Williams," the ER physician said. "Unfortunately there is not a plastic surgeon in this town. I am going to do my best, but there will probably be a scar here."

"Good. I was hoping there would be one," Nate responded.

The ER physician was surprised. He had never heard anyone say that before. "Are you sure you didn't get a small concussion back there?" he asked, smiling.

Nate laughed a little. "No, I'm in my right mind."

Sandy didn't know what to think. When they had finished, Nate was given some pain medication. Everyone thanked Nate for helping them stating that they wished he could be part of the hospital staff there.

Nate began to get groggy fast. He was a little dizzy from his injury and the pain medicine that was starting to work. Nate turned to Sandy. "I guess I will head back to my motel."

"No way," Sandy exclaimed. "You are in no shape to drive and you need a nurse to look after you tonight. I've got a real comfortable couch; you're staying with me. I'm not taking no for an answer."

Nate knew he could not refuse. He knew Sandy was just being kind to someone in need, but he felt a warm calm sensation that Sandy was going to take care of him. Sandy drove his car and took him by his motel to grab his suitcase, which had not been opened, before taking him to her apartment.

David's babysitter was waiting for them when they arrived. David was fast asleep. Sandy thanked her and wrote her a check before she left. Nate's head was still throbbing, but the pain medicine was helping. He was getting drowsy fast. He could see Sandy's face and her wonderful smile fade in and out. He wanted to say something to her, but his mouth did not want to cooperate. Then he was out. Sandy quickly tucked him in on her spacious couch as he fell asleep. With his eyes closed he started talking in his sleep. In a garbled voice he said, "Sandy you're a wonderful person. Did anyone ever tell you that?" After that he settled into a restful sleep with a slight smile on his face.

He lay asleep on his right side on the couch. Sandy sat on the floor next to his face with one arm around her bent knees while with the other hand she gently stroked his hair. She admired her handsome Nate with a black eye and stitches. She liked looking at him even though he was all banged up. *Just maybe*, she said to herself, *just maybe he could love me as much as Angela. Just maybe.* Her thoughts drifted off to somewhere very pleasant.

After a while Sandy said, "I love you Nate Williams. You are my hero." She got up and kissed him gently on the cheek and whispered, "Sweet dreams," and then left for bed. Nate did have sweet dreams that night. He dreamt that Sandy had said that she loved him. He hoped with all of his heart that it was true.

Chapter Forty-six

DAVID AWOKE NEAR DAWN. WITH HIS BLANKET IN ONE hand and his Star Wars sword in the other he walked into the living room to turn on the TV. He stopped short when he saw Nate sleeping on the couch. He stood there in amazement. Nate somehow sensed his presence and opened his eyes.

"Dr. Williams?" David said in a surprised voice.

"Yes, it's me, David," Nate answered as he sat up. His head was still throbbing but not as much as the night before.

"Mom said we probably would not see you again," David informed him.

"You know, David, sometimes parents are not always right," Nate said with a smile.

David approached him and looked closely at his swollen black eye and stitches. "Did you get in a fight?" he asked.

"Yes," Nate answered.

"Was it with Darth Vader?" David asked expectantly.

Nate thought a second and then said, "Yes, actually it was Darth Vader now that I think about it."

"Darth Vader is not real," David returned. "He's just made up."

Nate pointed at his black eye and stitches. "Well, this Darth Vader was very much real." David laughed.

Just then Sandy entered in her robe. "What are you two guys talking about?" she asked.

"Dr. Williams was telling me about his fight with Darth Vader," David said excitedly.

"Well let me take a look at Luke Skywalker here," Sandy said. She stood in front of Nate. With one hand gently behind his neck she examined him closely with her trained nurse's eyes. "You face looks terrible," she said and then added, "but the rest of you looks pretty good."

Nate smiled and didn't say anything.

"Come on into the kitchen while David watches TV," Sandy said, helping Nate get up. They went into the kitchen. Sandy closed the sliding door that separated the two rooms.

"How is your head?" Sandy asked seriously.

"As good as can be expected after a barroom fight," Nate said with a smile.

"I got news this morning that Joe is stable. They think he is going to make it," Sandy said.

"Thank God," Nate responded. *I didn't used to use that expression*, he thought to himself.

Sandy made coffee. They both sat at the kitchen table across from one another in silence. Nate did not look at Sandy but stared at his coffee. He was filled with remorse. He had barged in on Sandy's life uninvited, and it all turned out very badly. Not only had he interfered with Sandy's love relationship, but he also had wrecked a saloon and was indirectly responsible for Joe's heart attack. Nate had never felt so low before. He was ashamed and wanted to hide.

"Sandy," he finally said. "I am so, so sorry. I have made a complete mess of all this and a fool of myself. I'm sorry I may have messed up your relationship. I will go as soon as possible." He glanced up at her and then looked back at his coffee.

Sandy reached over and held one of his hands. "Nate, I can't believe that you came all this way just to see me. I can't believe you sought me out." She squeezed his hand. "I want you to know that cowboy and I were just dating. We weren't lovers in any sense of the word."

Nate looked up at Sandy and felt comforted.

"I don't want you to go. We need to talk, you and me," Sandy said, looking at him.

"Yes, I would like that," Nate responded.

"David has a party to go to this afternoon. If you feel like it, I know a place on the beach that we could have to ourselves," Sandy offered.

"That would be great," Nate agreed.

They dropped David off at his party and headed toward the beach, which was only a fifteen-minute drive away. Sandy insisted on driving even though Nate felt like he could. They parked on a slight overlook and walked down to the beach. Nate carried a folded-up beach blanket under his left arm that Sandy used when she visited the beach.

The beach was beautiful. A long stretch of white sand that seemed to go on forever had a gentle curve that would leave one to believe that it surrounded the whole ocean. A hundred yards or so offshore were giant boulders that almost seemed like small islands. White seabirds flew overhead held aloft by a gentle breeze and occasionally the sounds of sea lions that were sunbathing on the distant rocks could be heard.

Sandy walked by Nate along the shore; both were quiet. Nate stopped and closed his eyes and felt the cool breeze that cooled and soothed his swollen face. "It is heavenly here," he said, looking upward with his eyes closed.

"Yes it is," Sandy agreed.

They then spread the blanket on the sand. They both sat with their arms around their bent knees and looked at the ocean. Their hair moved gently at the mercy of the wind, Sandy's more so than his. Nate reached down and threw a few grains of sand up into the air and watched them as they were carried away by the wind. In some ways he felt like one of those grains of sand. Nate sat there in silence. He had never lost control before. His whole life had been about control. Then there was Joe. Worst of all, he was sure he had blown it again with Sandy and that he had lost her for good.

Sandy moved closer so that her shoulder touched his. "Are you ok?" she said.

"Not really," Nate answered.

"Still feeling bad about what happened?"

He glanced at her and then turned away. "I've never lost control before, plus I feel responsible for Joe."

"You know what I think about that?" Sandy returned.

"What?" Nate answered.

"I think Joe was about to have a heart attack anyway, and it was very fortunate for him that it happened with a heart specialist around who could save him."

Nate smiled and looked at her. "You're a wonderful person. Did anyone ever tell you that?" Nate asked.

Sandy smiled and thought about what Nate had said while he was asleep. "Yes, matter of fact, someone has told me that before." Nate wondered who it was.

Sandy's shoulder against his soothed him, and the heavy weight of guilt began to lift slightly.

"Why did you leave?" he asked softly.

Sandy looked down and slowly moved her finger through the sand. "I don't know. It's all so complicated," she answered.

"I missed you terribly. I feel so bad that I hurt you. I am so sorry," Nate said, still not looking at her.

"Oh Nate, you didn't do anything bad. I don't know what's wrong with me. I missed you too," Sandy returned.

"I would like another chance," Nate said, turning to look at her. "Is that possible?"

"Yes, it is," Sandy said as they both looked at each other. Nate turned back and looked at the sea. He had been granted a small reprieve. Sandy's heart went out to him. With both hands Sandy gently turned his head toward hers and kissed him gently on the lips.

Nate was surprised. He couldn't believe that Sandy had just kissed him. It wasn't a passionate kiss. It was a simple kiss that said I like you. Nate's burden was now even lighter. He looked at Sandy and said, "Thank you," because he knew her kiss was a gift, a gift from the heart. Nate reached and held her hand. They both sat there watching the endless rhythmic motion of the ocean while the touch of their hands helped their hearts communicate in the subtle ways that only hearts can when they are getting to know each other.

It soon was time to pick up David from his party. They got up, folded the blanket and started walking back to the car. Sandy put her arm inside his to hold his hand so their shoulders touched as they walked. Nate began to feel another thing he hadn't felt in a long time and that was hope.

That evening Sandy made a simple meal of meatloaf and vegetables and salad. The three of them sat around the table and talked and joked a little like any normal family would. Unlike most normal families, one of the members had a huge swollen black eye and stitches, but everyone acted like nothing had happened.

"Got any new facts about hearts you need to teach me?" Nate asked David.

"Not really," David replied. "Except, do you know what animal has the fastest heartbeat?"

"You've got me again. What animal is it?"

"It's the hummingbird. Do you know how fast a hummingbird heart beats?"

"No, I don't," answered Nate.

"It beats twelve hundred times a minute," David said with an air of confidence.

"David, you never cease to amaze me," Nate said. "I think I am going to be learning a lot from you."

"Does that mean we will get to see you more?" David asked.

Sandy spoke up. "We certainly hope so. David, I don't think Dr. Williams has ever seen the redwoods. Would you like to show them to him tomorrow?" she asked.

"Can we, Mom? That would be great," David responded.

"I'd love to see them," Nate joined in.

"Good. We will have a picnic in the redwoods tomorrow then," Sandy announced. Everyone smiled.

They left the next day a little before noon to go to The Redwood National Forest visitor's station, which was a thirty-minute drive away. During the drive David kept the conversation going with interesting facts he had gotten from his computer at home. The three of them watched the short video on the redwoods that Sandy and David had seen before. Afterwards, they decided to take one of the suggested trails. David was excited. He ran up and down the winding, flat, easily walked trail that led through a forest of giant redwoods. Nate and Sandy strolled behind David looking at the lush green forest vegetation between the unimaginably tall redwood trees. Walking among the redwoods made them feel like they had entered a land of giants.

There were a number of fallen redwoods in the forest that lay there dead. There were young trees growing up out of their sides reaching for the sky. Even on their sides they towered several feet above their heads. Nate stopped to look at one of the fallen giants. Sandy and David stood beside him.

"David," Sandy said. "Tell Dr. Williams what the park ranger told us about these trees. "

David was proud to be asked. "They are nursery trees. When the mother tree falls the baby trees grow out of her."

"So the death of the mother gives the baby trees a chance to live," Nate said with a slight tear in his eye.

David looked up at Nate and said, "That's what the ranger told us," and then he ran down the trail. Sandy held Nate's hand tightly because she knew he was thinking of Angela. For some reason it did not bother or threaten her, though she did not know exactly why. Later that night David asked his mom why Dr. Williams was about to cry in the redwoods. She said that someday she would explain it to him.

After their walk Sandy told him that she was going to take him to a special place that she and David knew about. They drove down a small dirt road through the redwoods that had only an occasional car on it. Sandy explained that the road is very busy in the summer when school was out, but now they more or less had the redwoods to themselves. She had Nate stop at what appeared to be a simple pull out where a car could park off the road. Sandy had prepared a big picnic basket. Nate carried a large tablecloth, and David had a plastic bat and ball. There was a small path that had a carpet of redwood needles on it that went around a huge redwood whose trunk looked like a small building. The path zigzagged down a slope behind the tree that could not be seen from the road. The path ended some twenty feet below in what appeared to be a room ringed with redwoods with a reddish brown floor soft with redwood needles. The trees were so tall they appeared to converge when they looked up. Their size guaranteed the room would be perpetually in the shade. Beyond the wall of redwoods some ten feet below was a streambed with a babbling brook that curved around a beach of small gray stones.

Nate spread out the large tablecloth in their redwood cathedral while Sandy opened her basket. She had fixed David his favorite sandwich, peanut butter and jelly, while she and Nate had lunchmeat sandwiches thick with lettuce, tomatoes, onions, and pickles. In the basket also were chips along with a thermos of tea. For a special treat Sandy had made chocolate brownies during the night, another one of David's favorites.

After eating David went to play and throw stones into the stream. Nate and Sandy lay on their backs and looked up at the ring of tall redwood trees that surrounded them. "These trees are so tall that I really cannot see the tops of them," Nate said.

"That's because they reach into the heavens," Sandy said.

"Is that one of the reasons you chose to come out here?" Nate asked.

"Yes, one of them," she answered.

Nate turned his head and looked at Sandy. "I like being here with you and David. I feel peaceful here." Nate looked up again at the trees that went right into heaven. "I never want to forget this place," he said with wonder in his voice.

"Me neither," Sandy said also.

That night after David went to bed they both sat on the couch, tired. Nate's eye was swelling even more. "Can I get you an ice pack?" Sandy asked.

"No, I'm fine. I want to look at you with both eyes," Nate answered and Sandy smiled.

Sandy asked Nate if he would like to watch a movie on TV. Nate said sure. Sandy turned on the TV to a classic movie channel that had an old-fashioned love story where the drama centered on whether the main two characters were actually going to kiss or not. Sandy set next to Nate on the couch. At first they were not touching but as the movie went on, they slowly moved closer until finally Nate put his arm around her. She snuggled against him, and his heart began to beat fast. They both laughed at the tension that built up as the two lovers finally were able to be alone and have their one kiss that ended the movie. When it was over, Sandy turned off the TV and sat back down in Nate's arms.

Nate looked at Sandy as she looked at him expectantly. He wanted to kiss her. From the look on her face he knew she wanted him to. He gently kissed her. The softness of her lips reminded him of their first kiss. Sandy put her arm around him and kissed him back. After a few minutes they were both flushed. Nate stopped and looked lovingly at her. He looked at her smile, her dimples, and her beautiful eyes. He gently ran his fingers through her hair exposing her ears. He couldn't believe that he was here with her in his arms.

"I've been wanting to kiss you for a long time," Nate said softly.

"You have?" Sandy said softly back.

"Do you know when I first wanted to kiss you?" he asked with the kind of smile one gets when a pleasant memory invades the heart and mind.

Sandy gently moved her head back and forth indicating she did not know.

"It was that night you stood by me on your porch. Actually, let me take that back. It was when you were doing that hula dance."

Sandy's heart leaped a little. She smiled and looked at Nate in amazement.

"Do you want to know why I didn't kiss you?" Nate asked.

"Yes," Sandy managed to say.

360

"Because you were so beautiful, inside and out, and I wasn't. I wasn't worthy enough to kiss you," Nate confessed.

"Oh, Nate, you were worthy! I'm so sorry if I made you feel that way. I wish you had kissed me," she answered.

"I never knew anyone like you before," Nate continued. "I didn't know a person could be that loving and open. My heart was small and hardened and I was afraid you would not love me when you found out."

"Oh Nate, you've always had a big heart. I knew it even if you didn't," Sandy replied.

"No, you're wrong. I know my heart and how it was. My heart is not as big as yours. It will never be as big as yours. But it has grown since that night."

Sandy thought to herself, *Could I have really been his first love? Maybe Nate can love me as much as Angela.* A smile came upon her face.

Nate looked down for a second in thought and then with a serious expression turned back to Sandy. "Angela and I met by accident and by some strange events we fell in love, and I learned what love was. Now I know in my heart that Angela wanted me to love you with all my heart after she died. She gave us that. She gave me you."

Sandy thought back to her conversations with Angela and how Angela told her Nate had a big heart and asked if she would she take care of him. What Nate said was true. Sandy felt the peace flow through her that one feels when a deep-seated conflict is finally resolved.

"I know," she said. "I know." Then she kissed him again.

"Will you come back home?" Nate asked in earnest.

"Yes, if you want me to," Sandy answered.

"Oh I want you to come home more than anything, and I want to take you out on that special date," Nate almost shouted.

"Will you take me dancing?" she asked.

"You bet!" Nate answered, remembering that was the one request she had asked for before.

"Ok, on that condition I will go. You are not going to stand me up without calling, are you?" she said kiddingly.

"Believe me. Never again. Of course I may have to pick you up on the way to the hospital," Nate said with a smile.

"And I would consider that one of the most special dates ever," Sandy said. She gave him a quick kiss that brought a smile to his face.

They sat on the couch in each other's arms until they finally had to go to bed. Sandy kissed him goodnight. Nate slept extremely well that night; better than he could remember, as did Sandy.

Sandy took Monday off to drive him to the small airport that morning. They walked hand in hand to the guarded entrance. Nate turned and kissed her.

"No more barroom fights, ok?" Sandy said with a smile.

"It's a promise," Nate returned. "And we've got a date?" Nate asked, knowing the answer but wanting to hear it again.

"We have got a date," Sandy said proudly.

Sandy stood and watched the small plane take off to San Francisco and as it did, she said, "Fly safely my love, fly safely."

Chapter Forty-seven

NATE GOT BACK TO EVERSTON AROUND EIGHT THAT evening. During the flight he could think of nothing but Sandy. He had another chance with her. It was a new beginning. They had known each other for two years, but now they had a chance to really know each other. He loved Sandy. He was sure of it. More sure than he had ever been before. He would count the days until she came home. She only had a little over two weeks left in Woodsville, and then she would come home. She had contacted the head nurse at St. Joseph's and they, like Nate, were overjoyed to have her back.

When he arrived at his apartment, Catherine was asleep. His mom and dad were sitting and reading as they usually did before going to bed. When his mom saw him she burst into tears and yelled, "Oh Nate my dear boy what has happened to you? Are you ok?"

Nate explained to them both that he had not gone to a medical meeting as he had said but that he went to find Sandy who was in California. He related that when he saw Sandy being treated roughly by the one she was with he gave the guy a shove, which started a fight. Nate's mom listened in horror, but his dad was totally fascinated and wanted all the details.

His mom hugged him. She had stopped crying but still looked very worried. His dad looked closely at Nate's swollen eye and stitches and said, "What does the other guy look like, Son?"

Nate couldn't believe his father had called him son. "Actually, he looks pretty good, but he was plenty scared," Nate answered.

His dad laughed and looked at Nate closely. "I bet you got in a few good blows," he stated. He seemed animated.

"Yes I did, Dad. After one of my blows he landed flat on his back on a table where two people were drinking." His dad's eyes opened wide upon hearing this, and his face brightened. Nate and his dad talked for twenty minutes as Nate recounted everything that happened in the saloon. Nate described every blow. It was a man-to-man talk. His dad seemed relaxed, very interested in every detail. He hung on every word as he looked at Nate smiling. Nate wondered if it had brought back some memories of when he was a young man. It was the kind of talk every son dreams of having with his father and one Nate dreamed of also. Nate felt accepted and loved by his dad. Oddly enough this conversation meant more to him than all the accomplishments he had achieved in the past to win his affection.

Finally for the first time that Nate could remember his dad hugged him. "I'm very proud of you, Son," he said. Nate thought to himself that there were definitely some advantages to getting beat up.

"What about Sandy?" his mom asked after Nate and his dad had finished talking about his saloon fight.

"Well Mom, I think she likes me," Nate said. A big smile appeared on her face. She hugged Nate again, trying to avoid his swollen black eye. Her grieving son had found love, so she hoped. "Is she coming back?" she asked.

"Yes, in two weeks," Nate answered.

"Praise the Lord," his mom said enthusiastically, not realizing what she had said. Nate and his dad looked at her in amazement. They had never heard her say such a thing before. She looked surprised herself for a moment. Then she acted like nothing had happened and asked Nate if she could get him something to drink.

The next morning he got up and did his usual routine of visiting Catherine before heading to the hospital. The nurses were aghast when they saw him but tried to pretend they did not notice. After a couple of hours one of the nurses told him that Dr. Archer and Dr. Allen wanted to see him in the conference room on the first floor. Nate thought *Not again* and headed down to join them.

Dr. Archer and Dr. Allen were sitting in the same seats that they sat in before when they informed Nate that his hospital privileges were suspended. Nate also sat in the seat he had been in before. He looked at them with a straight face with no emotion. His left eye was black and blue and swollen. The eight stitches below his eye had a slight redness around them.

Dr. Archer leaned forward and looked at Nate. "Nate," he began, "you look terrible." Then he smiled a little. "Did you ask some cowboy to step outside and duke it out?" he said jokingly.

"It was inside," Nate replied in a matter-of-fact way.

Dr. Archer looked surprised. "You mean you duked it out with a cowboy inside?"

"That's correct," Nate answered.

"Inside the hospital?" he asked again.

"No, in a bar," Nate returned.

Dr. Archer smiled even bigger and looked at Dr. Allen, who was also smiling. He then turned back to Nate. "Now, are you going to tell me that you got in a fight over a woman?" he said kiddingly.

"Yes, that's right," Nate said calmly.

Dr. Archer was speechless. Both he and Dr. Allen looked at Nate with their mouths half open, wondering if this was really real. Dr. Archer seemed to recover and said, "Nate, you are one of our best cardiologists, but you are definitely full of surprises. Everyone is worried about you." He thought some more. "There have been no complaints against you so I have no reason to order you to do anything."

"Feel free to test me for drugs and alcohol if you want. I'm clean."

"I know you are," Dr. Archer responded. "Here is what I want you to do. I want you to take a week off and recover. We will cover all of your patients. I'm doing this so you won't scare the hell out of the patients, ok?"

Nate smiled. "Thanks guys. I promise to look better when I come back." With that they shook hands and Nate went home to rest and to let his eye try to return to normal.

That evening he called Sandy long distance on her cell phone. "Hi Sandy," he opened.

Sandy recognized his voice. "Nate, oh Nate," she said enthusiastically.

"I just wanted to let you know I made it home without getting into any fights," Nate said with a smile.

"I'm proud of you," Sandy responded.

"There is one other thing though," Nate added.

"What's that?" Sandy asked expectantly.

"I'm out of the hospital for a week."

"Did you get kicked out again?" she asked.

"No, they asked me to voluntarily take a week off so I wouldn't scare the hell out of the patients as they put it," Nate answered.

Sandy laughed. "Yes, you do look pretty scary. In fact you look pretty mean and tough, but I know the real you."

"Thanks," Nate said. "Also I wanted to say thank you for a wonderful weekend and that I miss you."

"Yes it was wonderful, wasn't it," Sandy replied. "I miss you too."

"I may be calling you a lot if that is ok," Nate stated.

"Call me, please call me," Sandy returned with joy in her voice.

With that Nate told her he could not wait until she came back home. She said the same thing before they said sweet goodbyes that traveled instantly over three thousand miles to each other.

Nate called her every night for the remaining two weeks that she was there. They talked about everything and nothing at all. They both couldn't wait to talk to each other. They hated to say goodbye. Nate went back to work a week later. His eye was much better. The sutures had been removed leaving a linear scar on his left cheek below his eye that he was proud of.

Nate was at the airport the evening Sandy and David finally returned. As they entered the baggage claim area, David saw Nate and said with surprise, "It's Dr. Williams," after which he ran up and hugged him. Nate was also surprised. No little kid had ever run up and hugged him before. Then Sandy kissed him on the lips. David saw them and thought, *They really do like each other.* Two elderly ladies were watching the three of them from a bench where they were sitting waiting for the luggage. One turned to the other and said, "What a nice family. It's a shame more families are not like that." The other agreed.

Nate loaded up their suitcases as they all got into his car. On the way they talked and chatted and laughed like normal people do. Once they reached Sandy's house Nate carried in their luggage. Sandy and David were exhausted from the long trip. When Nate had done everything he could, David hugged him again and Sandy thanked him and kissed him goodbye.

Sandy was to go back to work two mornings later. When she arrived early, to her surprise there was a big white cake that said "Welcome Back Sandy." Around the cake were all the nurses, who said in unison, "Welcome back!" Then they all hugged her. Behind the nurses Nate stood leaning against the entrance to the doctors' charting room, holding a cup of coffee in his hand. He stepped through the nurses and said, "Here's a cup of coffee just like you like it," and smiled.

Sandy looked at Nate and said, "Thank you." She then turned to the nurses. "Thank you all. I am so happy to be back. Happier than you can imagine." Nate and Sandy then smiled at each other for only they knew their secret. Other than his parents Nate had told no one about them or that he had had a fight in a saloon over her. The nurses later commented that they had never seen Sandy so happy. She looked radiant and healthier than before. Her face had filled out a little and seemed softer without the lean look she had recently acquired.

Nate and Sandy looked forward again to their special date. Nate's mom was ecstatic that Sandy had come back and that Nate was taking her out. Nate had his clothes that he had bought before. He made reservations at the same restaurant and planned to go to the same nightclub afterwards. Sandy also had her dress from before. Their date was on Saturday night and she spent the afternoon applying the makeup that had made her so beautiful. Nate started worrying that Catherine might get sick again, but she seemed in perfect health the day of their date.

Nate arrived at ten minutes to seven and knocked on Sandy's door. When Sandy opened the door his heart seemed to stop for a second. The expression on his face was just what she had hoped for. Nate was speechless. Sandy looked like a Goddess. He didn't know whether to kiss her or to kneel down and worship her. He decided against the latter. As he slowly leaned to kiss her with his eyes aglow, he said, "I've just got to kiss the most beautiful girl in the whole world."

Sandy smiled and met his kiss with her soft lips. Nate did not know how he was going to make it through the evening. He recovered and then asked, "May I take the most beautiful girl in the world out on a special date?"

Sandy smiled and said, "You certainly know how to sweep a girl off of her feet," and offered him her arm. Nate walked her to his car and opened the door for her with a proud look on his face.

The restaurant was on the twentieth floor. Their table was by a floor-to-ceiling glass wall that revealed the beautiful night lights of Everston. The tables were set with expensive-looking tablecloths upon which sat shiny silverware. A waiter sat them down and unfolded their napkins for them placing them in their laps. Sandy was super impressed.

"Is this how the rich and famous live?" Sandy asked.

"Yes and the sad but true fact is that the rich and famous have completely forgotten how to put their napkins in their laps," Nate returned in a very serious tone meant to be funny.

"It's tragic, simply tragic," Sandy returned smiling still looking around impressed.

The waiter then brought out the menus that had the prices listed. Sandy gasped. "I can't believe these prices," she exclaimed.

Nate again looked serious. "Waiters and cooks in these places have to eat too. Think of their starving kids at home."

Sandy laughed. "You are a riot. I didn't know you were a comedian."

Nate smiled. "I'll be anything you want me to be," he said.

"Good because I want you to be both Nate Williams the doctor and comedian," Sandy replied.

After much speculation about what the names of items on the menu really meant, they decided on a French dish with meat simmered in a rich French sauce with exotic vegetables. As they ate Nate still couldn't get over how beautiful Sandy looked.

"Sandy, I need to ask you a personal question," Nate said, looking at her.

Sandy looked up surprised. "A personal question?" she asked.

"Yes, I want to know what things are the most special to you. I don't think you've ever told me before."

Sandy thought for a moment. "Well for one thing David of course is very special." She thought some more. "Starry nights are special and spring flowers are special. Romantic music is special and being with someone you love is special."

Nate's heart went out to Sandy. He was trying to make conversation with her, and what she said grabbed his heart. He wanted to burst inside.

"What about you?" she asked.

Nate, for some reason, had not anticipated being asked the same question. "You know, there are many things I've discovered of late that are special to me that I didn't realize before. Catherine is special for sure. I now know that my parents are really special people." He stopped and swallowed and then said, "You are the most special thing in my life."

Sandy reached across the table and gently held his hand. "And you are my most special thing." She then smiled and added, "We will never get to our dancing if we keep going on like this."

Nate laughed. "You're right."

They finished with an exotic desert and then went to the upscale nightclub. Here men in suits were playing saxophones. Along side a man playing a piano were to two men with violins. There was a dreamy atmosphere as dim lighting revealed the tables across from a dance floor. A few older couples were dancing along with a few who were Nate and Sandy's age who were very well dressed.

They picked a table and ordered drinks. The music was soft and romantic. Then Nate asked her if she would like to dance. Sandy smiled. "You know I would." He led her to the dance floor. As the dance began Sandy was impressed as he pulled her to him slowly.

"I thought you didn't know how to dance?" she asked.

"Well I guess I have to reveal my secret. I bought some DVDs on how to dance. My mom helped me," Nate answered.

"Your mom is special," Sandy replied. "Are there DVDs on boxing?" she inquired.

Nate laughed. "You make me laugh. After seeing me in action, do you think I need them?" he asked.

"No, you did great. It's just you might need a little help on how to duck." Nate laughed again. As the music played on Nate held her close with his cheek next to hers. He could see her lovely hair up close. The feel of her soft skin against his face was heavenly. The soft curves of her body seemed to melt against his chasing away all thoughts except those of her. He never expected he would enjoy dancing so much but then he was dancing with Sandy. There had been many unexpected things in his life recently, and he was thankful for them. They danced for a couple of hours. During each dance there was only he and Sandy and the music; nothing else existed in the whole world. In between each dance they would sit at the table and sip their drinks and look at each other and say unimportant things that made them both smile. Nate learned that night that dancing not only made Sandy extremely happy but made him happy as well. He made a resolution to take her dancing often the rest of her life.

They got home late. Sandy thanked and paid the babysitter. Then she turned to Nate. "I had a wonderful time. I think this has been the best night of my life."

"Me too," Nate replied. *I want you for my wife, and I want you to be with me forever*, he thought. He wanted in the worst way to ask her right there and then to marry him, but he knew it was too soon, but he could not keep that question within him much longer.

Sandy kissed him goodbye. As he left, she knew more than ever that she loved him. Deep down a feeling arose that said they should be married. But then she realized that she did not know if he believed in marriage or not. He had not married Angela, and now she had something new to worry about.

Chapter Forty-eight

WHEN SANDY ARRIVED AT WORK MONDAY MORNING Nate was waiting for her with a cup of coffee just the way she liked it. It was then that the nurses began to talk and rumors began flying. Nate and Sandy otherwise tried to act like two professionals, but soon everyone was on to their game. Everyone knew that Sandy joined Nate each day at lunch in the doctors' private dining room. They did not know but speculated that they kissed when they there were alone which in fact they did. Each evening when Sandy got off they saw the two of them talk in the parking lot and kiss goodbye.

This was their routine. They were very much involved in each other's lives. Even though they liked to kiss and hold their bodies next to one another there was no talk of marriage or of having sex. This was a strange time in their relationship. It was also strange for the times in which they lived, where everyone either jumped into bed with one another or got married the old-fashioned way, which in some quarters seemed to be going out of style. They both knew but pretended they didn't know that what they had between them had to change. Oh, there had been platonic relationships before where lovers only wrote poems to one another but nowhere had there been recorded two lovers who kissed and touched each other as intimately as they did who could resist the overwhelming passion to be one flesh for very long.

On Saturday Nate was invited to David's soccer game. He went with them just as any dad would, carrying folding chairs and a cooler full of drinks. Nate liked soccer. He remembered playing a little of it in high school. He and Sandy sat on the sidelines and yelled for David's team. They both saw several people they knew from the hospital there with their kids. The play was intense for eight year olds. A couple of kids were obviously overly aggressive. They collided with one another and one kid fell to the ground screaming holding his knee. All the parents became alarmed. One of the parents they had recognized from the hospital yelled, "Thank God we have a doctor here!" and then turned and looked at Nate. Nate actually had just settled down in his seat next to Sandy and gotten his diet coke opened when he heard her yell and understood what was going on. His first thought was that he was also glad that there was a doctor present before he realized that he was the doctor they were talking about. He stood up and wanted to shout that he was just a cardiologist and didn't know anything about kids' knees but thought better of it. He walked slowly and confidently out to the fallen player who had stopped screaming

"Let me see that knee, big guy," he said as the player began to move it. Nate felt the knee carefully, trying to remember what he had learned in medical school about the anatomy of the knee. The young man had stopped screaming and was looking intensely at Nate, as were all the parents. Nate began to slowly move his leg a little; it did not seem to hurt, which Nate was sure was a good sign. Nate helped him up slowly, and he was able to walk off the field. Once on the sidelines he began jumping around like nothing was wrong. As Nate walked back to Sandy all the parents stood up and gave him applause. Nate smiled in a very humble way knowing that they all thought he knew everything about knees since he was a doctor. He had never received applause in the hospital when he had successfully resuscitated someone or when he had saved someone's life by inserting a stent. *Maybe I should hang around these soccer fields more often*, he joked with himself.

When he had sat down again, Sandy whispered, "You put on a good show out there, Doc." They almost laughed because they both knew he knew nothing about kids' knees.

That evening when they put David to bed, he said, "Dr. Williams, thanks for helping my friend."

Nate smiled. "I'm glad I could help and that he is ok."

"Can you tell me a nighttime story, Dr. Williams?" he asked.

Nate's eyes narrowed, and his lips became firm. He had never told a nighttime story before. David was waiting anxiously for his reply. How could he say no? "Sure, I will give it a try," he answered. Sandy finished tucking David in and pulled up two chairs by his bed for her and Nate. She sat down wondering what Nate was going to come up with. Nate sat down also wondering what he was going to say.

"Can you tell me a story about the redwoods. That is my favorite place," David said.

"Mine too," Nate replied. "Well David, I'm not too good at this. I don't do it very often; in fact, I've never done it." Nate sat looking at them both. He thought back to how small he felt standing next to the redwoods. "Ok, here goes. Once there was this ant that lived in a forest and for some reason he was much smaller than all the other ants. His name was Peewee. He was so small that he could not see over them. That meant that all he could see was their undersides. When he asked the other ants what they saw they would laugh and say there is really not anything worth seeing around there. There were some tiny grass blades he tried to climb, but even these weren't tall enough for him to see over the big ants."

"Why was he so small?" David asked.

"No one knew. It was a mystery," Nate replied. "Peewee at first thought the other ants were right and that there was nothing more than the undersides of other ants to look at. Then one day he decided that he had to see for himself to make sure so he decided to do something none of the ants in his colony had done before and that was to climb to the top of a tree. The other ants said don't do it. It is impossible and besides there are dangers up there."

"Like spiders and stuff," David chimed in.

"Yes, like spiders and stuff. But that didn't stop him. So one morning he started climbing. He didn't know how long it took to climb a tree, but that didn't discourage him. He climbed and climbed. He got hungry but noticed in the cracks of the tree there was tree sap that he could eat. He climbed for two weeks, and finally he reached the top, and do you know what he saw?"

"What?" David asked.

"He saw mountains, and he could see the ocean with big boulders, and he could almost see the whole world, you know why?"

"Why?" David asked again.

"Because he had climbed a redwood tree, the tallest tree in the world."

"Wow," David exclaimed.

"Well, it took him another two weeks to climb back down, and he became a hero among the ants. They would ask him over and over again what he saw, and he would tell them over and over again. And this little ant grew old and became the wisest ant that had ever lived in that colony."

"Why didn't the other ants climb the tree after he did?" inquired David.

"For two reasons. First, they were not as brave as Peewee was and second, they really didn't need to because Peewee told them all about it."

"That was a neat story," David said almost asleep.

"Thanks,' said Nate.

They tucked David in. It was late and as they stood there David went to sleep quickly with a smile on his face. Sandy kissed him goodnight and stroked his hair and looked at him lovingly. Watching Sandy with David warmed Nate's heart. He thought how wonderful Sandy was. He was inspired by how much she loved David, and he thought back to a time when his heart was not moved by such things. They silently tiptoed out of David's room and went into the living room where they sat on the couch.

Sandy smiled at Nate and looked at him lovingly the way she had looked at David and asked, "Where did the wonderful story come from?"

"I have no idea. It just popped out. Who knows?" Nate replied.

Sandy put on some romantic music and poured them both a glass of wine and sat next to him on the couch. "Thanks," Nate said as she gave him his glass. "I never realized how much effort it takes to tell a nighttime story."

"You did great," she said. She lifted her glass to him and looked at him with eyes that seemed to sparkle. "Here's to a great bedtime story teller," she said enthusiastically. Nate could tell she was proud of him. Nate lifted his glass and took a sip and said, "Thank you." He began to feel very relaxed now that the story time was over and Sandy was next to him.

Sandy had a glow about her and her face seemed lit up with joy. After a few moments she looked at Nate and said, "It's about time, don't you think?"

Nate swallowed hard. He knew what she meant. Yes it was time.

Sandy put down her glass and kissed him passionately. He put down his and put his arm around her and pulled her to him. He then felt all her curves, and he kissed her until he was almost out of control. Sandy stopped kissing him for a second and looked into his eyes.

"Tell me what you want, just tell me," she said. She began kissing him again pressing her body against his. "I am all yours," she said between kisses. Then she added, "Anything, anything."

Nate knew what he wanted. He wanted her. He wanted her body, he wanted her love, he wanted all of her. He kissed her and held her closer than he had ever held her before. He did not want to let go. Sandy wanted him. She was open and willing. His hands began to explore parts of her that they had not explored before. However, amidst his passion somewhere deep inside a voice was whispering, do it right, do it right this time. He pulled back slightly to catch his breath. It was one of those times when a small part of you tells you do one thing while every other part of you is urging you to do something else. It was one of those times that takes courage and self-denial. Painfully, he pulled away. He recovered himself for a minute. Then with a cooler head, said, "I'll tell you what I want. I want you to marry me and live with me the rest of my life."

Sandy became even more animated. "Nate, my Nate yes, yes, yes," she said kissing him again. She didn't want to quit. Nate loved her. He wanted to marry her. Her dreams had come true.

In between kisses, Nate said, "I love you, I love you."

"I love you too, so much," Sandy said kissing him again.

"Oh Sandy, can we get married soon?" Nate asked.

"Yes my darling, as soon as we can," she exclaimed.

"Do you think Father Jim would marry us even though we aren't Catholic?" Nate said.

"I know he will," Sandy said happily.

They kissed more and finally had to stop. "I want to do this right," Nate said, "a real wedding and everything, that is if it doesn't take too long."

"It won't take long at all," Sandy said, smiling like she had never smiled before. She then added, "We must tell David."

"Yes, I hope it is ok with him," Nate said.

"It will be. He loves you," Sandy reassured him. "Can you come tomorrow afternoon? We will have a fun time and eat hamburgers. He will be excited when we tell him."

"Yes. I love David too," Nate said earnestly.

Nate did not want to leave. They were both giddy as they stood on the porch to say goodbye. They had so much more to talk about, their future, their fun times, their trips, and their times alone. It was late, but there was always tomorrow, and they both looked forward to it.

Chapter Forty-nine

NATE GOT UP EARLY THE NEXT MORNING TO TAKE CARE of Catherine and to give his parents a break. Catherine was standing up in her crib holding on to the railing smiling bouncing up and down on her legs. She had recently learned to pull up, to the delight of Nate and his parents. Nate picked her up and said, as he usually did, "Good morning sweet girl." He quickly got her into a fresh diaper and headed toward the kitchen. He put her in her high chair and gave her a spoon to bang with while he got her cereal and fruit sauce ready. He sat in a chair next to her and began the game they played every morning. That was to see how much cereal and fruit sauce would actually go into her mouth versus how much would cover her and everything else close by. Nate's ability to navigate a spoon full of cereal through a maze of waving arms to her mouth had greatly improved the last two months.

His mom soon entered the kitchen in her robe. Her hair was a mild mess. Nate noted that she looked very tired even though she had just got up. His mom managed to smile and say good morning with half-closed eyes as she headed straight for the full coffee pot that Nate had made. Next his dad came in fully dressed as usual. His dad never walked around in his pajamas and never left the bedroom unless he had shaved and was ready for the day. This made him look less tired, but he also headed straight for the coffee pot with a look that desert wanderers have when they discover an oasis.

They both sat down at the table and smiled at happy little Catherine. They were both thankful that they could now just watch the morning game and enjoy their coffee. Other than "hi" and smiles they didn't say too much. It was simply too early to engage in talk that required the mind to think.

"I have some news," Nate said as he fed Catherine.

"Good news or bad news?" his mom asked, barely showing any interest in what he was about to say.

"It's good news, Mom. Sandy and I are going to get married."

Nate's mom let out a shriek that probably woke up their neighbors and would have shattered the glassware if it had been expensive fine crystal instead of the cheap heavy stuff. Nate's dad sat back in his chair and almost fell backward. Little Catherine stopped all her arm waving and sat there wide eyed. Nate was surprised also. He looked up at his mom who was now standing and walking toward him. She swiftly hugged Nate's neck and kissed him on the cheek and kept repeating, "It's wonderful. It's so wonderful." His mom had long hoped that he and Sandy would marry someday but, like Sandy, she wasn't sure if Nate believed in marriage, judging from his relationship with Angela. In her heart she knew marriage was the right thing to do, but it didn't come from any religious belief or simple tribal custom. Her conviction that marriage was good came from somewhere deep inside but where exactly she did not know.

Nate's dad shook his hand and said, "Congratulations Son. Congratulations." Nate again noted that his dad had been calling him son more often and that it seemed to make his dad feel good.

"We are going to tell David this afternoon," Nate announced.

"I just can't believe it. My prayers have been answered," his mom exclaimed and when she did both Nate and his dad looked at her because they knew that none of them actually prayed as far as they knew. This didn't bother her though. She kept rattling on about the good news Nate had brought.

Nate arrived at Sandy's that afternoon. When Sandy opened the door, they immediately kissed briefly. "David is in the backyard. We've been playing. Come join us," Sandy said with a smile. When David saw Nate he ran up and hugged him and said, "Hi Dr. Williams." Nate hugged him back. This made him feel a little relieved about telling David that he and his mom were going to get married. David picked up a small soft football and threw it to him.

Nate caught it and said, "Go out for a pass, David." David ran just a few steps, and Nate threw the ball over his head. "I was never very good at passing," Nate confessed. David threw it back to him, and Nate started to run like he was going to a goal line. Sandy grabbed him around the waist, and David held tightly to one leg. Nate, weighted down, started walking with a limp dragging them both with a grim determination to reach the imaginary end zone. Finally though, he was overcome and tumbled down with the conquering heroes on top of him. They were both breathing heavily as they lay on him smiling. Nate looked up at these two who were looking intently at him. He wanted to remember the happy look on their faces and the feel of their bodies against his forever. After a few moments the victors decided to let him get up and resume his life.

The three of them played for over an hour under the huge arms of the oak tree in Sandy's backyard. They played baseball with a small plastic bat and ball. They ran kicking a soccer ball, all the while laughing and joking because it seemed Nate always lost and David always won. Sandy joined in also. Nate was impressed how in shape she was. It was at times hard to concentrate on David and look at Sandy at the same time.

After everyone was tired Sandy brought out hamburger patties to grill putting Nate in charge. Nate watched the patties with the greatest of care while Sandy set the small outdoor table on her back patio. When it was finally time to eat, all were hungry, especially David. There were hamburgers, chips, and baked beans and of course brownies.

"These hamburgers are just perfect," Sandy commented.

"Three cheers for Dr. Williams," David said between bites.

Sandy smiled. "He's been saying that a lot after the last cartoon he watched," she said.

"Here's three cheers for the winner of all the sports today," Nate returned, lifting his glass of coke to David who laughed.

They continued to joke enjoying everything Sandy had prepared. Finally Sandy turned to David. "There is something we want to talk to you about, David. Remember how I told you your father really loves you, but he is so busy with so many problems that he has to solve that he can't come around much?"

"Yeah Mom, you've told me that before," David replied.

"And do you remember that I said someday I might meet and marry someone and have a husband like everyone else?"

"Sure Mom. Can I have another brownie?" David asked.

"You bet," she said and gave him a brownie. "Well David, I want to tell you that Dr. Williams and I have decided to get married."

David kept eating his brownie and then said, "Does that mean we will all live together?"

"Yes it does," Sandy answered.

David thought some more. "Then will we live in his apartment with the balcony?"

"Well, we haven't figured that out yet," was her reply.

"So will Dr. Williams kind of be like my dad?"

"Yes," Sandy said.

"Will he go to soccer games with us and other places dads go?"

"Yes," Sandy said again.

"You bet I will," added Nate.

"Ok," David said. He finished his brownie then left the table to play some more. Nate and Sandy looked at each other with a sigh of relief and a small laugh. "What are you laughing at?" David said.

"Oh nothing," Sandy said. "Your dad, I mean Dr. Williams, makes me laugh."

"Will you always call him Dr. Williams?" David asked.

"I don't think so," was her reply. "I don't think either of us will call him Dr. Williams after we are married. He will be your stepdad, David."

David thought for a second and asked, "What will I call him?"

Nate began to get nervous. He was not good with all this family talk. Growing up, his family rarely used family terms like mom, dad, or son once Nate was older.

"Stepdads are called dads just like your real dad is called dad," Sandy answered.

"Oh, ok," David responded. It appeared evident that the problem had been solved. David resumed his playing.

While David was playing, Nate turned to Sandy and said, "Thank you for handling that." Sandy smiled. Then Nate added, "David brought up an interesting question we haven't talked about. Where are we going to live after we are married?"

"Where do you want to live?" Sandy replied.

Nate smiled. "That's easy. I want to live wherever you are living."

Sandy smiled. "Thanks. I appreciate that, but that doesn't help answer the question," she added.

Nate thought some more. "Sandy, your house is a home, and I feel at home here. This is where you grew up. It's your home. My apartment is simply that and nothing more," Nate replied.

"But it is much more modern," Sandy protested.

"Modern doesn't always win out, you know. I think often it takes a second place to the tried and true," Nate responded.

Sandy smiled. "I would like us to start off here. It would make me very happy. I know that our family may grow, and we will need to move, but for now it would be wonderful, plus David might feel more secure."

"Our family may grow?" Nate asked, repeating what he had heard.

"Well, yes, it might," Sandy responded.

"I guess that's something else we need to discuss. How do you feel about more children?" Nate asked.

"Oh, that would be wonderful," Sandy exclaimed and then stopped and looked a little worried. "That is, if you would like more children," she added.

Nate pulled her to sit in his lap and held her hand. "You're wonderful, Sandy. I would love more children." Nate didn't have to think twice about his answer. It came straight from his heart. There was no need to list the pros and cons of having more children. No need of deep self-analysis to see if this was what he really wanted. It was true that once he had no desire for children, but now he realized his desire was there and it was strong, though he did not really know where it had come from.

Sandy kissed him briefly and then noticed that David was looking at them from across the yard, but then he quickly resumed his playing.

After the talk of more children Nate realized that he did not know how strongly Sandy felt about her career. "How do you feel about your career?" he asked. "You know you won't have to work anymore if you don't want to," he added.

Sandy looked a little surprised. She hadn't thought about the possibility of not being a nurse nor had she thought about what Nate might want her to do.

"Do you want me to quit work?" she asked.

"Actually I know I am being very selfish, but I want to see you at work with me every day. I want to have lunch with you in the doctors' lounge and kiss you with the doors closed. I would miss you if you didn't work, but I would understand completely if you wanted to stay home," Nate answered.

Sandy smiled. "I love you," she said stroking his hair.

"You know Catherine is old enough to go to day care," Nate said.

"I'm going to be Catherine's mother," Sandy said as if it just occurred to her. She looked off with joy in her face. "I always dreamed of having a daughter. Oh Nate, I want to take care of her and raise her and help her grow up. If it's ok, I might work part time now and then to keep my skills up, but more than anything I want to make that happy home that our painting is about."

Nate hugged her, and each new day he loved Sandy more, which was a surprise because every day he was convinced that he could not love her more than he did already. Nate did not realize it but he would experience this surprise for the rest of his life.

Chapter Fifty

Nate picked Sandy up at 1:30 PM. They had both worked hard to be off the afternoon because they had a two o'clock appointment with Father Jim. Nate was a little nervous for some reason and told himself he shouldn't be. Father Jim was simply a friend who happened to be a priest, and he was sure he would help them out. Still, it seemed like they had an appointment with someone who had great authority, and that probably was the reason he was nervous.

They entered the church office a little before two, and the church secretary told them to go on in, that Father Jim was expecting them. As they entered Father Jim's office, they saw him behind his desk expecting them. The office was smaller than they thought it should be. All the walls except the wall behind him were covered from floor to ceiling with bookcases stuffed full of books of every kind. Not only religious books were in the shelves, and there were certainly plenty of those, but also Nate noticed books on philosophy, psychology, science, and even some fiction books, which were mostly mysteries. The wall behind him had a number of crosses of various sorts and sizes on one side and a picture of St. Francis of Assisi on the other.

Father Jim stood up with a happy look on his face and said,

"Come in, come in. It is great to see you two." He pointed to two very comfortable chairs in front of his desk. "Have a seat. I had sat down to work on my homily, and I noticed that you two had made an appointment. I was delighted. Can I help you in any way?" he asked.

"Father," Nate stated, "Sandy and I are going to be married."

"That's wonderful," Father Jim exclaimed.

"However, we have a problem," Nate added.

"Oh?" said Father.

"You see, I promised Angela to raise Catherine, my daughter, in the church, which I fully intend to do. Angela said that the choice of the church or even the religion was up to me, and that's the problem. "

"Go on," Father said.

"My parents are atheists," Nate continued. "I was not raised in any church or any religion, but since Angela became Catholic, I really want to raise Catherine as a Catholic."

"Ok, so far so good," Father replied.

"It's just that I must confess that I do not believe in God. I've tried, but it just isn't there. I'm open to the possibility of God because we can't disprove his existence so someday I might come to a belief in God, but honestly I'm just not there yet and I can't force it. So I guess I am what you call an agnostic. Can an agnostic raise a child in the Catholic Church?" Nate asked.

"Now that is one interesting question," Father said as he looked at them and leaned back. Nate and Sandy could tell he was thinking pretty hard, probably like he did when he was trying to solve a mystery in one of his novels. He looked at Sandy. "Sandy, I know you are Jewish. Do you mind me asking if you believe in God?"

"Father," Sandy said, "my parents tried to pass on the Jewish culture to me, but we did not talk of God much and did not go the synagogue often. I feel sure they did not really believe in God. As for myself, I don't know. I don't think about it much, but I am open to it. I guess I am an agnostic also."

"Ah yes, I understand," Father said. "That seems to be the common thing in our culture these days. There are very many who feel like you two." He sat quietly for a moment tapping one end of his pencil on the desktop. "So what I have here are two agnostics who want to raise their child Catholic. I must say again that is very interesting because I have a number of Catholic parents whom I have to encourage to take their kids to church and catechesis." Nate could tell Father was deep in thought. "So you don't think belief in God will come anytime soon?" he asked.

"No," Nate answered, "Not anytime soon."

"I really appreciate both of you being so honest. There are so many that aren't honest about it." Father again appeared deep in thought. "Isn't there a condition in children where if they don't use one of their eyes then part of the brain doesn't develop and they become permanently blind in that eye even though the eye is perfectly normal?"

"Yes, it's called amblyopia," Nate answered.

"I think the same thing happens in religion. I think there must be a region in the brain somewhere that has to do with belief in God that doesn't develop when children are not raised in the church. Then as adults I think they have some sort of faith disability that is often hard to overcome."

Not another disability, Nate thought to himself.

"However, it can be overcome, unlike amblyopia, which is permanent. I believe, maybe I should say I know, that all humans have a yearning deep down inside for God. It is like a fire that can never be completely put out. Some get the fire going again through an intense emotional religious experience, like at a camp meeting and that seems to cure them. I would imagine that is probably not up your alley," Father said, looking at them both.

Nate and Sandy smiled. "I don't think so," Nate answered. Actually, Nate knew so.

"In the Catholic church faith is like a family bond that grows and strengthens over time. Kids raised in most churches and in the Catholic Church develop that bond sometimes without thinking about it much. It's a bond that is more or less permanently there even when as adults they try to reject it, like Angela did. That bond can be developed later in life, but it usually takes time. It would be like adopting a twelve year old who had been raised in an orphanage and requiring him to know and love all the family traditions before he entered the family."

"So we are like that twelve year old then," Nate asked.

"Yes, I am afraid so," said Father as he smiled. "At least when it comes to religion. That is what I think anyway. Sandy, how do you plan to raise David?"

"I haven't given it much thought. I want him to know his Jewish roots. I don't have anything against Christianity though," Sandy answered. Sandy looked worried and then said, "I don't know, Father. What shall we do?"

Father thought for a minute. "You might consider the Hebrew Catholics. They are Catholics who were raised Jewish and keep all the Jewish traditions but believe in Jesus and the Catholic Church. You know of course that Jesus was Jewish and he said he came to fulfill the Jewish scriptures. As someone said, all the really big names in Christianity were Jews: Jesus, the disciples, and Paul."

Sandy smiled. "I would not be adverse to going to both the Hebrew Catholic Church and your church, Father. I think I would like David to be a Jewish Catholic. I would like David and Catherine to be together in their faith."

"If we were to raise Catherine and David Catholic, what would we need to do?" Nate asked.

"Of course the usual. Catherine and David would need to be baptized and then brought to church each Sunday. Catholics in general do not miss Mass, even when they are out of town. As they both grow up they would receive the sacraments and attend Catholic education classes and youth group. However, we believe that the main teachers of the Catholic faith are the parents, who both show the child God's love for them and instruct them. In your case your children will be exposed to God's love because of the love you have for each other. According to our theology your love for Catherine and David will teach them about God even if you don't believe in him. It's just that since you are agnostics I'm worried how you will be able to instruct them. That is what bothers me about all this." Father got up and got a Bible from the bookcase. "Some parents just pretend to believe for the sake of the children and then quit going to church when the kids grow up and leave home, and that is not good. Correct me if I am wrong, but I get the impression that you two are not really anti-religion but simply don't have a belief. Is that correct?"

"That about sums it up," Nate replied.

"I have known a number of atheists. I am sure deep down inside they occasionally have doubts about their atheistic beliefs, and of course agnostics are halfway there because they doubt both the existence and the non-existence of God."

Nate was starting to get confused. "Father, I think you may be losing me," Nate confessed.

"Ok, look at it this way. We believers have doubts occasionally. We can't deny that. So do atheists and agnostics, and thus since we both have doubts we really have more in common with one another than most people think. So what I am trying to say is that a person can have both belief and unbelief, which come and go at different times because we are only human."

Father Jim picked up a Bible and gave it to Nate. "I want you to look up one of my favorite verses. It is Mark 9:24."

Nate began to fumble with the Bible. "It's in the New Testament, you know, the second half of the Bible," Father said, trying to help.

"Oh yeah, I knew that," Nate said as he began turning pages in the New Testament. He finally found it and read:

> *Immediately the father of the child cried out and said,*
> *"I believe, help my unbelief."*

"I have a feeling," Father said, "that as you come to Mass with Catherine and David, you may slowly get help with your belief-unbelief ratio." *Belief-unbelief ratio? Father Jim, you take the cake,* thought Nate. *I have never met anyone like you.*

"So let me get this straight, Father Jim. What I need to do is to get my belief-unbelief ratio greater than one?" asked Nate with a smile.

Father Jim laughed. "Yes, it's hard to believe so much theology can be summed up in one simple mathematical formula."

Even Sandy laughed a little. "I happen to like math," she said.

They all sat around thinking of the implications of math and religion and then decided they needed to concentrate on what they had come for. Nate said, "Then do you think it is possible to raise them in the Catholic Church even though we are not Catholic or Christian?" Nate asked.

"I have come to believe that anything is possible with God," Father answered. "Of course you can raise Catherine and David in the Catholic Church, and we welcome them with open arms. I think you should be honest with them about your belief, or may I say, your disbelief. But I believe that telling Catherine about her mother's belief will be a great comfort and aid to her as she matures."

"I certainly plan to do that," Nate said seriously.

Father smiled. "You guys are wonderful parents, and you really love your children. And most importantly you love each other. It has been said, Nate, that the best thing a father can do for his children is to love their mother, and that goes for the mother also. So you guys are on the right track whatever you do. Go home and think about all this and whatever you decide is ok with me. But let me tell you something, as much as I would like for your family to be Christian and Catholic, I sincerely believe that God accepts all those who search for him, whether they be Christian, Jewish, Hindu, or Muslim."

Nate smiled. "Father, I've got too much on my plate to think of becoming a Hindu or Muslim right now." Father laughed.

"Yes, one thing at a time," Father added.

"There is one other thing we wanted to ask you, Father. Will you marry us?"

Father smiled again. "Are you sure you guys aren't really Catholic?" Father said kiddingly. "Are you sure you want a Catholic priest to marry you?"

"Yes, we want you and no one else," Sandy said.

Nate and Sandy could tell by the look on Father's face that it meant a lot to him. "Thank you. I am very honored that you have asked me to marry you. I was a chaplain in the army for several years, and I was authorized to perform what we call secular marriages. Yes, I would be more than happy to perform the marriage, but it wouldn't be an official Catholic wedding. It would be similar to being married by a justice of the peace. Where did you want to have the marriage take place?"

"We would like to have it in my backyard," Sandy answered.

"We would like to be married under the large oak tree that I grew up under."

"That would be fine," Father answered. "When is this joyous occasion going to take place?" Father asked.

"Next month, if that is possible," Nate asked.

"That would be fine."

Nate and Sandy stood up and shook Father's hand and thanked him ever so much. As they left, Father Jim thought to himself, *What a couple those two are. I wish I had more parents like them.* He then said a prayer for Nate, Sandy, Catherine, and David and welcomed his next appointment.

Chapter Fifty-one

NATE WANTED TO HAVE SANDY OVER TO HAVE DINNER with him and his parents Saturday night. Sandy was excited. She had arranged for David to stay with a friend and was ready when Nate arrived to pick her up. As usual, Sandy was breath taking. Nate still had trouble believing that all this was coming true. Sandy had gotten to know Nate's parents while Catherine was in the hospital. She looked forward to seeing them. They were really nice people. She liked them a lot.

Nate's mom and dad greeted them enthusiastically when they arrived. His mom's face was aglow, and his dad was smiling. Nate's mom handed him Catherine whom she had been holding and hugged Sandy right away.

"I think it is wonderful that you and Nate are getting married," his mom said. "You two are the perfect match."

"Well I think Nate's pretty perfect," Sandy replied, smiling looking at Nate.

"They say love is blind," his dad said in a rare moment of abandon. "I'm just kidding. I'm also happy you two are going to get married."

Sandy spontaneously hugged him and said, "Thanks both of you so much." His dad blushed a little.

As they walked into the living area Catherine began to get a little fussy. "I think it's bedtime for Catherine. She's already eaten. I think she just needs a little patting in her bed," Nate's mom said.

"Can I put her to bed?" Sandy asked.

"Yes," his mom said enthusiastically.

Nate handed Catherine to Sandy. Sandy hugged her and said, "Oh you sweet girl, I love you," and then walked with her into Nate's bedroom. As she entered, it all came back to her. She remembered how she felt seeing the pictures of Angela and Nate together. She paused for a second at the opening. Nate had loved Angela and that was good. *But now Nate is madly in love with me*, Sandy told herself. She knew it with all her heart. She put Catherine down and soothed her to sleep while sitting on Nate's bed next to Catherine's crib.

Sandy thought back to when Angela was admitted pregnant and in heart failure and how shocked and surprised everyone was. *One of the saddest things is that they never married,* Sandy thought to herself. She began to feel sorry for Angela like she never had before. Then she thought about her and Nate. *I was ready to give him anything he wanted and what he wanted was to marry me.* All of a sudden it didn't seem fair to Angela. It wasn't fair that she got so sick. It wasn't fair that she would not be here to raise her daughter. All that had been beyond anyone's control. But what seemed most unfair was that they never married.

She knew she had to look at Nate's bedside table. She had been avoiding looking at it while she sat there. *It won't matter if Angela's picture is still there,* she told herself. She was confident of Nate's love for her. Their love was strong. Nothing, no nothing could interfere with it. She again knew that with all her heart. With courage she slowly turned her head and saw an empty bedside table except for a lamp. There were no pictures and no card. She felt relief but not as much as she expected. She again felt sorry for

Angela. At the same time she had an overwhelming joy thinking of Nate and the love they shared. She was amazed that she could have both feelings at the same time. She got up and said a silent goodnight to Catherine. Then she said a silent goodbye to Angela, wishing her well wherever she was. She then joined Nate and his parents in the kitchen.

Nate's mom had fixed chicken spaghetti with salad and crunchy rolls along with some red wine. Everyone dug in. "This is delicious," Sandy exclaimed. "You must give me this recipe," Sandy said, looking at his mom.

"I'd love to," she returned feeling very proud.

"Mom and Dad," Nate said. "I really appreciate all the help you've given us. You guys are just super. Here's a toast to the best parents and grandparents in the world."

They both blushed. "Thank you," his mom said.

"We loved doing it," Nate's dad agreed.

"Now that Sandy and I are getting married, you guys can be regular grandparents. You know, you get to have lots of fun times with them and then bring them back to us spoiled." They all laughed a little.

"I confess we are looking for a break and a rest," his mom said. "Now that we have got out of our rut, your dad and I have been secretly planning to take some trips we have dreamed about. Maybe starting with a cruise."

"That's wonderful," Sandy said. Then added with a smile, "Will you please come stay with us and visit often? I can't remember my grandparents. I want David and Catherine to really know you. There's a love only grandparents can give." Sandy paused. Her eyes found Nate's. Nate could tell a feeling deep within had moved her. "David will now have grandparents," she managed to say with a voice that almost cracked.

Nate's mom teared up. She got up and hugged Sandy, who

also had gotten teary eyed. Both Nate and his dad also seemed to have moist eyes.

"You know, I'm sure, that our only daughter died in infancy. Now I have a daughter and a granddaughter. I am so blessed."

"And you have a grandson too," Sandy added.

"Oh yes, now we have David."

"And now I have a mother and also a dad," Sandy added again. Sandy got up and hugged Nate's mom. She then hugged his dad who blushed again.

"Mom and Dad," Nate said after Sandy had sat down. "Next Saturday we are having Catherine and David baptized by Father Jim. At that time they will enter the Catholic Church. We would very much like both of you to be there." His mom and dad looked at Nate speechless. Nate could tell that they were both totally surprised. They knew Sandy was Jewish and Nate, well, Nate was nothing.

"You see," Nate continued, "I promised Angela that I would raise Catherine in the church. She said I could choose any church so I chose the Catholic Church because Angela became Catholic before she died." His parents both nodded their heads slightly to pretend that they really understood.

"I decided that I wanted David and Catherine to share the same faith so David is going to be a Hebrew Catholic and keep his Hebrew culture," Sandy happily informed them.

Now Nate's parents were confused. They had never heard of a Hebrew Catholic. This was something they never expected. Not that they were against it or anything. It was just so surprising.

"Does that mean that both of you are now Catholic?" his mom asked in a weak voice.

"Oh no, Mom. Sandy and I don't really believe in God, at least not yet but who knows?" Nate said as if everything he had told them was perfectly normal and understandable. If Nate's parents had been confused before, now they were totally confused.

"Is this the new modern way of doing things?" Nate's mom asked.

"No, it's just our way, I guess," Nate replied.

"Well son, we will be there but I must admit, your dad and I don't understand the ways of this new generation. I guess we're just of the old school." They all laughed a little.

Nate, Sandy, Catherine, David, and Nate's parents met Father Jim in the sanctuary of Sacred Heart before noon on Saturday. Everyone seemed nervous except Catherine, David, and Father Jim. Before the actual baptism, Father Jim talked about the ritual. "We baptize infants and children because in baptism we enter the family of God and that is the age one usually enters a family. Catherine and David will be full members of God's family, and like the prodigal son, they will have free will and can leave the family if they so choose as an adult. However, like the loving father in the parable, God will be forever waiting to welcome them back if they want to return. But now we must hear God's voice saying, 'This is my son and daughter with whom I am well pleased,' as David and Catherine are baptized." Father Jim then turned to David. "David, you have the name of King David, the greatest king in the history of Israel. He was a great warrior and religious leader. The angel Gabriel told the Virgin Mary that she would have a son named Jesus and that he would be given the throne of David. You indeed have a great name." David smiled and looked very proud.

Father then looked at Nate and Sandy and Catherine. "Catherine is named after St. Catherine of Siena who lived in the thirteen hundreds. The Catholic Church has, as you know, at least I think you know, hundreds and hundreds of people who have been declared saints over the last two thousand years.

However, there have been only thirty-three who have been named doctors of the church because of their spirituality and influence. St. Catherine is one of the doctors of the church. She was not meek or mild. In fact she had to straighten out a couple of popes who, to their credit, did what she said. I think little Catherine may be like that, so Mom and Dad, be prepared."

Father Jim then conducted a beautiful baptismal service with pouring of water over their heads after which they were given a white baptismal garment. Nate thought back to the white baptismal garment that had been placed on Angela's casket and the sprinkling of Holy Water that symbolized baptism. While he still thought it was all superstitious ritual, deep down he felt a soothing of his soul like he had never experienced before. He wished Angela could see Catherine being baptized. He felt proud he was keeping his promise to her. Everyone clapped afterwards and was full of smiles. Sandy gave Nate's parents her small digital camera to take pictures during and after the ceremony. They all thanked Father enthusiastically and invited him to lunch, which he was sorry to decline since he had other duties calling him. Thus two atheists, two agnostics and two new members of the Catholic Church went out to a restaurant to celebrate such a wonderful event in the life of their family.

Chapter Fifty-two

NATE TOOK SANDY TO A JEWELER'S SHOP TO PICK OUT an engagement and wedding ring after they had let everyone know about their marriage. Sandy insisted on a pair of rings that were not expensive but had a simple elegant beauty about them. Nate also chose a simple but beautiful gold band for himself. Sandy put on the engagement ring and could not keep from looking at it.

"This ring will not have to be by itself for very long," Sandy said, still looking at it. "Soon it will be joined to its soul mate when we are joined to each other," she said dreamily.

"Yes, and I look forward to joining with my soul mate if I can wait that long," Nate said with smile. "A month seems like a lifetime, you know."

Sandy put her hand on his cheek. "Oh my poor suffering darling. To think that I can drive a man mad thinking about me."

"I think you kind of like watching me get all torn up inside when I look at you," Nate replied.

"Yes I do, matter of fact. It's one of the pleasures of being desired," Sandy said kiddingly as she ran her hand along her side as she looked off.

"Well, I'm glad to provide you that pleasure," Nate returned.

"Speaking of pleasure, we must now plan our honeymoon." Sandy held out her hand. "With pleasure," she said as they both laughed.

They did plan their honeymoon, which was to be in a very pleasurable all-inclusive resort in the Caribbean for four days. Nate's mom and dad turned out to be saints and volunteered without being asked to babysit Catherine and David while they were gone on the promise that Nate would check out the resort for them so they could take a second honeymoon themselves. All the wedding details finally were taken care of and all that was left was to await that very special day.

The night before their wedding, Father Jim helped them go through a rehearsal in their backyard under the huge oak tree. There was only Father Jim, Nate's parents who were in charge of Catherine, little David, Sandy's bridesmaid, and of course Nate and Sandy. Father Jim knew exactly what everyone was to do and when they were to do it. Afterwards they all went to Tony and Rita's restaurant for the rehearsal dinner. Cindy, Rick and Samantha joined them there and as usual Gregg came separately. Tony had reserved a special side room for such occasions.

When they were all seated wine was served along with rolls in baskets. Tony stood up as usual and began. "I, I mean we, Rita and myself, are greatly honored to be the hosts of Sandy and Nate's rehearsal dinner at our humble restaurant. I would like to make a toast to the bride and groom." He held up his glass and everyone joined him.

"I would also like to say the name of my restaurant, The Silver Lining Restaurant, does not apply here because there are no black clouds to have a silver lining around," Tony added with a smile. Everyone laughed a little.

Cindy got up next. "Sandy, I may have known Nate longer than you, but I want you to know that I love you both and wish you all the happiness in the world." Nate and Sandy both said "Thank you" together.

Then to everyone's surprise Gregg stood up and looked at Nate. "I just wanted to say how much I respect you and Sandy and what you have together. You are an inspiration to us all." Samantha looked shocked, as did everyone else.

After Gregg sat down Nate couldn't believe his eyes: His dad stood up. "I want to say something I have wanted to say for a long time and I don't know why I haven't said it up until now." He turned to Nate. "Son, I am so proud of you. You've turned out to be one of the most loving fathers I have ever known, more than I ever was." He then turned to Sandy. "Sandy, I know Nate will be a good husband. He is the luckiest man in the world to have you." He then sat down. Nate was in tears. He felt closer to his dad at that moment than he ever had before. He got up and hugged his dad and said, "I love you, Dad." His dad said, "I love you too, Son." Nate sat back down shaken, but shaken in a good way.

Tony served up delicious lasagna and salad with cheesecake for desert. The dinner was filled with stories interspersed with laughter. Everyone including Father Jim at one time or another got up and wished both of them the best in their marriage. During all this Nate held Sandy's hand below the table and did not want to let it go. He would glance at her and every time he did he could not believe his good fortune. He could not believe how an empty, shallow, hard-hearted person like himself could be where he was. He could not believe how he had changed. He could not figure it out but knew it had something to do with love.

After the rehearsal dinner Nate took Sandy home. He kissed her as they stood outside her door. "I'd better not come in. I think you know why," Nate said with a smile.

Sandy smiled back. "So do you think you can wait that long?" she asked.

"No, but I must," Nate replied and kissed her again.

Sandy looked up at him. "Do you know you have got the most wonderful father in the world and of course the most wonderful mother?"

"I know," Nate replied. "I have also got the most beautiful bride in the world."

"You had better go quickly before I drag you into this house," Sandy said still smiling. At that Nate said a sweet goodbye and left not knowing how he could endure being without her another day.

The October weather was clear with a hint of fall in the air the next day, which was the day of the wedding. Unlike most brides and grooms, Nate and Sandy chose to get married in the morning to begin their marriage at the beginning of what they hoped would be a beautiful day and it turned out to be just that. Rented chairs and tables with white tablecloths were positioned strategically in Sandy's backyard A hired disc jockey had set up large speakers next to a table that his equipment sat on to play music for dancing. A number of chairs were arranged with an aisle in between leading to where Father was to stand under the oak tree. A large wedding cake from the bakery had arrived that morning. White ribbons adorned the house and backyard.

The guests began getting there early. They included Nate's mom and dad, Tony and Rita, Cindy and Rick, and Samantha. Greg came separately. There were some distant relatives of Sandy who came and a few nurse friends from the hospital. David was dressed in a very special grown-up suit since he was to be the ring bearer. Catherine sat in Nate's mom's lap wearing a Sunday dress with ribbons.

Nate and his dad arrived both dressed in black tuxedos. Nate had asked his dad to be his best man knowing that it would make him proud to be honored in that way. Father Jim arrived with a special robe for the occasion that he put on as he took his place under the huge oak tree. He had asked Nate and Sandy if there could be a religious song at the wedding even though they themselves were not all that religious. They both said definitely since their children were now members of the Catholic Church. Also some of the guests were religious. As far as to what religious song it would be, they left that up to Father who said he had a favorite song in mind already. Father Jim had arranged for a vocalist from Sacred Heart to sing the song at the start of the wedding.

Nate and his dad stood beside Father Jim at the front as they waited for the vocalist to start the ceremony with a song. With a beautiful voice she began to sing *Morning Has Broken*. When Nate heard the second verse, "Like the first morning," he thought to himself, *Father Jim chose the perfect song for us. This is the first morning of our life together.* The sunshine, the blue heavens overhead, the giant oak tree that they were under and everything else in the world seemed more beautiful than ever to them as they listened to the lovely lyrics that filled the air.

After the song the disc jockey started playing the wedding march softly as Sandy's bridesmaid, one of her friends from the hospital, started to walk down the aisle. Following her was David carrying the rings on a small pillow. Everyone thought he was one handsome cute little guy as he walked with an air of confidence. Then everyone stood up waiting for Sandy. Sandy appeared holding a bouquet of flowers. She wore a white wedding dress that a cousin had loaned her that was more of the modern style, which was not so full but very stylish. She had a thin lacy veil and white shoes.

Nate could not believe his eyes. Sandy looked more lovely and beautiful than she had ever before. She was beautiful from her head to her toes. There was a lot that Nate could have thought about at that moment. He could have thought about the journey that had led up to all this. He could have thought about all the joys and sorrows his heart had experienced of late. He could of thought of how his heart had changed. But he didn't. None of those thoughts were in his mind. Only Sandy was there. Her beauty and her smile filled his heart. There was no room left for anything else. Nothing else mattered but Sandy. The wedding march increased in intensity. Their eyes quickly found each other as she walked down the aisle between the chairs toward him. It seemed that there was no one else there but them. When she reached Nate they both turned toward Father.

Father Jim had a very welcoming smile that made them both feel that they had come home. He then turned to the audience.

"We have come here this beautiful morning to celebrate the marriage of Sandy Abraham and Nate Williams. I would like to start off with a reading from scripture that I have picked out especially for them from the book of the *Song of Songs.*" He then opened his Bible to the verse that he had marked and began.

My lover speaks: he says to me,
"Arise, my beloved, my dove, my beautiful one, and come!
For see, the winter is past, the rains are over and gone.
The flowers appear on the earth,
The time of pruning the vines has come,
And the song of the dove is heard in our land.
The fig tree puts forth its figs,
And the vines, in bloom, give forth fragrance.
Arise, my beloved, my beautiful one, and come!
O my dove in the clefts of the rock,
In the secret recesses of the cliff,
Let me see you, let me hear your voice,
For your voice is sweet, and you are lovely."

Father Jim closed his Bible. Nate and Sandy trembled a little.

Father Jim began again. "The marriage of Nate and Sandy is a joyous occasion as all weddings are. We at this time should ask ourselves why this is so joyous not only for Sandy and Nate but also for all of us." He waited for a second so everyone could ponder this question.

"The answer is that love is contagious. The love between two people affects all those that they encounter. Their marriage is like a small pebble dropped into a still pond that makes waves that spreads throughout all of it. In a similar way their love, their marriage, their commitment sends waves of love through us all giving us a joy that we cannot help but pass on to our family and others. Thus we have many, many reasons to be thankful for the love of Sandy and Nate."

After a few more words, Father Jim had them turn to each other for the wedding vows. Nate held both of Sandy's hands and looked into her eyes. He began without Father Jim's help and spoke in a strong but not loud voice:

I Nate, take you, Sandy, for my lawful wife, to have and to hold, from this day forward, for better, for worse, for richer, for poorer, in sickness and in health, until death do us part.

Nate's voice seemed strongest when he said, "until death do us part." Sandy began next again without Father's help and spoke in an equally strong voice:

I Sandy, take you, Nate, for my lawful husband, to have and to hold, from this day forward, for better, for worse, for richer, for poorer, in sickness and in health, until death do us part.

Father Jim then said, "What God has joined, men must not

divide." He just couldn't help but say these words even though the two in front of him didn't really believe in God yet. He then asked David to bring the rings and without thinking said a blessing over them. Later Sandy and Nate would recall that the blessing of the rings was very special to them for some reason. Nate then took Sandy's ring from the pillow held by David. As he gently placed it on Sandy's finger next to its soul mate, he said,

Sandy, take this ring as a sign of my love and fidelity.

Sandy took a deep breath and seemed to tremble a little. Then she took Nate's ring and said,

Nate, take this ring as a sign of my love and fidelity.

Father Jim then said, "I pronounce you man and wife. You may kiss the bride." Nate slowly lifted up Sandy's veil. He looked at her lovingly then gently kissed her soft lips longer than was customary because he did not want that moment to end. Father Jim then had Nate and Sandy face the audience and said, "I present to you Dr. and Mrs. Nate Williams!" Everyone clapped enthusiastically.

Nate almost pulled Sandy down the aisle making everyone smile. Afterwards the chairs were pulled back to make room for dancing. Sandy and Nate were to have the first dance. As everyone gathered around, glasses of champagne were handed out. Nate and Sandy stood in front of everyone and held their glasses to make a toast to each other. Nate began first.

"I want to say that I promise to you that I will always respect you and your wishes." He cleared his throat. "I say this because I love you with all my heart and soul, and because I want you by my side for the rest of my life. I promise to do everything in my power to win your love each and every day. I never want to lose you, Sandy. I am yours forever."

Sandy stood there with tears in her eyes. It took her a second to regain her composure. "Nate, I also love you with all my heart and soul. I was going to say more but you said it for both of us. I promise everything you promised. Know that I am yours forever." They then locked their two arms together and sipped their champagne. As they prepared for their first dance, someone announced that after the first minute or two Nate and Sandy would like whoever wanted to, to join them.

Nate led Sandy to the center of the yard. He pulled her close to him with one arm around her waist. Their eyes were aglow as they looked at each other. Nate whispered in a voice only Sandy could hear, "Have I told you lately that I love you?" Sandy looked a little surprised. It was a verse from her favorite song. Then she heard the song begin softly in the background. She smiled. "You knew," she whispered.

Nate whispered back, "Yes." Then looking into her eyes he said, "Sandy, you know there's no one else above you."

Sandy knew what he meant. Her eyes seemed to radiate with joy. "I love you Nate," she said as she put her head on his shoulder. After a moment she looked back up at him. "There is someone who is above both of us," she said with an earnest look in her face.

"I know," Nate replied.

"I would like to thank Angela for giving you to me," Sandy said softly.

"And I would like to thank Angela for giving you to me," Nate returned. They both raised their heads slightly and together said softly, "Thank you, Angela." They then again became absorbed in one another lost in each other's embrace.

Soon Cindy and Rick began to dance followed by Tony and Rita. Gregg got up and walked slowly over to Samantha, who returned to help his parents run their restaurant but also opened a very successful restaurant of his own. He followed the example of his parents who had followed the example of their parents of trying to force his kids to go to church without actually going himself. Rick was successful as a college professor publishing more papers on the mating behavior of frogs that resulted in his work being cited in several major biology textbooks. Their two children grew up to become responsible loving parents who, like their parents, did not go or take their children to church thus passing on a relative recently established family tradition of leaving religion out of their lives. Samantha was so impressed by Angela's decision to be Catholic that she decided to become Catholic herself. Gregg resisted this, but after a few years of reading almost everything he could get his hands on concerning the existence of God, joined the Catholic Church as well. He had to get his first marriage annulled. After the deep introspection that resulted from all the questions he had to answer in the process he finally experienced a peace he had not known. After the annulment he actually looked forward to going to confession to express his sorrow for all his past actions.

Nate smiled as he thought about the fiction reading disability that Angela had diagnosed him with. She was right; it was incurable. He never got over it. However, he and Sandy in remembrance of Angela began reading fiction books out loud to one another each evening soon after they were married. Each would take turns reading a page while the other listened. In this way Nate was able to keep his mind on what they were reading. To his surprise he developed a real liking for fiction. They used Angela's bookmark with each book. Over the years together they had read several hundred works of fiction from classics to modern novels. *Angela, I know that you are proud of us reading all that fiction*, he said to himself as he sat there because he still occasionally talked to her.

About the Author

Carl Turner is a retired pediatrician who has authored poetry and works concerning nature and theology. He enjoys reading classics and studying nature. He and his wife, Diane, have three grown married children and seven grandchildren and live in East Texas.